THE MISSING MEMSAHIB

Also by Arjun Raj Gaind

A Very Pukka Murder

Death at the Durbar

THE MISSING MEMSAHIB

THE THIRD MAHARAJA MYSTERY

ARJUN RAJ GAIND

HARPER FICTION

First published in India by Harper Fiction 2026
An imprint of HarperCollins *Publishers*
HarperCollins *Publishers* India, Cyber City,
Building 10-A, Gurugram, Haryana – 122002, India
www.harpercollins.co.in

2 4 6 8 10 9 7 5 3 1

P-ISBN: 978-93-6569-209-9
E-ISBN: 978-93-6569-652-3

Typeset in 9.5 pt/13.5 HC Arc
by HarperCollins *Publishers* India Pvt. Ltd

Printed and bound at
Nutech Print Services Pvt. Ltd.

This book is printed on FSC® certified paper
which ensures responsible forest management.

HarperCollins *Publishers*, Macken House, 39/40 Mayor Street Upper,
Dublin 1, D01 C9W8, Ireland

For my Masumeh.
My universe and my infinity.

'From Britain, yearly hundreds sail to try their luck in Asia's kinder lottery.'

—John Hobart Caunter, *The Cadet* (1814)

'... there are few, if any of our readers, whether in this country or in England, who have not heard much and read much on the subject of Female Adventurers, and the Marriage Market, and young ladies going out to India, on what was vulgarly called "a spec"[speculation].'

—*Calcutta Review* (1846)

'Even this homely face would charm, they say,
Amongst the copper beauties of Bombay;
And she who in a croud would scarcely pass
With us, would be a Venus, at Madrass.
Pantheon, Opera, Playhouse, Fantoccini,
Farewel—I'll go, and be a Nabobini: Or, if that scheme, perchance, should not succeed,
E'en wed a Seapoy chief, and mend the breed.
What if one's husband is a little frightful,
Where every thing besides is so delightful.
'Twill be so charming, on a summer's day,
For forty slaves to fan me as I lay,
Or on rich carpets free from noise and hurry,
Sit cross-legg'd with my spouse, and feast on Cury.
If I've a taste for baubles, my good man,
Will load me with old China and Japan.
Diamonds on diamonds heap'd, and pearly rows,
For hair, ears, neck, and breast, perhaps my nose.'

—Elizabeth Griffith, *A Wife in the Right: A Comedy* (1772)

PROLOGUE

He was dead. That much was certain.

But how had he died?

That was the question which nagged at me as I leaned over to study the corpse.

'Shouldn't we wait for the police, Huzoor?' Charan Singh, my faithful shadow, suggested from behind me.

I ignored him, narrowing my eyes. When it came to investigating a dead body to ascertain if it was an accident or foul play, there were six things a detective had to look out for. As luck would have it, I had devised rather a useful mnemonic for it some years earlier.

ROCPET.

R for rigor. His eyes were shut, his jaw was clenched tight and the skin was supple, still warm to the touch when I laid one hand on his forehead.

O for odor. I leaned forward and sniffed deeply, searching for the tell-tale scent of necrosis. As I had suspected, there was only the faintest hint of decay. The corpse was still fresh.

C for color. I looked for any indicative marks of post-mortem lividity, first on his neck and then his extremities. His face still had some pink and had not yet acquired the etiolated pallor of someone long dead. A closer examination revealed just a few splotches around his heels and back, more crimson than purple, which suggested his demise had occurred less than four hours ago.

P for posture. The body had definitely not been moved. He had died here, in this very bed, judging by how he was still swaddled by the sheets and how the blanket was crumpled around his legs. Most likely in his sleep, I concluded.

E for environment. A half-empty bottle of Gordon's gin stood atop the bedside table. An empty glass lay beside him, its contents staining the bedsheets, an acrid smear that was still slightly damp beneath my fingers.

T for trace. Poison, I surmised. Strychnine perhaps? No, his face lacked the characteristic leer, the macabre risus sardonicus associated with strychnine poisoning. A cursory examination of his nails showed the absence of Mees' lines, which ruled out arsenic. Not cyanide either, because I could not smell even a hint of bitter almonds. Something more exotic then, a nightshade perhaps, or ricin. Once again, my eyes skipped across the stain on the bed before settling on the overturned glass. I picked it up, realizing there was a faint blue residue speckling its base, something I had failed to notice earlier.

Running one finger around the bottom of the glass, I brought it to my lips. The taste made my tongue go numb immediately. Frowning, I parted his eyelids and peered into his eyes. The pupils were contracted, not dilated, which could only mean ... morphine, I thought. He had overdosed on it, which meant this was a case of suicide, not murder.

'Huzoor,' Charan Singh said, interrupting my investigation, 'that's enough! Come away now. I will take care of it and make sure he is buried with respect.'

Placing one gentle hand on my shoulder, he tried to steer me away from the body. Part of me was offended by such brazen intimacy, even from my oldest friend. I was tempted to brush him off, to remind him to remember his place. Instead, I let him lead me out of that grisly room, as docile as a dog on a leash.

Outside, I sagged wearily against the doorframe. The detachment I always assumed when confronted by a crime scene was fading fast. In its place, a farrago of conflicting emotions assailed me, shock warring with outrage, sorrow battling with bewilderment.

Charan Singh, ever faithful, pressed a glass into my hand. 'Here, drink this.'

'What is it?'

'I don't know, some vilayeti liquor or the other. Drink it. It will make you feel better.'

I sniffed the glass briefly and then bolted it down in one gulp. The caramel taste of cognac flooded through my mouth, a Croizet by the taste of it, its heat perfectly matching the raw ferocity of my mood.

Another, I was about to demand when a voice interrupted me.

'Mr Singh, could we have a word please?'

Turning, I was greeted by the one person I did not want to see at that moment.

'Not now, Commissioner Edwardes,' I rasped, biting back my impatience. 'This is not a good time for a social call.'

'I am not here on a social call, I'm afraid,' the commissioner replied. 'I'm sorry to be such a raven, but I have another bit of bad news for you.'

He offered me a very official-looking sheet of bond paper, anointed with what looked to be the Governor of Bombay's seal. 'This is an order of externment. By imperial gazette, Your Highness, you have until tomorrow to leave the Presidency and return to Rajpore.'

'This is ridiculous!' I exclaimed, giving him a perplexed frown. 'Can't you do something about this, Commissioner?'

'You were warned, Mr Singh. Not only did you not apply for a permit from the Native States Agency to leave your kingdom and travel to Bombay, but you also failed to ask permission from the governor before entering the Presidency. And then, of course, there is the small matter of the entirely illegal investigation you have been carrying out illicitly under my department's nose, not to mention the dead gentleman you have in there.'

'Please, Commissioner,' I tried to plead. 'I only need a few more days ... two at the most, and I will get to the bottom of this mess.'

Commissioner Edwards smiled sympathetically. 'Look, Sikander, if I may call you that, I have always admired your reputation and appreciated your skills as a detective, but I cannot help you. The powers that be have spoken, and my hands are tied.'

With that pronouncement, he gave me a shallow bow before departing rather precipitously. I glared at his retreating back and let out a curse so florid that it made Charan Singh turn as red as a beet.

Damn him, and damn the English!

'What are we to do about this?' asked Charan Singh, holding up the letter. 'Shall I pack up and get us ready to return to Rajpore?'

'No, do nothing. Stay here and make sure,' the words caught in my throat, 'make sure our friend inside is taken care of. Don't let the police take his body away.'

Angling my neck, I cast a despairing glance at the door behind me, unable to stop myself from shuddering.

'What a god-awful waste!' I said. 'Why resort to something so drastic? Why choose the coward's way out?'

'Who knows what was going on in his mind, Sahib,' Charan Singh, ever stoic, said with a shrug. 'If one thing is certain, it is that love makes fools of us all.'

ONE WEEK EARLIER

CHAPTER 1

'Do you love me, Sikander?'

I was seated at my piano, as is my habit on most mornings following breakfast, when the door to the music room slammed open, and Helene came storming in.

My mood was already rather sour, considering I had managed to squander the better part of two hours trying to master the same piece of music only to fail rather miserably. Chopin's 'Winter Wind', is one of my favorite compositions. It is a madness, a cataclysm so tremendously involving that a man can lose himself in its intricacy. Unfortunately, it also happens to be perhaps the most challenging orchestration ever written for the piano, so complicated that it can defeat even the most seasoned of virtuosos from time to time.

In my youth, I had always thought it an easy enough piece, but now, I found myself struggling through my third attempt to get it right. The first two had come to an embarrassingly premature conclusion when my fingers had cramped up each time I approached the final fortissimo. Still, even though my knuckles felt like they were on fire, I refused to give up.

Sadly, just as I was nearing the most crucial moment in the final variation, Helene barged in. Taken entirely by surprise, my concentration wavered. The music faltered, leaving one single glassy note lingering between us, as sharp as a dagger.

Biting back an irritated curse, I swiveled to face her. Helene had been my companion now for the better part of two decades, but still, as always, my heart could not help but skip a beat when I saw her. Though she was firmly on the wrong side of forty, she remained a very handsome woman, tall and slender, with an elegance of posture that only the French can master. A few desultory streaks of grey had only just begun to lace the russet of her hair, and if I squinted, I could discern the faintest webwork of wrinkles around her eyes. Those imperfections though only made her more desirable to me. A beautiful woman, I have always believed, is like a Montrachet. They only grow finer with time.

'I asked you a question, Sikander,' Helene repeated, enunciating each word, as if it was a threat. 'Do you, or do you not, love me?'

'It is eleven in the morning, Helene,' I said, letting out rather an exasperated sigh. 'A gentleman does not speak of matters of the heart until after the sun has set.'

Sadly, this jest, while clever enough, fell on deaf ears.

'Why must you always insist on being so difficult? Can't you give me a straight answer for once?'

'Very well,' I said, easing shut the piano's lid. 'Although I must warn you, you may not like what I have to say.'

Rising to my feet, I crossed over to place my hands on her shoulders, so that we were standing face to face.

'I do love you, Helene, insomuch as I am capable of love.'

'What is that supposed to mean?'

'I guess what I am trying to say is that as I grow older, I have come to realize that it is not in my nature to believe in abstracts. I have neither the time nor the patience for it. What is it that Descartes said? The senses deceive from time to time, and it is prudent never to trust wholly those who have deceived us even once. Truth be told, that is why I find mysteries so involving,

Helene. They are real. They are palpable. There is always a villain to be caught, a suspect to chase down and a clue to uncover. There is always an answer simply waiting to be found. That is what makes sense to me. Not the metaphysical, but the corporeal. Do you understand?'

Even as I said those words, judging from the way Helene's upper lip curled with disdain, I knew I had made a mistake.

'You really are a dreadful man, Sikander Singh,' she hissed. 'There are times when I cannot help but despise you utterly.'

With that announcement, she spun on one foot and stormed toward the door, brushing past my manservant Charan Singh, who had chosen that unfortunate moment to make an entrance.

Charan Singh was a veritable behemoth, some seven feet tall in his socks, towering over Helene who was just over five and a half feet in height. Nevertheless, he scurried out of her way with the greatest of haste, not unlike an elephant retreating before a mouse.

'The memsahib seems more annoyed than usual,' he observed when Helene slammed the door shut behind her, hard enough to make my teeth rattle.

'I can't understand it,' I said quizzically. 'Something is obviously bothering her. I wonder what it could be.'

'Well, Huzoor, if I may hazard a guess,' Charan Singh said. 'While I am not as experienced as you in the ways of love, even I possess enough common sense to understand that no woman is happy when you forget to celebrate the day on which she was born.'

'Damn it!' I exclaimed. A shudder of dismay coursed through me as I realized the old man was absolutely correct. 'Why didn't you remind me it was her birthday, you oaf?'

I gave Charan Singh an accusing sneer, to which he responded with a sardonic chuckle.

'From the day you were born, Huzoor, I have served you loyally. Through thick and thin, through hardship and strife, I have stood by your side. I have polished your boots and pressed your trousers and taught you how to tie your pugree. When needed, I have even bathed you and wiped up your vomit. But I have not, and will not, ever involve myself with whatever happens between you and Helene Memsahib.' He sniffed volubly and shook his head. 'Only a fool sticks out his head when a lion and lioness are roaring.'

I rolled my eyes. 'Oh, get lost, won't you! And spare me your homespun homilies, you oversized baboon.'

Sitting back, I let out a Vesuvian sigh. *How was I to extricate myself from this quagmire? How could I mollify Helene and make up for such a dreadful faux pas? An emerald necklace perhaps?* No, that wouldn't work. She had plenty of jewelry already, many a shiny reminder of my innumerable gaffes in the past. *A holiday maybe?* Yes, that might work. She was always carping on about how utterly boring Rajpore was. Maybe I could promise her a trip to the Continent for a few weeks come summer. Venice perhaps, and Paris, of course. Surely that would convince her to forgive me for forgetting her birthday.

A muted cough behind me made me realize that, rather than leaving, Charan Singh was still lurking about.

'Is there a reason you are still here, hovering about like an oversized vulture, you decrepit old fossil, or are you merely trying to annoy me?'

His reply was a self-satisfied smirk. 'As a matter of fact, Your Highness, I thought you may wish to have this.' Reaching into his cummerbund, he pulled forth an envelope that he waved at me. 'It arrived this morning, addressed to you, and is marked urgent.'

'A letter!' I exclaimed. 'Why didn't you say so earlier? Hand it over immediately!'

Snatching it from his outstretched hand, I peered down at the postmark. The letter's point of origin seemed to be Bombay. The stamp, in particular, caught my eye. It was one I had not seen before, featuring a garishly painted portrait of George V in bright green. Licking my lips, I used one of my thumbnails to carefully pry it off the thick manila beneath.

Charan Singh watched curiously for a moment before retreating to a nearby bench. Settling down with a sigh, he unfolded a copy of the *Lahore Tribune* and began to peruse its pages with a squint. As for me, I let out a delighted laugh when the stamp finally came loose, that too without a single tear. Rising, I shuffled over to my writing desk and tucked it away between the pages of my diary, so that I could add it to my stamp album later, before picking up an ivory tusk with which I proceeded to tear open the envelope.

Inside, I found a single sheet of coarse paper. Unfolding it, I saw it was covered by a neat, spidery script that I recognized immediately.

Sikander, my dear boy,

I do hope that this letter finds you in the halest of health. What has it been since we last corresponded? Nine, no, closer to ten months, I think, but not a day goes by that I do not fondly remember you and the time I spent in Rajpore as your tutor.

The truth is that I have been meaning to write to you for some weeks now, but what can I say? Life inevitably is what ensues while we are busy laying plans, and it is only now that I have been able to find the time to put pen to paper.

As you may recall from my last letter, I had taken the decision to retire from the business of private tutoring last May. I am not a young man any more, and in recent years, I have not been able to find the satisfaction I once cherished in teaching. You were always the favorite among my wards, quite as clever as you were obstinate, but this new generation of princes area disappointing lot, even more arrogant than they are privileged.

In any case, I had retreated to my cottage in Landour, hoping to enjoy a quiet retirement cultivating roses, when out of the blue, a most unexpected offer turned up on my doorstep. Much to my surprise, I was approached by the trustees of the Mayo College in Ajmer, asking if I would care to take over as their Master of Classics. Needless to say, I did not tarry too long before jumping at the chance. Who would not? A position at one of India's finest institutions, a fine salary and an assured pension, not to mention the chance to teach Virgil to a generation of intelligent young gentlemen. It is, to say the very least, a dream come true.

However, that is not the sole reason I am writing to you, to appraise you of this unexpected change in my fortunes. To the crux then, without further ado. I do hope you're sitting down, for the news I have for you is nothing short of flabbergasting.

Along with this new opportunity, it seems fate had one more surprise in store for me. You see, at the ripe age of fifty-two, I have decided at last to take a wife!

I can imagine the look on your face, how shocked you must be, wondering if I have taken leave of my wits at last. As I am sure you may recall from our many discussions on the subject, in my youth I chose to hold rather a dim opinion of the merits of marriage, but now, as my twilight beckons, I find myself wondering if I was being unnecessarily hasty. Hard to believe, yes, but I have been considering the possibility for some time. Perhaps you might remember that poem by Emily Dickinson I often read to you:

Hope is the thing with feathers
That perches in the soul
And sings the tune without the words
And never stops at all.

The truth, my dear boy, is that not only does the thought of being alone in my dotage terrify me, but I also cannot help but feel that I have failed my family in some way by not siring a son of my own, an heir to carry forward the Rowan name. In either case, what held me back from seeking a companion for the longest time was the fact that I had no fixed address. India is, as you know, a difficult place for an Englishwoman, but to drag her from kingdom to kingdom, like a piece of baggage, that was not a life any respectable young lady would accept. As a result, I had resigned myself to being a confirmed bachelor, but now, faced with the chance to put down permanent roots, I realized I could at last seek out a partner for myself.

The main obstacle that stood in my way was the fact that I have never been skilled with the opposite sex. Thus, I decided to take the arranged marriage route and wrote a letter to the parish priest at my birthplace in Edinburgh, asking him to find me a suitable bride.

As Mr Wilde said so perspicaciously, there are only two tragedies in life: one is not getting what one wants, and the other is getting it. Frankly, I forgot I had even drafted such a missive, so little did I expect any success. But wonder of wonders, a little over eleven weeks ago, Father Snowdon wrote back to inform me that he had contracted an engagement on my behalf.

Her name is Mary. Miss Mary Hartley of Pitlochry, a village on Loch Rannoch. Isn't that a puissant, salt of the earth, altogether dependable name?

I paused, stifling a smile. Mary Hartley indeed! Good heavens! She sounded like something straight out of a Walter Scott novel!

> *She is an orphan, much like myself. Thirty-one years of age, and until recently a governess in Aberdeen. You must be wondering what she looks like. Well, I haven't a clue. In my mind's eye, I have imagined a tall, Highland lass, strong-boned, with a straight back and a joyful laugh, but I fear I will*

have to wait another six days to discover if I am indeed correct in my assumptions.

Even as you read this letter, you see, my Mary is safely aboard a Peninsular and Orient (P&O) vessel, well on her way to India to become my wife. The ship is due to dock in Bombay on the morning of the fourth of May, and the very next day, I intend to have the banns read at St John's. That is the very reason why I have written to you, Sikander. You once told me that if ever I needed you, you would be there for me, no questions asked. Well, now is the time to make good on your vow. I want you here when I walk down the aisle, not only to bear witness to and share in my happiness, but also because I am scared, old friend. Yes, I confess it. I am terrified. What if Miss Hartley dislikes me? What if I dislike her? What if she thinks me old and boring, and spurns me at first sight? That is why I would be truly grateful if my favorite student was here, by my side, to provide some much-needed support.

I can only hope you will be able to find the time to leave behind the many responsibilities of running your kingdom for a few weeks and come down-country to Bombay to oblige this most humble of wishes.

I look forward to seeing you soon.

Fondly yours,

Your old comrade in quills,

Peter Rowan

When I saw that signature, my mouth crinkled into a smile. Peter blasted Rowan, of all people! That was a name I had almost forgotten, but now a flood of pleasant memories came rushing back.

I had scarcely been eleven when Peter came to Rajpore. My tutor before him had been a very dour Presbyterian gentleman named William Dall who believed fervently that to spare the rod was to spoil the child. He was forced to quit his position and evict himself from Rajpore with the greatest alacrity after Charan Singh found him beating me with a bamboo switch one afternoon and broke his right arm.

Peter arrived a month later as his replacement. He came highly recommended. A Canterbury and Cambridge man, he had previously been retained as my cousin Bhupinder of Patiala's Latin instructor. Unfortunately, as those who know Bhupinder will be quick to testify, he possesses no interest in anything he cannot eat, drink or mount. As a result, he had been a most unreceptive ward. So, when my mother offered Peter a position as my tutor, he decided to accept only too eagerly.

I had been quite cold with him at first, expecting him to be much like his predecessor, but Peter—a tall, shy, merry-eyed man with enormous horse's teeth, a braying laugh and a sense of curiosity very nearly as boundless as my own—had managed to surprise me. We hit it off thoroughly. My father, God bless him, rarely had time for anyone but his horses. As a result, it was my mother, Amrita Devi, and Charan Singh who had raised me. It was from the former I learnt to play the piano, speak French and do the waltz, and from the latter, to shoot and ride and fence. But it was Peter who taught me how to be a gentleman and how to appreciate the finer things in life. Besides Latin, he taught me how to appreciate the Italian masters and write in iambic pentameter, and how to tell a Merlot from a Beaujolais. He taught me how grammar maketh a man, how to always pair my socks with my tie and that ostentation would never quite be as elegant as understatement. He showed me how to fight chestnuts, and bowl a googly and even box Queensbury rules, a skill which has served me in good stead more than once in the years since.

Grinning, I refolded the letter and replaced it inside its envelope.

'Charan Singh!' I exclaimed. 'Where are you, you dozy dolt?'

'Not so loud, Huzoor.' The big Sikh put down his newspaper and lurched to his feet with a pronounced groan. 'I am old, yes, but not yet deaf.'

'Oh, stop your moaning! Go have my private carriage prepared immediately. And tell the stationmaster to arrange to have it attached to the next express train going south. Oh, and have my trunks packed, and the memsahib's as well, for a journey of at least two weeks.'

To his credit, the big Sikh was so accustomed to the capriciousness of my moods that he did not miss a wink.

'And where, might I inquire, is it that we are off to in such a hurry?' he inquired, giving me his usual scowl of disapproval.

'For once, stop asking stupid questions and do as you're told, won't you?' I growled. 'You have two hours, old man. I want to leave before sunset, so make yourself useful.'

With that imprecation, I dashed out of the music room to find Helene. It took me almost twenty minutes to track her down. She wasn't in any of her usual haunts, neither the library nor up in her private suite, nor was she seated in her favorite gazebo out on the grand lawns, where she enjoyed reading Molière and Dumas and the like, especially on days like this, when a cool breeze was blowing in from the nearby Himalayas, bringing with it the scent of fresh snow.

In the end, I found her in the terrarium, up on the roof of the killa. To be honest, that was rather a grandiose name for what was really a small greenhouse housed beneath a domed marble chattri, just above the western corner of the palace. In my grandfather's time, it had served rather a different purpose, as a pied-à-terre where he could retreat with his favorite concubine when the urge to make love beneath the full moon happened to seize him. But once Helene had come to stay with me, she had cleared it out and instead turned the place into her own private sanctum, replacing the low divans and muslin curtains that had once decorated the enclosure with rows of clay pots in which she had nurtured an extensive variety of exotic flowers.

'There you are,' I said, coming up behind her. She was hunched over a row of dendrobiums. I thought at first that she was pruning them, but then, as I inched closer, I saw her shoulders shudder and it dawned upon me that she was crying.

'You know,' I snaked one arm around her waist, 'the salt in your tears will kill your flowers. You do realize that, don't you?'

'Leave me alone,' she murmured, choking back a sob. 'I don't want to talk to you!'

'Helene,' I wheedled. 'Don't be like this!'

I slipped my other arm around her as well and pressed up behind her. Her closeness was infinitely reassuring to me. It never ceased to amaze me how well we seemed to fit into each other, like two adjoining pieces of a jigsaw puzzle.

To my dismay, Helene remained unreceptive. Instead of slumping into me, as she normally did when I embraced her, she remained stiff, her back as rigid as an iron rod.

'I said go away, Sikander!' she snarled, pushing my arms apart with a strength that took me by surprise.

'What if I was to tell you that I have a surprise for you?' I said, grinning slyly.

Her gaze narrowed. 'I really am in no mood for your games, Sikander.'

'Really? Then I'd better tell Charan Singh to cancel the trip, I guess.'

That was what finally did the trick.

'Trip?' she said, looking at me suspiciously, wiping her cheeks clean with the back of one hand. 'What trip?'

'Well, I came up here to tell you to pack your bags because I am taking you to Bombay for two weeks, but if you don't want to go I can have Charan Singh cancel everything.'

'Bombay!' she exclaimed, her eyes widening. 'Are you serious?'

'Of course! Surely you didn't think I would forget your birthday?' I feigned an expression of sanctimonious outrage. 'Helene! I'm hurt. I'm wounded. I'm mortified.'

With each word, I leaned in closer and closer until I was just inches away from her. 'I wonder, how are you going to make it up to me for distrusting me so completely!'

'Oh, Sikander!' Helene leaned forward to close the gap between our mouths with a groan that was one part frustration and two parts desire.

Smiling, I stifled a sigh of relief as she settled her head into the crook of my shoulder, resting her forehead against the curve of my scapula.

Crisis averted! I thought happily. Things were coming up trumps at last for Sikander Singh.

CHAPTER 2

You can smell Bombay long before you see it.

There are poets who insist that cities have souls, but I haven't the patience for such sophistry. I am a hunter at heart, and what I have come to realize after a lifetime of travelling is that cities, like animals, are defined by their scents.

Every great city has a perfume, an essence which when distilled, personifies all that it represents. Take London as an example, which stinks of ash and secrets. Or Paris, which smells of bones and lust. Rome is redolent with the aroma of cold stone and murder, while New York reeks of ambition, cabbage and iron. As for India, Calcutta is a strange mixture of paper, rot and regret, while Delhi smells of dust, and sorrow and longing. Madras stinks of arrack, fever and gunpowder; and in Simla, no matter where you turn, you are assailed by the stench of homesickness, so unavoidable that it brings tears to your eyes.

But Bombay? All that Bombay smells of is fish and greed.

It comes upon you very quickly. One moment you are amidst the Western Ghats, surrounded by dust and black slate, and then suddenly, as you cross the Thane creek, it assails you, a miasma so palpable it seems to be as impenetrable as a wall.

Bombay is a many-layered cache, quite as complex as one of Monsieur Dralle's fragrances. First comes the base note, the stink of salt and the sea, of rotting fish, wet mud and pungent mangroves. Then the stench of raw sewage mingling with the acrid smoke belching from the mills and foundries, and the unwashed reek of too many people crammed into far too little space, all blending into an assault on your senses so fetid that you begin to choke. And beneath that, if you close your eyes and take a deep breath, you can smell the sour scent that makes Bombay what it is—hope, quite as intoxicating and inescapable as raw olibanum.

That is what no poet will ever tell you, that hope stinks—of sweat and desire and sex and longing, of impossible dreams and nauseating ambition and, most of all, of the sweet and unnerving odor of disappointment.

It was this very stench that assailed my nostrils as the gaudy edifice of Victoria Terminus finally hove into view. Even though I had never bothered to keep my disdain for Bombay hidden, I let out a sigh of relief, glad to see that the end of our journey was finally in sight.

To say the trip south had been onerous would be the grossest of understatements. My kingdom, Rajpore, is located almost seventeen hundred kilometers north of Bombay, deep amidst the fertile heartland of the Punjab. On one side, we are bordered by the Himalayan foothills. To the other lies the alluvial floodplain of the Sutlej, and beyond that is Delhi, the new capital of British India. In terms of the hierarchy of princely India, I am rather an insignificant monarch. Compared to the bigwigs like Baroda and Hyderabad, who are entitled to twenty-one guns, I am only permitted a measly fifteen. Still, in contrast to the average Indian, I am impossibly wealthy, certainly well-off enough to travel in my own private coach, which is a Pullman with all the comforts of home: carpeted flooring, iced air conditioning, two fully functional bathrooms with hot and cold running water, sleeping cabins for twelve with electric lights and fans, and even a wet bar and gramophone.

In spite of this excess of luxury, after spending almost a week rattling across the length and breadth of the Indian subcontinent, I was understandably sick and tired of being cooped up like a bird in a gilded cage. All I wanted was to be off this damnable train and to get myself a stiff drink or two, before taking a nap so long that it would put Epimenides to shame. To my consternation, we were forced to wait yet another hour as our carriage was unshackled from the train and shunted to a private siding, where Charan Singh had managed to arrange for us to disembark on an unused platform, away from the cynosure of prying eyes. By the time we finally managed to dismount, it was almost dusk. After five days on a train, my knees were understandably wobbly. I took a minute to stretch my back and grow accustomed once more to having the firmament of solid ground beneath my feet. Behind me, Helene let out a sigh of relief as she stepped down on to the platform, assisted by Charan Singh. Poor thing, she had weathered the journey with her usual forbearance, never once uttering a word of complaint, no matter how cloying the heat and dust.

'Are you all right, my dear?' I inquired, giving her a concerned smile.

'I need a proper bath, Sikander,' she said, wrinkling her nose. 'I smell as pungent as a fishwife.'

'That can wait,' I retorted. 'What I need first and foremost is a drink.'

As if on cue, a young Sikh clad in Rajpore livery stepped forward and gave me a respectful bow.

'Welcome to Bombay, Huzoor, Memsahib,' he said, before offering us a silver salver atop which two chilled tulips awaited.

After raising one inquiring brow at Charan Singh, who nodded in affirmation, I took one glass and passed it to Helene, before helping myself to the second. Taking a sip, I let out a sigh of absolute satisfaction. It was my favorite, Pol Roger, chilled perfectly to exactly ten degrees centigrade, just as I preferred. To my parched tongue, it tasted quite as sweet as ambrosia.

After another larger sip, I studied the young retainer intently. He certainly seemed familiar, but I couldn't remember hiring him, although it was obvious he worked for me. That much was apparent from his uniform, which was in my colors, black with bands of red and gold at the throat and sleeves. He was in his early twenties, I guessed, and very tall, with a handsome face that had only just begun to harden with maturity. It took me a minute to realize why I knew him, only after I noticed the look of paternal pride that decorated Charan Singh's weather-beaten visage.

'One of your myriad offsprings?' I asked him.

'This is Uday Singh, Huzoor,' Charan Singh confirmed, clapping the boy on his back so hard that he nearly fell over. 'Son number four. He is taking care of your property and business here in Bombay.'

The boy grinned, first at his father and then at me. 'If you would care to come this way, Huzoor, your chariot awaits.'

Returning his smile, I followed the boy. I could see why Charan Singh was proud of him. He seemed to be a smart and well-mannered young man, even if he was unnecessarily attractive, as evidenced by the admiring glances Helene directed toward him when she thought I wasn't looking.

'If he continues this way, old man,' I said, giving Charan Singh a nod of approbation, 'you'll soon be out of a job.'

'I think not,' the big Sikh snorted. 'You wouldn't survive five minutes without me, Huzoor. Besides, Uday Singh is destined for greater things than being an overbred brat's personal valet.'

Before I could come up with a suitable scathing retort, I was distracted by something quite unexpected.

At the south end of the platform, a trio of vehicles was parked. Two were Ford lorries, on to which our luggage had already been loaded, I noticed approvingly. However, it was the third vehicle that caught my eye. I let out a low, surprised whistle. Ordinarily, I favor Rolls-Royces; in my experience, there are few automobiles more reliable, but this was something else. It was longer than my Silver Ghost, squarer and somehow still sleeker, with an aggressive wedge-shaped grille that made it look like a snarling predator about to pounce. What it lacked in elegance it made up for in the suggestion of raw power, an impression that was only magnified by the startling shade of yellow in which it was painted.

'This is definitely not a Rolls-Royce,' I said to Uday Singh.

'It's German, Sir, not English,' the boy replied. 'A Mercedes Tourer with coachwork by Henri-Labourdette. It was imported for the Khan of Kalat. However, he changed his mind and put it up for sale, whereupon I snapped it up.' He offered me another, even more cheeky, grin and added, 'I thought you might enjoy it.'

'Well done!' I said.

I took a slow circuit of the car, admiring its lines. I was tempted to open the bonnet and make a careful inspection of the engine, but before I could indulge myself, Helene interrupted me with an exasperated snort.

'Oh Sikander, do hurry up! You can fiddle about with your new toy later. Please, can we get going now?'

As if to illustrate this rebuke, Charan Singh hurriedly pulled open the passenger door for her. Helene climbed in, settling back into the leather seat with a groan. I paused, tempted to drive, but common sense quickly prevailed over excitement.

Not only was I a stranger to Bombay's byways, but I felt close to the brink of exhaustion, which was why I joined Helene in the back, leaving it to Uday Singh to take the wheel. After Charan Singh had mounted as well, taking his customary position in the front seat, Uday Singh cranked the car to life with practiced ease.

The engine growled, as throaty as a panther. When he released the parking brake, the Mercedes rolled smoothly into motion, without a single creak or rattle.

Peering out, I tried to get my bearings straight as we slowly swung out of the rear entrance and trundled past the new General Post Office with its half-constructed black basalt dome. It had been just a few years since my last visit to Bombay, but in that brief expanse of time, the city seemed to have undergone quite a drastic change. Business was booming, by the looks of it. There was new construction everywhere, buildings I did not recognize, all bedecked by the skeletons of scaffolding reaching toward the heavens like grasping fingers.

Even though it was early evening, the streets were very crowded. A teeming mass of people thronged the streets outside the terminus, where the tram lines intersected with the broad avenue of Bori Bunder. They numbered easily in the hundreds, all waiting impatiently for the last trains of the day to depart. Our convoy was forced to slow to a crawl. Though Uday Singh pressed down on the car horn with shrill abandon, and Charan Singh opened his door and leaned out to shout '*Rasta do*! Give way!,' the crowd refused to budge. Instead, many of them turned to peer at us with idle curiosity, as is the Indian way, shoving and jostling against the car, rocking it back and forth on its springs.

Abruptly, we were surrounded by beggars, a horde of filthy skeletal creatures clad in a mismatched motley of rags. They surged forward, seeming to appear from nowhere, far too many to count. My eyes flickered across their faces—a wizened old man, his nose eaten away by leprosy; a broad-shouldered soldier whose height rivaled Charan Singh, except his right arm was amputated; a slender girl with no eyes, holding a mewling baby at her hip; a fat eunuch, clapping her hands and clanking her bangles at us; a trio of toothless old women, as ancient as Macbeth's witches;

and a dozen ragged urchins, all clamoring in different languages, Urdu and Hindi and even one who spoke reasonable English, all mouthing the same monotone: '*Paisa de do*. In God's name, give us a penny.'

My lip curled with disgust, and I began to roll up my window. Beside me, Helene let out a squeal of dismay when one of the beggars, a cherubic boy with filthy fingers and a runny nose, made a grab for her necklace. Charan Singh was quicker though and struck him a resounding slap that sent him scuttling away.

Thankfully, that served to thin the crowd. A narrow path opened ahead of the car, which Uday Singh took gratefully, twisting the throttle as hard as he could.

'My apologies, Huzoor!' he explained as the Mercedes sped up. 'It gets worse every year. It is because of the mills. Every day, more and more people arrive, looking for work. Sadly, most of them end up on the streets.'

'Are you okay, my dear?' I said, turning to make sure Helene was unharmed.

'I'm fine, Sikander,' she replied, smiling weakly, unable to hide her shock. 'It's just ... I'm not used to so many people, not anymore.'

Frowning, I leaned over to wind her window up as well. This incident, albeit mundane, had served to remind me exactly why I disliked Bombay. There were far too many people here, over a million souls packed into a space the size of my smallest hunting estate. And if the congestion wasn't bad enough, there was the noise, a constant barrage of sound assaulting my ears and nearly overwhelming my senses. That was what I abhorred most about the city, along with the endless poverty that surrounded us. It was unavoidable, so omnipresent that it seemed as obvious as a slap to the face. Everywhere I turned, I could see the poor and homeless congregating on the streets, mainly natives, sleeping on the pavements and living in shanties and hovels so squalid they were not fit for animals, much less human habitation. That was the clearest evidence of the innate callousness of the English, one of the starkest ironies of the British Empire. It suited the India Office to style itself as India's enlightened rescuer and cast us, the princes of India, as wastrels and sybarites. But in my experience, I had found that the maharajas and nawabs cared for their people far more deeply than the British ever would. Take the Gaekwad of Baroda, for instance. He provided his citizens with free education and healthcare and had even founded a bank, as had Bhupinder of Patiala, my maternal cousin, who was a great lout but made every effort to ensure that his people were kept safe from famine. Even in Rajpore, my citizens had electricity, hospitals, pukka homes, water and even a free library. But here, in the wealthiest province of British India, all that greeted my eyes was the direst of poverty. Back home, we had no beggars, no indigents, no homeless; I made sure of it, regardless of the expense. But in Bombay, the English did not seem to give a hoot, not as long as they continued to turn a healthy profit.

I suppose I am being a dreadful hypocrite. The truth, however unsavory, is that none of us maharajas could have existed without the English. This was particularly true of the Phulkian kings of the Punjab. It was the British who had made us, who had provided us with the income and status of which we had become so fond. That meant my own family was as culpable as all the rest in the slow entropy that was gripping British India, the massive social divide that had come to separate the rich from the poor. That was the primary contributor to my sour mood; even though I was well aware of this irony, it did not mean I relished having it rubbed in my face. And then, of course, there was the fact that I could not help but be assailed by the same unease I always felt when I left the confines of my kingdom and entered British India, a sense of wary circumspection. In Rajpore, I was untouchable, as good as a demigod, but here, to the burra sahibs, I would always be a jumped-up native, a second-class citizen, a darkie.

Suddenly, I felt myself stricken by a pang of homesickness so intense that it made me shiver. I fought the temptation to order Uday Singh to turn the car around. Instead, I glanced over at Helene, who was gazing out of the window with shiny eyes, devouring every glimpse of the city as it flickered past.

'What a glorious idea this was!' she exclaimed exuberantly. 'I'm so glad you came up with this plan, Sikander. It feels so good to be in a proper city for a change,' she laughed, a joyful chortle. 'I mean, I love Rajpore, and you always make sure I have everything I want or need, but this is so much more exciting. There's so much to do in a place like Bombay, so much to see.'

Her eyes sparkled with anticipation. 'I have the whole week planned out for us. You simply must take me to the new opera house and to the races, and then, this weekend, we shall go sailing. You still own that sloop, don't you? Or did you get rid of it? And I warn you, I intend to spend an entire day shopping at Whiteaway and Laidlaw.'

'I do hope you've left time for me to visit the bathroom,' I said sarcastically.

'Oh, stop being such a stick-in-the-mud, won't you?' She let out another laugh and mock-punched my shoulder.

I intercepted her hand, enfolding it into mine. On most occasions, I abhor physical contact, but with Helene, it felt different. She always managed to make me feel complete, at peace, my natural impatience somehow held in abeyance by her proximity.

'This is going to be so much fun,' she said, nestling her head into my shoulder. 'A proper adventure. It's been so long since we have had an adventure, non?'

As we approached the junction of Esplanade and Queen's Road, she continued to natter away, listing out an even more elaborate litany of plans. I tuned out her voice , craning my neck instead to cast an admiring glance at the steeple of the University Clock Tower, which I could see in the near distance, rising up like a warning finger. And then, on our right, I caught my first glimpse of the sea, an azure expanse stretching to the horizon, so implacably placid that it seemed to be made of silk.

Greeted by this magnificent vista, I found myself ruminating over what I could recall of the city's origins.

Curiously enough, the story of modern Bombay had begun with a marriage. Originally, what was today British India's largest and most prosperous city had once been an archipelago of seven small islands just off the Konkan coast. The Marathas and the Mughals had shown little interest in inhabiting them, preferring to leave the islands to the Angria pirates and the Koli fisherfolk, who had migrated there long before Christ was even born.

It was the arrival of the Portuguese, which had laid the foundation stone for modern Bombay. They were the ones who had named the largest of the islands Bom Bahia, which meant 'good bay', and recognized that it was one of the finest natural harbors in the world. And it was when they had signed the Treaty of Bassein in 1534 with Bahadur Shah of Gujarat that all seven islands—Bombay, Parel, Mazagaon, Mahim, Colaba, Worli and Old Woman's Island—had officially passed into European hands.

The Portuguese had been content to treat Bombay mainly as a victualling station for vessels outbound from Surat to Goa. Rather than encouraging a permanent settlement, they had built forts in Bassein, Bandra and Salsette, and intermarried with the locals, thus giving rise to the Bombay Catholics.

The first Englishmen had arrived in Bombay in 1583, eager to break the Portuguese monopoly on trade with Mughal India. It was not long before the East India Company recognized its value as a strategic naval port and tried several times to purchase the islands, only to be rebuffed. After three decades of inconclusive skirmishing, it was only when the English had emerged as the dominant power in the Arabian Sea, after trouncing the Portuguese at the Battle of Swally in 1612, that Bombay finally passed into their hands.

In 1662, when Catherine de Braganza of Portugal had married Charles the Second of England, the island of Bombay had been ceded to the English as part of her dowry. It was then that the story of the city had begun in earnest. Over the next fifty years, the East India Company had slowly acquired the other islands. It had taken another six decades to rid them of pirates, and to build the Bombay Castle, thus attracting a spate of Parsi, Gujarati and Bohra traders who flocked to the city in droves. By 1750, Bombay had eclipsed Surat as the center of shipbuilding and commerce in western India. When Salsette was ceded to the Crown with the Treaty of Salbai in 1782, it was the English who had initiated the spate of reclamations that had united the seven islands together as one, thus giving birth to the cosmopolitan metropolis that surrounded us now.

'Are you even listening to me?' Helene exclaimed, interrupting my reverie.

'Of course, I am,' I responded, even as she mock-punched my shoulder again.

'Liar! You haven't heard a thing I said.'

'That's not true. I heard every single word, I swear it on my honor.'

'Good, then we are in agreement. We are having lunch at the Byculla Club tomorrow. I shall have Charan Singh call ahead and make a reservation for noon.'

'Ah!' I shifted uncomfortably, realizing that I had been caught out. 'Everything in good time, my dear,' I said. 'Unfortunately, the Byculla Club shall have to wait until the day after. You see, as it happens, we are scheduled to attend a wedding tomorrow.'

This announcement caused Helene to sit bolt upright. 'A wedding? What wedding? Whose wedding?'

I offered her a weak smile. 'Did I forget to mention it to you? My old tutor, Peter Rowan, is tying the knot. I thought we could make a brief appearance at the festivities.'

Helene was not pleased. Her face clouded, growing stormy with consternation.

'Sikander Singh, did you plan all this?' She gave me a very suspicious glare. 'Is that what this trip was all about, not my birthday?'

'Of course not. It's just fortuitous, that's all. A stroke of good luck!'

'I don't believe you! *Sacré bleu!* How could you do this to me, Sikander? How can I possibly attend a wedding? Why, I haven't a thing to wear.'

'You have three trunks filled with dresses, Helene.'

'Yes,' her frown deepened into a scowl, 'but not one of them will do for a formal occasion. I am not a crow like you, Sikander. I can't wear the same clothes every day. I am French. We have style! We have panache!'

I rolled my eyes. 'How about this, my dear? I shall have Bombay's finest seamstress come and knock together a frock for you by tomorrow morning, no matter the price. Will that make up for me forgetting to tell you about Peter's wedding?'

Even as I uttered those words, I realized it was entirely the wrong thing to say. Rather than mollifying her, it only served to make her angrier.

'*Nom de dieu!*' she spat in French. Her eyes flashed with such fury they seemed like sapphires. 'I am not some Montmartre trollop to be bought off with the promise of a pretty dress.'

'Helene,' I said hastily, trying to backtrack, 'let's not ruin the whole trip.'

'You've already done that,' she snapped.

'Please, my love, don't be like this. Look, let's just get through the wedding. Afterwards, we can do all the things you want to. Day after tomorrow, I will be all yours. I will be at your every beck and call, I swear it.'

Her expression did not change. Instead, if anything, the disgust in her eyes seemed to intensify, almost to the point of loathing. For a heartbeat, it felt like Helene hated me, like she wanted to hit me. I decided I would let her, if that would serve to calm her down.

Thankfully, as quickly as it had manifested, this revulsion subsided, morphing into resignation, a crestfallen acceptance.

'You are very good at making promises, Sikander Singh,' she sighed. 'I only wish you were equally good at keeping them.'

'This time will be different.' I offered her my most winsome smile. 'I promise!'.'

My attempt at charm fell flat, met instead by an impervious hauteur.

'You are a horrible, horrible man,' she declared, fixing me with a look so frosty that I could not help but shiver.

'I know, Helene,' I replied, reaching for her hand. 'What I simply cannot understand is why you choose to put up with me.'

Thankfully, she did not rebuff me and allowed me to wrap her slim, manicured fingers around my own.

'One of these days, Sikander, I warn you, I will not be quite so accommodating.'

CHAPTER 3

Our destination lay at the distant end of the Colaba Causeway, past Sassoon Dock and the Bombay, Baroda & Central India Railway Terminus, located barely a stone's throw from the towering steeple of the Afghan Church. Until the mid-1800s, both Colaba and the quaintly named Old Woman's Island had been all but inaccessible unless the sea was at ebb tide. It was only in 1839, when the causeway was completed, that these two southernmost islands were linked to Bombay proper. Within the next decade, several successful projects had been engineered by the English, most famously the Hornby Vellard that filled the great breach between Bombay and Worli; and the Mahim Causeway, which joined Bandra and the rest of the city.

Not only had all three reclamations played a pivotal role in uniting the seven islands into one cohesive land mass, but they had also created vast acreages of residential space available for the land-hungry migrants who were flocking to Bombay in droves.

It was this endless desire for new space that inspired several more private reclamations just before the turn of the century. The most famous of these was the Backbay Scheme, which was started in 1860 during the cotton boom with the ambitious goal of pushing back the sea from Malabar Hill to the distant tip of Colaba. Sadly, with the end of the American Civil War in 1865, the cotton trade collapsed and land prices plummeted, and the Backbay Bungle, as it was now remembered, came to a premature and altogether ignominious conclusion.

A few years later, in spite of the Backbay debacle, the Bombay City Improvement Trust had undertaken to reclaim around ninety thousand yards of land lining the western shore of Colaba island. The result was a paved road adjoining a seafront promenade, not unlike the Thames Embankment, that began at the end of the broad avenue of Queen's Road and ran straight across Wodehouse Bridge down to Prongs Lighthouse. It had been completed just seven years previously and named Cuffe Parade, after the gentleman who was the president of the trust at the time.

It was here that I had acquired a house some two years ago. Why, you might wonder, would someone who dislikes a city purchase a residence there? My reasoning was simple enough. While I have never hidden the fact that I think Bombay to be a crass and provincial entrepot, filled with hustlers and swindlers, smooth-talkers and charlatans, I am pragmatic enough to recognize that it has become, without a doubt, the financial capital of British India. And I am certainly not the sort of man who is comfortable staying in hotels. The very thought of sleeping swaddled in second-hand sheets, and using a bathroom that has been patronized by other travelers, is enough to give me the shudders. Add to that the sad truth that even the most expensive hotels in Bombay, whether Watson's or the Great Western, were second-rate at best. While they may be comfortable enough for itinerant box-wallahs, for a man of my breeding and taste, they would never be quite as satisfactory as the Ritz or Claridges.

That is why, during my last visit to the city, I had decided to invest in a property of my own, a handsome twelve-room mansion that had originally built for a minor Parsi cotton baron. When his fortunes dwindled and the estate was put up for sale, I snapped it up, and after an extensive renovation—where it was refitted with every modern amenity, —I had it rechristened as Rajpore House.

'Here we are, Huzoor,' Uday Singh declared when the Mercedes drew up before the ornate front gate embellished with my royal seal, a stag with antlers of gold. 'Welcome home, Your Highness!'

Leaping down, he hurried to hold open the passenger door for me. Even as he moved to help Helene alight next, I spared a few moments to inspect the property. It was obvious the boy had made a concerted effort to get the place ready for our arrival. The ironwork was newly painted, the walls freshly whitewashed, the roof capped with new tiles and the garden in excellent trim. Even the bannisters that lined the twin verandahs had been polished to a sheen recently, as had the window shutters.

'Oh, it looks so lovely,' Helene said, her face finally flowering with a reluctant, if somewhat beatific, smile.

'It will look even lovelier after a magnum of Bollinger,' I retorted. 'Charan Singh, see to it, won't you?'

'Everything is ready and waiting, Huzoor,' his son interjected, waving us toward the front door. 'If you will follow me, I will show you to your rooms.'

Sadly, before we could oblige, a tall Englishman came rushing through the gate and marched up to accost me.

'Sikander Singh!' he exclaimed. 'There you are at last! I have been waiting for you for hours.'

It took me a moment to realize that this cadaverous creature was none other than my old friend and tutor. Peter had never been handsome, but the passage of time seemed to have turned him into something out of Dickens. He looked like Sowerberry come to life, a tall question mark of a man with a hunched back and a skeletal body.

That wasn't the only thing that had changed about him. The Peter I remembered from my childhood made up for his lack of pulchritude with an almost obsessive fastidiousness. He had always taken great pains to make sure he was impeccably groomed and coiffed, his hair and moustache combed slick with pomade, his suit pressed so perfectly that you could slice fruit on the creases of his trousers. But this hapless fellow who confronted me now was clad in a Norfolk jacket so rumpled it looked like it had been put through a wringer. He wore no hat; his hair was all but gone now, just an unkempt auburn fringe remained above his ears, and he had taken to cultivating a chaotic spade of a beard that hung nearly to his chest, as dense as a bird's nest, making him resemble a prophet from the Old Testament.

Charan Singh did not recognize him. Letting out a growl, he moved forward to intercept him, but I forestalled his advance with one curt wave.

'Wait!' I said, still unable to believe my eyes, 'Peter? Peter Rowan, is that you?'

'I can see your powers of observation have remained undiminished by time,' he replied, his lips twisting into a sarcastic smile.

'It *is* you,' I laughed, recognizing that insolent smirk immediately, and offered him my hand to shake.

To my surprise, he swept it aside and instead threw his arms around my shoulders, enveloping me into a sweaty embrace. I shuddered. I have never been comfortable with physical contact. More often than not, I disdain it, permitting only the occasional handshake. In this instance, it took all my strength to keep myself from pushing Peter away. Not only had his urgency taken me completely by surprise, but what also made it doubly worse was that he smelt awful, of sweat and body odor, and beneath it, the bitter, sour tang of stale gin, so noxious it made me want to gag with revulsion.

'Oh, what am I to do, Sikander? I feel so helpless,' Peter bleated piteously. And then, to my dismay, he burst into tears, sobbing as shamelessly as a child.

Overt exhibitions of emotion make me cringe, almost as much as extended periods of physical contact. If I can, I try to avoid histrionics like the plague. That is why Peter's unexpected display made me even more uncomfortable. The man I remembered so fondly from my childhood had always been preternaturally calm, collected to the point of being one of Hephaestus's automatons, but this older Peter was so frantic that I could not help but feel a flutter of embarrassment.

'Steady on, Peter!' I growled, unable to hold my tongue. 'You're making a fool of yourself.'

This outburst came out more curt than I had intended. An expression of betrayal flickered across my friend's face, abject grief at being treated so brusquely. A sliver of guilt wracked through me and I began to apologize, but before I could find the right words, Helene surged forward, elbowing me aside.

'Sikander Singh!' she exclaimed. 'How can you treat your old friend so churlishly? Can't you see he is distraught?'

She reached out to place one delicate hand on Peter's wrist. 'Mr Rowan, is it?'

Gently, but firmly, she steered him toward the front door of the house. 'Come along. Let's step inside, shall we, and then you can tell us properly what is bothering you?'

From bitter experience, I knew better than to come in Helene's way once she decided to take charge. When she got into one of her moods, instead of arguing, the smartest course of action was to surrender meekly, which was exactly what I did, following her lead as she herded all of us indoors like a gaggle of recalcitrant geese.

It was like watching a virtuoso conduct a domestic symphony. With one flick of a wrist, she settled Peter on a chaise in the parlor. With another wave, she had Charan Singh's son scurrying upstairs with our luggage. A tilt of her chin commanded the day maid to wrestle open the thick damask curtains and let in some sunlight, and a curt snap of her fingers sent Charan Singh scurrying to find us a pot of tea, a task he set about with unusually grim urgency, as if he were herding troops to fill the breach at Serangipatnam rather than have a servant put some water to the boil.

Stifling a smirk, I plopped down opposite Peter, waiting patiently until Charan Singh returned with not one but three steaming pots of tea and quite enough jam biscuits to feed half of Bombay. Helene wasted no time in pouring each of us a generous measure, handing a mug first to Peter with a comforting smile, then one to me with another frown, and finally one to Charan Singh, which he accepted gratefully.

My grin widened. It was rather ironic really. I would have thought her Gallic heritage would have compelled Helene to offer us cognac, but it seemed that her time in India had managed to make her indomitably English, at least in regard to the curative powers of tea.

Regardless of my amusement, her plan worked admirably. As soon as Peter imbibed a couple of sips of Assam's finest, he seemed to regain his composure quite admirably.

'Sikander is a very lucky man to have you in his life, Madam,' he said, offering Helene a grateful nod.

'Of course, he is,' Helene let out a little laugh. 'Although,' she angled one sarcastic brow in my direction, 'it would be pleasant to have him say so once in a while.'

'Enough of your fussing, Helene!' I interjected before she could launch into a detailed description of my many failings as a partner. 'Now you are feeling a bit better, Peter, tell me, what is it that has you so shaken up?'

'That is exactly what I was trying to explain, Sikander. It's my fiancée, Miss Hartley. She has disappeared.'

If he was expecting sympathy from me, Peter was sorely disappointed. The rigors of the journey had already left me rather irritable, and now, coupled with his theatricality, my only response was a snort of manifest disbelief. 'Surely you're exaggerating! People don't just disappear, not in this day and age. It's 1912, for heaven's sake.'

'I am most certainly not exaggerating!' Peter's voice rose three octaves, coming close to cracking once more. 'I swear it is the truth. Mary is gone. She has vanished without a trace.'

'Come now.' I offered him a cheeky grin. 'Are you sure she didn't take one look at you and change her mind about getting married?'

I was trying to be funny, of course, to lighten the somberness of the mood just a bit, but to my chagrin, it misfired quite badly. Peter let out a gasp of outrage, which was echoed in turn by Helene, who turned a dangerous shade of puce, utterly aghast at my effrontery.

'Let me apologize on Sikander's behalf, Mr Rowan,' she hissed, shooting me a grimace so acidic it could have curdled milk. 'He imagines he is amusing, but it is a misapprehension, I am afraid. If only he realized that he is just not funny! Not at all!'

Rising to her feet, she leaned forward to refill his mug. 'Here, have some more tea.'

'I'd like some as well,' I chimed in, but all I received was another, even more pronounced, scowl.

'Don't you worry!' she assured Peter, caressing his shoulder reassuringly. 'Sikander will find your fiancée for you in a trice.'

She then gave me a challenging look, as if to dare me to refuse. I am more intelligent than most men, but even if I had been impaired in some way, it was only too apparent that I really had no choice in the matter.

Resignedly, I let out a sigh of surrender. 'Very well, Peter, let us start at the beginning, shall we? What makes you so sure that your Miss Hartley has disappeared?'

'I feel it in my bones, Sikander,' Peter declared. 'I don't know if you remember, but I told you once that I am sensitive to the attenuations of the spiritual world. Well, I have had a premonition,' he let out a most unmanly groan. 'My Mary is in grave danger; I am sure of it. You must help me find her, Sikander, before something awful happens.'

'Calm down,' I snarled before he could succumb to yet another fit of melancholia. 'I do not care to know about your feelings or instincts, Peter. They will not help me locate your Miss Hartley for you.' I rose to my feet. It was like a switch had gone off inside me. My demeanor changed completely in the blink of an eye, all affectations of humour melting away, replaced by an absolute seriousness.

'Facts, man,' I exhorted. 'Give me facts.' I loomed over Peter, locking my eyes with his. 'Now, in your letter, you said she was due to arrive yesterday morning. Am I correct?'

'Yes, she was supposed to arrive on the *Caledonia*.'

'And you are sure of that?'

'I am. I booked her ticket myself.'

'Good. Start there and tell me everything that has happened since.'

Peter paused, taking another sip of tea before launching into his story.

'As I mentioned in my letter, it was my intention to greet Mary as the ship docked. I made it a point to arrive at Ballard Pier almost two hours early. I was planning to wait for her on the quayside, but the security johnny on duty was this jumped-up prig who refused to grant me access. He said that only ticketed passengers were allowed to enter the docks, and that I would have to wait with all the others at the visitor's pavilion next to the customs shed. I tried to reason with him, even offer up a bob of baksheesh, but he was absolutely adamant, and thus like Napoleon in Russia, I had to beat a retreat. Anyway, it was a bloody hot day yesterday, and I was feeling very nervous, so instead of loitering about, I decided to have a brief drink at Rowland's Hotel nearby. To fortify my courage, so to speak.'

'When did you start to drink?' I interjected. 'You used to be a teetotaler, unless I am mistaken.'

'Yes, in my youth, I was very strict about my habits. But in recent years, I have come to enjoy a pint from time to time.'

'Is that all you had, Peter? A pint?'

'Well, that and a dram or two of gin.' He offered me a sheepish shrug. 'As I said, it was infernally warm, and I was bloody well nervous. Anyway, by the time I returned to the pier, the *Caledonia* had just docked.'

'Could you be more precise? Did the ship dock before or after you arrived?'

'Just before. It didn't dock actually. There were no berths available, so it anchored just off the coast. When I turned up, they had just announced the imminent arrival of the first ferry, I recall that very clearly, which was why I hurried to the designated pier.'

'Which pier was that? Do you recall?'

His brow wrinkled. 'Pier 3, if you must know.'

'Very good. Do carry on.'

'As I was saying, I got there just as the first lot of passengers was disembarking. I searched for Mary amongst the crowd, but she was nowhere to be found.'

'Hold on a minute. In your letter, you said you have never met Miss Hartley, yes? Then how did you know what she looked like?'

'I have a portrait of her. She sent it to me.'

'May I see it, please?'

'Of course.' Peter fumbled around in his jacket pockets, first the left and then the right. 'I have it here somewhere. Oh, where has it gone?' He let out a triumphant cry. 'Aha! Here it is.'

He offered me a small square cameo locket, quite a tawdry piece, rose gold engraved with a filigree of enamel lilies. Before I could accept it, Helene snatched it from his grasp. Unclasping it, she revealed a miniature framed within, an old-fashioned portrait in the style made popular by John Smart.

'What a lovely young woman!' Helene exclaimed and handed it to me.

I studied it intently, taking a moment to try and commit the visage to memory, even if it was hazy and somewhat out of date. She seemed a benign enough creature, with features that were quite forgettable—rouged cheeks and deep-set eyes surmounted by a halo of dark hair primped into curls. *Was she truly capable of betraying a man, of buoying his hopes and then shattering them mercilessly? Or had something bad genuinely happened to her?* A flicker of doubt clawed at me, but I refused to surrender to such abject conjecture, based merely on a drab and somewhat faded portrait.

'Can I have that back, please?' Peter asked.

'Of course.' I handed the locket to him, which he took almost reverently, putting it away in his inside pocket as if it were a relic of Saint Thomas himself.

'Let us go back to your story, shall we? You said she was not on the first ferry.'

'Yes that's right, ' Peter let out a florid sigh. 'I waited patiently for the rest of the afternoon, and most of the evening. There were four more ferries that came in, but she was not aboard any of them. Finally, I lost my patience and decided to approach the officer on duty, to ask him for help locating her.'

'And what did he say?'

'He was terribly rude. I tried to explain the situation, that I was Mary's fiancé and had come to receive her. I asked him very politely if he could examine the manifest and confirm that she had disembarked, but he rebuffed me quite soundly, saying that it was none of my business, that it was against P&O policy to share the passenger manifest with anyone who was not a member of the crew.'

'What did you do next?'

'Well, I tried my level best to plead with him, but he was a hard-headed sort who refused to listen to reason. So, I gave up trying to talk to him, went straight to the harbormaster's office and asked for his assistance. Sadly, he was even more unsympathetic and suggested that I stop wasting his time and go home, that Mary would contact me if and when she chose to.'

'But you had no intention of giving up quite so easily?'

'Of course not. In fact, that was when I had the premonition that something awful had happened to Mary, which was why I marched right back to the quay and waited until the last ferry of the day brought in the *Caledonia*'s crew. As it was discharging them and their baggage, I accosted the captain and insisted he help me, that he let me examine the passenger manifest so that I could see if Mary had left a forwarding address.' Peter shook his head. 'Unfortunately, he was even more brusque. Not only did he refuse outright to help me, citing that he was not at liberty to divulge a passenger's private details, he also told me that I was behaving like a fool when I tried badgering him.'

'Let me guess what happened next. He thought you were drunk, didn't he?'

I was right, judging by the remorseful nod this observation elicited.

'I may have become a little belligerent,' Peter confessed. 'I admit, I was rather irate by then, quite tired from wasting half my day waiting, which was why I lost my temper and gave the captain a right earful. Naturally, he was not at all pleased and had three of his sailors restrain me. They dragged me off the quay and marched me over to a nearby constable who forcibly escorted me out of the pier, like I was a common criminal.'

'And you came straight here, to see if I could help you out?'

'Not quite,' Peter said diffidently. 'I decided to go see the police first. You see, I told the constable the whole story. He was kind enough to take me to the nearest police station, the chowki near the Town Hall. Once there, I tried to write out a complaint, but the duty sergeant refused to help me as well. I even insisted on speaking to the deputy inspector in charge, but he said that technically, according to the tenets of the law, Mary wasn't a missing person, at least not yet. He suggested that I wait a few days and sent me packing.'

Peter fixed me with a look so abject it made my stomach turn. 'I know what you are going to say. That I am being unreasonable, that Mary will turn up sooner or later. But I can't wait, Sikander. I just know something has happened to her, something dreadful. I can feel it in my bones. You have to help me,' he pleaded. 'You have to find her, tell me you will, before it's too late.'

CHAPTER 4

Furrowing my brow, I considered all that Peter had just recounted.

My every instinct raged at me, warning me that this was a waste of time. It sounded less like a mystery and more a story straight out of a bodice-ripper. And while I do take great pride in my deductive abilities, I have always thought of myself as a solver of conundrums, not a seeker of lost cats and absconding fiancées.

Before I could articulate my concerns though, Helene chimed in yet again. 'Of course, he will help you! Won't you, Sikander? Tell him not to worry!'

I pursed my lips, annoyed by her impetuousness. Briefly, I was tempted to refuse, to tell Peter that I hadn't the time to help him, perhaps even suggest that he forget Miss Hartley and move on with his life. Unfortunately, the hopeful look that he gave me made me realize I could not be quite that callous. This pitiful wreck of a man, he may no longer be the larger-than-life hero I remembered from my childhood, the confidante I had cherished so deeply, but he was still the man who had made me the person I was today. That meant I owed him a debt so profound that I could not turn him away in such a cavalier fashion, not without causing him an equal amount of harm as the absconding memsahib already had.

'Very well, Peter,' I offered him a brisk smile. 'I'll see what I can dig up tomorrow.'

'Oh, wonderful.' Peter's face sagged with relief.

'Excellent!' Helene exclaimed, giving me a nod of approval. 'It is settled then. Tomorrow, Sikander will help you find your fiancée. As for tonight, Mr Rowan, you must stay here with us.'

'Oh no, I wouldn't want to be any trouble.'

'Please,' she silenced him with a curt wave. 'I insist. As you can see, we have more than enough space.'

Peter looked like he was about to offer a further argument, but Uday Singh stepped forward to forestall his objections.

'I have taken the liberty, Memsahib, to have a room made up for Rowan Sahib,' he said. 'If he would be so kind as to give us the address of his lodgings, I shall have his baggage fetched at the earliest.'

Realizing that he had been neatly outmaneuvered, Peter sagged back. 'Very well! I would be delighted to stay.'

'Good, it is settled then.' Rising to her feet, Helene offered Peter a warm smile. 'Now, if you will excuse me, I think it's time for me to retire for the evening.'

'How can I ever thank you, Madam? I am in your debt.'

'Nonsense! I should be the one thanking you. By all accounts, if it wasn't for you, my Sikander would not be the wonderful man he is today.'

Reaching out, she patted his shoulder reassuringly. 'I shall say a prayer for your young lady. And don't you worry, Sikander will track her down. This is what he lives for.'

With that promise, Helene made her exit. As for me, I was about to follow when Peter stepped forward to bar my way.

'It's not quite 7 p.m., Sikander. Why don't you stay for a while? Let's have a drink and catch up, shall we? We have so much to talk about.'

It was a tempting proposition, I admit. The thought of a cool glass of champagne was difficult to resist. But somehow, as I looked at Peter, I felt an ennui wash over me, an intense fatigue. Perhaps I had not realized how bone-tired the rigors of our journey had left me, or perhaps it was the earnest expression on Peter's face that put me off, but I decided, for once, to decline the offer of a drink.

'Another time, Peter,' I said. 'For now, what I need desperately is a bath and a change of clothes.'

A crestfallen expression flashed across his face. I could tell that he was disappointed, maybe even hurt by my refusal. Unfortunately, I had neither the energy nor the patience to placate him. Avoiding his dejected eyes, I hastily summoned Uday Singh and tasked him with showing Peter to his bedroom, before beating a hasty retreat myself.

As I climbed the stairs to my own bedroom, a wave of fatigue washed over me, leaving me weak at the knees. I realized I was near exhaustion, barely able to string together two coherent thoughts, much less spend an evening exchanging fond remembrances with this stranger who had once been my closest friend.

Judging by the neat pile of clothes on the bed and the sound of running water coming from the bathroom, I concluded that Helene had beaten me to the punch. Briefly, I toyed with the idea of joining her in the bath, but then dismissed it with a sigh. After a week spent cooped up on a train, I doubted she was in the mood to play at being amorous. I certainly was not, a realization that was accompanied by rather a strong pang of self-recrimination. In my youth, such thoughts would never have given me a minute's pause, but now, the notion of curling up in bed was infinitely more palatable than a soapy escapade with my beautiful paramour.

Leaving Helene to enjoy a few moments of privacy, I unfurled my pugree and let loose my joora. It is a particular torment that only gentlemen of the Sikh persuasion can understand, but after almost a week of travelling, my hair felt matted and knotted, sorely in need of some care and attention.

Picking up an ivory-backed brush from the dressing table, I began to comb out my hair. It was a ritual that had always calmed me, one I remembered and cherished from my childhood, which now seemed to be a lifetime away. When I was a boy, it was my mother who combed my hair out every night, a routine that always brought with it an impeccable sense of peace.

As I ran the brush through my hair with long and practiced strokes, easing away the tangles, I found myself contemplating Peter's situation. *What were the chances that his Miss Hartley had actually gone missing? Slim to none*, I thought dogmatically. As far as I could envision, there were only two possibilities here. One, Miss Hartley had decided to jilt Peter, perhaps even run off with someone else. Two, she had developed a case of cold feet, a condition that was not unheard of, especially for someone who had an entire voyage out to India during which to consider the decision to marry. In either case, there was one only foregone conclusion to be made: whatever came next, my old friend was going to end up with a broken heart. I could see no real way to avoid that, which was the very reason I would have preferred not to become involved in this affair.

I was so caught up in these ruminations that I did not hear Helene come up behind me. She smelt damp from her bath, and fresh, a delightful bouquet of Guerlain and talcum powder that made me smile. I did not resist when she took the hairbrush from my grasp. Instead, I let myself lean backwards, nestling into her as she carefully began to comb my hair. I could feel her warmth, the soft curve of her body obscured only by a diaphanous silk robe. As always, her proximity soothed me, like laudanum. I felt my fatigue recede, replaced by a sense of contentment.

'How is your friend?' she asked.

This question, however innocuous, managed to break the spell. An involuntary shudder ran up my spine, causing the comb to snag in a knot, tugging at my scalp. Helene's fingers deftly unknotted the tangle, but her eyes, ever sharp, saw the wince that had made my lips twist, recognizing it for what it was, not discomfort but reticence.

'What's wrong, Sikander?' she inquired, pursing her lips primly. 'Something is bothering you.'

'Why did you ask him to stay?'

'He's your friend, Sikander, and he needs your help. Of course, I had to ask him to stay.'

'He *was* my friend,' I groused. 'Now ... I barely recognize him, Helene.' I paused, shaking my head. 'He used to be so different, so confident. The Peter I remember was an extraordinary man, a scholar and an autodidact, but this person ... I don't understand it. How could he have changed so much?'

'People change, Sikander. It is one of the inevitabilities of life.' She smiled and caressed my neck. 'Do you remember what you were like when we first met? So hesitant, so nervous, so careful? Do you remember what it was like? The life we had in Paris before you claimed the throne of Rajpore, before you even solved your first case?'

She sighed. 'Sometimes I wish we could go back to being those hopelessly uncomplicated people, living in our dirty little garret in Montmartre, you trying to be a poet and me supporting you by working as a nurse. But I am honest enough to admit that I have changed too much to ever be that girl again. And so have you. You have changed as well, Sikander, haven't you?'

'Not into a bitter old drunk!'

'Be kind, Sikander. Your friend has suffered a great loss today. That's enough to make any man turn to drink.'

'Oh, I'll find him another wife. There's a hundred eligible women out there. It shouldn't be too much of a task.'

Helene frowned. 'If only it was that simple. Don't you realize, he is in love with this Mademoiselle Hartley?'

'Love! Surely you're joking. How can he be in love with her? He hasn't even met her yet.'

Helene rolled her eyes. 'It doesn't matter, Sikander,' she said with a laugh. 'You aren't French, you wouldn't understand. What was it that Pascal said: "*Le cœur a ses raisons que la raison ne connaît point*." 'The heart has its reasons, my love, of which reason knows nothing.'

'You're right. I don't understand.'

She sighed. 'Put yourself in your friend's place for a moment, Sikander. Imagine how it feels, to be far away from the land of your birth, to be a stranger in a strange land. You come here to India in your youth, when anything seems possible, when everything seems so exotic, so exciting. But then time whispers by and hope withers. All the dreams you cherished and all the plans you made, they all fizzle away slowly. And one day, all you feel is tiredness. Not pain. Not regret. Just the dull ache of resignation.'

She shuddered. 'Don't you see? That is why your friend is so cut up. For Monsieur Rowan, this memsahib is what we call in France a symbole de l'espoir. She represents hope. Possibility. A future. That is what he is afraid of losing.'

She caressed my arm. 'You have to find the girl, you do realize that, don't you? Not just another girl, but this Miss Hartley, all right? If you care about your friend, you must find her, and soon.'

'Oh, stop being so dramatic, Helene! You're as bad as he is.' Even as I said those words, I knew I had crossed a line. Helene's brow knit with a familiar consternation I knew so well. Generally, such an expression presaged an angry outburst. I girded myself, preparing for an impending onslaught of vitriol.

Sure enough, a moment later the hairbrush came flying through the air, aimed in the general direction of my head. Thankfully, my reflexes were quick enough to avoid it, if only narrowly. It bounced off the wall and clattered on to the floor behind me, even as Helene fixed me with a poisonous scowl.

'*Merde!*' she exclaimed. 'It's astonishing that a man as intelligent as you, a man who claims to be an expert about human nature, is so clueless when it comes to matters of the heart.' She shook her head. 'You poor man! You're extraordinary in so many ways, Sikander, but you really don't understand what it is to love, do you? Love is not a choice. It is a need. It is not sublime or poetic; it is ecstasy. It is selfish, an agony, Sikander, as desperate as a drug. Like a cripple needs a crutch, we need to love. That is what makes us human, because it is love that gives you meaning and purpose in a world that often seems pointless. You think you know everything, Sikander, but you *know* nothing if you do not know how to love. Without love, you *are* nothing.'

CHAPTER 5

With that declaration, Helene turned and marched over to the bed.

Without another word, she lay down and switched off the lamp, leaving me swathed in darkness. I stood there for a minute, trying to understand what I had done wrong. *How had this become a fight?* All I had said was that Peter was being overly dramatic.

At the same time, my temper couldn't help but flare. Helene's words, though harmless, had cut deep. I knew her well enough to understand that beneath the acid there hid a hint of pity. That thought rankled me deeply. *Who did she think she was, to have the gall to pity me?* I felt my irritation rising, and it took every ounce of my willpower to keep it under control.

As I stood there, clenching and unclenching my fists, I realized where I had failed. It wasn't just Peter she had been talking about, it was herself.

That realization made my anger leach away. Crossing over to the bed, I lay down beside her. 'Helene, I'm sorry. Please, let's not fight.'

This apology was greeted by an uncomfortable silence. Helene's spine remained as rigidas an iron rod. Gently, I started to stroke her hair. To my relief, she did not push me away. Instead, after a few minutes, her diffidence seemed to subside and she moved to nestle into me, fitting herself into my supine body.

I lay there quietly, unwilling to say another word, afraid it would only make things worse. Instead, I simply continued to caress Helene's hair until she fell asleep, her face curled into my shoulder and one arm thrown across my chest. Trying not to fidget, I listened to the steady sound of her breathing, as regular as a metronome. Ordinarily, this soft rhythm reassured me, but on this occasion, I found myself much too unsettled to sleep. My ennui grew, magnifying with each passing tick of the clock. It wasn't the familiar melancholy I often felt when I was weary. No, I was seized by an unlikely foreboding, a *pressentiment* as the French called it, a sinking feeling in the pit of my stomach that something bad was about to happen.

My earlier exhaustion seemed to have vanished, replaced instead by a nervous energy that made me shiver.

I found myself thinking of Peter's memsahib once again. As I lay there, it occurred to me that there was a third possibility I had failed to consider. *Could Peter be making it all up? What if he was so desperate for attention that he was lying, playing the victim for sympathy? What if his real motive was to find a way to get back in with me, to come back to Rajpore?* No, I thought, dismissing that thought outright. That was just my paranoia talking. Peter was too good for something quite so underhanded, far too much of a gentleman.

Finally, my restlessness got the better of me. Slipping out from under Helene's arm carefully, so as to not disturb her, I belted on a silk dressing gown and set out in search for a drink. A quick peek into Charan Singh's quarters revealed that both he and his son were fast asleep, snoring as loudly as a pair of rival foghorns. I stifled a smile and eased the door shut, deciding not to disturb their slumber. I wandered around a bit, searching for the kitchen. When I did manage to find it, I spent another ten minutes blundering about looking for a suitable bottle. Unfortunately, all I managed to locate was a rather plump cat, which gave me a forlorn meow when I stepped on its tail, as if to chastise me for daring to intrude into its territory.

After five more minutes of fruitless rummaging, I decided to give up and headed to the music room instead. Inside, to my delight, I was thrilled to find that Uday Singh truly was a chip off the old block. Not only had he made sure that my piano—a Bösendorfer Imperial—had been polished to a high gloss and tuned exactly how I liked it, but the boy had also displayed the uncommon perspicacity of uncorking a bottle of Taittinger and having a chilled glass ready and waiting for me.

Taking an appreciative sip, I settled down, staring at the keys speculatively. It took a few minutes before inspiration dawned. Almost of their own accord, my fingers began to skitter across the pale ivory of the keyboard. What emerged finally was a most unexpected choice. Schumann's 'Fantasie in C', or the 'Wanderer' as it was nicknamed, was a charmingly elegant piece of music but certainly not one of my favorites. I have never been a fan of the Romantics; my tastes run more toward the Baroque, Handel, Bach and Purcell. And this composition, in particular, was one that I had not played in decades. It had been one of my mother's favorite pieces. After her death, I had almost managed to forget it entirely.

I found my thoughts turning back to the last time I had seen her. That had also been the last time I had played the piano for her, this very movement in fact, the night before I had departed for England. Less than a year later, she was gone, just six weeks after my father fell off a horse while playing polo and broke his neck. After his passing, my uncle Lal Singh had quickly laid claim to the throne and tried to snatch away my birthright. By all accounts, it had been touch-and-go for a bit. While Charan Singh had been dispatched to fetch me from university in England, my mother had managed to outmaneuver Lal Singh and made a compact with the English, thus assuring me the throne of Rajpore. But it had not come without an inestimable cost. On the eve of her victory, Lal Singh had poisoned my mother, cutting her down in her moment of triumph before absconding to Europe with the Rajpore jewels.

As always, that memory made me grimace. I had a score to settle with my uncle, a debt that had gone unpaid too long. Not only had he taken my mother from me, what also made it worse was that I had not been able to say goodbye, to thank her or tell her I loved her. Instead, I had arrived just in time to set fire to her funeral pyre and to be anointed as the Maharaja of Rajpore.

I have little to no memory of the weeks that followed that ominous day. All I recall is drinking, bottle after endless bottle. For almost four months after I was crowned, I refused to leave the Sona Killa or make a public appearance. Instead, I lost myself in a haze of alcohol, unable to quench my grief, no matter how many jeroboams of champagne I guzzled.

Neither Charan Singh nor Ismail Bhakht, my trusted chief minister, had been able to get through to me. I was lost, adrift in a sea of self-pity and self-loathing, at least until Peter turned up to talk some sense into me. When he arrived, I was drunk out of my wits, stinking, covered in my own piss and vomit. The last thing I wanted was for my old mentor to see me like that, which was why I tried to refuse to see him, to have my guards get rid of him. Thankfully, Charan Singh chose to disobey me, as he is wont to do from time to time, and insisted that Peter be allowed into my private chambers.

I thought he would be ashamed, disgusted by how far I had fallen, but to my surprise, Peter had reacted exactly the opposite. 'The truest test of a man's character, Sikander,' he had said to me, 'is not how he behaves when he falls down, but how readily he is able to find the resolve to get back on his feet again.'

I am much older now, experienced enough to understand that there are pivotal junctures in a man's life, watershed moments when he faces certain choices that will define him. '*Luctor et Emergo*,' as Peter would have quoted, 'I struggle, and I emerge stronger.' In many ways, that was exactly one such critical moment for me. *If Peter had not sought me out, if he hadn't come all the way to Rajpore to help me in my hour of need, who knows where I would be now?* I may very well have kept on drinking. I might never have accepted my responsibilities. I might never have solved a mystery, never saved the Durbar or untangled the most pukka of murders India has seen. If not for him, I may never have become the man I am today.

I have always believed that Peter saved me. He rescued me, in a way, from the worst of myself, and for that, I will always owe him a debt that can never be absolved. *However*, I thought, *if I could find this woman who had caused him so much anguish and heartache, perhaps the balance might be settled, if only a whit.*

Even as I contemplated that thought, a knock on the door surprised me, disturbing my reverie. 'Come in,' I said, not at all happy at being disturbed.

The door cracked open, and Peter peered into the room.

'Might I join you?' he asked, giving me a guilty smile.

He looked much better now, bathed and perfumed, his hair and that bird's nest of a beard now neatly combed and trimmed, dressed in a pair of silk pajamas and a velvet dressing gown that matched my own. To my relief, he looked like my old tutor once more, the gentleman I remembered so fondly.

'Of course. Sit, have a drink.' Rising, I poured out a slender flute and offered it to him.

He accepted it with a grin, his eyes widening with appreciation as he tasted its contents. 'Gosh, I had almost forgotten what good champagne tasted like.'

He sank onto a nearby Louis Quatorze bench and gulped down the rest of the glass in one mighty swig. 'Pour me another, won't you?'

'Help yourself,' I said, waving at the bottle.

Peter reached for it greedily and poured himself a very generous double measure, which vanished down his throat with even greater alacrity. I resisted the urge to frown. Not only was it a tragedy to treat good champagne so shabbily, as if it were little more than cheap arrack, but his appetite also was surprising. The Peter I remembered had been a reluctant drinker, rarely imbibing more than a glass of claret, but this new avatar seated in front of me was as eager as a sot. And by the looks of it, a morose one at that, which was always the worst kind.

As we sat there, I studied my old friend more carefully. At first glance, I had assumed he had aged badly, but now I realized it wasn't just time that had left its indelible imprint upon his features, but something more. Too much drink, I guessed, judging by the pouches beneath his eyes and the way his shoulders and hands trembled, and too many disappointments.

'Are you well, Peter? You look tired.'

'Age, my friend! Time is a cruel mistress who makes fools of us all.' He offered me a smile. 'I have followed your adventures with great interest. What an interesting life you have lived, Sikander,' he said with a grimace. 'I, on the other hand, have had a very boring go of it.'

He let out a vast sigh. 'When I was your age, I thought I would look back at my life and congratulate myself, that I would see a long line of boys who made something of themselves because of my teachings. But I am sad to say that I am a dreadful failure. All my wards are brats and scoundrels. You were my only success, Sikander. You are the only one I am truly proud of.'

Leaning forward, he refilled his flute and raised it in a toast. 'Here's to you, Sikander, and your adventures!'

'No,' I responded. 'Here's to you, Peter. You are not a failure, not at all.'

He shook his head. 'Let's raise a glass to Mary instead. The sooner you find her, the sooner she will be Mrs Rowan.'

I paused. 'About that. Might I be frank, Peter?' Putting down my glass, I leaned forward. 'You do realize that we may never find her, don't you? I feel I must warn you.'

'I understand,' Peter said.

'And, of course,' I continued, 'there is the likelihood that if we do find her, she may choose to repudiate you, to reject your offer of marriage. I will not compel her to be your wife, not against her will. I hope you realize that, too.'

'Of course! I would expect nothing else from you.'

'Very well!' I gave him a piercing glare. 'There is one more thing I need to know. Why, Peter? Why do you want me to find her?'

He looked at me coldly for a long moment, his expression so austere I thought I had offended him.

'Did I ever teach you about entropy?' he finally asked.

'No, you did not.'

'Entropy, my boy, is that slow, inevitable decay into nothingness that every object in the universe faces, the gradual decline that comes with old age, when all the grand plans you have made slowly unravel and go awry, when all you have left is regret and sorrow.'

'I'm not sure I understand.'

'I truly pray you never have to. In any case, that is why I need to find Mary, Sikander. She is the only way I can stave off entropy. She is my last chance to be happy.'

'Surely you're exaggerating, Peter. All is not lost yet. You are young still and have much to look forward to. This new position. And a new wife to go with it. I mean, even if we fail to find Miss Hartley, there are plenty of women out there.'

'No,' he said, rather too vehemently, 'not for me, there are not. This was my roll of the dice, my salvation. But look how things turned out! I should have known. With my luck, what else could have happened?'

'And that is your only reason to find her, the fact that you don't want to feel old?'

'No, not quite. The truth,' he laughed, a bitter cackle, 'if you must have it, is pride, Sikander. I have to know why she deserted me. If this is indeed a rejection, I *need* to know!'

Much to my dismay, he began to sniffle, his eyes blurring with a hot flush of tears.

'It's not fair. It's just not fair,' he groaned.

'Steady on old chap,' I said, unsure of how to react to this extravagant display of emotion. 'You must stay strong.'

'I'm so lonely, Sikander,' he gasped. 'I thought if I could find someone, a woman, I could start again.'

Biting back my revulsion, I offered him my handkerchief.

'You said something to me years ago, Peter, that I have always held in high regard. Do you remember?'

'I'm afraid I don't.'

'You told me that a man's character is defined not by how he behaves when he falls down, but how readily he is able to find the resolve to get back on his feet again.'

I had hoped those words would bring him solace, as they had often done for me in trying times, but to my chagrin, Peter rolled his eyes and let out a scornful snort.

'God, I was a pompous git when I was younger!' he exclaimed.

I felt a sudden loathing for him. In just one second, he had ruined the fondest recollection I had of him. My whole life I had cherished the memory of his strength, but now, seeing him sitting in front of me, sniveling like a spineless schoolboy, it dawned on me that he was as weak as I was, as human. Much to my surprise, that made me hate him.

'God,' I hissed even before I knew it, 'what happened to you, Peter? When did you become so ... so weak?'

Peter flinched, like I had struck him across the face. I regretted it immediately, but before I could apologize, before I could offer a single conciliatory word, he rose to his feet. Gathering what little dignity he had left, like a tattered robe, he gave me a frosty smile.

'I'm going to call it a night,' he said. 'Thank you for the drink.'

I'm sorry, I wanted to say. Instead, I nodded gruffly, matching his curtness. 'Yes, I think that's a good idea. Try and get some rest. You'll feel better in the morning.'

He frowned and nodded back, refusing to meet my eyes.

'Peter,' I said, as he opened the door, giving him pause before he could depart. 'I'll find your memsahib. You can count on it. I give you my word.'

CHAPTER 6

The Bombay Police had a long and somewhat checkered history.

The origins of the department lay in the late seventeenth century, when Gerald Aungier—the same governor who had ordered the Fort walls to be demolished—decided to employ a troop of five hundred Bhandare tribesmen to keep the peace in Mahim, Sewree and Sion. The Bhandares had been little more than thugs themselves, but through a combination of intimidation and brute force, they had proven to be remarkably effective at keeping the crime rate low, at least crimes against Europeans.

The first official police chief of Bombay had been a man named Frank Tod, a name that became so synonymous with corruption that he had finally been tried for bribery and dismissed from office in 1790. Following his ignominious tenure, the post of superintendent of police was officially created, and the English set out to reorganize the constabulary into a more effective force, one capable of dealing with the myriad of criminal activity that accompanies a booming metropolis.

Finally, it was in 1864 that Frank Souter was appointed the first proper commissioner of Police, a post he held for twenty-four long years. It was under his formidable leadership that the

Bombay Police emerged as a professional organization, second in reputation only to Scotland Yard.

The current commissioner happened to be a gentleman I was somewhat familiar with. His name was Stephen Meredyth Edwardes, a fine fellow I had met some years ago, when I had come to the city to solve a rather unexpected case. A young impostor had ensconced himself at Watson's Hotel and tried to pass himself off as me, so that he could run a swindle on several unsuspecting marks. When I found out, I delayed my trip to the Continent long enough to expose him to the police. It was then that I had first encountered Edwardes. While what had commenced could not quite be described as a friendship, it had certainly amounted to a grudgingly respectful acquaintance.

In the brief time I had spent talking with him, I had come to quite respect Edwardes. He had turned out to be a taciturn and scholarly sort, with the bespectacled countenance of a college professor rather than the pugnacity one expected from a policeman. In fact, he had confessed to me once, over a glass of Pol Roger at the Byculla Club, that his real ambition was to write a series of books about the history of the city, a dream he most fervently hoped to accomplish upon retiring.

The headquarters of the commissioner of Police were located about half a kilometer away from Victoria Terminus. To the east lay a tangled warren of crowded gullies and bazaars spread across the districts of Pydhonie, Kalbadevi, Bhuleshwar and Khetwadi, teeming with so many people that, at noon, it was hard to move more than a few inches without bumping shoulders. To the west lay the wide-open expanse of Esplanade and a mile-long avenue that led to the Fort district and its grand colonnade of government buildings, home to the very heart of the Bombay Presidency.

It was at the junction of these two very different worlds that the headquarters of the Bombay Police had been constructed, a towering two-storeyed building wrought of yellow basalt, constructed in the same Indo-Gothic style as the Victoria Terminus. Inside, it was surprisingly elegant—Burma teak ceilings held up by polished pillars and a floor paved with Victorian Inverlochy tiles that made it seem more like an upscale club than a police precinct.

The commissioner's office was on the second floor, overlooking a wide courtyard enfiladed by arched corridors. I had sent Uday Singh ahead earlier that morning to secure an appointment for 10.30 a.m. Naturally, I arrived at 10.15, as was my habit. I am, and always have been, a firm believer in punctuality. Not only do I subscribe vigorously to the adage that manners maketh a man, but honestly, I can think of no greater insult than to arrive late for a meeting, which is why I always try to make an appearance at least fifteen minutes early.

Unfortunately, in spite of my timeliness, I was made to wait. Rather than showing us straight into Commissioner Edwardes' office, when Charan Singh and I presented ourselves, an orderly ushered us into a small anteroom. *It might as well double up as a holding cell for interrogations*, I mused, judging by the iron grilles in front of the windows and the drab furnishings, just a cheap hayrake table flanked by three very uncomfortable-looking chairs.

'Please wait here,' the orderly instructed. 'The commissioner will be with you shortly.'

I have never been a patient man. Not only am I not accustomed to having people waste my time, but I am also the sort of person who is reduced to fury by inactivity. I cannot help myself. It is not in my nature to be still. In some ways, it is the defining crux of my character. Like a shark, I must keep moving.

If I am made to sit still for more than a heartbeat, it feels like I am suffocating, like I will lose my mind.

Even as Charan Singh lounged against one wall, watching me simmer with a bemused smirk, I began to pace the room. It did not take long to establish that it was exactly eleven steps to get from one wall to the other, a circuit I repeated once, twice and then thrice, my features settling into a scowl. The fan overhead was too noisy, clacking steadily with each revolution, a metronomic tympanum that matched the rising cadence of my irritation. *Clack, clack, clack.* Eleven steps, turn and eleven more. *Clack, clack, clack.*

To add insult to injury, it was turning out to be an exceedingly torpid day. Though I had taken great pains to dress suitably for Bombay's humidity, eschewing an achkan in favor of a light linen band-gala and ivory trousers, unfortunately, within the stifling confines of the waiting room, my clothes were soaked through with sweat in just a matter of minutes, leaving me in an even damper mood.

I was very nearly at the end of my tether when the door finally creaked open. However, it was not Commissioner Edwardes who finally deigned to make an appearance. Instead, another gentleman came striding in. He was tall, almost the same height as Charan Singh. However, unlike my manservant, he was slender, as lanky as a scarecrow. Rather than a uniform, he was wearing a checked cheviot suit, paired with a red tartan vest so bright that it made me blink. As if that wasn't bad enough, he was rather young, in his mid-twenties I guessed, and much too oleaginous for my liking. His face was smooth and unlined, his cheeks covered with a smattering of freckles that made him resemble an overgrown schoolboy, and he had rather too much pomade in his carefully waved hair, which was parted neatly down the middle.

Actually, that was the first reason my initial impression was decidedly negative. If there is one thing I have learned through bitter experience, it is that you cannot trust a man with a middle parting. The second reason I took an immediate dislike to him was because of his manner. He was much too sleek and self-assured, his posture far too swaggering for my taste, all of which suggested to me that he was a bit of a dandy, the sort of fellow who thought rather too highly of himself.

'Why, hello!' he exclaimed. 'I hope you haven't been waiting too long, Mr Singh.'

Without bothering to introduce himself, he crossed over to the table at the center of the room. Pulling out one of the chairs, he sank into it with languid grace and placed the manila folder he was carrying in one slim hand squarely between us before inviting me to take the chair opposite him.

'How dare you keep me waiting?' I started to growl at him, but before I could get to venting my spleen properly, he forestalled me with one slim finger.

'Just a moment, Sir,' he said and clapped his hands.

A moment later, a brown-shirted bearer came rushing in, carrying a tray upon which lay a kettle and three cups, accompanied by a platter of biscuits.

'Tea?' the young Englishman asked. 'A Shrewsbury biscuit perhaps? They are freshly baked, I believe.'

'No, thank you.' I struggled to control my irritation. 'As I was saying, I had an appointment to see Commissioner Edwardes at 10.30 a.m. It is now coming up at a quarter past eleven. Where the bloody hell is he?'

'Ah, yes!' His shoulders rose and dipped in a noncommittal shrug that could have been either apology or disinterest. 'I regret to say, Your Highness, that the commissioner will be unable to see you,' he said with a thoroughly insincere smile.

'He has been called away on urgent business. Perhaps I can be of service instead.'

'I don't see how you can.' My lip curled, and I did not bother to disguise my disdain any longer. 'What good are you to me? You barely look old enough to tie your own shoelaces without assistance.'

I was trying to insult him, but it failed, and miserably at that. The smile did not waver a whit. Instead, if anything, it grew even more diffident.

'Forgive me! I haven't even introduced myself properly,' he said. 'My mistake! I am Albert Hall-Caine.'

Delving into his breast pocket, he removed a sterling silver case embossed with a cinquefoil, from which he extracted a calling card and offered it to me.

I examined it cursorily. It was very ordinary, a simple white square upon which his name was printed. Beneath it were the words: Senior Manager, Messrs. Rasen, Falcon and Company, Import and Export.

As I read that seemingly innocuous title, a shiver ran down my spine, and then right back up again. To a layman, this may have seemed an innocent enough name for a trading company, the sort of cut-rate box-wallah establishment that engaged in transcontinental shipping and the like, but I recognized it immediately for what it actually was.

'You're with Vauxhall Bridge,' I whispered. 'One of Mansfield Smith-Cummings' chosen acolytes.'

'Indeed,' he said with a smirk, 'although we are at Whitehall now. C sends his regards, by the way. He wanted me to thank you for the ivory sword cane you sent him last Christmas.'

I frowned. Mansfield Smith-Cumming, or C as he liked to style himself, was London's spymaster. He headed the Secret Service Bureau, which had been founded just three years previously, in 1909.

The English were relative latecomers to the shadowy world of cloak-and-dagger. For decades, the Tsar and the Kaiser had steadily been infiltrating agents into Eastern Europe, the Levant and Central Asia, slowly building up a network of spies that reported every occurrence within the British Empire to their masters in Saint Petersburg and Berlin. In India and Afghanistan, this game of cat-and-mouse had come to be called the Great Game, and the stake being wagered was India itself, the jewel in the British Crown.

It was only after the Dreyfus affair in France that the English woke up to the invisible danger that faced them, both at home and in the colonies. As a result, the Home Office, the Admiralty and the Foreign Office combined forces and two new intelligence agencies came into existence overnight—the Special Investigation Branch , headed by Vernon Kell, which was tasked with unearthing spies within England; and the SSB, run by C, which handled the unenviable task of counter-intelligence and curtailing espionage overseas. Personally, I had rather a low regard for the lot of them, especially when it came to Indian affairs. Unlike the Russian Okhrana, who were stone-cold killers; or the German Abteilung, who were as devious as devils, the English were just a bunch of overeducated schoolboys playing at being agent provocateurs. Not only did they still believe they could operate by an archaic system of gentlemanly rules, but in my opinion, they also lacked the bloodthirsty resolve it took to hold on to the empire in India, especially as the notions of home rule and nationalism were slowly taking root across the subcontinent.

Still, regardless of my general disdain for Britain's India policies, I had to admit that selecting Mansfield-Cumming to head this nascent spy service was the one good choice they had made. In spite of his foppish monocle-wearing exterior, he was as ruthless as a Borgia. Not only was he more than willing to get his hands dirty, but he also was more than ready to go out there and make a bloody mess himself if he had to. I had known him casually while I was at Eton. Even back then, he had been rather an insufferable fellow, a slender prig of a boy who was convinced he knew better than everyone else. However, if there was one thing he could not be accused of, it was a lack of good judgement. C was one of the finest judges of character I had ever met. He was famous for picking only the best of the best as his agents, the smartest and bravest and best-educated. If this fellow was one of the chosen few, well then, perhaps it was time for me to reevaluate my opinion of him.

On a whim, I decided to test Hall-Caine, see how far I could push him before his equanimity began to crumble.

'Tell me, how long have you worked for C?'

'Almost two years. He got me straight out of Canterbury. I was reading to be a priest when he turned up and convinced me to jump ship.'

'Ah! So you are not an Eton man then. I thought as much. You can tell if a man is a gentleman by his breeding, by how he dresses and the way he speaks. Take you as an example. From your accent, I can infer you are from Staffordshire, around Stoke, I should guess, from the way you drop your h's and elongate your diphthongs. And your suit, while decently tailored, is distinctly workman-like, which suggests you are not a man of means. Your father was a teacher, I am guessing, or a civil servant. You grew up with a classical education, but most of what you know of the world comes from books. Also, you have never had the benefit of traveling and enjoying the benefits of first-hand experience, have you?'

I was trying my level best to get a rise out of him, and it almost worked. For a moment, Hall-Caine's eyes clouded over with the dull patina of rage, but to the man's credit, he stayed well in control of himself. The effort showed, but he managed to tamp down his irritation and regarded me with a smile so serene it would have looked at home on a Japanese buddha.

'C warned me about you.'

'Did he now?'

'Yes, he said you enjoyed eliciting reactions from people when you met them for the first time.' Offering me rather a glib grin, he reached for the manila folder, snapping it open crisply.

'Maharaja Sikander Singh of Rajpore,' he read, holding up a typed sheet of paper, 'entitled to fifteen guns, which makes him rather a minor sort of king. Son of Dilawer Singh and Amrita Devi, both of whom were most likely murdered by his uncle, Lal Singh, the guilt of which he bears to this day and which probably explains his macabre interest in mysteries. Extremely well-educated. Eton, Oxford but sent down, Heidelberg and the University of Turin. Speaks seven languages fluently. Expert with a pistol, knife, and sword. Trained in several obscure oriental martial disciplines. Fancies himself a bit much but is neither as dashing nor as clever as he likes to believe.'

'That is not in there!' I exclaimed. 'You made that up.'

Hall-Caine let out a chuckle. 'I did,' he admitted. 'Forgive my presumption, but I simply couldn't resist.'

As far as insults went, I had to agree it was admirably well played, even if I was the victim of that particular sally. This Hall-Caine was rather a clever fellow, even if his manners were quite atrocious. I studied him carefully, trying to decide how to respond. I could continue to remain antagonistic, or I could swallow my ego, backtrack and start over.

Hall-Caine held my gaze with absolute sang-froid, his green eyes so cold they reminded me of the North Sea. Leaning forward, he lifted up the kettle, and very deliberately, poured out a measure of steaming hot tea into one of the cups before offering it to me.

After a very long moment, I picked it up and took a brief sip.

'Very well,' I said 'Let us call a truce. You obviously didn't come in here to insult me, Mr Hall-Caine. Shall we stop fencing and come to the point?'

'So be it,' he responded. 'On to business then, without further ado.' He studied me with great gravitas. 'I am sorry to say, Sir, that the Bombay Constabulary will not help you. Nor will the Governor's Office, I am afraid, or your friends at the India Office.'

'What? Why ever not?'

'Well, there are several reasons. The first, and most pressing, I am afraid, is that you have enemies in high places,' he said with an apologetic shrug. 'It seems you made quite an impression on Michael O'Dwyer last year at the Durbar. He has gone to great lengths to have you proscribed as a Person of Interest, I am sorry to report. That means, as far as the British government in India is concerned, you are persona non grata.'

I let out a curse. *Michael high-and-bloody-mighty O'Dwyer! Damn the man!* I had embarrassed him, quite badly at that, when our paths had crossed the year before. Obviously, he was still carrying a grudge. And while I had expected some sort of retaliation, especially when he had been designated as the next lieutenant governor of the Punjab, to have me declared a POI was just too much to swallow. That sort of classification was normally reserved for threats to the empire—nationalists, nihilists, subversives and the like. Not only did that brand me as untrustworthy as far as the government was concerned, someone who was to be watched constantly, but it also made me a pariah to the English establishment in India. No matter how wealthy I was, or how well-connected, they couldn't help me, not without endangering themselves. I realized now why the commissioner had refused to see me. Because I was as good as carrying the mark of Cain.

'It's all trumped up,' I tried to argue. 'O'Dwyer has it in for me. He's a petty tyrant.'

'I am sure you're right, Mr Singh. However, there is a more pressing problem we cannot ignore. You see, it is the official position of the police department that a person must be unaccounted for for at least a week before they can be declared missing. They cannot, and will not, consider Miss Hartley as a police matter, at least not for another five days.'

'That's downright ridiculous.'

'Is it, Mr Singh? Do you have any idea how many of these complaints the police receive every day, or how many people supposedly vanish only to turn up a few weeks later? They simply cannot investigate every single complaint. They do not have anywhere nearly enough resources, not to mention the manpower.'

'For God's sake, man, how can you be so nonchalant?' For once, my frustration got the better of me. 'A young woman has gone missing. Why, she may be lying in some dark alleyway with her throat slit even as we sit here wasting time, chattering away like fools!'

'Ah! That leads us to the third reason why the police are unwilling to help you.' He let out a low sigh. 'Frankly, we cannot be sure that Miss Hartley has actually fallen victim to foul play, can we?'

'What do you mean?'

'Could it not be that the young woman merely changed her mind? That she decided she would rather seek her fortunes elsewhere instead of marrying your friend?'

'I do not believe that is the case,' I said doggedly. 'I do not think she would jilt Peter, not quite so wantonly.'

'Are you sure of that, Mr Singh? With all due respect to your friend—I am sure he possesses many fine qualities—it is not unheard of for women, especially young women, to develop cold feet at the last moment. And that is especially true of the fishing fleet, isn't it? These young girls are only too eager to come out here looking for husbands, but the moment they set foot on Indian soil, they change their minds quicker than chameleons change their colors. I have seen it happen a hundred times, to be honest, as has Commissioner Edwardes. As far as he is concerned, he would prefer to treat this as a domestic dispute, I am afraid.'

I grimaced, unhappy at his use of the term 'fishing fleet'. It was a dreadful pejorative, but unfortunately it was one that summed the phenomenon up only too accurately. That was how most residents in India referred to the droves of young women who arrived in Bombay and Madras from England each year, angling for husbands. Some were orphans, sent out from the Home Counties as contracted brides, bonded into matrimony in exchange for the price of a second-class P&O ticket. Others were matches made on behalf of unattached bachelors, chosen either by their families back home or by their local parish priests. And many came out on their own, hoping to find a better life in the tropics, or to have a bit of adventure, or to make a fortune for themselves. In the end, most of them fell victim to the curse of the subcontinent. India was notoriously difficult on white women. It wore them out very quickly. It aged them prematurely and broke them down; almost half perished within five years of landfall. Those Englishwomen that did survive and flourish in India were a unique lot, as tough as nails, and practical to the point of being indomitable. And yes, Hall-Caine was right. This was no place for wilting willows. India was the kind of place where the strong survived and the weak fell by the wayside, which was exactly why it was not incomprehensible to think that Miss Hartley had chosen a path different from the one intended for her.

'I would still like to track her down,' I said. 'If that is indeed the truth, if Miss Hartley has changed her mind and decided to repudiate Peter, I would like to hear that from her own lips.'

'And you have no intention of forcing her into wedlock against her will?'

'Of course not! What do you take me for? Some kind of sheikh?'

'Very well!' he smiled. 'In that case, I will be only too happy to assist you however I can.'

'I thought you said the police would not assist me.'

'Ah, then it's a good thing I do not answer to the police.' He smiled archly. 'I work directly for the India Office, Sir. I answer only to the Great Dane.'

At the mention of that name, my own lips couldn't help but curve into a grin. Now there was one of the few Englishmen I genuinely admired. Louis Dane was the outgoing governor of the Punjab, a gentleman of the same school as Nicholson and Lawrence, who genuinely loved India and the Indians. He had been a close friend of my grandfathers' and a great admirer of my mother, and it was due in no small part to him that I had been able to hold on to my throne and title when my uncle had tried to steal both after my father's untimely demise.

'How is he?' I asked.

'Still blundering along, Sir, as he likes to remind us all. He is due to retire next year, and is not looking forward to leaving India. In fact, I saw him just last week. We came out from London together, on the *Maloja*. When he heard you were on your way to Bombay, he asked me to stay behind and look in on you, so that I could pay his warmest compliments. He offers his most profuse apologies and, by the way, wants you to understand that he tried his best to block O'Dwyer's efforts to blacken your name. Sadly, he remained unsuccessful in spite of his best efforts.

After offering me a convivial grin, Hall-Caine added, 'He also said that he has not forgotten the invaluable assistance you provided us last year at the Durbar. And he commanded that I was to make myself available in case there was anything you needed, so here I am!'

I started to thank him, but he held up one finger to stop me.

'However, there is one condition, Mr Singh. You must make every effort to be discreet. If you make a public spectacle of yourself and stir up a hornet's nest that results in any undue embarrassment to Her Majesty's government, or the governor, both you and your friend will be asked to leave the city with the utmost of haste. Is that clear?'

I was not in the least bit happy about being spoken to like a naughty schoolboy, but I swallowed my pride and nodded briskly. 'I understand.'

'Good! I'm glad we are on the same page.' Pulling a piece of paper from the folder, he offered it to me. 'Here, you will need this. It is a letter of introduction signed by Commissioner Edwardes, explaining that you are conducting your investigation in assistance to the Bombay Police. I would suggest you use it sparingly, Mr Singh, only if absolutely necessary. It will hold up to a cursory perusal, but I doubt it will survive a close examination.'

'Why not?'

'Well, because it is a forgery, of course. I slapped it together about twenty minutes ago.' His grin grew wider. 'I am quite proud of how well I managed the commissioner's signature, if I may toot my own horn. Even he will think twice before denying it's not genuine.'

I took the letter and glanced at it, before folding it in half and tucking it into my inside pocket. He was correct about the signature, I observed. It was a very decent forgery. Used sensibly, this document could prove to be very useful indeed. In Rajpore, I was well-nigh all-powerful. But in Bombay, I was just another visitor, and Indian to boot. Having a credential endorsed by the commissioner himself would simplify my task immensely, not to mention open doors that were firmly shut to most Indians.

Hall-Caine wasn't quite done being generous. 'I think you will find this equally helpful,' he said, offering me another folded sheet of paper. 'I took the liberty of sending one of the constables down to Ballard Pier to make a copy of the dockmaster's disembarkation register. It contains the addresses of where most of the passengers that arrived on the *Caledonia* are staying. As you can see, your Miss Hartley's name is right here,' he said, tapping the middle of the page, 'which confirms beyond a doubt that she did indeed disembark from the ship.'

Sitting back, he folded his arms across his chest. 'Might I say something, Mr Singh? Though I fear that you may not wish to hear it?'

'Of course!' I responded. It was the least I could do, after all that he had done for me. 'Please, speak your mind.'

He let out another, more forceful sigh. 'Personally, I do not believe your memsahib has gone missing. I am convinced she simply changed her mind and decided to do a runner, so to speak. India does that, Sir, to a person who visits these far-flung shores for the first time. There is adventure in the air here. It causes people to forget who they are and succumb to grandiose dreams.

'That is why I suggest you don't waste any more of your time. Abandon this wild goose chase you have decided to embark upon. Instead, enjoy your stay in Bombay. Take in the theater, perhaps get in a spot of shopping with your lovely partner, and then head back to Rajpore before the rains arrive and turn this city into a bigger cesspit than it already is.'

'I'm afraid I cannot do that,' I said, unmoved by his eloquence, persuasive though it was.

'I owe Peter a debt that I cannot dismiss quite so easily, and I have made him a promise which I intend to keep, for better or worse.'

'Very well!' he said. 'If you are bent upon continuing your investigation, then far be it for me to stand in your way.'

'Wait a minute! Before you leave, might I say something to you as well, Mr Caine, is it?'

'Hall-Caine,' he said, turning to face me, that unwavering smile remaining fixed, as if it was painted on his face. 'Of course, how may I be of service?'

'Why are you helping me?' I inquired suspiciously. 'What is it you really expect in return?'

I made no effort to be polite. In fact, my tone was almost hostile.

However, Hall-Caine remained unruffled, looking me squarely in the eye. 'Patience, my dear boy,' he said. 'Surely you of all people know that one doesn't give away the answers until the very end.'

CHAPTER 7

After departing from the police headquarters, I decided to begin my investigation at the most logical place, which was with the captain of the *Caledonia*.

A quick check of the manifest that Hall-Caine had handed me revealed that he was staying at the Royal Bombay Yacht Club. I had never visited that most venerable of institutions before. It was 'Whites Only', not the sort of place I ordinarily had any interest in patronizing. However, Uday Singh informed me that he knew exactly where it was located, directly opposite the Wellington Pier, close to the grand triumphal archway that was being erected to commemorate the king's visit to the Delhi Durbar.

Construction on the grandiosely named Gateway of India had begun just a year and a half earlier. From a distance, the edifice looked to be as magnificent as the Arc Du Triomphe or Constantine's Arch in Rome. Up-close, though, it was revealed for the monumental folly it really was. Like the King-Emperor, it had been constructed to celebrate, the gateway was rather less than overwhelming. I had attended the Durbar and solved rather a devious murder which had occurred there, thus saving the day and earning the privilege to meet the king face to face. Unfortunately, he had turned out to be a mousey bearded man with a lisp, who looked more like he belonged tending bar in a public house than on the throne of Great Britain. The gateway was much the same, built not of basalt as intended, but of cardboard and papier mache. After the king's departure from India's shores, it had been left to rot, white sagging to brown with the passage of each monsoon, slowly decaying until all that was left was a moldering heap, covered with fungus and pigeon droppings.

The Yacht Club itself was housed in a very handsome Gothic building, with a commanding view of the Arabian Sea. Inside, quite naturally, I was greeted by a surfeit of nautical themes, given the club's seafaring antecedents. The walls were paneled in burnished oak, not unlike the wardroom of a steamship, and the floor underfoot was lined by intricately patterned Minton tiles. Everywhere I turned, the eye was greeted by mounted ships' wheels and framed portholes, interspersed with a myriad of marine themed art, mainly lithographs of sailing vessels and a few seascapes done in the style of Eakins and Dutton. Elsewhere, it may have seemed somewhat hokey, but here, when combined with the high ceilings and arched oriel windows that let in an abundance of light, it managed to create a very comforting atmosphere, that sense of homecoming that sailors so desperately craved after months at sea.

There was, to my dismay, a touch of unpleasantness when we entered. As I strode into the vestibule abutting the front verandah, a turbaned Sikh porter, clad in blue and gold livery, scurried to intercede.

'No Indians are permitted entrance,' he announced, throwing up one hand to block us from proceeding any further.

'I am Maharaja Sikander Singh,' I said, 'and I am here on official business.'

'I am aware of who you are, Sahib,' the porter replied. 'My mother was born in Ranigarh, just west of Rajpore.' He offered me an apologetic nod. 'Unfortunately, rules are rules. No natives, even those as famous as you, are permitted to cross beyond the foyer.'

I took out the letter Hall-Caine had given me for exactly such situations, but before I could unfold it, Charan Singh stepped forward.

'I will take care of this, Huzoor.' He advanced on the Sikh, frowning so menacingly that I thought he was going to assault the man.

Thankfully, instead of knocking him aside and causing an unholy scene, he burst into a stream of voluble Punjabi. A moment later, the porter chattered back at him, shrugging his shoulders. This back-and-forth went on for a few more minutes, both men gesticulating and shouting at each other, until finally, the porter let out a sigh of surrender.

'Please wait here, Your Highness,' he said with a bow. 'I will go and fetch Captain Carruthers Sahib for you from the breakfast room.'

As he spun and marched away, I shot Charan Singh a quizzical look.

'He is family, as it turns out, Huzoor,' Charan Singh explained. 'My wife's third cousin's son. I thought I recognized him.'

'Of course, he is,' I said, stifling a smile and settling into one of the palm chairs that lined the vestibule. 'I should have expected nothing less.'

Thankfully, the captain did not keep us waiting quite as long as Hall-Caine had at police HQ. In a matter of minutes, the porter came scurrying back, followed closely by a tall, slender gentleman with sun-bronzed skin and a pair of well-trimmed whiskers. I had been expecting an older man, someone in his late forties, but Captain Carruthers was my age, perhaps even younger. Also, rather than naval whites, which would have been very much in keeping with our surroundings, he was wearing a tropical worsted suit in dun beige with a matching Terai hat, which made him look more like an African explorer than the captain of a passenger liner.

'Yes?' he inquired, not bothering to offer me a hand. 'You wished to speak with me?'

'Forgive me for interrupting your breakfast, Captain, but I am here on a matter of the most vital importance,' I said and handed him Hall-Caine's letter.

He glanced at it briefly, his brow wrinkling with a mixture of curiosity and wariness. 'What exactly is it you want?' he said, returning the letter to me, obviously unimpressed.

'I believe you had a passenger on your vessel, a young woman named Miss Mary Hartley, outbound from England. Unfortunately, she has gone missing it seems, and it has fallen to me to try and ascertain her whereabouts.' I offered him a comradely grin. 'I was hoping we could speak about her for just a few minutes.'

'Oh, not this again!' the captain's brow knit with consternation. 'I've had this chat already, first with her very ill-mannered fiancé and then with the police.'

He gave me a long, calculating glare. It was neither disdain nor a challenge, but something more akin to curiosity, like a prizefighter weighing up his opponent. 'I have said all I have to say about Miss Mary Hartley,' he growled, squaring his shoulders.

My first instinct was to bluster, my second to harangue him and my third to threaten, but one look at the obdurate expression on his face was quite enough to convince me to hold back. Bullying would not work with the captain, nor remonstration. I knew his type—hard men, as unyielding as the teak of their decks, in whose veins flowed the blood of Raleigh and Hawkins. He would not cave in to threats or intimidation. *How then was*

I to inveigle him to speak with me? Money perhaps, a bribe of some kind? No, I thought, biting my lip, *he would not succumb to any blandishments I could offer. What option did that leave me?*

I saw that he had a slim Bible tucked away in his breast pocket, a calfskin-bound volume that looked well-thumbed. I realized that was the answer I was seeking. It was his conscience that I would have to appeal to, his Christian compassion.

'Please, Captain, there are two lives at stake here,' I laid it on a bit thick for his benefit, making my voice quaver with entreaty. 'Surely you understand that?'

'Two lives?' he echoed, visibly dismayed.

'Indeed! First, of course, there is Miss Hartley. She could have been abducted, spirited away to who knows where. This is Bombay, Sir, not England. It is not a safe place for an unaccompanied white woman, especially one who has no prior knowledge of India. But there is another person whose feelings we must consider. Her fiancé, Peter Rowan, who happens to be a close friend of mine. He is bereft, Captain, to say the very least.' Clicking my tongue, I gave the captain a very poignant glare.

'Put yourself in his place for a moment. To live your life out without ever knowing what has become of the woman you set your heart upon, whether she came to a gory end, or if she simply decided to desert you! Is that a fate you would wish on anyone?'

This salvo obviously hit home. The captain's shoulders sagged in surrender.

'As I told the police, Miss Hartley disembarked when we arrived. I even provided them with a copy of the passenger manifest.'

That would be the document my new friend, Hall-Caine, had shared with me, I thought. My heart sank. The captain's confirmation that the manifest was genuine pretty much put paid to any possibility that Miss Hartley had suffered a mishap on board the *Caledonia*, which meant that the likelihood that she had jilted Peter was becoming more palpable by the minute.

'Couldn't the manifest be wrong?' I asked, instantly regretting it. It was an amateur question, not fitting for someone of my quality and experience.

'Not in this instance, no,' the captain replied.

'What makes you so certain of that, Captain?'

'Because, as I explained to her fiancé, I saw her stepping aboard a tender with my own two eyes.'

'You're sure of that?' I frowned. 'That it was Miss Hartley, not someone else.'

'Whatever else my defects, Mr Singh,' he replied, not bothering to disguise his condescension, 'I am blessed with excellent eyesight.'

Still, I refused to give up, in spite of his adamance. There was something there, something vital waiting to be uncovered. My every instinct was shouting that out at me.

'Did you speak to her?' I asked doggedly. 'To bid her adieu perhaps?'

'There were six hundred and fifty-four passengers on board my ship, Mr Singh,' the captain replied dryly. 'It is not my habit to wish every single one of them goodbye in person, especially not those traveling by second saloon.'

'How about on the journey out, Captain? Did you have much occasion to interact with Miss Hartley on the journey out?'

'What do you mean?'

'Did you socialize with her at all? Did you speak often?'

'Not really, no. I did have her at the captain's table one evening for supper, as is the custom, but that was the sum of it.'

'And what was your impression of her?'

Captain Carruthers hesitated momentarily, but it was as good as a grimace. 'A fine young woman. She had a charming smile.

Unfortunately, I don't know what more I can say beyond that. I really did not interact with her much.'

His expression and body language, however, conspired to convey something quite different. The way he pursed his lips, how his eyes crinkled at the corners and how his fingers tightened into involuntary fists told me he was hiding something.

Even to a dilettante, and I was not one, it was patent that Captain Carruthers did not care for Miss Hartley. *But why? Was it personal, a rejected overture perhaps, or a failed advance? Or had she done something to get on his bad side, an impropriety of some sort, or an argument?*

'What aren't you telling me, Captain?'

'I beg your pardon.'

'It is very apparent to me that you disliked Miss Hartley.'

'I barely knew the woman—' he started to bluster, but I cut him off mid-sentence.

'You seem like a fair man to me, a man of fine Christian morals. I can only imagine she had to have done something rather unforgivable to have ended up on your bad side.' I gave him a leer and a wink. 'Were you involved with her? Or is this a case of unrequited love?'

He frowned, unmoved by these accusations. 'You're barking up the wrong tree, Mr Singh. I am a happily married man, and I have been one for twenty-one long and fruitful years.'

'Then why, pray tell, do you go red in the face each time you speak of Miss Hartley?'

The captain clenched his jaw and let out a long cold breath before replying. 'Yes, it is true. I had rather a low opinion of the young woman.' He tweaked his moustache. 'She would better have been named Salome than after the Virgin.'

'What do you mean?' My ears perked up, sensing a hint of scandal.

'From the moment she set foot on my ship, she was a troublemaker.' This time, the grimace was unmistakable. 'A swallow, Mr Singh, a summer bird. Are you familiar with the term?'

'*Timon of Athens*, isn't it? "The swallow follows not summer more willing than we. Nor more willingly leaves winter. Such summer birds are men."'

'And women,' the captain replied, giving me a nod of approbation. 'I have been ferrying passengers out to India for eleven years, Mr Singh, and every passage, we see two or three women like your Miss Hartley. The popular term for them is the fishing fleet, I believe.'

The grimace became a scowl. 'I should not say any more. I have no right to malign her, or damage her reputation, no matter how little I thought of her.'

'Please, do continue,' I insisted. 'I assure you, everything you say to me is in the completest of confidence.'

The captain studied me pensively before sighing. 'In my experience, Mr Singh, there are three types of women that travel out to the colonies. The first, of course, are the wives. They are the easiest to manage and by far the best behaved. And yes, while there are occasional,' he cleared his throat, 'entanglements, they go to great efforts to keep their shenanigans discreet, and rarely become my problem.

'The second variety are the sisters and the matrons. They can often be dreadfully difficult and demanding, but if you treat them well, with courtesy and patience and respect, they keep to themselves and don't make trouble.

'The most dangerous passengers, however, are the single women. The spinsters and the widows, in particular. They set out for the colonies eager to leave their mundane lives behind, seeking excitement, driven by the lure of the exotic and the unknown, the call of the mysterious Orient. And money, of course. They are all looking to make their fortunes, to find the big fish, so to speak, to land a fellow who has his three hundred pound in income, or more. That is why they take on contracts of marriage with men they have never met, never seen.

'But like the birds of summer, Mr Singh, they are fickle creatures. The moment they are on board, with the White Cliffs behind them, they change their minds. They decide to seek out new arrangements, new affairs, new attachments. And the further that England recedes into the horizon, the more their thirst for adventure grows,' he shook his head. 'Such women, the broadsheets often describe them as adventuresses, but I much prefer calling them summer swallows.'

'What makes you believe that Miss Hartley was one of that lamentable breed?'

'Because she had me duped!' he exclaimed. 'Just as surely as she had everyone else on board hoodwinked.'

He let out a mournful sigh. 'As I said, Mr Singh, I have been doing this for a while, ferrying brides out to India, and I always take a paternal attitude toward them. I have no daughters of my own, which is why I feel so protective of these young women and try to watch out for them as much as I can. That is what drew me to Miss Hartley, at least at first. I thought her to be a simple country girl, someone who needed to be protected. She was rather demure, you see, obviously from a rural background, as a result of which she was quite timorous and did not socialize much with the other passengers. But oh, was I wrong? It was all an act, Sir, just a facade.

'As the journey progressed, she underwent a rebirth, so to speak,' he said, giving me a very frank look. 'The voyage to India, Mr Singh, affects a person, particularly the first time. When you spend an extended period at sea, you discover many truths about yourself. Twenty-one days may not seem like much on land, but on a ship, it is as good as a year. After you have weathered a storm or two, it alters the way you look at yourself. It makes you understand what you really want from your life. I believe that is what happened to Miss Hartley. She discovered who she truly was, the true essence of her character, and it certainly wasn't a spinster coming out to Bombay to marry a stranger. And that, Sir, is when she began to play her merry games quick enough.'

'What sort of games?' I asked, my interest piqued.

'You are a man of the world, Mr Singh! You know the webs women weave with their wiles! Batting their eyelashes, rolling their hips and enticing men with come-hither smiles. Miss Hartley may have looked naïve, as innocent as a lamb, but by the Gods, she could play the temptress with the best of them.'

'Personally, I did not think her attractive, but I can see how some men would desire her. She had something about her, a coy manner that far exceeded her beauty. And there was something about her bearing, the way she carried herself, a mixture of diffidence and approachability that made you want to take care of her, Mr Singh. It's difficult to explain.'

Shaking his head again, the captain let out a sigh. 'The only way I can describe it is as a vulnerability. That was what drew men to her, regardless of age, like moths to a candle.'

'But it was not the truth, was it?'

'Oh no, not at all. Miss Hartley was no innocent. On the contrary, she was as cold and conniving a creature as Lucrezia Borgia herself,' the captain shrugged, an antipathetic shudder. 'I am not an easy man to take advantage of, Mr Singh, but I am sorry to say, I did not realize what she truly was until much later. When I first met her, I felt an instant affinity toward her. That was why I had her at my table for dinner the very first night of the voyage. I rarely do that, you know, with people traveling by second-class. Ordinarily, I wait until after we enter the Med before inviting them to join me. But for Miss Hartley, I decided to make an exception.' His mouth tightened. 'That was my first mistake.'

'Why do you say that?'

'Well, not only were her manners dreadful, but she also caused an appalling scene. She drank enough champagne to drown a duck, and then she had the temerity to lecture me about the rights of women, that too in front of my first-class guests.'

I bit back an involuntary snigger. The thought of an inebriated Miss Hartley lecturing this pompous prig of a man tickled my sense of humor to no end. Thankfully, Captain Carruthers was too caught up with his diatribe to notice my bemusement.

'I should have had her thrown out,' he huffed, 'but regardless of her impertinence, she was a passenger. As a result, I was honor-bound to suffer her company for the rest of dinner.' He bristled like an aggravated cat. 'Frankly, I thought that was the last I would see of her for the rest of the voyage, but that was my second mistake. You see, once she had a taste of first-class, there was no going back for her,' he said with a grimace. 'It was very different when I started out. We kept the passengers strictly segregated, each to his or her own class, but nowadays things are much more informal. Your Miss Hartley refused to stay down on 'B' Deck where she belonged. Why, the very next morning, she was back on the promenade deck, parading about as if she owned the whole boat. And that was only the beginning, Mr Singh. She was forever turning up in first-class. Somehow, she found a way to be invited up every morning for whist and every evening for dinner. It was well-nigh intolerable.'

'I'm guessing you decided to intervene?' I asked, raising an inquiring brow.

'She left me no choice. I forbade her from coming up-deck and warned her that if I caught her in first-class again, I would have her put ashore. To be honest, I thought that would be the end of it, but yet again, I was mistaken,' he said with a shiver. 'The nerve of that woman! Immediately, she went crying to her patron, an Italian princess of some kind who was occupying the Peninsular suite and who had taken an inordinate liking to her.'

'Do you happen to recall this Italian princess's name, perchance?'

'Forsa, I think it was. The Countess of Forsa, or some such.'

I sat up. 'Do you mean the Contessa di Sforza?' I exclaimed, exaggerating both the sibilant 's' and 'f' as one sound. 'Katerina di Sforza of Forli?'

'Aye, that sounds about right,' he replied. 'Anyway, as I was saying, this contessa came along and gave me a proper talking-to, like I was a bloody third-rater.' His expression was thunderous. 'It was an absolute embarrassment. I have never had any passenger talk to me like that, like I was a blasted servant and not the captain of my own vessel. Why, if it had been anyone other than her, I would have given them a proper piece of my mind right back.'

'What did the contessa say exactly? Do you happen to recall?'

'She informed me that Miss Hartley would be moving up from second-class into her cabin, and insisted that I permit her access to the first-class deck and salon. When I refused, she offered to pay the difference in fare. I refused again, but then she threatened me. She said that she was a close friend of Sir James Mackay and warned me that she would have me shored if I did not acquiesce to her wishes.'

'And that is why you backed down and allowed her first-class access?'

'What choice did I have?' He said dolefully, 'I've never heard such a thing, a captain being bullied on his own vessel? It was bloody well ridiculous. And if that wasn't bad enough, I had to endure it silently as she set out to make doe eyes at damn nearly every single man on board.'

'Is that so?' I leaned forward, intrigued.

I have always enjoyed a good piece of gossip. Most people are rather dismissive of it, declaring it a waste of time and breath, but in my experience, there is no better place to find a clue amidst a mound of seemingly insignificant hearsay.

'It was shameful, Mr Singh. She had half a dozen bachelors, dancing to her tune, catering to every whim, like puppies on a string and a few of the married gents as well. My goodness, how they fell for her "lost little girl" act I will never understand! I could not believe how ready they were to throw all propriety to the wind and chase after her in droves, like hounds coursing after a hare. Why, she even had one of my crew members following her around, acting like a lovelorn fool.' He sniffed, his nostrils flaring with voluble disapproval.

'He is my second mate, Michael Mascarenhas. A fine young fellow, and really very intelligent for a native.'

Even as he said those words, his face turned puce, realizing he had made rather an immense faux pas.

'Oh ... my apologies, Mr Singh, I mean no offence.' The captain offered me an apologetic grimace. 'What I was trying to say is that young Michael, he's as smart as a whip. I've been grooming him, and he has a fine future ahead of him. Why, in a few years, he might even be the first Indian to captain a vessel, if he plays his cards right.'

'And Miss Hartley endangered these prospects?' I asked, ignoring his apology.

'She did. The poor boy became quite enamored with her, and she did nothing to rebuff him, certainly not as a woman who had a prior arrangement ought to have done. On the contrary, she led the unfortunate chap on a merry dance. Why, he nearly came to blows with one of the passengers because of her.'

'A brawl with a passenger! Really?'

'It was hardly a brawl. More like heated words being exchanged. And it was hardly poor Michael's fault. The passenger in question was a bit of a twit, this jumped-up brat called Billimoria who kept chasing after Miss Hartley like a dog in heat. He got into a dreadful argument with Michael because of her, some rubbish about monopolizing her dance card at the Arabian Nights ball, or some such nonsense. Anyway, I nipped it in the bud as soon as I found out. Before it could turn into a scandal, I warned Michael off and ordered him to keep his distance from Miss Hartley.'

I mulled over this snippet. As I had hoped, while venting his spleen, the captain had inadvertently given me a half-decent clue. Peter's description of Miss Hartley had led me to perceive her as a shy, ageing spinster, unaccustomed to the ways of the world. I had built up a preliminary theory based on that notion, a variation of the classic trope where a single woman falls victim to the many perils of the Orient. But the captain's account changed all that. Miss Hartley, it seemed, was not a wilting willow after all. She was a confident, headstrong woman who was more than capable of jilting Peter in case a better offer came along. *In fact*, I thought with a sinking feeling in my stomach, *it sounded like that was exactly what she had been angling for. A better offer.*

'Tell me, Captain, just to satisfy my curiosity, are such shipboard romances common?'

'Not quite as common as you would think, and certainly not on my vessel. In fact, just last year I had a young gentleman put ashore at Aden because he had become much too persistent in his amorous pursuit of a young memsahib bound for Calcutta,' he said, pursing his lips as primly as an ageing dowager. 'Generally, most people, especially single women, try to keep such entanglements discreet. They don't want to risk their reputations, you see. British India is a small place, and once you acquire a reputation for being fast, it follows you like the mark of Cain emblazoned across your forehead.

'I even took the trouble to meet with Miss Hartley, tried to explain that to her that she would ruin her reputation if she persist with such unseemly and flirtatious behavior. And do you know how she responded?' he harrumphed, unable to keep his consternation to himself. 'She laughed, Mr Singh! She said she didn't give two whits about her reputation. And as if that wasn't bad enough, she had the gall to tell me to mind my own business, to say that it was none of my concern even if she chose to bat her eyelashes at every single man on board.'

'Is that so?' I leaned forward again, lowering my voice to a whisper. 'Would you happen to recall the names of any of these gentlemen? More importantly, would you know if any of them could have become enmeshed in a romantic entanglement with Miss Hartley, to use your words, which may have led her to decide to dissolve her marriage contract with my friend?'

It was a shot in the dark, I knew that when I took it. Still, I could not help but feel a flicker of dismay when it missed by a mile.

'I have no idea,' the captain replied frostily. 'As I already told you, I am a merchant mariner, not a housewife. I don't deal in gossip. If that is what you wish to know, I suggest you speak with the lady who shared Miss Hartley's cabin. A Miss Bennett, I believe. They were quite close and spent a considerable amount of time in each other's company.'

With that, he lost the last of his patience. 'Now, if you will excuse me, I have wasted quite enough of my time on the subject of Miss Mary Hartley.' He offered me a brisk nod of farewell. 'I shall leave you now, before my breakfast goes cold.'

'Of course, Captain, but would you be so kind as to answer one last question? This young officer of yours, Mascarenhas, do you have an inkling where I can locate him? I would dearly like to have a word with him as well?'

'Why?' the captain glared at me, even more suspicious than before. 'What do you wish to speak with him about?'

'Well, it is not illogical for me to think he might be involved with Miss Hartley's disappearance in some way. I mean, if he was as passionate about her as you have suggested, even willing to engage in an altercation with a passenger, it is not beyond reason to speculate that he would be willing to help her break off her engagement with another man.'

'I refuse to believe that.' The captain's mouth knotted into a frown. 'Young Mascarenhas is a good lad, a decent and rather shy fellow. Besides, as I told you, I gave him a proper talking-to. I told him to stay well away from her, or I would have his license suspended.'

'And you are sure he listened to you?'

'Of course,' the captain pursed his lips. 'My crew is my family, Sir. My officers are as good as sons to me. They dare not disobey me.'

'So, you are absolutely convinced that there is no chance your young officer may have decided to abscond with Miss Hartley? Perhaps he decided to spirit her away?'

'Absolutely not! He would never have truck with such nefariousness, I assure you!'

'Would you be willing to stake your reputation on that? And that of your vessel?'

Captain Carruthers wrestled with this question silently, his forehead furrowing. His expression grew steadily more pensive until, at last, he let out a groan of surrender. 'Very well!' Pivoting, he beckoned the doorman close. 'Have them keep my breakfast warm, will you? I will be back shortly.'

Turning back to me, he gave me a brusque nod. 'Come along then. Let's get going.'

'And where is it you're taking me, if I may ask?'

'To speak to Michael, of course. He is just down the road, at the Royal Alfred Sailors' Home.'

Squaring his shoulders, he straightened his hat determinedly. 'Let us go and put this mess to rest once and for all, shall we?'

CHAPTER 8

The Royal Alfred Sailors' Home was just a stone's throw away from the Yacht Club, located at the intersection of the Colaba Causeway and Frere Road. It was a monstrosity of a building, designed by F.W. Stevens, the same architect who had constructed the Victoria Terminus. Like the aforementioned building, it was a bit of an eyesore, a mishmash of arches and turrets in that ghastly style that Stevens had grandiosely dubbed Indo-Saracenic.

There were two wings; the west wing, which comprised permanent residences, mainly for officers, and enlisted men from His Majesty's Navy, who had suffered injuries during the Empire's many wars; and the east, which was earmarked to accommodate sailors still in active service.

'The higher floors,' the captain informed me, 'are reserved for captains and ranks above that, but the ground floor houses a dormitory and chummery where unmarried officers can seek temporary accommodation while on shore leave.'

It was here that Captain Carruthers led me without further discussion, striding along determinedly. I followed him with a smile, studying the fanciful sculptures that decorated the building's pediment, which included a rather morose-looking Neptune surrounded by a covey of very shrewish nymphs, flanked by a pair of plump sea lions, each fancifully holding up pennants. We cut across a dusty courtyard and went down a wide corridor before finally entering a large and airy room. Judging by the long wooden tables and benches that lined its granite floors, this was a shared mess where the sailors congregated for meals. At the moment, however it was deserted, except for a small group of six or seven men who had pulled aside a table in the far corner to make space for them to squat on the floor, where they were engaged, it seemed, in a rather spirited game of Crown and Anchor.

'Mr Mascarenhas,' Captain Carruthers thundered when he took in this scene, 'how many times have I warned you about the evils of gambling?'

One of the men leaped up in surprise as this announcement boomed through the room. This was Michael Mascarenhas, I presumed. From the name and the captain's narrative, I had expected a tall, well-proportioned young tyro, but this gentleman was very short, just over five feet in height, with a complexion dark enough to be sub-Saharan rather than Anglo-Indian. He looked more like a schoolboy than a rake, an effect that was only added to by his choice of clothing, which was a pair of worsted trousers and an ill-fitting pea coat.

'Forgive me, Sir! A thousand apologies!' he exclaimed, squirming with shame as the captain fixed him with a withering glare. 'We were only having a bit of harmless fun.'

'I am profoundly disappointed in you, Michael,' Captain Carruthers proclaimed. 'I thought you were a godly, Christian man. Dice are not harmless. They are the device of the devil. Do you wish to lose your immortal soul, and be damned to purgatory for all eternity? Does that sound like fun?'

Even as the captain launched into this sermon, the rest of Michael's compatriots used this opportunity to scatter, beating a hasty retreat and leaving the three of us alone.

'I am a fool, Sir,' Michael whispered, shifting from foot to foot. 'Please, give me another chance. I shall never gamble again; I swear it on all that is holy.'

'Very well,' the captain's tone softened. He gave Michael a friendly pat on the shoulder. 'I have faith in you, my boy. You are better than this.'

He probably remembered that I was standing behind him, watching this scene unfold with a sardonic smirk.

'Perhaps we could get to business, Captain,' I commented.
watching this scene unfold with a sardonic smirk.

'After all, your breakfast awaits, yes?'

'Of course,' the captain replied. 'Michael, my boy, this is Mr Singh. He is working with the police and would like to speak with you. I want you to cooperate fully with him.'

Michael Mascarenhas had been eyeing me curiously up to the moment the word 'police' was uttered, at which point his eyes widened with unease.

'Talk to me?' he exclaimed, thoroughly perturbed. 'What about?'

'Do not be alarmed,' I responded. 'I only want to inquire about one of your passengers, Miss Hartley.'

'Mary?' he asked, bewildered. 'Do you mean Mary Hartley?'

The way he said Mary, with an easy familiarity and palpable emotion, told me two things. First, they had been close, if not intimate, then at the very least an abiding involvement. Second, he cared for her deeply, that much was obvious, even if you ignored the lovelorn look that crossed his face. It was an observation not lost on the captain either, judging by the way his mouth tightened with disapproval.

'I am afraid to report that Miss Hartley has gone missing,' I said, watching the second mate carefully to see how he would respond.

'Oh no! How terrible!' He paled, turning puce with dismay.

His reaction seemed genuine enough, but was it concern, or was it fear?

'Wait a minute,' he said, noticing my vigilant expression. 'Surely you don't think I had something to do with it?'

'Well, the captain did say you were inordinately interested in her. Is that true? Were you involved with Miss Hartley, Mr Mascarenhas?'

It was a very direct question, I know, tactless to the point of being rude. My instincts were telling me to take the path of the battering ram. That was the sort of gambit I normally eschewed. Not only was it unsubtle; it lacked finesse. But sometimes, with men like Mascarenhas who were used to following commands, being direct could work wonders.

Unfortunately, it backfired completely on this occasion. Rather than being intimidated by my hectoring, Mascarenhas responded by squaring his shoulders, perhaps remembering some vestige of ancestral pride.

'That is none of your business,' he hissed. Turning to the captain, he gave him a plaintive look. 'Must I speak of this, Sir? It is a personal matter I would prefer to keep private.'

'I don't see that you have a choice, Mr Mascarenhas,' the captain spoke up. 'This looks very bad indeed. I must insist, if you have anything to do with this nonsense, tell us everything now.'

The way the captain phrased it was more a command than a request. Much to my chagrin, where I had failed, he managed to do the trick.

Michael sighed and shook his head in surrender. 'Yes, I knew Miss Hartley, he said. 'And no, I was not involved with her.'

It was a half-hearted denial, even a rank amateur could see that. I seized upon it.

'But you wish you were?' I said. 'You were in love with her, weren't you?'

It was an even more gauche tactic than the last one, so crude that the captain let out a squawk of consternation, rather like an aggrieved rooster.

'Mr Singh!' he exclaimed, aghast. 'This is a breach of all boundaries of propriety. Don't answer him, Michael. He is being terribly rude.'

'No,' the boy whispered. 'I'll answer him.' He fixed me with a level gaze. 'Yes, I was in love with Mary.'

Turning to the captain, he gave him an apologetic frown. 'Forgive me, Sir. I know you told me to keep my distance, but I could not. What is the old saying? The heart has its reasons, of which reason knows nothing.'

The captain blanched. 'This is most alarming, Michael. I had such plans for you, but to become involved with a passenger? Oh, that is a cardinal sin. I will have to have you beached, my boy. There's no two ways about it.'

'It doesn't matter any more, Sir.' Michael sighed haplessly. 'I will accept whatever fate you choose for me.'

He looked so utterly heartbroken, his demeanor so bereft, that a part of me could not help but sympathize with the poor fellow. I am not a romantic, not by any stretch of the imagination, as my Helene is quick to remind me, but in this case, I knew exactly how Mr Mascarenhas was feeling. I had felt it myself once, a long time ago. Coup de foudre, the French called it, the thunderbolt. Love had no rationale, no rationality. When it came, it swept you away. It broke you. It unmade all certainties, all absolutes, all sureties. And when it was gone, all that remained was a hollow shell, an empty silhouette of what had once been a man.

Beneath his hangdog manner, I sensed something else, an apathy that was more reminiscent of a disappointed teenager than a Lothario.

'Forgive my presumption, Mr Mascarenhas, but was this affection you felt for Miss Hartley one-sided, or did she happen to reciprocate your ardor?'

Michael winced at this question. 'She broke my heart, to tell you the truth.' His eyes brimmed with anguish. 'Ordinarily, I am very careful to keep my distance from female passengers, especially the spinsters. The captain has been very clear with us that he will brook no scandals aboard his vessel. But it is very difficult, even for an officer as junior and unattractive as myself.'

'Surely you're exaggerating? Are your female passengers really that forward?'

'Oh, you have no idea!' The captain interjected forcefully.

'It's true, Mr Singh,' Michael said. 'These buccaneer girls throw themselves at men in uniform like we are pieces of gold, just waiting to be snapped up.'

'Buccaneer girls?' I echoed. 'I haven't heard that phrase before.'

Michael's face turned purple, realizing he had committed a bit of a gaffe. 'I'm sorry, I didn't mean to sound insulting. It's a dreadful term, and I'm ashamed to use it, but that's what all of us call these young women who come out to India looking for husbands. They are like pirates, you see, each waiting for a big fat target to plunder, a suitable prospect with a decent income and some rank. And they will do anything to get what they want, so to speak.'

He shuddered, but I could not tell if it was disdain or embarrassment. 'Some of my mates enjoy their attentions immensely. They chase after them readily, only too eager to take advantage of their overtures, but I am ordinarily rather shy, especially in my interactions with the opposite sex. This time, however, I don't know what overtook me. It was like I had no choice in the matter. I had never experienced love before, but when I met Mary,' he shook his head diffidently, 'I found myself attracted to her with a passion I could not have imagined. I am no poet, but it overcame me like a madness, a disease, or whatever metaphor you may think best! All I know is that it consumed me whole.'

'Preposterous!' The captain sniped. His outrage made his voice shrill. 'You barely knew the girl!'

'Perhaps you're correct, Sir,' Michael responded bashfully. 'But from the moment I met her, I thought her possessed of every quality a man may desire in a wife. She had such excellent posture, such fine skin and teeth, and a gait that was almost regal.'

I stifled a grin. It sounded like he was describing a mare, not a woman.

'As I said, I have never been good with women,' Michael continued. 'More often than not, they bewilder, even scare me. Their caprice, their mutability ... somehow I always end up with my foot firmly in my mouth. But with Mary, it was different. She was different, quite unlike any woman I have ever met.'

'How do you mean?'

'Well, for one, she was very patient. And she was not a talker, as most women tend to be. She preferred to listen, Sir. In fact, she had this way of listening, this way of angling her head and looking straight at you, which made you feel like you were the only man in the world, like every word that came out of your mouth was of monumental importance. I can't explain it, but every man she encountered felt it. You couldn't help but want to take care of her.'

His earlier reticence seemed to have receded entirely, replaced now by what was almost an eagerness. I was tempted to interrupt, to try and steer the conversation back to something more germane to my investigation, but after a moment's consideration, I decided to let him talk. *It was patent that he had a lot he needed to get off his chest, a form of expiation*, I told myself. *Who knew where it would lead?* Perhaps, somewhere amidst his ramblings, a clue would emerge.

'I tried to resist the urge to pursue her, Captain,' Michael said apologetically. 'I truly did. I tried to tell myself I was being a fool. I resolved every morning to stay away from her, to keep my distance as you commanded, but every time I saw her, when I gazed into those eyes, Sir, my resolve turned to dust.'

He turned to me, his voice wistful. 'She was beautiful, Mr Singh, as lovely as a sunrise.'

'That's not how I have heard her described,' I said. 'I was told she is rather a plain, unassuming creature, somewhat of a frump.'

'That's a lie!' he retorted hotly, his voice strident. 'I thought as much when I first met her, at first glance, but it was just an affectation, a facade she hid behind. It was only as the journey progressed that the real Mary came to light, as scintillating and exquisite as a cereus, Mr Singh.'

I tried not to chuckle at his enthusiastic, if somewhat ham-handed, attempts at mixing metaphors. Only two kinds of people compared women to flowers, armchair poets struggling to find an eloquent turn of phrase and men who were hopelessly lovelorn. Still, clumsy metaphors aside, it was unequivocal that Mr Mascarenhas felt a deep passion for Miss Hartley. But, at the same time, I couldn't help but feel a nagging doubt that there was something I was missing, a piece of the puzzle I had not yet grasped. *What could it be?*

The answer to that question fell into place a moment later.

'Just to satisfy my curiosity, how did you two even meet? You are the second officer, correct? I imagine your duties kept you occupied and gave you very little time to socialize with passengers.'

'As of this moment, he is the *third* officer,' Captain Carruthers piped up. 'And no, he is not supposed to socialize with the passengers at all. His duties are to stand watch at night and make sure the lifeboats are kept shipshape, not chase after single women.'

'I will accept the demotion, Sir, but let me make one thing clear. I didn't chase after Mary,' Michael objected, his cheeks turning a bright shade of red. 'As a matter of fact, she approached me.'

'Is that so! You should have fobbed her off, like you are supposed to.'

'I couldn't, Sir,' Michael nodded empathically. 'She sought me out and asked for my help.'

'What about?'

Michael's face hardened. 'I don't know if it would be correct for me to speak of it. It was a private matter. She came to me in confidence.'

'For God's sake, man, speak up!' Captain Carruthers snarled even before I could say a word. 'This is no time to be close-mouthed.'

Michael gritted his teeth. 'As you wish, Sir! She came to me because she was having some trouble with one of the crew members and asked me to intervene on her behalf.'

'What? Trouble aboard my ship? What sort of trouble?'

'It seems, Sir,' Michael dropped his voice an octave, 'that she was being harassed by one of the crew.'

'On my vessel?' Captain Carruthers growled, his expression thunderous. 'Why was I not told of this before?'

'I deemed it best to handle it myself, Sir,' Michael replied. 'You had enough on your plate, what with the passengers and that storm that came upon us as we left the Canaries.'

'Hold on a minute!' I interjected. 'Who is this crew member? Is he one of your fellow officers?'

'He's the first-class porter,' Michael replied. 'His name is Hamid Ali. A thoroughly shifty fellow, I am sorry to say. There have been complaints about him before as well. Small things mainly, missing items of luggage and the occasional rudeness, but this was the first time he has been accused of something serious.'

'What exactly did Miss Hartley say he did?'

Michael's mouth wrinkled, as if he had swallowed a bitter lemon. 'Allegedly, he accosted her and tried to force himself upon her.' He bristled visibly. 'Ali denied the accusation, of course. When I cornered him, he spun an outlandish tale about how she was the one who had made an overture toward him. What balderdash!' Michael frowned, his distaste at such a suggestion more than evident. 'As if any respectable woman would ever do something like that!'

'I'll have him whipped,' the captain thundered. 'I'll have him hanged from the yardarm, the scoundrel.'

'Don't worry, Sir,' Michael assured him. 'I handled it. I gave him a proper talking-to and let him know that he should find another berth after we reached Bombay, that there was no place for the likes of him aboard the *Caledonia*.' His frown deepened to a grimace. 'I would have liked to do much worse, put him ashore at the nearest port and file a complaint with the police, but Mary was most insistent that we keep things quiet. She did not want to risk a scandal, Sir, especially anything that could besmirch her reputation or damage the ship's good name.'

'Well done, my boy,' the captain said grudgingly. 'You handled this affair very well, better than I would have myself. Unfortunately, that doesn't absolve you of your stupidity for becoming enamored by a passenger. I will let you hold your rank, but still, I shall have to censure you formally for your behavior. It will have to go in my log. I have no choice. You have broken the oldest oath that every merchant sailor swears to obey when he puts on his whites. As Noah was bound to the denizens of the ark, so are we bound, by duty and by God, to protect those in our charge. You should not have seen Miss Hartley as a woman, only as a responsibility, as sacrosanct as the Holy Grail itself. How many times have I taught you that?'

'Captain,' I interjected, 'before you decide to have him drawn and quartered, I have one more question for Mr Mascarenhas.'

Obviously annoyed at being interrupted, Captain Carruthers gave me an irritated frown, even as Michael offered me a wry smile, grateful for being rescued before the captain's invective could gather its full momentum. 'Tell me, do you think that Hamid Ali would harm Miss Hartley? I mean, he certainly has ample motive to wish her ill, considering she cost him his job.'

'Oh no, Mr Singh,' Michael replied. 'He is all piss and wind. He wouldn't dare harm a hair on her head. I have held on to his travel pass, you see. Besides, he knows if he tries anything, he will have to deal with me.' Michael squared his shoulders and gave me a steely nod. 'I may not look like much,' he announced, 'but I was the welterweight champion at Bishop's Cotton School for six years running.'

I couldn't help but grin when he made this unlikely declaration. 'For a man who claims to be rather shy, you really are quite the Lancelot, aren't you, Mr Mascarenhas?'

He blushed, turning very nearly as scarlet as my pugree. 'It was all Miss Hartley's, Mary's, doing. Ordinarily, I run a mile away from a confrontation, but she made me want to be a knight in shining armor.'

'You were the one who helped her gain access to the first-class deck each evening, weren't you?'

His eyes widened with surprise, and he shot the captain a guilty glance.

'I was.'

'Was that your idea? Or hers?'

His brow wrinkled with confusion, as if it was the first time that consideration had occurred to him.

'Hers actually, now that you mention it! I didn't see any harm in it. Frankly, it was the least I could do to make up for Seaman Ali's impropriety.'

'And the fact that you were attracted to her had nothing to do with that decision? You weren't trying to court her favor?'

'Not intentionally, no. As I have already explained, Mr Singh, I am not a forward man. Rather than making a fool of myself, I was willing to keep my feelings concealed. Honestly, Sir, I just wanted to see more of her, to spend more time with her. That is why I switched shifts with Mr Jones. Ordinarily, he is the one responsible for the first-class passengers. I took over his duties and timed my rounds to coincide with her appearances on the foredeck. Whenever she came up each evening to take a turn, I made it a point to bump into her,' he said with a smile. 'It worked quite well, if I might add. We became good friends, after a fashion. She always made it a point to stop and inquire after my health, and to gossip a bit. It really was the best part of my day, even if it meant working both day and night shifts. I would happily have left it at that, a harmless infatuation. I would have been content with the occasional hello, I assure you, but everything changed after Marseilles.'

'In what way? What happened in Marseilles?'

'Not in Marseilles, Mr Singh,' Michael responded. 'The night after we departed for Port Said. Much to my surprise, Mary asked me to squire her to the Arabian Nights ball, to accompany her as her partner. A most unexpected development, if I may say so.

Not only was it the first time I had ever been invited to escort a passenger, but also where I come from, it is unheard of for any woman to take the initiative so openly and approach a man. That was when I realized that she must care for me quite as deeply as I did for her.'

Michael let out a school boyish chuckle, his Adam's apple bobbing up and down like a cork. 'It was the most astounding evening of my life. I went dressed as Ali Baba, complete with those pointy slippers. And Mary, she was resplendent, Mr Singh. She came as an Egyptian princess.'

He let out a doleful sigh. 'I cannot describe how wonderful she looked. She was like a dream, Sir,' he said, grinning at the captain who remained unmoved. 'A vision come to life, all done up in gossamer taffeta and muslin. She was the most beautiful woman there by far. All the unattached gentlemen were dazzled by her, and a great many of those who were attached as well, if I might add. They swarmed after her, like bees to honey. But Mary ignored them all. She spent the whole evening on my arm. No matter how many gents wanted to get on her dance card, she only had eyes for me.'

Michael preened like a gangly peacock. 'You have to realize, Mr Singh, it was the first time something like this had happened to me, the first time I had been the center of attention. I am not a handsome man, nor am I particularly clever, but with Mary on my arm, it was like I mattered, like I was someone special, a prince and not just a lowly second mate. The very next morning, I decided to court her.'

'You did not?' Captain Carruthers exclaimed, aghast.

'I am sorry, Sir, but try to understand. I wanted to spend my life with her, which was why I asked her to break her marriage contract and become engaged to me.'

'For God's sake, Michael, have you no shame?' the captain was close to apoplectic. 'I warned you that she was spoken for. Did that give you no pause?'

'It did, briefly.' Michael frowned, as if he was still struggling with what a particularly difficult choice it had been. 'At least until I realized she had no intention of marrying her fiancé.'

'She said that to you?' I leaned forward so sharply that I damned nearly toppled over. Here it was, the clue I had been waiting for so patiently. 'With her own lips, she said those words?'

'She did. Not once, but many times, Mr Singh. The thought of marrying a stranger sickened and terrified her. It was a fear that had grown immeasurably as the voyage progressed, accompanied by a sense of helplessness that she was trapped. She confided that much to me on several occasions, along with the confession that she had no intention of going through with it. She told me that she was going to jilt him as soon as we arrived in Bombay, confront him and tell him that she had changed her mind, that she could not go through with the contract any longer.'

The captain shook his head, his face as grim as a hurricane in the Bay of Biscay. 'The nerve of that woman! How dare she get the *Caledonia* involved in such a mess! I should have had her confined to her quarters after that first embarrassment,' he snarled. 'That dreadful, money-grubbing witch!'

'Please don't speak of Mary like that, Captain.' Michael's voice was deceptively soft, but at the same time, as cold as steel. 'She was not like that at all. Think about it for a moment. Try to envision how monumentally unfair her situation was! She had never even met the man. All she knew of him was his name and age, and the little she had been able to piece together from two letters. She hadn't seen so much as a photograph,' his voice grew strident, passionate with barely repressed outrage. 'You tell me, Sir, how is it right to be sold to a man twice your age, like a prize heifer, and sent halfway around the world so that you could spend the rest of your life keeping his house and hearth, slowly frittering away your youth, your dreams, your very hopes?'

'Nobody sold Miss Hartley to Mr Rowan,' I retorted. 'She chose to accept his proposal, of her own free will.

'Did she? Or was she pressured into it by her parish? Mary was an orphan, Mr Singh. When she accepted the offer of marriage made to her, it seemed to be her only chance, the only way to have a better life. But once she embarked, as England's shores receded behind her, she came to realize that it wasn't her only option. She grew convinced that she deserved a better fate, one of her own choosing. And frankly, Mr Singh, I agreed with her. She was special, Sir, and she merited more than being forced to marry a stranger.'

A mournful look flashed across his face as he said these words, a palpable regret.

'She rejected you, didn't she, when you asked her to marry you?' I asked.

His mouth tightened, the regret darkening to despair. 'Yes, she did. When I pleaded my suit, she thanked me but refused outright. She told me she had no intention of being a sailor's wife, of staying ashore by herself for months on end while I was away at sea,' he said. 'I don't blame her, Mr Singh. Nothing would have made me happier than if she had accepted my suit, but I am enough of a realist to understand she made the right choice. Why would she want to settle down with someone as penniless and lacking in prospects as a humble second officer? Why would any woman?'

'You do realize, Mr Mascarenhas, that gives you a halfway decent motive to harm her?'

Michael's eyes widened. Clearly, this consideration had not occurred to him.

'Oh no!' he gasped, giving me, and then Captain Carruthers, a stricken look. 'I could no more harm her than I could hurt myself. I was pained, I admit it, at being rebuffed so coldly, but I am not a violent man. Besides, if I wanted to get even, it would be with that bloody Captain. He was the one who had turned her head, Mr Singh, the real reason she turned me down. I know it.' His mouth twisted into a scowl. 'Captain Malcolm bloody Gordon of the Highlanders. After the Arabian Nights ball, he got right after Mary, sniffing after her like a dog in heat.'

'Mr Mascarenhas!' the captain interjected. 'Mind your language!'

Michael winced. 'Forgive me, Captain. It's just, he was a complete and utter berk, and you know it. A dreadful cad, Mr Singh, chasing half the girls on board from the moment we left Southampton. He didn't even care if they were married or not, just made a sally at anyone below forty. The fellow had no shame.' His brow darkened with outrage. 'I tried to be civil to him, I really did. I even approached him, one gentleman to another, and told him about my interest in Mary, asking him very politely to step aside.'

'And how did he respond to that request?' I asked.

'He laughed at me,' Michael growled. 'He called me a callow fool and told me he would give Mary a kiss from me.' His hands tightened into fists. If he hadn't been a passenger, I swear, I would have given him a proper drubbing right then.'

'I take it that Miss Hartley found him somewhat more irresistible than you ,' I said dryly.

Michael nodded. 'I have no idea why. He was the worst kind of bounder, with an oily charm that only someone truly naive would fall for. But Mary,' he stifled a sigh, 'she bought it, hand over fist. I caught them kissing one evening, can you believe it, behind one of the lifeboats on the starboard deck. I confronted her after that, tried to explain to her that he was not good enough for her, that his interest was not,' he blushed bright red before saying, 'honorable.'

'She was not happy about that, was she?'

'She was downright furious!' he exclaimed. 'She told me to keep my distance from her, or she would complain to the captain about my behavior.' His face hardened. 'I only wanted what was best for her. I don't know what happened, but after we left Port Said, she ... she changed, Mr Singh. It was like she became a different person entirely. She had no time for me anymore. We barely exchanged two words. It was like she was determined to avoid me completely.'

'And you felt betrayed?'

'Not betrayed,' he said, shaking his head. 'Disappointed. I was deeply disheartened by her behavior, but I realized that was what she wanted, which was why I kept my distance.'

Everything about his manner—his hangdog expression and his slumped shoulders—proclaimed he was telling the truth, but still something made me doubt him.

'I think you are hiding something, Mr Mascarenhas. You know more than you are letting on.'

'I ... I am not,' Michael stammered. 'I swear. I have told you the whole, undiluted truth.'

As far as denials went, this was even more unconvincing, so specious that not even the captain was swayed.

'I demand you tell us everything immediately, Mr Mascarenhas.' The captain's voice was adamant, making it clear that he was unwilling to brook any further obfuscation. 'If you know anything about this woman's whereabouts, you must tell us right now.'

Michael's jaw stiffened, his teeth grinding audibly. At first, it looked like he would refuse, but after a brief staring match with Captain Carruthers, his shoulders sagged.

'I know exactly where Mary is, Sir,' he whispered. 'She has not gone missing, not at all.'

This admission took me completely by surprise, and the captain as well, judging by the astonishment I saw mirrored on his face.

'What?' I took one menacing step forward, deeply irritated at being made to look a fool. 'Where is she? Tell me, damn you!'

'At the YWCA, Sir. Lady Willingdon's hostel in Churchgate,' Michael explained hurriedly, taking a hesitant step backwards. 'She has taken up lodging there.'

'Are you certain?' I barked. 'How do you know that?'

'I had her followed,' Michael said shamefacedly, 'after she disembarked. I paid one of the lascars to trail her and find out where she was staying.'

'You did not!' The captain looked like he was about to explode. 'That's not cricket, Mr Mascarenhas, not cricket at all.'

'What else could I do?' Michael wheedled. 'I needed a little time to figure out how to redeem myself. I wasn't going to let her just get away without a fighting chance.'

'She is at Lady Willingdon's hostel?' I said, 'You are absolutely certain of that?'

'Yes, I am.' He reached out to me desperately, grasping at my sleeve with one finger. 'Please, Mr Singh, when you talk to her, will you tell her I still think of her very fondly? Will you tell her that I still want to marry her? Please, will you do that much?'

CHAPTER 9

'Back to Rajpore House, Huzoor?' Uday Singh inquired when I emerged from the Royal Alfred Sailors' Home.

'Helene Memsahib said you were to return home for lunch,' Charan Singh cleared his throat, giving me an imprecatory frown.

'Lunch and Helene can wait,' I responded. 'Take me to Churchgate, and make it quick.'

'Very well, Huzoor,' he grumbled, 'but you can be the one to explain why her orders were disobeyed, not me.'

The locality of Churchgate derived its name from one of the three gates that had once allowed entry into Fort St George. Because of its proximity to St Thomas Cathedral, it had come to be known as the Church Gate, a name that stuck on even after Gerald Aungier ordered the fort's walls to be torn down in 1862.

Once, this area had also been called the Pawan Chakki, named after an ancient windmill that had stood nearby, bordering the ramparts of the Bombay Castle and the moat that had surrounded it. But the windmill was long gone, and the moat had been filled in, resulting in a vast open space called the Esplanade. At its westernmost corner stood two greens, or maidans, as they were called in India. The smaller of these was known as the Cooperage, while the larger was called the Oval.

Measuring some twenty-two acres, the Oval's eastern boundary was lined by a panoply of imposing edifices, including the Bombay University with its Big Ben-like clock tower, the secretariat and the high court. On the other side, near the northern boundary of the maidan, stood the massive black-and-white domed headquarters of the BB&CI Railways, which in turn was flanked by the Churchgate railway station, an odd little structure made of wood and capped by three peculiar pagodas. Beyond it, a silvery webwork of tracks headed toward the distant suburbs, enfiladed by a hodgepodge of ramshackle buildings, mainly boarding houses and lodges for travelers headed up-country, spreading outwards from the station like a sore slowly turning scabrous.

It was here, overlooking the railway tracks, that Lady Willingdon had established a hostel for Christian girls. Marie Adelaide Brassey, better known as Lady Willingdon, was said to be perhaps the poshest woman in England, and certainly the pushiest. Born the second daughter of a minor politician, she had married a retired major of Sussex Artillery named Freeman Freeman-Thomas, some ten years previously. Since then, thanks in large part to her bullheaded determination to further her husband's career, not only had he become King George the Fifth's favorite tennis partner and been elevated to the peerage as Baron Willingdon, but she had also somehow managed to wrangle him a plum appointment as the new governor of Bombay. Rumored to be on the fast track to becoming the Viceroy someday, Willingdon was said, by all accounts, to be rather a gormless sort, more interested in cricket than politics. However, his wife, if my dear friend the Gaekwad of Baroda was to be believed, was a veritable force of nature whose very name caused most maharajas to turn pale and scurry off to bury their state jewels lest they became victims of her grasping fingers.

Nonetheless, in spite of this rather rapacious reputation, in the few short months since her arrival in the city earlier that year, the redoubtable Lady Willingdon had proceeded to earn the sobriquet of First Lady of Bombay many times over. The very day after landing at the Apollo Bunder she had embarked on a grand whirlwind of charitable donations and hospital constructions and land reclamations, not the least of which was this hostel that had come to be named after her.

A nondescript three-storeyed structure with a neo-classical façade; before it had been appropriated by her ladyship to serve as an accommodation for poor and destitute Christian women, the hostel had belonged to the Railways, who used it to house outward-bound laborers. In spite of a fresh daubing of whitewash that made the building's edifice gleam as white as bone in the noonday sun, it was obvious it had seen better days, with damp-stained walls and a rickety array of balconies that looked ready to collapse.

Barely had Charan Singh and I set foot inside the foyer when we found our way barred by an immense woman the size of a buffalo. She was well over six feet tall, dressed in a nun's habit at least two sizes too small, with hair cut short and dyed carelessly with henna.

Fixing me with a frown that could have curdled milk, she held up one flabby forearm to keep us from proceeding any further.

'No men,' she barked, pointing to a nearby signboard that declared in large red letters, 'Gentleman prohibited. Women only.'

'Forgive me, Madam,' I tried to say, 'but I am here on official business. I am looking for a young woman, you see.'

'This is not that sort of place,' she cut me off. 'And I am not that sort of madam.'

'You misunderstand me. What I meant to say is that I am looking for a young lady who has gone missing. Her name is

Miss Mary Hartley. She arrived the day before yesterday on the *Caledonia*. I am trying to locate her for her fiancé.'

Even as I offered that explanation, the virago's face hardened with suspicion. I realized I had put my foot in it quite squarely. In my haste, I had managed to say precisely the wrong thing. This was a refuge for women, after all, and the last thing they would be receptive to was aggressive, inquiring men, especially those of the native variety.

'Didn't you hear what I said?' she squawked, shaking one ham-sized fist at me. 'I said no men allowed. Get away from here before I call the watchman and have him throw you out.'

I shot Charan Singh a desperate glance. Hurriedly, he extracted a ten-rupee banknote and offered it to try and placate the amazon. It was a tactic that had worked very well in the past, but unfortunately, on this occasion, the gambit backfired rather spectacularly.

Rather than accepting the money, the giantess exclaimed, 'You dare to offer me a bribe? This is not a brothel. It is a safe haven, and I am Sister Milla, the matron of this sacred institution. I am a servant of the Lord, and it is my hallowed duty to protect these girls from the rapacious attentions of vile creatures such as you. Do you think I would betray that most holy of trusts for a few measly rupees?'

With that thunderous declaration, Sister Milla reached for the nearest weapon at hand, which happened to be a broom resting against a wall in a nearby corner. Brandishing it, she advanced upon us, like Quixote spurring at a windmill. Charan Singh and I backed away with the greatest alacrity, even as she continued to admonish us, reverting to impeccable Maharashtrian in her fury, her language so colorful that it would have made a sailor blush. I struggled to calm her down, to try and tell her she had misjudged us, but it was impossible to get a word in edgewise. With each step, the good sister's torrent of invective grew ever more effusive, as furious as a river in spate.

I have been accused once or twice of being a brave man, but it is a bravado well-tempered by pragmatism. In this instance, it was just good sense to retreat when faced with such an absolute termagant, especially one who was brandishing her broom as if it were a medieval maul. Charan Singh obviously agreed with me, because after giving me one frantic grin, he turned tail and ran for the door, with me following close behind.

Outside, we paused to gather our wits.

'By golly, Huzoor, that was quite a close one!' Charan Singh said with a vast belly laugh. 'I did not realize they made women that large.'

I glanced around, trying to figure out my next step. It was obvious that the direct route was out of the question, not with Sister Milla guarding the front door like Horatius at the bridge.

Thankfully, it did not take me unduly long to spot another way to get into the hostel.

'Stop standing around, you old oaf, and give me a boost,' I said, pointing at a nearby drainpipe.

It took Charan Singh a minute to understand exactly what I had planned. 'Oh no, Huzoor,' he protested. 'Surely you're joking! You are a king, descended from the moon god himself, not some sorry excuse for a second-story man. Not only is this exceedingly unbecoming for a man of your upbringing and stature, but you might fall and break your head! Then what will I say to Helene Memsahib?'

'Oh, shut up for once and help me!' I quashed his objections with a slash of my hand.

Realizing that there was no changing my mind, Charan Singh reluctantly held out his hands, cupping them together. I placed one booted foot in this ersatz stirrup, and he hefted me up, propelling me off the ground with such momentum that I very nearly missed my mark.

It was a close-run thing. I felt my spine creak as I reached for the bend in the drainpipe above. Only the tips of my fingers closed around it. For one precarious heartbeat, I almost lost my grip. Thankfully, in my youth, I had been quite an ardent tree climber, not to mention an avid mountaineer. I braced my shoulders, tightened my stomach muscles and slowly pulled myself up, first into a chin-up and then up and over to drag myself on to the pipe properly. Gingerly, I rose to my feet like a tightrope walker, pressing my back to the wall, gathering myself before making a quick hop over to the adjoining balcony.

Hauling myself over the railing, I tried the balcony window. Much to my delight, it was unlocked. Turning, I gave Charan Singh a whistle, indicating for him to stay put and wait for me. It took him a moment to understand before he shrugged and retreated to a nearby wall, leaning against it and trying rather hard to look nonchalant. I stifled a chuckle. It was laughable really, a seven-foot Sikh pretending to be incognito. He couldn't have been more noticeable if he had tied a cowbell to his neck and done a Highland fling!

Leaving him to his devices, I clambered through the window and found myself in a narrow, deserted corridor that smelt of lye and linseed oil. After taking a tentative step forward, I realized there was rather a large flaw in my clever plan. *How was I to ascertain which room was Miss Hartley's?*

Thankfully, a quick poke around revealed that someone, most likely the ominous Sister Milla, had taken the trouble to post name cards on each door, identifying each occupant in bold italics.

Miss Hartley, as it turned out, was in room 202, which was just two rooms down from the balcony where I had made my entry. I skulked down the corridor furtively, hoping my luck would hold for a few moments longer, and tried the doorknob. Unfortunately, this was where the gods of good fortune decided to desert me. Unlike the balcony window, it was firmly locked.

Leaning over, I examined the lock. To my relief, it was a simple mortise. After a quick bit of jiggery-pokery with one of my turban pins, I had it open in a jiffy. Inside, the room was sparsely furnished, just a wrought-iron bed in one corner and an almirah in the other, flanked by a small wicker table and an iron folding chair. Other than that, it was empty. And by the looks of it, it had been empty for a while. A quick scan revealed that the bed hadn't been slept in, the counterpane stretched as rigid as a shroud, and there was a thin coating of dust on the table, which confirmed my inference that the occupant had not returned to the room for at least two days.

I took a second to pull the chair across the room and wedge it firmly under the doorknob, just on the off-chance that someone decided to disturb my investigation. Once that was done, I turned my attention to Miss Hartley's possessions. There were only four pieces of luggage. The first was a battered steamer trunk that, when opened, revealed a small heap of immaculately folded clothing. It was a meager collection—five nondescript dresses that were at least two years out of fashion, a chintz bag filled with drab unmentionables, two cotton nightgowns, six pairs of rolled socks and stockings, three sets of gloves, five handkerchiefs, a dreadful straw hat, a riding jacket with worn sleeves, a pair of purl knit sweaters, several petticoats and a heavy tweed skirt that smelled strongly of mothballs.

Next to the trunk lay a ubiquitous bistar band, a canvas bedroll which when unraveled revealed a set of threadbare sheets, a blanket and pillow, and a chipped chamber pot. Beside it was a matching canvas hold-all, inside which I found two towels, an oilskin satchel containing a toothbrush and a sponge, a calico bag with an ivory backed hairbrush, several jars of face powder and face cream, a mish-mash of assorted pins and needles, a cracked enamel mirror, a hand-knitted woolen shawl, two pairs of sensible shoes and a well-worn pair of riding boots.

Lastly, I turned my attention to a battered carpet bag, inside which I found a well-thumbed copy of a racy novel titled *Five Nights*, a tin of Peek Frean biscuits, a half-consumed bottle of Bovril, a bottle of permanganate of potash and another of camphor, several rolls of bromo paper, and finally, at the very bottom, a flask which turned out to contain some very forgettable brandy.

As I finished rifling through the valise, I was struck by the certainty that I had overlooked something important. Obviously, Miss Hartley was a woman of modest means, judging by the quality of her trousseau. *But where was her wallet? Her money and her jewelry? What woman traveled without jewelry?* Not to mention her passport, her letters of introduction and her tickets, all important documents that any international traveler could not possibly journey without.

Returning to the trunk, I gave it a closer look. It was one of the newer flat-topped variety, leather and canvas with wrought-iron rivets. At first glance, it seemed entirely ordinary, but then, upon closer inspection, my suspicions were confirmed. Once I removed all the clothing inside, the lining near the bottom turned out to be concealing a hidden compartment, a feature undoubtedly designed for circumspect travelers to keep their most valued belongings safe and sound.

Tucked away behind the lining, I uncovered a small oilskin chatelaine. Unrolling it, I saw it contained an array of assorted earrings and brooches, a modest bundle of paper money—about twenty pounds—an equal number of sovereigns, a very handsome gold Elgin pocket watch and a sheaf of documents, which included a creased birth certificate, and most importantly, a bill of passport issued by the Foreign Office, made out in Mary Hartley's name.

I unfolded it and glanced through the array of brightly colored stamps emblazoned across the back, chronicling her journey out—Gibraltar, Marseilles, Cairo, Port Said, Aden. Flipping it over, I was greeted by a much better picture of Miss Hartley, a sepia photograph of a pale woman with dark curls and wary eyes. It was very different from the cameo Peter had shown me. There she had seemed introspective, shy, as wistful as one of Dante Gabriel Rossetti's portraits. But this woman looked brittle, skittish and ready to bolt, certainly not the person described to me by the passengers I had been able to interview thus far.

I studied her face briefly, trying to deduce what she might have been thinking. *What was going on behind those deceptive eyes? Which one was the real Mary Hartley? Who was she? The brazen creature that Captain Carruthers had spoken of, or the ingenue who had so enticed the second officer? Or was she both, able to change guise as easily as a chameleon?* And then, of course, there was the question of motive, or rather motivation. *Why had she disappeared? Had she suffered an accident or come to harm, or had she, as Hall-Caine put it so brutally, done a runner on my friend?*

I was about to put the wallet back when I realized I had missed something else. There seemed to be another object secreted in the compartment, a canvas pocketbook by the feel of it. It had slipped down the lining and become wedged behind one of the wooden joists that held the trunk's base rigid.

I managed to get a tenuous grip on one corner. After a few minutes of pulling and cursing, I was able to pry it loose. To my surprise, it turned out to be a canvas-bound journal. Miss Hartley's diary, I realized as I opened the first page. A prurient shiver ran up my spine, immediately followed by a pang of guilt. For a moment, I found myself torn between curiosity and reluctance. After all, it was the grossest invasion of privacy, to go leafing through someone's most private of thoughts, and most certainly not the sort of thing a gentleman of quality did.

As always, my inquisitiveness won out over my hesitation and I decided, manners be damned, that I would go through the diary. I was hoping for a clue in there, something revealing, salacious even, a secret or a confession that would crack the case wide open, but as I quickly leafed through the pages, I was sorely disappointed. I found no mention of the journey out at all, not of the *Caledonia* or any of the passengers. In fact, the diary came to an abrupt end some two weeks ago. The last entry was dated 7 June, exactly three days before Miss Hartley had departed England by my calculation.

That last entry, however, caught my eye.

As the date of embarkation draws closer, I find myself even more confused.

Shouldn't I feel a sense of excitement, an anticipation at the thought of this new adventure that beckons. A new life awaits me in India, a whole new world, waiting to be discovered. Surely that is more than any woman could hope for, isn't it?

Is there something wrong with me? Somehow all I can manage to feel is dread, a hollow feeling in the pit of my stomach that refuses to go away. I do not know this man to whom I have become betrothed, this Peter Rowan. He is a stranger to me. We have never spoken, never met face to face. From his letters he seems to be a good man, a kind man, but what if it is all a lie? What if he mistreats me? What if he is a brute? How will I escape him? I am not strong enough, I think, to make my own way, not in a strange country where I have no friends, no family.

I cannot help but wonder, have I made a mistake?

Looking down at the diary, I felt my hopes sinking, replaced instead by a sense of foreboding. Something just did not smell right. If Miss Hartley had been so filled with fear at the prospect of marrying a stranger, it was only too plausible that she could have run away and jilted Peter. Still, that did not explain the matter of the travel documents or the money. No sane person in control of themselves, or their circumstances, would leave their papers or money unguarded, especially someone who had just arrived in the colonies from overseas. A passport was more than a form of identification in India. It was intended as a declaration of protection within the demesne of the empire, the king's own guarantee to each of his subjects. But to find Miss Hartley's documents here, apparently abandoned in this squalid little room, could only mean one of two possibilities. First, she had left in a hurry and abandoned her identity; or second, and by far the more realistic possibility in my opinion, she was in genuine trouble and had fallen victim to a fate so unexpected that it had forced her to leave everything of value behind.

Leaning forward, I replaced the diary in its hidden receptacle and then shut the trunk before spending a few minutes rearranging everything until the room looked exactly how I had found it.

It had been my intention to leave the same way I had entered, retracing my steps through the door and sneaking down the stairs at the back to make an exit through the rear of the building, keeping as far away as I could from Sister Milla and her broom.

Unfortunately, just as I was about to push the chair away from the doorknob, an angry rattling shook the door, half scaring me out of my skin.

'Who's in there?' a voice shouted. 'Open this door immediately. I know it's you, you villain.'

It was her, the gigantic Sister Milla. By the sound of it, she was out for blood. I looked around desperately, seeking another way to escape. My eyes fell upon the window at the far end of the room. I rushed to it and yanked open the shutter, only to find my egress obstructed by a mosquito grille. Thankfully, it was of the variety that was not fixed. Grabbing the handle, I tried to shove it open, only to find that the bolt was rusted shut, even as the good sister's efforts to breach the room became more raucous. Bunching my hand into a fist, I hammered the bolt once, twice, thrice. To my relief, the grille gave way after the third attempt. In a trice, I was out of it, before the door behind me could give way.

Outside, I balanced precariously on a narrow parapet, which I saw ran along most of the circumference of the building. Peering to my right, I tried to discern if I could make it to the pipe from which I had made my entry. There it was, only a few meters away, but there was a gap of some seven feet separating the edge of the ledge from the drainpipe.

I started to shuffle toward the pipe. Unfortunately, before I could get there, Sister Milla managed to get the door open. She came barging in and looked around the room, bewildered to find it empty. Spying the open window, she made a beeline toward it. Realizing I had mere seconds, I tried to speed up, but I wasn't quick enough to dodge the determined nun, who leaned out and jabbed at me with the broomstick.

That was what pushed me over the edge, quite literally. Desperately, as I lost my balance, I reached for the drainpipe with one outstretched hand but it was just out of reach. My fingertips brushed against the pipe, but it was not enough to let me get a grip, and then, a heartbeat later, I was falling.

Luckily, as it happened, Charan Singh was loitering about directly below me. I landed squarely atop him, sending him sprawling in a most unceremonious fashion.

'God in heaven, Huzoor!' he exclaimed, adjusting his pugree that had come awry 'I am getting too old for your antics.'

I laughed and stood up, dusting my trousers even as Sister Milla glared down at us, hurling down a torrent of abuse from the window above.

Charan Singh took a while longer to follow, cursing profusely in Punjabi, stretching his back with an audible creak.

'Well,' he asked as we beat a hasty retreat toward the car, 'did you find anything, or have you broken my back just for fun?'

Before I could answer, who should come sauntering up like he was out for a stroll in Hyde Park but the preposterous Mr Hall-Caine.

His outfit was even more curious than before—a pair of plaid herringbone knickerbockers with matching gaiters and a rakishly cut belted gabardine jacket that looked like it belonged on a golfing green than in India. To top it all, he had on a straw Mallory, which he doffed at me rather too jauntily for my liking.

'Ah, there you are, Mr Singh! Have I caught you at an inopportune moment?'

'Oh, what do you want now, Hall-Caine?'

'Well, as it happens, I have a clue for you, and rather a juicy one at that.'

CHAPTER 10

'A clue, you say! Well, what is it?'

'I can't exactly tell you, my dear fellow. I will have to show you.' Hall-Caine flashed me a toothy grin. 'If you would care to join me!'

I exchanged a look with Charan Singh, who shrugged and rolled his eyes, as if to say 'Why not?'

'Very well! Lead on, I guess.'

Snapping my fingers, I called for Uday Singh to bring up the car.

'No, leave it here,' Hall-Caine said. 'It's a lovely, warm day. Let's take the tram, shall we?'

He led us across the street and past the Churchgate station.

Letting out a whistle, Hall-Caine hailed a horse-drawn tram as it trundled by. When it rattled to a stop, I climbed aboard, followed by Hall-Caine and Charan Singh, who had insisted on tagging along. We each found a seat: Hall-Caine sat next to a thin munshi, while I squeezed in beside a tall Englishman with a homburg hat, who was perusing a copy of the *Bombay Gazette*. Charan Singh had to make do with the rearmost bench, where he found himself sandwiched between two fisherwomen who looked him up and down like he was a deva come to life before cackling and exchanging ribald jokes in Marathi.

'Good day,' I said to the Englishman when he swiveled his neck and looked at me curiously.

'Are you off to some sort of fancy dress?' he asked, offering me a pinch of snuff. 'Dressing up as a maharaja? That's rather a cliche, don't you think?'

'You're right, of course,' I said, refusing the offer. 'Sadly, it's the only outfit I own.'

He shrugged and returned to his newspaper, leaving me to stare out of the window as the driver snapped his whip, and, with a lurch, we set off.

The tram cut across the Esplanade, weaving its way toward the imposing dome of the Post Office, which was visible in the distance. The horses made surprisingly fast progress. The driver sent passersby scrambling out of the way with a combination of abuses and a loud bell, which he clanged at with gay abandon. The crowds seemed endless, bullock carts jostling against horse-drawn Victorias and the occasional honking car. Everywhere I turned, I saw a horde of people, brown and white and every shade in between, packed so dense that it felt like I was drowning in an ocean of humanity.

We passed Bombay Gymkhana and approached the Victoria Terminus. I gazed up at it with a grimace. Up-close, it was even more hideous than I had imagined, a peculiar mishmash of the Gothic and Italianate styles, as if someone had mated Notre Dame with St Pancras Station.

At the next stop, the Englishman vaulted up and doffed his hat at me before disembarking. Following his departure, Hall-Caine crossed the aisle to fill the vacant seat. Taking out a sterling silver case embossed with a lion and unicorn rampant, he offered me a cheroot. I declined, pointing at my turban. He smiled and placed one between his lips, lighting it with a matching lighter before making it disappear into thin air, a blindingly quick bit of sleight of hand that made me grin appreciatively.

'Now where do you learn how to do that?' I asked.

'I read a book once,' he replied, taking a deep drag before exhaling a cloud of aromatic smoke. 'Might I ask, why do you do it ... all this *detecting*? If I was quite as wealthy as you, I wouldn't waste my time with all this nonsense.'

'It's a character flaw,' I said. 'I have always believed that money becomes pointless after a while. A man needs more to excite him.'

'You enjoy a thrill, I surmise.'

'It is not the thrill that compels me, but the puzzle.'

'It's interesting how only the very rich have time for puzzles. The rest of us ... we are much too busy trying to earn a living to think of mysteries.'

'I did not take you for a Fabian.'

'I'm not, Sir. I'm nothing at all. That's my specialty.'

'An agnostic?'

'Not quite,' he grinned. 'Call me an opportunist. That's a much better word for the likes of me.'

As I pondered this cryptic declaration, he pointed out the window. 'Ah, there's our destination.'

As the tram slowed at the next stop, Hall-Caine hopped off. I followed, pausing to look up at the towering structure that dwarfed us. Completed in 1869, the Crawford Market was even more eccentric than the Victoria Terminus. The brainchild of another Parsi baron, Cowasji Jehangir, it was named after the first municipal commissioner of Bombay, Arthur Crawford, an odd man who spoke flawless Marathi, despised Brahmins and was quite crazy for open-air markets. Built in imitation, perhaps of the Grand Bazaar of Istanbul or the Rialto in Venice, the end result was the largest indoor market in India, a vast warehouse made of bright yellow Kurla stone, fronted by a gabled Tudor facade complete with a clocktower, its exterior lined by Moorish arches and capped by an enormous skylight.

Without a word of explanation, Hall-Caine led us through the grand entrance, and into the bazaar, a teeming labyrinth of stalls and shops and sheds that sold everything from Nagpur oranges to Goan vinho do Porto, from Marmara almonds and fresh mutton and ripe pears imported from Afghanistan to, it was rumored, more exotic delicacies like rhino horns, shark fins and elephant tusks.

After a bewildering series of turns, he came to a stop next to a small shop in the distant recesses of the third lane. It was much posher than the rest of the market, with Venetian glass windows and an ornate sign outside that declared: Lalljee and Sons, Purveyors of Fine Goods and Antiques.

'Mr Hall-Caine,' I snarled, nearing the end of my patience, 'I've had quite enough of all this traipsing about. Stop wasting my time! What is this clue of yours? Just tell me, this instant, I demand it. Tell me this instant, I demand it!'

'Very well,' Hall-Caine replied. 'The day before yesterday, the same evening that the *Caledonia* docked, one of my sources saw a white memsahib at the Terminus, trying to buy a ticket to go up-country to Agra. According to him, she was redirected by a tout to visit this establishment. Naturally, he was somewhat surprised to see a memsahib traveling unattended, without an ayah or a guard, especially after sunset, which was why he decided to follow her.'

'Is that the only reason?' I asked.

'He may have been planning to pick her pocket,' Hall-Caine said, smiling sheepishly.

'You know the finest people, don't you?'

'This is Bombay, Mr Singh. Everyone here is trying to make a quick penny. If you're poor, you're a thief. If you're rich,' he shrugged, 'then you are an entrepreneur. Besides, in my line of trade, I have found it is more important to have friends in low places than in high ones.'

I smirked. By god, he had a clever tongue. He had summed the city up very succinctly, capturing the essence of Bombay much better than any poet or artist.

'I don't see what is so odd about a memsahib coming to a market, I ventured. 'Even if she happened to be unaccompanied. That's a perfectly respectable thing to do, isn't it? '

'Oh, I assure you, the gentleman we are about to meet is not respectable, not in the least.'

Holding open the door, Hall-Caine bid us to enter. Once inside, we found ourselves in a cramped room whose walls were lined by glass-fronted cupboards stuffed full of a peculiar assortment of bric-a-brac, everything from gold candelabra to an array of china plates decorated with Mad King George's frowning face.

'A thousand salaams to you, Sahibs!' An elegant Bohri with a well-trimmed goatee, wearing a filigree skull cap and a monocle, emerged from the back room to greet us. 'How may I, your humble servant, be of service today?'

Hall-Caine did not return this florid greeting. Instead, he sank down on a nearby divan and made a great show of dusting his trousers.

'This here is Lalljee, Mr Singh. Don't fall for his well-groomed, civilized exterior. He is a rogue of the first class, descended from a clan of notorious Afghan bandits.'

'That is a scurrilous lie,' Lalljee objected. 'I am a humble businessman.'

'What you are, old boy, is Bombay's most notorious pawnbroker. You specialize in objets d'art and jewelry, especially items of dubious provenance.'

Lalljee frowned, giving Hall-Caine a look of great affront. 'I have been known to speculate from time to time, and to buy the occasional piece of gold or statuette. However, that is not illegal.'

'Very true. What is illegal though is not paying your taxes and also the little side business you have been running.'

'I do not know what you are talking about.'

'Come now, Lalljee, don't play coy. I know what you have been getting up to, duping travelers and then having them robbed.' Hall-Caine turned to me and gave me a broad smile. 'His modus operandi is really quite ingenious. He has set up his nephew as a tour agent with a legitimate business. They have even printed a brochure; can you believe it? What they do is promise new visitors to India a tour of the scenic bits like the Taj Mahal or the Himalayas—the whole package, train bookings, meals, even security—but then they inform a gang of local ruffians who rob the unwary bastards somewhere along the way. And what no one guesses is that it is Lalljee who is behind it all, the mastermind who then pawns their possessions and sells them in his shops in Bombay,' Hall-Caine picked up a cumbersome-looking astrolabe. 'Whose was this, I wonder? It looks expensive.' With a laugh, he flung it to the ground. 'Or this?' he mused, picking up an expensive-looking lacquer snuffbox. *Crash!* He threw it against the wall, where it shattered to a thousand shards.

Lalljee let out a piteous whine. 'Stop, please stop!' he bleated. 'You are destroying my stock!'

'That's not all I am going to do, Lalljee, unless you tell me what I need to know.'

'Anything! I will tell you whatever you want. Just stop breaking my things.'

'Very well!' Hall-Caine grinned and put down the antique-looking wall clock he had just picked up. 'I heard a bit of gossip. that you had a memsahib in here yesterday, looking for a tour with an escort up-country. Is that true?'

'Yes,' Lalljee nodded, taking the clock and placing it as far away from us as he possibly could. 'There was a white woman here. She came to sell me some gold ornaments and to inquire about arrangements to travel to Agra, and then onwards to Calcutta and Assam.'

'And what did you say to her?'

'I told her we could assist her, as long as she was able to pay our fees. I quoted a number, and she agreed to pay it. However, since she did not have much cash, she offered me some trinkets instead. I told her I would have to have them assayed to calculate their value, and suggested she come back tomorrow so that we could make all the arrangements for her, provided of course that the value of the gold proved to be adequate.'

'I have a question,' I chimed in. 'Would the memsahib have ever reached her destination?'

Lalljee frowned. 'There are no guarantees in life, Sir. The ways of Allah are strange and no one can predict what misfortune one may meet on the highway.'

'You dirty bugger!' Hall-Caine clapped the man on the back so hard that he nearly fell over. 'You were going to swindle her, weren't you? What was the play? Were you going to keep the gold, or were you going to pull a fast one and desert her somewhere out in the wilderness?'

Lalljee did not answer. Instead, he gave us a wounded look. 'You malign me, Sir. I had no intention of letting the memsahib come to harm.'

'That's a load of codswallop. You were going to rob her and then sell her, I'm sure of it.'

'As I said, I am just a businessman. I was only trying to help the memsahib. In fact, I am even paying for her hotel until we are able to conclude our business suitably.'

'Wait a minute!' I exclaimed. 'Are you saying you happen to know where she is right now?'

'Indeed, I do. She is staying at a lodging house not far from here, which is owned by my third cousin.'

Hall-Caine vaulted to his feet. 'You will take us there this instant!'

'I cannot leave the shop, Sir,' Lalljee objected. 'I will lose customers. Then who will feed my children and grandchildren?'

Hall-Caine loomed over him. 'Oh, stop playacting! You don't have any children, Lalljee, so the question of grandchildren simply does not arise. Besides, you know who I am and what my reputation is. If you don't do exactly as I say, you know you will lose much more than your customers.'

Grimacing, Lalljee realized he had no choice. Mumbling to himself, he set to closing up his shop, slamming cupboards shut and pulling down shutters with a frustrated aggression.

As he prepared to lock the door, I interrupted him.

'Wait a minute,' I said. 'I will have the memsahib's jewelry, if you please.'

Lalljee stifled a curse in Gujarati. Reluctantly, he pulled open a drawer and handed over an oilskin pouch. I unrolled it and peered inside to find an assortment of sundry chains and bangles, which I passed over to Charan Singh.

'Keep this safe!' I said to him.

'I will guard it with my life,' he promised.

Behind us, Hall-Caine commanded Lalljee to hurry up. Once the man had locked up his shop securely, he set off toward the back entrance of the market. We emerged very close to the loading docks, and he led us across the street toward the Muslim quarter of Bombay. Clustered around the Minara Masjid, this area was known as Bhendi Bazaar, a chaotic maze of lanes, each named after the different trades conducted within their respective confines. On one side was Null Bazaar, named after the pipes and taps sold there; and Cooper Street, where one could buy barrels of all shapes and sizes; and Tokra Galli, with its basket weavers. On the other side lay Attar Galli, for perfumes; and Champa Galli, for flowers; abutting the Zaveri and Meena bazaars that were lined by shops that sold jewelry and fine stones. and finally, Lohar Chawl, the lane of the ironsmiths.

Once we had passed Lohar Chawl, Lalljee cut across a small maidan crowded with hawkers selling their wares from blankets spread on the ground. I looked around, trying not to stare, dazzled by the vast array of goods on display. From ornate statues to antique swords, from casks of brandy to brass Victrolas and piles of leather boots, they seemed to have everything under the sun for sale.

'Welcome to the infamous Chor Bazaar,' Hall-Caine explained. 'This is the thieves' market. Every house that is robbed in the city, every pocket picked, every crate stolen from the docks, it all ends up here.' He gave me a grin. 'Do keep an eye on your billfold, old man. Some of these fellows will steal your very soul before you realize it.'

We shouldered our way through the milling crowds until Lalljee came to a halt outside a shabby looking boarding house named the Pearl of Asia Hotel. It was a rough-looking establishment, the sort of place inhabited by sailors and laborers and journeymen, certainly not a place for memsahibs of any quality. The doorway was guarded by a bearded Pathan ruffian, armed with a stout cudgel, who jumped up to confront us when we approached. Charan Singh grinned and stepped forward, but before he could indulge in his favorite pastime and lay him out flat on his back, Lalljee squealed, 'Please don't hurt him. He is my nephew.'

Turning to Hall-Caine, he gave him a baleful glare. 'Your memsahib is staying on the second floor, in room 203. Now that I have done my part, Sahib, I really should be returning to the shop. What if there is a customer?'

He turned to leave, but Hall-Caine cut him off neatly before he could take more than a couple of steps.

'Come now, old boy, you've come this far. Why leave now? I think we shall enjoy your company a bit longer, just in case there are any untoward surprises waiting for us upstairs.'

Lalljee looked like he wanted to argue, turning to first frown at me and then at Charan Singh, who leered and made a great show of cracking his knuckles indolently. Realizing there was no escape, he groaned and tramped up the steps. We followed close behind, Charan Singh leading with one hand on his trusty revolver, and Hall-Caine and myself trailing close behind.

Keeping Lalljee around turned out to be a smart decision after all. There were two more Pathans and a terrifying old woman with a squint lying in wait at the top of the stairwell. Before they could try and cause any trouble, Lalljee barked out a string of orders in Pashto and sent them scampering.

He came to a stop in front of the last room on the floor. 'She is in there,' he mumbled.

I gave Charan Singh a brisk nod. Reaching out, he tried the doorknob, only to find it was firmly locked.

'Break it down,' I commanded.

Charan Singh laughed and did as ordered. Raising one size 12 boot, he let loose a mighty kick, sending the door flying open with a resounding crash, even as Lalljee belatedly screeched, 'Wait, I have the keys.'

We barged inside en masse, only to be confronted by a very surprised memsahib. We had managed to disturb her as she slept, judging by the dazed look on her face as she sat bolt upright in her bed. I could tell right away that she was not Mary Hartley. One look was all it took. She was a decade too old, for one, and ten inches too tall, I realized when she leaped up to her feet. She was very nearly as tall as Charan Singh, not to mention blessed with proportions so Amazonian that I blushed and averted my eyes, for she was clad only in a satin slip that left little to the imagination.

'What is the meaning of this?' she squealed. 'Who are you?'

That was the clincher. Her accent was not Scottish; it wasn't even Welsh or Irish. She was decidedly American, which could only mean that this detour had been a complete waste of time.

Even as I arrived at that conclusion, the memsahib let out a shriek when she realized her state of deshabille and hurriedly shrugged on a dressing gown. 'I asked you a bloody question. Why are you in my room?'

I was about to launch into an explanation, but Hall-Caine beat me to the punch. Stepping up, he gave her a courtly bow and held out his identification papers.

'We are with the Home Office, Miss, and this is a rescue.'

'But I am in no need of rescuing,' the memsahib exclaimed. 'And why on earth is my travel agent here?'

'Tell me, Miss, how did you hear of Mr Lalljee here?'

'One of the touts at the railway station showed me an advertisement in the *Gazette*. He said he runs a reputed travel agency, and I was in need of a rail ticket up-country to Agra. To be honest, he has been very helpful. I did not have enough cash on me, you see, so he very kindly offered to help me liquidate some jewelry.'

'Well, Miss, I'm sorry to say, but this bastard had some rather nefarious plans for you.' Turning to Lalljee, he said, 'Go on then. Tell her the truth.'

Lalljee responded by shaking his head and shifting his weight from one foot to another. And then, all at once, he made a dash for it, turning and running off with an astonishing burst of speed.

We watched him go and exchanged an amused glance.

'He's quick for a small fellow,' I said.

'I'd hazard he's had plenty of practice,' Charan Singh added. 'Do you want me to go get him?'

'No, let him be,' I replied, even as the American memsahib let out another yelp of consternation.

'Can someone please tell me what the bloody hell is going on?'

I gave her a wry smile. 'We were looking for someone else, Madam. My apologies!' I gave Hall-Caine a poisonous scowl. 'It seems I was misinformed. Please forgive the intrusion!'

'But ... but I don't understand. That gentleman was my tour guide. He was to escort me to Agra. That was the arrangement.'

'I'm afraid he was going to dupe you,' I explained. 'It's what he does. He's a charlatan, you see, a flimflammer!'

'God,' she whispered, shuddering palpably.

No doubt she was about to burst into tears, I thought, *filled with dread at the prospect*. But the American memsahib surprised me.

Rather than crying, she dissolved into a gale of manic laughter. 'Oh, that's just perfect! First my fiancé. Then this. Gosh, I knew I was up for an adventure, but this is too bloody much.'

Hall-Caine waited until she had managed to calm down a bit before taking out his cigarette case.

'Would you care for a fag?' he asked.

'No, thank you,' she refused. 'I'd rather have a drink, to be honest.'

He turned to me, raising one inquiring eyebrow. Pulling out a slim chased silver flask from my jacket, I uncapped it and offered it to her. She accepted it warily and took a tentative sip, her eyes widening with delight when she tasted the cognac it contained.

'Gosh, that's splendid!'

She was about to pass the flask back to me, but I shook my head.

'Please, keep it ... as a small token, as an apology!'

She nodded gratefully and took another, longer sip.

'I am Eunice, by the way. Eunice Ogilvy, late of Hartford, Connecticut.'

'It's very nice to make your acquaintance, Madam,' I said. 'This is Mr Hall-Caine of the Foreign Office, as you already know. That large fellow over there is Charan Singh, and I am—'

'Hold on a minute,' she cut me off. 'I ... I know you. You're one of them maharaja chaps.'

Darting across the room, she grabbed a canvas valise that lay atop a nearby sideboard. Pulling it open, she rummaged about before pulling out an old magazine, a well-thumbed issue of *Harper's Bazaar*, and riffled through the pages until she found what she was looking for.

'That's you, isn't it?' she exclaimed, holding up a faded photograph.

I recognized it, a portrait of myself with my cousins Kapurthala and Patiala, which had been taken the year before at the Durbar. In a rare moment of weakness, I had let myself be talked into posing. Unfortunately, the final product had turned out to be dreadfully gauche, a twelve-page feature called 'Exotic India' with all the maharajas on display in full regalia, like preening peacocks.

'Indeed, it is,' I said, trying to hide my embarrassment even as Hall-Caine bit back a chuckle.

'Gosh, a real-life maharaja!' Miss Ogilvy let out a giggle of delight. 'If only the girls in Hartford could see me now!'

'I take it this is your first visit to India,' I said, hurriedly trying to change the subject.

'It is. My first visit anywhere, to be honest. This is the first time I have traveled abroad.'

'And what brings you here, Madam, if I may inquire?'

'What brings any of us here? India is as good as hell for a white woman, isn't it? The sun burns our skin, and we turn to bitter old crones, lonely and sour before our time. There is no society to speak of here, no conversation except about tea and indigo, no company but soldiers and merchants. But still we come in droves, don't we? Because there are fortunes to be made here, Sir, husbands to be found.

'I was working as a waitress in New Haven when I heard about the marriage season in India. There was a gentleman who had just returned from Darjeeling, a tea importer. I overheard him saying that there was only one woman per seven gentlemen in Assam, that even a girl of middling beauty could have a chance to get ahead. That was all I needed to hear. In Connecticut, Sir, sadly I was dismissed as Miss-Too-Tall. Since most of the unclaimed gentlemen were shorter than me, it led to rather a paucity of offers. At best, I would have had to settle for a farmer or a tradesman from Pennsylvania. But here, in India, there are enough prospects from which I can pick and choose. That is why I came out, Sir, because this country is a place where even an ordinary girl like myself can become the mistress of a hundred acres and be waited on hand and foot like a great lady. So, without further ado, when I heard about the shortage of brides in Assam, I decided to take matters into my own hands and find my prince myself. After searching an atlas and finding out exactly where Assam was located, I wrote to the Salvatorian mission in Dibrugarh and Guwahati, listing out my meritorious qualities as a wife. To my delight, a few short months later, they were only too eager to arrange for a gentleman to correspond with me.'

Behind me, Hall-Caine cleared his throat, unable to hide his patent disapproval. I gave him a sidelong frown, signaling to him not to interrupt her, but it was too late. She had already noticed the scandalized look on his face.

'I see your expression, Mr Hall-Caine, is it? You think me to be blasé, perhaps even forward. Thankfully, Sir, I am American and not English. If we worried unduly about social propriety and manners, why, we would still be a British colony!' She gave Hall-Caine an impish smile. 'Tell me, why should I play the wilting violet? What is the shame in making my own way in the world? I wasn't born with a silver spoon, Sir. Everything I have, everything I am, I have fought for it every inch of the way. I feel no need to hide that I am here to find a husband. And I almost had a good one, let me tell you!

'The Salvatorians matched me with a gentleman named James Ballantyne. Jim, he said I should call him. He is an estate manager at McLeod Russel. We began corresponding last year, and I took to him immediately. He was clever, witty, acerbic, and most of all, kind. And he took a shine to me, too, saying he found me charming and that he could not wait to meet me. We wrote to each other once a month for a year, and even exchanged portraits, until he finally suggested that I come out to India. I took that as good as a proposal, Sir. I withdrew my savings, gathered what little jewelry I had inherited from my mother and booked my passage out on the very next steamship.'

'Ah, yes! That reminds me.' I snapped my fingers at Charan Singh. He stepped forward and handed her the oilskin pouch we had retrieved from Lalljee.

'It's my things! Thank you so much!' she exclaimed, rewarding him with a smile that made the old man blush and bow his head.

'It's nothing, please,' I said. 'Do continue your story.'

'As I was saying, I wrote to Jim and told him I was coming out to India. He was even more excited than me and said he would take a leave of absence to come down and meet me in Bombay.' She shook her head sadly. 'He was waiting for me on the dock when I disembarked, Sir. It was almost the perfect love story, except for one tiny problem.'

I hid a knowing grin. It was an old story. Caveat emptor. Buyer beware!

'What was wrong with him?' I asked. 'Was he cross-eyed, or club-footed?'

'Did he have bad breath?' Hall-Caine added. 'A lazy eye perhaps?'

'Or he was balding?' Charan Singh chimed in, not wanting to be left out.

'No, none of that. He looked exactly as he did in the photograph he had sent me, as handsome as I had expected. The only problem,' she swallowed, shaking her head mournfully, 'was that in our haste to be together, there was one detail that we had overlooked, quite literally. You see, what neither of us had ever talked about was our respective heights. As a result, when we finally came face to face, we simply could not see eye to eye. Poor Jim, he was much shorter than me, by almost five inches.'

I smirked and exchanged a guilty look with Hall-Caine, who was also trying his best not to laugh. It was a delightful pun, a too-tall woman unable to see eye to eye with her too-short beau. Still, it would have been cavalier to be amused by her discomfort.

'I take it that Jim decided to break it off,' I said.

She nodded. 'I tried to tell him it did not matter to me, but he was terribly unkind, Sir. He said he would be the joke of Assam if he married someone like me, that they would say he had wed a giraffe! What a farce! Why should I be punished for how God has made me? Rejected because I am too tall! What kind of a reason is that, and that too after I came halfway around the world for him? How is that fair?'

'What are you going to do now, Madam, now that your engagement is off? Head back to America?'

'Good god, no! I have no intention of being the laughing stock of my town, poor Miss-Returned-Empty. And why should I allow a man and his shortcomings to determine my future?'

Once more, I struggled not to smile. As far as puns went, this was even better, a real crackerjack. Shortcomings indeed!

'I am a strong woman, Sir, and I will not allow any man to sell me short.'

This was just too much. I couldn't help it. I burst into laughter, as did Hall-Caine a moment later.

'You're doing that on purpose, aren't you?'

She began to laugh as well. 'Yes, I couldn't resist it!'

'You really are rather delightful, Madam. This is the most I have enjoyed barging into someone's room for a while!'

'Well, there certainly is a lot more to me than most women!' she retorted.

'That I agree with,' I said, shaking my head. 'So, it is your plan to stay on in India, I presume?'

'Yes, I think I shall travel around the subcontinent for a while. I have a second cousin in Agra. He has offered to show me the north. I have a hankering, Sir, to see the Himalayas, and Darjeeling, too. I think I shall go out there and see the snow, perhaps paint the mountains. I have always wanted to learn how to paint,' she said, her eyes sparkling. 'And then perhaps, when I am bored, I shall go to Assam in time for the planter season. Can you imagine Jim's face when I turn up in Chittagong? Now that is a sight worth waiting for!'

She grinned. I could not help but feel a deep affection for her, almost an affinity. Who knows, in another life, if I hadn't been so attached to Helene, it may even have been an attraction. But for now it was merely empathy, something I have rarely been accused of.

'That sounds exciting, Madam. Is there something I can do to help you?' I reached for my billfold. 'A small donation perhaps to help you on your way.'

Her brow knotted with suspicion. 'Now why would you show a stranger such generosity?'

'Let's just say I cannot resist a woman who needs to be rescued!'

'That's very kind, but I am sorry to say I will have to reject your offer. You see, I am neither in need of charity nor in need of being rescued, as I have already mentioned,' she said with a solemn sniff. 'Whatever I do, wherever I may end up, I would rather do it on my own terms.'

I replaced my wallet with a shrug. 'Very well! I appreciate that. However, I insist that you at least let us make the arrangements for your safe passage to Agra to meet your cousin. Mr Hall-Caine here will take care of it for you, won't you?'

I gave him a pointed look. He rolled his eyes and nodded. 'Of course! Leave it to me; I'll sort it all out for you. And if you would care to pack your things, Miss Ogilvy, I'll make sure you find better quarters until you leave Bombay.'

'Now that offer I will accept very gratefully. This isn't exactly the Waldorf, is it?'

'Good! Now that this is settled, we really should take our leave. Once again, my apologies, Madam! Thank you for your time, and let me wish you the very best of luck.'

She surprised me once more, by leaning forward and giving me a kiss on the cheek.

'I do not believe in luck,' she said. 'Women like me, we make our way in the world on the strength of our wits and our willingness to adapt. If we fail to do that, Sir, all we will end up is as thralls to men who are much smaller than us.'

Those words rang through my ears as we bid farewell to Miss Ogilvy. How true! As men, we had been educated to think of women as the weaker sex, taught from childhood that we had to protect and coddle them, but that was only an insidious way, I realized, to diminish them, to keep them weak and dependent on us. *What was wrong with a woman claiming power for herself? Why should she not be accorded the same rules as a man?* My mother had never played the role of the subservient, and neither had Helene. In fact, that was what I had always personally found attractive in a woman, a spine of steel and a heart of iron.

'Well,' Hall-Caine interrupted my stream of thought. 'Aren't you going to thank me, Mr Singh?'

I gave him a withering scowl. 'That was a complete waste of time, Mr Hall-Caine. I think you should stick to your job and leave me to mine.'

'You wound me,' he said. 'I was only trying to help. In any case, even though you're being terribly churlish, I will share one more snippet of information with you.' His voice hardened, his airy manner all but dissipating in the blink of an eye.

'I hate to sound like the proverbial white rabbit, but ticktock, ticktock!' Hall-Caine pantomimed, tapping his wristwatch. 'A little mouse who works for me informed me this morning that Commissioner Edwardes received rather an irate call from your old friend in Punjab, He who we shall not name. Unfortunately, it seems he has discovered you are up to your tricks in Bombay and has commanded the commissioner to give you a stern talking-to, so I am afraid you can expect a visit from him shortly. What I am trying to say, Mr Singh, is that you will have to hurry up. You are running out of time, and quickly.'

CHAPTER 11

The Great Western Hotel was a blocky jigsaw puzzle of a building, all iron pillars and angular porticoes.

Positioned directly across the Naval Clock Tower and adjacent to the Scots' Kirk, it was one of the oldest structures in the city. Originally constructed to serve as the residence for the governor of Bombay, the Navy had taken over the building in 1764 and renamed it Admiralty House. Then, in 1800, it had been converted into the premises for the Recorder of Bombay's courthouse and had served as an assizes for almost seven decades until 1883, when the building had been purchased by an enterprising Parsi named Jewanjee.

He had renovated and expanded it, and transformed it into a hotel he hoped would rival the Raffles in Singapore or the Peninsula in Hong Kong. Sadly, in spite of the building's storied history, Jewanjee's vision was neither as grand nor as elegant as either of the aforementioned establishments. Upon entering, I found myself standing in a rather drab lobby. The floor was layered with white and black Worcester tiles bordered by a pattern of embossed fleur-de-lys. The walls were lined by oak panels that hadn't been polished for a while. The decor was equally musty, typically colonial with whitewashed colonnades everywhere, surrounded by an excess of bamboo furniture and rather too many potted plants for my taste.

Nodding at Charan Singh to stay put by the entrance, I made a beeline for the reception desk, which was manned by an officious-looking man clad in tie and tails. Another Parsi, I guessed, judging by the size of his nose and the fairness of his skin, an inference that was confirmed a moment later as I peered at his nametag, which proclaimed, F. Bamanji, Esq.

'And what is it you want?' he inquired, gazing at me with that supercilious imperiousness that only the Zoroastrians can master.

'I am the Maharaja of Rajpore,' I explained, hiding a smile at the 'Esq.' part and ignoring the disdainful sneer that made his lip curl. 'Mr Bamanji, I would very much like to interview one of your guests. A Miss Eloise Bennett.'

Bamanji cleared his throat and opened his mouth, most likely to shoo me away, judging by my experience with hotel clerks. Reaching into my pocket, I extracted a ten-rupee banknote, which I placed squarely atop the granite counter. I imagine it was about three months' salary for him, judging by the way his eyes widened and how quickly his lips snapped shut, choking back a cough.

'Here is my calling card,' I said with a grin, tapping the money. 'Perhaps you could ring up to her room and see if she is available to meet with me.'

I must give the chap credit, he recovered admirably. After casting a quick glance left and right to make sure that he was not being observed, he made the banknote disappear as skillfully as a cardsharp.

'My apologies, Sir,' he said, his manner now as sweet as saccharin. 'I failed to recognize you. Miss Bennett is presently in the salon, enjoying a cup of tea. If you would care to follow me, I shall take you there.'

Without further ado, he ushered me to a restaurant located at the far end of the hotel, a small parlor done up in imitation of a Viennese coffee house, with rows of narrow teak-lined alcoves separated from one another by still more ferns.

'That is the lady you seek,' he said, pointing at the first alcove on the right, which was occupied by an English couple.

Rather than approaching the table directly, I paused and studied the pair from a distance. The woman sat facing me. My first impression was one of overwhelming frailty; from her pale complexion that suggested she spent little if any time outdoors, to her choice of dress, an ivory taffeta Lucile with a cinched bodice that did little to accentuate her waiflike figure. She was about thirty, I presumed, though she could have been younger. She had an aristocratic nose and a severity to her lips that some men may have found becoming, but which I found rather cold. This air of wintry reserve was added to by her hair, which was dyed a bright silvery blonde and cut very short in the new bob made famous by the French actress Polaire. On most women, such a daring style would have seemed mannish, but in this case, the young lady managed to carry it off quite as effortlessly as one of Mr Gibson's eponymous girls.

As I admired her, I could not help but think how well her name suited her. Eloise Bennett. Like Abelard's paramour, there was a tragic grandeur about her, an inescapable sense of despair. In many ways, it was the most irresistible thing about her, a tired romanticism that surely attracted men like flies to honey.

The gentleman she was dining with had his back to me. I could see him only in partial profile. He was much older than his companion, nearing fifty, judging by his hair and whiskers, which were almost completely gray. A soldier, I guessed, based on his unyielding posture and how uncomfortable he looked in his suit, which was badly cut, bunched across his waist and shoulders. Also, he was well tanned, almost sunburned, which made me conclude that he served with a frontier regiment. Most likely infantry, I mused, for he lacked the stiff posture of a horseman, and because of his hobnailed ammunition boots that were army issue.

How was I to get past this rather ominous sentinel and talk to Miss Bennett alone? I hatched a rather clever plan on the fly. Returning to my new Parsi friend, I placed another ten-rupee note squarely on the countertop and said, 'My dear Bamanji, I shall require one more service from you.'

Pointing sidelong at Miss Bennett's companion, I asked, 'You see that fellow over there, the pugilist with the face of a Rottweiler?'

'That, Sir, is Colonel Boothroyd of the 121st. A famous soldier from the north. I most certainly would not like to get on his bad side.'

'Well, this is what I need you to do,' I explained. 'Tell him he has an urgent telephone call. Say it is from Army HQ.'

'And what should I say it is about?'

'I don't care, man. Just get him away from the table for five minutes.'

Pursing his lips, Bamanji considered my request before making a great show of offering my money back to me.

'I'd rather not, Your Highness. Colonel Sahib has a rather grim reputation; he is said to be very ready with the whip.'

Letting out an exasperated sigh, I produced another note from my waistband. Once it had exchanged hands, Bamanji was only too willing to cooperate.

'I shall tell him he has a call from General Allenby in Cairo. That should do the trick.'

'Very good. You do that.'

Giving me a broad smile, Bamanji waddled off to execute this plan. I watched him cautiously, peering out from behind my sheltering fern. Thankfully, it worked like a charm. As I had hoped, the large colonel leaped up and scurried away, leaving Miss Bennett by herself.

I waited just long enough to make sure he did not change his mind and come back before making my move.

Emerging from my ersatz refuge, I fixed my most genial smile on my face and swaggered over to greet her.

She looked up as I approached, holding my gaze with such absolute equanimity that I was a bit taken aback. I had expected her to blush and glance away, as any mannered woman would have been taught to do when confronted by a staring man. Instead, what I received was a careful, measuring look as she proceeded to give me a proper once-over, quite as brazenly as I had her.

Up-close, I found myself revising my initial impression. What I had taken to be pallor was actually a thick layer of Tetlow's face powder and carmine lip rouge. Beneath the mask of make-up, what I had mistaken for plain was actually quite striking—fine cheekbones and a pert nose surrounded by a smattering of freckles that seemed incongruous in contrast to her hair that was dyed blonde, I realized, because I could see dark roots beneath the peroxide.

And her body, I noticed, beneath the sack-like cut of her dress was not fragile at all, merely slender to the point of being athletic, a slimness that came from a lifetime of outdoor activity. *There was steel in her*, I thought, *a most alluring hauteur*. This was a woman who was sure of herself, who knew exactly what she wanted and had no intention of letting any obstacle get in her way.

'Miss Eloise Bennett, I presume,' I said, offering her a brief bow by way of greeting.

'Of course, I am Miss Bennett,' she retorted rather too partly. 'Who else would I be?'

'Of course. I just wanted to be sure that you were the same Miss Bennett who arrived the day before yesterday aboard the *Caledonia*.'

'I do believe I am, as far as Monsieur Descartes will allow me to be.'

I laughed, amused by this rather clever bon mot. 'Well done! It's always a delight to meet a fellow rationalist!'

'What choice do we have, surrounded by such an irrational world, but to laugh and do what we can to survive!' she said, waving me to the chair opposite her, recently vacated by her large companion. 'Oh, do sit down! Your looming is giving me a crick in my neck.'

Smiling, I took the indicated seat. 'Please allow me to introduce myself.'

'There's no need for that. Just tell me what you want, and be quick about it. I'd suggest you make yourself scarce before my fiancé comes back. He's rather possessive, I'll have you know.'

'Of course! I'll do my best to be brief. I am here trying to locate a Miss Mary Hartley. I believe you know her.'

Her smile wavered and then turned ashen. 'Why have you come to see me? What makes you think I know where she is, that I have a clue about Mary's whereabouts?'

'Oh, come now! Didn't you share a cabin for the journey out, Madam? Surely that resulted in some sort of friendship?'

'Yes, we did share a cabin, but only till Gibraltar. After that, she moved up to first-class to stay with an Italian contessa who had taken a shine to her. I barely saw her after that. As for a friendship,' she paused before adding, 'were we friends?' A wistful look drifted across her face.

'Yes, I suppose we were, as much as she was capable of friendship, although I think it would be more accurate to describe us as passing acquaintances.'

'What do you mean exactly?' I asked, intrigued by this cryptic answer.

'I guess what I am trying to say is that I knew her well enough, but we were not close. Frankly, I don't think Mary had it in her to be close to anyone. She was, for lack of a better word, complicated. Most women my age, Sir, live for small talk, for gossip and chit-chat. But Mary was decidedly different. All the fripperies most of my friends back home adored, our talk of dresses and fashion and society and eligible gentlemen, seemed so banal to her. It made her difficult to connect with. She had a good heart, yes, a kind heart, but at the same time ... she was driven, Sir, like a wolf on the hunt, as if she had seen too much in her life to care for pleasantries and polite conversation.'

'Is that a hint of resentment I sense, Madam, in your voice? It sounds like you and Mary had a falling out? Was it over one of these eligible gentlemen you just mentioned?'

She responded with a mordant little laugh. 'Gosh, you're like something out of *Vanity Fair*! I hate to dash your expectations, my dear fellow, but this isn't the 1850s. This is the age of Edward. We women don't fight over gentlemen. We have far more important subjects to worry about, like suffrage, for instance. Do you know that women are permitted to vote in New Zealand, Australia and more than half of the American territories, but in the home counties we are still denied the right?'

I tried not to roll my eyes. Miss Bennett was obviously one of that breed who affected the word 'modern' before the word 'woman'. And while I had nothing but sympathy for the suffragette movement—Helene and I had even marched with Miss Pankhurst on Black Friday, and I had earned a black eye for my efforts—I couldn't help but feel that, in this instance, the notion of women's rights was being used to obfuscate my investigation rather than further any meaningful dialogue.

'That may well be, Madam, but I think you are trying to change the subject. There is definitely more to the story than you are telling me.'

She gave me an evaluative look, followed by a confident half-smile. 'Perhaps there is. To be honest, Sir, Mary and I did not part on pleasant terms.'

'And why was that?'

She sighed. 'The journey out to India; it changes you. For some, it is an adventure. For others, it induces immense panic, a fear which grows and grows until it threatens to consume you. But for a rare few, it is the chance to blossom and grow. Mary was one of those rare few. The further we traveled from English soil, the more she metamorphosed, as Shakespeare put it so well, a sea change into something dark and strange.'

'Could you be more specific?'

'It's difficult to explain. Personally, I had a terrible voyage out. I am a poor sailor and spent most of the journey in my cabin, wrestling with a crippling bout of seasickness. It took until Marseilles for my stomach to settle, and then, just when I was starting to feel shipshape, I was struck by a bout of malaria.

'When I first met Mary, we were sharing a cabin. She was meek, nervous to the point of being mousy. I will not deny that she was very kind to me. She brought me my meals, nursed me and helped me wash my clothes, but the further we sailed from the shores of England, the more she changed. She grew more assertive, less demure, more sure of herself, more resilient. And as she changed, Sir, the chasm between us grew larger, more difficult to bridge. I am glad she moved cabins, to be honest. Had she not, we would have been at each other's throats sooner rather than later.'

'She did something to offend you?'

'Oh no! Forgive me if I gave you that impression. What I meant to say is that while I was fond of her, certainly at least of the naive young girl who boarded the *Caledonia* in England, the young lady who arrived in Bombay was a very different creature, someone so relentless that she scared me, Sir. I assure you *that* Mary Hartley is more than capable of taking care of herself.' She let out a bitter little laugh. 'I don't think you have to worry about her. I am sure she is just fine.'

'That sounds like more than a guess, Madam. It feels like the assertion of someone who knows exactly where she is.'

Another laugh followed, this time laced with acidic disdain. 'Really? First, you accuse us of having a falling out, then you suggest the opposite, that I am so close to her that I am somehow part of her plan to abscond. Is that the best you can do, Mr Sikander Singh? Aren't you supposed to be a famous detective?'

'You know who I am?'

'I have been known to read a newspaper from time to time, Mr Singh. You're supposed to be better than Sherlock Holmes, Monsieur Lecoq and Dupin all put together. Frankly, I'm a bit disappointed.'

If it was her intent to rattle me and offend, it didn't work out quite to plan.

'Quite right,' I said sarcastically. 'I'll try harder to be more inventive.'

A third laugh erupted from her throat, throaty and charming this time, full of joie de vivre. 'Oh, this is fun. I've never been investigated before.'

Her delight was infectious. Hiding a grin, I strove to stay professional and not fall victim to those captivating dimples.

'To return to what you were saying, you mentioned Mary was resilient. What does that mean exactly?'

'I am sure you are aware how difficult it is to be a lone woman in India, especially one who is Caucasian. The heat, the weather, the language barrier and the endless social taboos, not to mention the men, who are more rapacious than the hungriest of predators. The colonies are an unkind place, Mr Singh. It takes a certain strength of will and character to make your own way here. I fear I don't possess it. I am much too used to comfort and security. Without my fiancé, I would probably be lost. But Mary was a survivor. She had seen the world.

'You know,' I said, 'I have always thought that to be a very curious phrase. To have seen the world! People say that a lot, but I can never quite tell what it means exactly?'

Miss Bennett frowned. It was a precipice. She teetered at the edge for a moment. Then, with a shake of her head, she took the leap and decided to confide in me.

'Tell me, your friend, Mr Rowntree, is it?'

'Rowan. Peter Rowan.'

'What did he tell you of Mary's past?'

'Not a lot, to be honest. Peter is a romantic. I don't think it occurred to him that Mary could have a past, nor did he bother to investigate it.'

'Well, more fool him!' Miss Bennett hissed. 'I assure you that girl had quite a past, and a checkered one at that.'

'Is that so?'

'Let's compare notes for a minute, and I will endeavor to fill in the gaps as well as I can.'

'Peter said she was a Highland girl from Perthshire, a priest's daughter. I know she had a rocky relationship with her father. When he passed, she came to live with an uncle in Edinburgh, and sought employment as a governess in Aberdeen, I believe. And, of course, that she was introduced to Peter by a priest and became affianced to him without ever meeting him, and that he paid for her passage out.'

Miss Bennett pursed her lips and gave me a mournful frown. 'That's only half the truth, I'm afraid. The whole story is somewhat more colorful.'

Like a ghoul, my ears perked up, not just because they had sensed a hint of tragedy and scandal, but also because this was exactly what I had been waiting for. To most people, this may have seemed idle gossip, but for me, it was the beginning of a hypothesis that granted me some measure of insight into Miss Hartley's personality. That was what most people failed to understand about the art of deduction. It was not a game of chess, where you planned one move after the next. No, it was more like a game of bao. You had to move in all directions at the same time, notice every detail, consider every alternative and every pattern, no matter how minuscule and insignificant.

This, I was sure, was the key to understanding Mary Hartley. That was the one thing in common with every interview I had conducted so far. While I had been painted a myriad of portraits, from a grasping gold-digger to a nymph, the one thing nobody had been able to tell me about was her past. Until now, at least.

Frowning, I tried to stifle my excitement. 'Could you share her story with me, Madam? Or would that be overstepping?'

Miss Bennett paused for one long minute before letting out a sigh.

'I don't see how it would hurt to tell you. Mary did not swear me into confidence. On the contrary, she almost seemed proud of how much she had suffered. She wore it like a badge of pride, as if it ennobled her in some way.' Miss Bennett's face softened, not just with empathy but with something deeper. Pity perhaps, or sorrow, I could not be sure.

'You have the first part right,' she said. 'Mary was indeed a clergyman's daughter. Her father was a vicar, the rector of a small church not far from Pitlochry. Unfortunately, he was also a drunk and a gambler, and by all accounts, a violent man who often beat her and her mother. When she was nine, her mother ran away with a sailor and was never heard from again, abandoning poor Mary and exposing her to her father's cruel excesses. A year later, he was defrocked for stealing from the tithe box. As a result, he lost the vicarage and, with it, their home. They were forced to move to Edinburgh where he found employment as a knacker. Do you know what a knacker is, Mr Singh?'

'I do not.'

'They are paid by the borough to remove animal carcasses from the streets and dispose of them by boiling them down to tallow and fat and grease, which they then sell to candle and soap makers. Can you imagine it, to live in a house that smelled perpetually of death and decay, to be given the duty to watch carcasses boil down to skeletons and then gather up the fat into blocks for sale?' she shuddered. 'Well, that was Mary's childhood. Three months shy of her twelfth birthday, her father was knifed over a debt and left to rot in a ditch. Mary found herself an orphan. The only choice she was given was to move to Dundee and be fostered with her mother's brother. He was a scrivener for a legal firm, and a pederast, it seems, who enjoyed tormenting her, not to mention the other horrible things he did,' Miss Bennett's voice choked in her throat. But she did not need to elaborate. The anguish on her face was enough to tell me everything.

'That's only the half of it, sadly. When she was seventeen, she ran away and became a nursery maid for some minor laird up in Aberdeen. Not a governess, that was a piece of fiction she devised to make herself seem respectable. She was a lowly skivvy, tasked with polishing the floors and cleaning the chamber pots. Her master was a brute, a proper Heathcliff, who became entangled with her romantically. She said he mistreated her horribly, like she was his property, and was prone to dreadful rages, especially if she so much as cast a glance at another man.

'So, two years later, she stole a small sum from him and ran away again, back to Edinburgh. There, she decided to try her hand at being an actress and managed a few small roles. In the meanwhile, she subsisted by finding work as a milliner and took up residence in a Magdalene Asylum in Canongate, you know, the sort of institutions that house prostitutes and fallen women. That was when your friend's offer of marriage found her, through one of the nuns there, a Sister Bridget. She was at her lowest point then, struggling to scrape together two pennies to survive,' said Miss Bennett, letting out a plangent groan, as though she was pained by recounting Mary's story.

'The truth, Mr Singh, is that Mary did not accept your friend's proposal because she wished to marry and settle down. She accepted it to escape, to flee from the life she was trapped in, and make a new beginning in the colonies, a fresh start.'

I sat back, shaken by these revelations. The story that Miss Bennett had recounted was more than shocking; it was nothing short of scandalous. Why, even the merest hint of such depravity was enough to ruin a woman socially, not to mention destroy her marriage prospects entirely and leave her unweddable. This made me wonder if Peter was aware of the truth about his fiancé's past. No, he could not possibly know. The Peter I knew was not a forgiving man, a stiff Presbyterian who had never believed in second chances. He would never agree to marry someone with such a picaresque past.

And then, of course, there was the matter of Miss Hartley's personality. After my previous interviews, I had built a biography painting her as a Sarah—a nervous, shy girl out on her own for the first time, with steadfast morals and an indomitable spirit. But this changed the picture considerably. If Miss Bennett was to be believed, it seemed that Mary Hartley was more of a Salome—a bold, seductive creature who would stop at nothing to get what she wanted.

'Are you sure of all this?' I asked. 'Is this hearsay or fact?'

'Oh, I am certain of every single word. Think of it to be as good as from Mary's mouth herself,' Miss Bennett shrugged. 'I'm sorry to say, but she was what we call damaged goods. No matter how much she tried to change the way she dressed and looked and spoke, no matter how mightily she endeavored to pretend to be a fine lady, she could not escape her past. There was always a touch of the gutter about her. Why, you only had to see her behavior at the Neptune Ball to realize she had no breeding and no class.'

'What happened at the Neptune Ball?'

'She made a complete fool of herself, of course. Swanning about in scarlet, looking like Bathsheba Everdene, batting her eyelashes at every man on board, dancing with them one after the other like she was a hostess at a music hall,' Miss Bennett shivered. 'I was embarrassed for her.'

'Was that the reason you distanced yourself from her? Because of her, what was the word you used, "checkered" past?'

'In part, yes. A ship is a closed world, Mr Singh. I could not risk my reputation by getting caught up in her affairs, especially after what I happened to witness in Cairo.'

'And what exactly was that?' I asked, my ears perking up again.

Miss Bennett paused, deliberating whether to answer or not. Another long minute passed before she opened her mouth, but to my chagrin, before she could say a word, we were interrupted very rudely.

'Who the blazes are you? What do you think you're doing sitting at my table with my fiancé?'

It was the large colonel. By the look on his face, he was about to have an apoplexy. Ordinarily, I would have matched such blatant insolence with equal rudeness of my own, but since Miss Bennett was present, I decided to behave. Fixing a convivial grin on my face, I rose and started to introduce myself, but before I could get any further than 'good afternoon', he cut me off savagely.

'Oh, do buzz off, won't you?' he said.

'There's no need to be unpleasant,' I said, refusing to back down, even as the colonel took one stolid step forward to try and intimidate me. He was taller than I was and considerably broader across the shoulders and chest, but it was old muscle, now running to fat. Instinctively, I found myself calculating how to take him down. It would be easy enough, a stiff palm to the Adam's apple and a kick to his knee. Finally, as he toppled, a hammer blow to the temple; that would put him out for the count.

From the corner of my eye, I could see Charan Singh moving toward us, his face thunderous, but I delayed his progress with a discrete nod.

'As I was trying to explain, my name is Sikander Singh. I am trying to find—'

Before I could finish, he cut me off again. 'Didn't you hear me the first time? I said go away and leave us alone.' Colonel Boothroyd squared his shoulders belligerently and gave Miss Bennett an apologetic nod. 'Why, I've a good mind to teach you a lesson.'

It was obvious that he was itching for a confrontation. I knew the type only too well, bellicose bullies who had never been put in their place. Why, he was probably the sort of fellow who had whipped his juniors at school.

It would have been only too easy for me to sink to his level, to match insult with insult and make a proper scene, but where would that get me? No, I would have to hold my tongue this once and play the passive, a role entirely unsuited for my temperament but which, when forced, I could manage quite as well as the best of the Barrymores.

'Again, as I was trying to tell you, I am here expressly at the request of the police,' I lied without a blink. 'You are welcome to check with the commissioner if you please.'

The colonel frowned, stymied by this unexpected declaration. I could almost hear the clock in his head ticking away. *What was he to do? Should he take a stand and risk offending the commissioner, or should he back down and risk looking like he had been bested by a native?*

Even as he struggled to make up his mind, Miss Bennett forestalled him with a wave of her handkerchief.

'Oh, do calm down, Malcolm. You're making a scene. That's quite enough!'

The colonel gave her a wounded scowl. 'This is preposterous, Eloise. Here we were, enjoying a nice cup of tea and this plumed fellow, this jumped-up native, has the temerity to disturb us. Surely you can't expect me to allow such a flagrant breach of good manners?'

Miss Bennett's only response was a snort. 'I said, behave! Have a seat, both of you.'

It was more a command than a request, and nicely done at that, quite as effortless as a lion tamer cracking a whip. Immediately, all the belligerence hissed out of the Englishman. With a muffled grunt, he obeyed, sitting down as meekly as a recalcitrant schoolboy.

Stifling a grin, I followed suit, but not before offering Miss Bennett a bow of respect.

She responded with rather a cool smile. 'Forgive my fiancé. He is a marvelously passionate man. That is what makes him so special.'

She patted his hand, causing the colonel to turn an even brighter shade of red. It was obvious that he was utterly besotted with her, and Miss Bennett knew it, judging by the way she had him wrapped around her little finger. The poor fool!

'Anyway,' she said, 'where were we?'

'You were about to tell me what happened in Cairo?'

'Ah yes, Cairo! Have you been, Mr Singh?' She stifled an obvious shudder. 'They call it the Paris of the East, but I thought it was simply awful. The heat, the dust, such dreadful crowds everywhere and the flies, as if it were an abattoir! And let me say this much, the Pyramids ... I found them rather disappointing. What's to appreciate in a giant pile of rocks?

'Anyway, we shored there for a day. I decided to venture forth with the rest of the passengers and explore the city a bit. Unfortunately, as I mentioned, it was all rather tedious. By mid-afternoon, I was feeling exceedingly poorly. A touch of the vapors coupled with the onset of heatstroke. As a result, I decided to return to the ship early. I was looking forward to a bath and taking to my bed early, but it was much too humid to get any rest, so I decided to take a turn around the lower deck. That was when I caught Mary in a very compromising situation with a gentleman behind a lifeboat.'

'You did not!' The colonel exclaimed, utterly outraged. 'Good heavens! How scandalous!'

I stifled a smile at the excessiveness of this reaction. It was not often that one heard three exclamations in a row, that too from a man built like a rugby prop forward.

'Who was this gentleman?' I asked. 'Did you happen to recognize him?'

'Of course, I did. Captain Gordon of the Highlanders, I believe. Another Malcolm, just like my fiancé. Rather a handsome fellow, and a bit of a ladies' man. I had seen him flirting about with all the other eligible memsahibs on board; he had even taken a pass at me during the Neptune ball. He was a scoundrel, Mr Singh, the sort of man they call a bounder, which is why you can imagine I was dismayed to see Mary locked in an intimate embrace with him. I was absolutely shocked, let me tell you. I separated them immediately, before dragging Mary back to our cabin and giving her a stern talking-to. I warned her that she was endangering her engagement and that no man would want to marry her if she acquired a reputation as a fast woman, that she would be ruined if word got out.'

'How did she respond to that?'

Miss Bennett's voice quivered with barely restrained emotion. 'She laughed at me, can you believe it? She scoffed and said it was easy for me to play the prude since I was marrying a good prospect, a man with power and wealth. She said she had no choice but to find a better match than an aging schoolmaster.'

'Those were her exact words?' I asked, sitting up.

'She called me a fool, Mr Singh, and said I was weak to want little more than to be married. She said she had no intention of surrendering tamely to any man, that she was destined for greater things than to be a teacher's wife, that she intended to make her own way in the world, on her own terms. I tried to reason with her, but she was adamant. She told me she had no intention of surrendering to fate as meekly as a mouse and insisted that she would do as she pleased, convention and society be damned.' Miss Bennett shuddered visibly. 'Frankly, she scared me a little, which is why I decided to avoid her. As I said earlier, a ship is a small world, a closed world, and I could not afford to risk having my reputation and my engagement damaged because of her shenanigans.'

'Was that the last contact you had with Miss Hartley for the duration of the voyage?'

'Not quite. She came to see me the night before we docked in Bombay. I had been feeling particularly wretched that day, vomiting my guts out, and she very kindly brought me a bowl of soup.' Miss Bennett frowned. 'She seemed distraught, Mr Singh. In fact, she broke down and started to cry bawl her heart out.'

'Did you ascertain why?'

'Yes, I had a long chat with her. She said she was not happy with the marriage contract. She told me she had been pressured into it, that Sister Bridget had been very insistent she accept, even though the groom in question was elderly, even though it meant coming to India to marry a man without ever setting eyes on him. She revealed she had accepted because it seemed like the only course for her to take, the only way she could escape, but as we drew closer to Bombay, her trepidation was becoming too much to bear. She was scared, Mr Singh, afraid that she had made the wrong decision. She said that she was filled with despair, that she didn't see the point in going on, that she was sickened by the thought of being some schoolmaster's chattel, that she would rather die than be trapped in a loveless marriage.'

'What are you trying to insinuate, Miss Bennett?'

'I ... I don't know. All I know is that she asked for my help, if she could come up-country with me, if I would help and protect her until she found a way to support herself.'

'And what was your response?'

'I refused, of course. I could not risk my good name and my future for her.' She paused, giving me a stricken look. 'I made a mistake, didn't I? I should have been there for her, helped her when she needed it. She wouldn't be missing then.'

'Tell me, Miss Bennett, do you think Mary Hartley was the sort of woman who would harm herself?'

Miss Bennett looked torn, her mouth opening and closing as she struggled to find the words to answer me. I was about to press her on, but her oaf of a fiancé decided to intervene.

'That's quite enough, I think. Can't you see she is exhausted, the poor thing?' The colonel leaned forward and patted her hand. 'It would be best if you would excuse us. As you can see, my fiancé is not feeling too well.'

'I only have one or two more questions,' I tried to say, but as if on cue, Miss Bennett let out a gasp and dabbed at her eyes.

'Malcolm is right. I am afraid I have told you all I can about Mary Hartley. It would be best if you let us get back to our tea, Mr Singh, before it grows too cold to drink.'

It was a polite dismissal, but an absolute one. I was not so dense not to see that nothing would be gained by overstaying my welcome.

'Very well. I am grateful for your help, Madam. Might I call on you when you are feeling better?'

The colonel's whiskers fluffed like an irate buffalo. 'I am afraid that is quite impossible. We will be leaving for Peshawar on the night train. The banns have been read, and we are scheduled to be married, you see, three days hence in front of my entire regiment.'

'In that case, congratulations on your upcoming betrothal, Miss Bennett.'

I nodded at Charan Singh, who stepped forward and offered her my actual calling card.

'If you happen to think of anything else, anything at all, please don't hesitate to call on me at this address. Or, in this case, since you are off to the frontier, perhaps you could telephone, if you can find one up there in the mountains!'

'Of course, I will,' she said, taking the card even as the colonel glowered at me poisonously. 'Oh, poor Mary! I do hope you find her.

I hope she is safe, wherever she is.'

CHAPTER 12

For a brief period in the mid-1800s, Bombay had enjoyed an economic boom of titanic proportions.

The cause for this unforeseen prosperity, curiously enough, had been the civil war in America. When the North had moved to blockade Confederate ports, the flow of cotton from Virginia and the Carolinas had reduced to a trickle. As a result, England's textile mills had turned to India, to the fertile fields of the Deccan Plateau and the crowded dockyards of Bombay, from where Indian cotton was shipped to Birmingham and Sheffield to feed the forever-hungry looms of the Midlands.

It was the cotton trade that had turned Bombay from a town into a metropolis. It was cotton money that had funded the sprawl of Girangaon, the village of mills, that had steadily lured migrants to the city in droves, in search of steady employment. It was cotton that had financed the reclamations and ultimately stitched the seven islands together as one and paid for the grand monuments of the Fort, from the Victoria Terminus to the Gothic campus of the University with its imposing clock tower. If not for cotton, Bombay would have remained a provincial backwater, home only to sailors, shipbuilders and thieves.

Watson's Hotel was very much a by-product of this short-lived cotton boom. Opened in 1869 by a tailor who had amassed a fortune selling draperies, in its heyday it had enjoyed a glamorous reputation as one of the finest establishments east of the Suez. In fact, Mark Twain, who had resided there briefly during his tour of India, had described its cast-iron facade, which had been designed by the same architect who had constructed the Crystal Palace in London, as a gilded birdcage.

Sadly, Watson's heyday was a thing of the past. The ornate birdcage was rusting and looked more a prison than a paradise and the steady flow of grandees that had once patronized its passages had been reduced to a trickle of traveling box-wallahs.

It had been almost five years since I had visited Watson's, not since my last trip to Bombay. That time around, I had come to expose an impostor who had been pretending to be none other than myself, an adventure that had ended in a most satisfactory result.

I remember being quite unimpressed by the decor, thinking it to be rather dated even back then. As I dismounted from the Mercedes and strode into the lobby, followed by Charan Singh, who trailed in my wake like a turbaned shadow, I saw nothing to change that previous opinion, though the hotel seemed to have undergone a recent renovation. The smell of paint still lingered in the air, and the black and white parquetry was gone, replaced instead by a preponderance of white granite. Only the oddly shaped glass atrium remained untouched, I observed with a dour smirk, still fighting a losing battle against a relentless flock of pigeons.

Almost immediately upon making our entry, we were approached by a plump Anglo-Indian with slicked-back hair and a sleek moustache. I knew him, an odious little man named Marshall who had previously been the reception clerk at the Bombay Gymkhana and was currently the day manager of this establishment. The last time I had been here, he had been excessively rude, almost churlish. This time around though, he surprised me by giving me an unctuous bow.

'Your Majesty,' he exclaimed, 'what a pleasure it is to welcome you back to Watson's!'

Taken aback by this one-eighty in his demeanor, I couldn't help but wonder what had brought about the change until Charan Singh leaned forward and whispered in my ear.

'I had a word with him, Huzoor, after his bad behavior last time.'

'You didn't rough him up, did you?' I whispered back, trying to hide my amusement.

'Oh no, I am not a bully, Huzoor,' the big Sikh replied with a grin. 'Actually, I put him on our payroll. As you always say, the best gossip comes from the staff, doesn't it?'

I feigned clapping my hands, as though to applaud him for his initiative, before turning back to Marshall, who was waiting patiently with a questioning look on his face.

'Would you care for a room? I can make a suite available if you give me an hour.'

'Thank you, no. I will not require accommodation, not this time.' I nodded at Charan Singh who took out a small wad of banknotes from his cummerbund and offered them to Marshall.

The manager's face reddened. His eyes darted left and right before he accepted the money eagerly, tucking it deftly into his jacket pocket.

'How may I be of assistance in that case? Please, you have only to ask,' he said, his fake smile blooming into a real one.

'Actually, Mr Marshall,' I responded, 'I am looking for a woman.'

He misinterpreted my intentions, that much was apparent, from the way his face fell.

'I am afraid, Sir,' he sniffed. 'Watson's is not that sort of establishment. Might I suggest you try Green's? It tends to attract that sort of crowd.'

'Oh, don't be silly,' I shook my head. 'I don't mean a companion. I am here to speak with one of your guests, Contessa di Sforza. Do you know her?'

Marshall's response was a shudder that made him quake all the way to his brogues.

'By George, I do,' he groaned. 'I warn you, Sir, she is a horrible creature, utterly terrifying, an unholy terror and a Catholic to boot.'

'Should you be speaking about your guests like that?' I retorted.

'I cannot help it, Sir,' he scowled. 'We have had some demanding guests over the years, but this memsahib is the worst of all. A dreadfully loud woman, she likes to shout as much as she enjoys a drink. Why, last evening, she had the better part of two bottles of port and then got into an argument with our barmaid when she tried to cut her off. She made her cry, Sir. I haven't heard such language, not even from the fishwives who bring us our daily pomfret.'

In spite of his patent outrage, I couldn't help but chuckle. 'She sounds bloody marvelous,' I said. 'Send a message telling her I would like to meet with her, will you, and inquire if she can find the time to speak with me?'

'Of course,' Marshall replied. 'As you wish.'

'Excellent! I will be waiting in the lounge.'

The lounge, as it turned out, was the one part of the hotel that had not changed. It was a drab parlor abutting the lobby, done up in a style that could only be described as mock Georgian. At this early hour, it was entirely deserted. An array of battered satinwood tables were scattered across the room, matched by a variety of brocade-covered gentlemen's chairs. I took the one furthest from the door, looking out over the green expanse of the Oval. As was his habit, Charan Singh took up a position nearby, staying just out of my eyeline, far enough to assure me a modicum of privacy but close enough to come to my aid in case of any trouble.

Summoning a bearer, I tried to order a Sazerac but was apologetically informed that no alcohol was served until after 4 p.m. Instead, I had to make do with a pot of Lapsang Souchong and that morning's edition of the *Gazette*.

I sat back, expecting a bit of a wait. As I leafed through the newspaper, I found myself reflecting upon my previous interview. I was not sure how I felt about Miss Bennett, about how reliable she was as a witness. She was a bewilderingly breezy creature, as capricious as quicksilver, sometimes warm, sometimes venial. I could not classify her, which made me doubt her testimony.

However, after speaking with her, there were two things I now knew beyond a doubt. First, Mary Hartley had lied about her past. Well, perhaps not an outright lie, but she had certainly concealed the more racy bits. *But was that a crime in itself? Who did not have secrets, skeletons in the closet to hide?* And simply because she had chosen to hide the truth of her antecedents did not necessarily mean she had chosen to desert Peter. The only evidence I had of that was pure hearsay, which was Miss Bennett's recollection of their last conversation, an account I had difficulty trusting beyond face value.

The second point of interest that Miss Bennett had revealed was that Miss Hartley had been drawn in by Captain Gordon, a known womanizer. *But was that a seduction, a shipboard romance, or something more? After all, it wasn't out of the ordinary for women outbound to India for marriage to sow their wild oats, so to speak?* But how that affair had ended was crucial for me to find out. *Had Miss Hartley fallen in love and chosen the Captain over my old friend, or had it ended badly with Gordon looking to do Mary some harm, thus resulting in her disappearance?*

Thankfully, my patience was not tested for too long. After about five minutes, just as I was enjoying an article about a large hyena that had been seen prowling the western side of Malabar Hill, Marshall made a comeback, followed closely by a behemoth of a woman I presumed was none other than Contessa di Sforza.

I don't know why I had imagined that she would be an elegant creature, with the dark coloring and delicate beauty for which Milanese women are so renowned. The suggestion of her name perhaps, the fabled Sforza cachet, was what had led me to this presumption, but it was promptly dispelled when she entered the lounge, letting out a voluble 'yoo-hoo'.

What confronted me was a rangy mare of a woman, at least a head taller than me, with a profile quite as equine as last year's Derby winner. She was well on the wrong side of forty, with a chaotic thatch of iron-grey hair cut to her jawline and skin so leathery that it told me she was the outdoorsy sort who cared little for her appearance. This impression was only added to by the excessively sensible way she was dressed in the style affected by the horse and hound set—a belted jacket and skirt, both Harris Tweed, paired with ankle-high walking boots. It made her look more like she planned to climb the Kanchenjunga than make a social splash.

'Buon giorno!' I said, rising to my feet and giving her a curt bow. 'Contessa di Sforza? Katerina di Sforza of Forli?

She did not respond to my greeting. Instead, she studied me very carefully, from the top of my turban to the tips of my Balmorals.

'You!' she said at last, after making me endure well-nigh a minute of uncomfortable scrutiny. 'You are the maharaja who has come to see me?' Her mouth twisted into a scornful sneer. 'But where are the jewels? Where is the grandeur? How to say it? *La splendore?*'

Her English was excellent, if somewhat accented, with a broad Lombardo cadence that made every word she uttered seem like an exclamation.

'I must say, I am very disappointed. I was hoping for something exotic, but you're rather ordinary looking, aren't you? Haw-haw! I mean you're handsome enough, but nobody will believe you're royalty unless you have at least an emerald or two, my plum fellow, and perhaps a plume on your turban and some silk robes, eh?'

Absently, I rubbed the lapel of my band-gala, trying not to feel self-conscious.

'Forgive me, Madam,' I quipped. 'I am only a very minor maharaja. My name is Sikander Singh of Rajpore, in the Punjab.'

I nodded at Charan Singh, who shuffled forward and offered her my calling card. She ignored it, choosing instead to eye the big Sikh with undisguised admiration.

'Now this is more like it!' Her lips curved into a sly smile. 'My-my! What a striking specimen you are! Tell me, do you like Italian women?'

The old man blushed. 'I shall wait for you by the car, Huzoor,' he declared and beat a hasty retreat, as if he had been confronted by a mythical churail.

The contessa watched him go with a gleam in her eyes. 'I think I may have scared your man off,' she said with a glib chuckle.

'Madam,' I started to say, but she cut me off, refusing to allow me a word in edgewise. 'Oh, sit down, won't you? I don't like looking down at men.'

With that imprecation, she plonked herself on my chair and took out a sterling silver cigarette case from her pocket. She offered it to me, but I refused, waiting patiently as she took out a slim Gitane and fixed it on to an ivory holder. When she brought it to her lips, I leaned over to light it with a Lucifer before crossing over to take the other seat.

'As I was saying, I was hoping we could have a brief chat,' I said to her.

'Of course!' She waved one dismissive hand at me. 'We will speak about many things, but first, I really must have something to drink. This humidity has me parched!'

With that declaration, she turned to snap her fingers at a passing waiter. 'You there, bring me a cup of black tea, no sugar and none of that rotten Darjeeling rubbish, you hear?'

Turning back to me, she let out a braying laugh, revealing an expanse of square, white teeth. I have acquired a taste for the Earl of Grey. I must say, I dislike the English rather much, but my goodness, do they know how to grow fine tea!'

In another person, the robust and brash manner she liked to affect may have been tiresome, but much to my surprise, I found myself quite liking her.

'I take it this is your first trip to India,' I said.

'Oh yes! And you're my first maharaja, you know, even if you're rather a disappointment.' Her eyes shone, gleaming with barely restrained enthusiasm. 'I have waited my whole life to come here, and I cannot wait to get out of Bombay and see all the sights. A tiger! The Taj Mahal! An elephant or two, the Himalayas and a proper maharaja, one who is more glamorous, more meraviglioso! My apologies,' she giggled, 'for saying so!'

'Not at all! Tell me, what do you think so far? Do you like it here?'

'It's magic,' she gushed. 'The colors, the sounds, the people! I feel like I'm in the Arabian Nights.' She arched an eyebrow and waggled a finger at me. 'But that's not why you're here, is it, to inquire so solicitously about my impressions of India. I'm too old and too impatient to beat about the bush, Mr Maharaja. Come right out with it, what do you want from me?'

'I am here, Madam, about a young woman named Mary Hartley,' I said, mirroring her expression and raising an eyebrow of my own. 'I believe you knew her quite well. You sailed out on the *Caledonia* together, didn't you?'

At the mention of Miss Hartley, the contessa's lips thinned, as if she had swallowed a bitter lemon. Her gaiety disappeared, replaced by a sudden suspicion.

'What is your interest in Mary?' she asked, her accent thickening even further with wariness, making the name sound more like 'marry'.

'Ah, so you do know her? You admit it?'

Her jocularity evaporated, replaced by a dour circumspection that seemed quite out of character.

'Are you trying to interrogate me?' she rasped. 'I was not aware that you are a policeman.'

'I am not, Madam, but I occasionally dabble in small mysteries from time to time.' I gave her a polite smile, trying to allay her suspicions. 'In this case, I am working with the permission of the Bombay Police. You see, unfortunately, Miss Hartley seems to have gone missing, and since she was affianced to a dear friend of mine, I have decided to investigate the matter.'

'Your friend? He is the schoolmaster?'

'Yes, Peter Rowan. He is the one who paid for her to come out to India. They were to be married, but she never turned up.'

'What if she does not wish to be found, Mr Maharaja?' The contessa hissed. 'What if she has not gone missing? What if she simply changed her mind and does not desire to be wed to your friend any more?'

'In that case, Madam, I assure you, I have no intention of forcing her to do anything she does not wish to do. I merely want to ascertain her whereabouts, for the sake of my friend's peace of mind. I mean, does he not deserve to know what happened to her? Is he not entitled to at least that much courtesy?'

The contessa pursed her lips, considering what I had said briefly, before giving me a curt nod.

'I knew Mary, yes. We became quite close during the voyage,' she said with a sigh. 'I met her the first night out, at the captain's table. He had her up from second-class, for dinner, as is the practice.'

She shook her head .'The poor child. It was all too much for her, I'm sorry to say.'

'Would you care to elaborate?'

'Well, she got very carried away. First of all, she decided to get rather too dressed up in an awful pink chiffon concoction that was at least three seasons out of style and had her looking like a giant toffee. It was, as I am sure you understand, an absolute faux pas.'

I nodded. It was common practice to never dress for dinner in formal wear the first night out on a sea voyage. I could imagine how embarrassing it must have been for Miss Hartley to turn up at the captain's table looking completely overdressed, quite enough to undermine her social standing for the rest of the trip.

'As if that wasn't enough,' the contessa continued, 'Mary had rather too much champagne and then decided to lecture the captain about how women deserve the same rights and opportunities as men. As you can imagine, Captain Carruthers (which she pronounced as three syllables: care-you-theres, bringing a smile to my face) was none too impressed. He is a rather staid fellow, one of those awful chaps cut from Victorian broadcloth. Luckily, I decided to step in before matters could get too unpleasant and managed to steer the conversation back to a safer, more sedate subject.

Tea, actually!' she exclaimed. 'That is another thing I intend to do while I am here, visit Assam and see the plantations for myself. Who knows, perhaps I shall buy some land and become a planter myself. Can you imagine it? The world's first Italian tea! I'll make millions!'

'Madam, we were talking about Miss Hartley,' I interjected, trying to steer the conversation back toward familiar ground.

'Ah, yes! Needless to say, that was the last time she was invited to take dinner at Captain Carruther's table.'

'But you took a shine to her?'

'Indeed, I did. My own trip was off to a dreary start, I admit it, and I was bored. My fellow passengers had not taken warmly to me. You know how the English are when it comes to foreigners, especially the middle classes. They distrust Italians very nearly as much as they dislike the French. Honestly, I had all but resigned myself to an excruciatingly dull voyage when Mary turned up. By God, she made me laugh. And she had something special; a fire, faccia tosta, or what the English call bottle. All she needed was for someone to encourage her, to teach her how to reach her potential.'

'The captain told me you intervened on her behalf, that you insisted he grant her access to the first-class deck. He said you even offered to pay the difference in her fare.'

The contessa smiled. 'What can I say? I decided to take her under my wing. She reminded me of myself when I was her age, although I doubt I was ever that unworldly. And then, of course, there was her story,' she said, clucking her tongue. 'The poor thing had a terribly sad story, a tragedy worthy of Ariosto himself!'

'I know some of it, yes.'

'Then you will surely understand the reason she decided to accept your friend's offer of marriage. She told me she was desperate for a fresh start. And what better place than India, eh?'

'Did she say anything else about Peter? Did she ever mention to you if she intended to repudiate her contract with him?'

The contessa scowled. 'Yes,' she replied diffidently, 'she did. Several times, as a matter of fact. And I supported her choice. In fact, I encouraged her to do it.'

'You do realize that is a crime, don't you, Madam? Aiding and abetting someone to break a legally binding agreement?'

I was trying to intimidate her, but the contessa was not one to be so easily cowed.

Rather than being dismayed, she let out a mordant laugh. 'Don't be ridiculous, Mr Maharaja! Where is the crime in encouraging a girl to go out and find her own way in the world? What is the offence in helping her find happiness? Women are not chattels, to be bought and sold. The only wrongdoing here is forcing a woman to marry a man when she has no wish to do so.'

She gave me a level look. 'The truth of the matter is that Mary was special. She deserved more than a loveless marriage to an ageing schoolmaster. She deserved a chance to make something of herself on her own terms. That was exactly why I decided to help her, not just because I was touched by her tragic story and took pity on her, but also because she deserved a chance.' Her voice thickened before she continued, 'Every woman deserves at least that much. That is why I offered to be her chaperone and decided to make her my little project. It wasn't very difficult, really. She had good cheekbones; If you have good cheekbones, mio amico, anything is possible. All that was left was to teach her some manners and a bit of polish, to turn her into something special,' the contessa grinned. 'My motives weren't purely unselfish, I confess. As I said, I was lonely and somewhat bored, and it felt good to have someone to talk to, a companion to keep me diverted from the monotony of shipboard life.

'She was such a smart child, decidedly naive, yes, and rather unworldly and much too stubborn for her own good, but with a brain as sharp as Toledo steel. Of course, that was the first thing I taught her, that it would be best if she kept the fact that she had a mind of her own well-hidden. Most men, especially those who are looking for wives, prefer women who can cook and clean but who profess not a single original thought in their dainty little heads. I told her as much. And I also suggested that if she wanted to get ahead, it would be best to hold her tongue and hide behind a pretty smile.'

I tried not to roll my eyes. *How different this woman was from my Helene!* They would never get along, not in a million years. For one thing, Helene would never warm up to such brisk arrogance and brassy self-confidence. And then, of course, there was the fact that she would be deeply offended by the thought of any woman pretending to be submissive merely to get a man.

'What else did you teach Miss Hartley, if you don't mind me asking?' I inquired sardonically.

'Oh, more than a thing or two. She was attractive enough, just lacking in confidence and breeding. Women are not born beautiful, Mr Maharaja. They are made. Sophistication is an art. It must be learned, not imitated. When I first met her, Mary didn't know how to carry herself or use her natural gifts to her advantage. I taught her a little about making herself up, how to affect an elegant posture and how to dress for effect. She would come up and see me for tea every afternoon, and I enjoyed talking to her. It was deeply satisfying to watch her transform from a shy, mousy creature into a confident young woman.' She sniffed wistfully. 'I guess it was my maternal instincts at work, but I felt responsible for her somehow. In some way, she was my creation, my masterpiece.'

'The Neptune Ball,' I said softly. 'That was your handiwork, wasn't it?'

This question elicited a narrowing of her eyes, almost as if I had managed to surprise her.

'Yes,' she said. 'I helped Mary prepare for the Neptune ball. It didn't take much to transform her, just a dab of some rouge and a smattering of powder. I lent her one of my old dresses, a red House of Worth piece that she altered to fit her. I loaned her some of my jewelry, just a necklace and some earrings, and a pair of decent shoes. They were rather too big for her feet, so we stuffed newspaper down the toes. She spent hours wearing them, practicing how to walk like a lady, until she had it down perfectly.'

Smiling sadly, she continued, 'In a way, it was her debut, at least in what passed for high society aboard the *Caledonia*. Mary was like Cinderella that night. Before the ball, she had been plain and easy to ignore, but after,' the contessa said, her smile widening, 'all the men on board, every single one, from the old codgers to the young bucks, had eyes only for her. She was resplendent, Mr Maharaja, as alluring as a bird of paradise.'

Her voice wavered a twinge of regret so palpable that it bordered on bitterness. A less acute man might have missed this cue, but I seized upon it as surely as a hunter sensing the scent of his prey.

'You sound like you resented her success, Madam,' I observed. 'Did it annoy you that she stole so much of the limelight?'

I had expected a denial, or something theatrical. Instead, she responded with a discreet shudder. 'No, not at all. It isn't that at all. The truth is,' her voice dwindled to a whisper. 'It doesn't matter, not any more. What's past is past.'

It was quite uncharacteristic, this sudden melancholy on her part. However, it lasted only a heartbeat. Within moments, she managed to regain her composure and come back to her brash, blasé self.

'Now I am bored,' she declared. 'That is all I am willing to say about Mary, Mr Maharaja! I hope it has helped you.'

'It was very enlightening, Madam,' I sat back, pursing my lips and studying her intently. 'There is only one problem. I don't believe I can accept a single word you have said at face value.'

'What?' she exclaimed, her insolent grin wavering. 'Why ever not?'

'Well,' I replied nonchalantly, 'quite simply because you're a liar and a charlatan. You are no more a Sforza than I am Queen Victoria.'

The last remnants of her smile disappeared, replaced by an impressively thunderous outrage.

'How dare you?' she started to bluster, but I cut her off brusquely.

'You can certainly try to deny it, Madam, but I am absolutely certain you are not who you say you are. You see, I happened to have met the real Contessa Katerina di Sforza seven years ago, while I was on a grand tour of the Continent. I had the pleasure of attending a lunch hosted by the Duke of Savoy, where she was in attendance.' I gave her a knowing grin. 'She was three years old at the time.'

'This is preposterous,' she exclaimed, rising to her feet with a grandeur so stately that it bordered on magnificent. 'I'll have you arrested for slander, you ... you rascal! I ... I shall have you clapped in irons! You rogue! You knave!'

It was a masterly performance, all brows a-shaking and bosom a-quivering, but it left me unmoved.

'Sit down,' I said. My voice was so cold that it could have frozen water to ice. The effect was instantaneous. The contessa, or whoever she may have been, let out a startled squeak and obeyed immediately, sinking back into the chair bonelessly.

'It is quite obvious to me, my dear lady,' I said, keeping my voice calm, 'that you are what is known as an adventuress, an impostor, a pretender who is up to some sort of nefarious scheme. However, what that scheme may be is of no interest to me. My only interest is to find out what happened to Miss Hartley. Do you understand?'

She watched me silently, holding her tongue for a very long time, every vestige of her brazen facade now gone, replaced instead by a vigilant wariness. Finally, just when I was about to lose my patience, she offered me a nod of surrender.

'Ah, hell's bells!' It was like magic. Her accent and demeanor changed in an instant. The thick lilt of Milanese receded, replaced by pure Irish.

'You've got the better of me, you cheeky sod. Who would have thought it? In bloody India, of all places, I find the one fellow who manages to see through my act. You're right, of course. I'm no contessa, nor am I Italian. I am just as common as mud, I am. As to why I'm here, it's to make my fortune, and what better way to get by, I thought, than as a toff. People look at toffs differently, especially the English. They worship the ground beneath their feet, like they are god's chosen few. So why not, I thought? And I was getting away with it. I bloody well was until you turned up, Mr Maharaja!'

'You're an actress, aren't you?'

She laughed, a very different laugh from the one she had employed while playing the contessa. This one was much earthier, more heartfelt and infinitely more likeable.

'Oh, that's very good. How did you guess it?'

'You have talent, Madam,' I said grudgingly. 'You almost had the better of me, and that is not easy to do. Your demeanor, your manners, your accent were spot-on. And you never once broke character. That kind of attention to detail can only mean you're a professional.'

'I've been many a thing and many a person, Mr Maharaja,' she said. 'I've roped horses in America and dug for gold in the Klondike. I've danced for pennies in Australia and read fortunes for an Austrian duke. I've hunted impalas in the Kalahari and preached the Bible to the savages in Sudan.' Holding out her hand, she invited me to shake it. 'But yes, a long time ago, in one of my past lives, I was Miss Clara Olson, as fine a player as the great Nell herself. They called me the pride of Donegal, Sir, when I strode the boards at the Gaiety in Dublin town.'

I let out a chuckle, delighted by her effrontery. 'It's a pleasure to make your acquaintance, Miss Olson,' I said, taking her hand lightly. 'You can rest easy. I have no intention of ratting you out. All I ask is for you to tell me the truth about Miss Hartley. Why did you come to resent her?'

'Because she stabbed me in the back,' she snarled. 'The little bitch stole from me, Mr Maharaja. A gold pendant in the shape of a fleur de lys. It was a gift from a gentleman I was once acquainted with, a token of his lasting esteem.' Her face colored, turning beet red. 'After all I did for her, after I took her under my wing and taught her everything that I knew, that is how she repaid me!'

'How do you know it was her?'

'Who else could it be? I saw her admiring it one evening, just a few days after the ball, and then, the very next day, it was gone.' Her jaw clenched with outrage. 'I knew she took it, even though she denied it when I confronted her. The nerve of the girl! I couldn't prove it, of course, but I knew she did it.' Miss Olson grimaced. 'I cut her off after that. I had her evicted from my cabin and refused to speak with her any longer, or help her in any way.'

'There's something you are not telling me, isn't there?' I asked, sensing she was holding back.

'Oh, all right!' Miss Olson exclaimed, letting out a grand sigh. 'I whipped her. I did. I let her have it right and proper. She couldn't wear short sleeves for a week. What else could I do? It's not like I could go to the captain, not without giving my secret away. That's the first rule of the grift, Mr Maharaja. Keep a low profile and don't ever get noticed,' she said with a shrug. 'Anyway, that was the last time I interacted with her.'

I considered what she said. It presented a very different picture of Miss Hartley from all of my previous interviews. Most of the people I had spoken with so far were male, and quite infatuated with her, all too ready to praise her many merits. At first, I had thought that was the case because of her beauty and innocence, which was a combination that almost always proved irresistible to that breed of middle-aged men who liked to imagine themselves as knights in shining armor, only too eager to rescue a maiden. But now, it seemed the truth was quite something else. Miss Hartley was not a naif after all. On the contrary, if the contessa, or rather Miss Olson, was to be believed, she was a siren, accomplished at beguiling men. And a thief to boot, which suggested to me, along with her tragic story, that she was an amoralist, infected by the condition that Émile Durkheim had described as anomie.

'There is one more thing you could help me with, Madam.' I said, choosing my words very carefully. 'Can you tell me if Miss Hartley, if Mary, became involved with any of the gentlemen from the Neptune ball? Anyone who gave her special attention, who she may have chosen to elope with? Surely, she would have confided in you, yes?'

Miss Olson sniffed. 'She did mention a couple of fellows she liked the look of. There was an Indian she was interested in, the scion of a wealthy family, Percy something or the other.'

'You must mean young Mr Billimoria.'

'Yes, that was his name. Porky Percy, we called him, because he was a bit of a podge.' Her brow wrinkled. 'And there was an officer of some kind, a stuck-up ruffian with far too much a sense of himself. He was always sniffing about her, every evening at tea, trying to strike up a conversation.'

'I think that is Captain Gordon. I know about him. Were there any others?'

'Well, there was one more chap. An older man, rather ugly. He had very little hair and dreadful teeth. He spent a lot of time with her, even before the ball. She would often take a tour of the promenade deck with him on most evenings. Once or twice, I even saw her visiting his cabin.'

'Would you happen to remember this gentleman's name, Madam?'

'No, not really,' she frowned. 'All I recall is that he had one of those dreadfully Scottish surnames. Yes, he was a Scotsman, I am sure of that. He wished me a good day once, and I distinctly recall that accent of his.'

I made a mental note of this detail, even as Miss Olson's face stiffened, becoming almost hostile.

'May I be candid, Mr Maharaja?' she said. 'If you find Mary, and I doubt you will—'

'Oh, I will find her, Madam,' I interrupted. 'You can be sure of that.'

'Don't be overconfident,' she warned me. 'Mary is a very intelligent woman. If she doesn't want to be found, I doubt you will locate her.' She shook her head. 'Might I offer you some advice, from a woman who has some experience with matters of the heart?'

'Of course.'

'Go back to your friend and tell him to forget Mary, to find another woman to marry. She is not the girl for him. She is destined for far more than being a schoolmaster's wife. Even if you do find her, it will only cause more heartbreak. Just leave it well alone.'

'I can't do that, Madam. It is anathema to my nature. I cannot leave a riddle unsolved. I will find Mary Hartley, whether she wants to be found or not.'

'I am sure you will,' Miss Olson repressed a shudder. 'I would not like to have you on my tail, Mr Maharaja. You are rather terrifying.'

'Not at all, Madam. My bark is much worse than my bite.' I gave her a genial grin and rose to my feet. 'Thank you, I am very grateful for your time.'

Giving her a brief bow, I turned to leave, but before I could go more than two steps, she stopped me.

'One moment,' she said, unable to hide the tremor in her voice.

I paused and turned back to face her.

'What you said about not ratting me out, you meant it, didn't you? You aren't going to tell the police about me, are you? Please, I have to know,' she asked, her eyes wide with apprehension.

It was something that I had not contemplated, but now that the words had been spoken, I found myself wondering what was I to do with the duplicitous contessa? She was a mountebank and a professional liar, and a bit of a termagant to boot, but I liked her far more than most of the actual gentry I had met, almost all of whom were jumped-up dullards with an overinflated sense of their own importance and their inbred lineages. To be honest, I admired her impudence and energy. And the more I thought about it, the more I couldn't help but conclude it wasn't really my job to grass her out.

'Have you ever heard of the Khanate of Kalat, Madam?' I asked. 'It is rather a dreary place, up in the dusty reaches of Balochistan, not far from Quetta.'

'I am afraid I have not,' she replied, confused.

'Well, the reason I happen to mention it now is that I know the current ruler, Mir Mahmud Khan the Second, rather well. He is a bit of a nutter, I am sorry to say, but still a terribly important and wealthy man, one of the English government's most valued allies in the north-west. In fact, he is absolutely mad for everything European, big or small, but his three particular passions are polo ponies, the aristocracy and white women, in that order.' I gave her a smile and added, 'I met him at the Durbar just last year. He confided in me that he wanted only two things in the world: the first a personal crest from the College of Arms and the second a European mistress who can ride.

'Perhaps,' I gave her a very deliberate wink, 'it would be best if you visited Kalat once you quit Bombay. It isn't much of a place, just acre upon acre of farmland, but I think you might like it very much. And might I suggest that when you get there, you introduce yourself as Magdalena di Sforza and not Katerina. She is the contessa's aunt and roughly your age.'

Even as I finished, Miss Olson's dour features flowered into a vast grin.

'Kalat, is it?' she said, giving me an even bigger wink. 'Why, I do believe I shall leave for Lahore this very evening, Mr Maharaja.'

'In that case, let me be the first to wish you a safe journey and all the very best for the future.'

'Thank you,' she surprised me by leaning forward and planting a kiss on my cheek. 'I am in your debt, it seems. You have my word. Someday, somehow, I will find a way to pay you back.'

'I am certain you shall, Madam,' I said, raising one hand to offer her a slow salute. 'Or shall I say Begum Sahiba?'

CHAPTER 13

A cursory examination of the passenger manifest revealed that other than the notorious Captain Gordon, there had been three other gentlemen with Scottish surnames booked aboard the *Caledonia*.

The first of them was one Duncan Macmillan, who had given an address close to the docks, Pallonji's Adelphi Hotel. Uday Singh informed me that it was just about ten minutes away, which was why I decided to go see him first. As it was, he turned out to be an elderly fellow, well over seventy, whose sole interest seemed to be lepidopterology.

When I asked him if he knew Miss Hartley, his reply was that he had no time for women, followed by a rambling lecture about the breeding patterns and taxonomy of the Kaiser-i-Hind butterfly, which was the reason he had traveled out to India, to see this rarest of species. As a result, I dismissed him immediately as a suspect. If Miss Hartley had been born with wings, he would only have been too eager to chase her down. However, since she had none, he hadn't a clue, which meant a wasted hour for me.

The next person on the list, a sergeant of the Borderers named Murray, was somewhat more difficult to track down. It ended up entailing a trip to the Bombay Cantonment. Unfortunately, when I arrived there and checked with the quartermaster, it turned out that he had already left for Ranikhet the night before.

That left me with two options. Either I could hare off to the United Provinces chasing after him, nursing the forlorn hope that he was the Scotsman I was looking for, or I could roll the dice and try my luck with the last name on the list, which was exactly what I decided to do.

The address provided by the third gentleman, a Herbert Ross, turned out to be a lodging house located at the tail end of the Apollo Bunder, a rather nondescript establishment named the Waldorf Hotel. Sadly, other than a grand art deco sign atop its entrance, there was no other resemblance to its New York namesake. This Waldorf was small and somewhat dusty, precisely the sort of establishment that catered to bachelors disembarking in Bombay before continuing their journey up-country. The manager, a wide-shouldered, phlegmatic-looking Parsi named Bharucha, refused to cooperate when I tried to question him.

However, after I had Charan Singh slip a generous gratuity to the doorman, a plump Maharashtrian with an effusive smile named Vijayakar, he was only too quick to reveal that the man I had come to seek had summoned a carriage not one hour earlier to take him to the Town Hall, where he intended to attend a lecture of some kind.

Bombay's Fort precinct derived its name, quite simply, from the fortress that had once stood there. The Bombay Castle, as it had been known, had been built by the East India Company to protect their investment from the depredations of the French, the Dutch and most importantly, the Marathas. Its ramparts had originally been a mile in length and a quarter of a mile wide, a rough quadrangle whose walls had been twenty-seven feet tall on the landward side and forty-two feet on the seaward. Three fortified gates had led out of the fort: the Apollo Gate, which had been directly opposite where the statue of Lord Wellington now stood, bordering the Colaba Causeway; the Bazaar Gate, which had been located at the northernmost end of the fort and was now hidden away behind the sprawling expanse of Victoria Terminus; and the Church Gate, named so because it had been located close to St Thomas Cathedral.

According to British custom, while the fort's walls had stood tall, each of these gates was shut at dusk and opened only at sunrise. No natives were permitted to stay within the fort walls overnight, other than servants and sepoys quartered in the garrison barracks. At least that had been the case until 1863, when the then-Governor, Henry Bartle Edward Frere, had ordered the ramparts to be pulled down and the moat to be filled, thus creating an entire new quarter for the city, beginning its transition from a fortified port into what had come to be known as Urbs Prima in Indis, the first city in India.

It was here, at the heart of this new Bombay, not far from the Mint and the Post office's half-constructed black basalt dome, that the Town Hall had been constructed. Once, this had been the true epicenter of British Bombay, its unyielding and marbled heart. Now, it was the headquarters of the Asiatic Society who maintained a museum on the premises, as well an extensive public library of over a lakh books, which included rare works in Persian, Sanskrit and Urdu, and even a first edition of Dante's 'Divine Comedy', supposedly one of only seven left extant in the world.

It was also probably my favorite building in the city, an elegant neoclassical structure that reminded me very much of the British Museum. They both had similar, equally striking facades, a long row of eight towering Doric colonnades beneath a sparkling Palladian portico, fronted by a sweeping rampart of thirty broad steps.

'I am afraid you will have to stay here, old man,' I said to Charan Singh as his son brought the Mercedes to a halt opposite this magnificent entrance. 'They will not let you in.'

'But, Huzoor,' he insisted, making to follow me when I dismounted, 'what if you find danger inside? I should stay by your side. That is my duty.'

'The only thing I will find inside,' I reassured him, 'is a crowd of stodgy old Englishmen who are about as threatening as a passel of pigeons. Stay here,' I repeated, 'and keep the car running. I will be back before you can say Dante Alighieri.'

With that out of the way, I marched up the steps and strode into the Town Hall as if I owned the place. Once inside, I paused, looking around the foyer curiously. This was my first visit, and my immediate impression was very positive, from the polished Burmese teak floors to the vaulted ceilings above. I grinned as a delightful mélange of smells filled my nostrils—the reassuring odor of linseed oil, old paper and leather. Briefly, I was tempted to spare a moment and inspect the admirable collection of statuary on display, but before I could take more than half a look around, a clerkish young man hurried up to me and inquired if I was there to attend the Asiatic Society's monthly lecture.

When I affirmed I was, he impatiently ushered me straight through to the Grand Hall, chivvying me along as if I were a tardy schoolboy. Upon entering, I found, to my dismay, that the lecture had already begun, judging by the pointed looks several of the gentlemen in attendance gave me when I blundered in. Thankfully the room, which could easily have seated at least two hundred, was sparsely populated. There were only about thirty attendees, an elderly and rather scholarly lot judging by the threadbare look of them. I managed to find an empty chair without much ado, in the back row, and scanned the people seated in front of me, wondering which of them could be the Scotsman I was seeking.

Up on the stage, a middle-aged man stood poised behind an oaken dais. Clad in a tweed cheviot suit, he was portly and extremely bald, except for a bushy Vandyke that made him seem like a phlegmatic goat. From behind a pair of pince-nez glasses, his bulbous eyes glared down at me, obviously irritated by the interruption.

I offered an apologetic smile, which only served to make him frown more deeply. Clearing his throat, he proceeded to resume his disquisition. When I heard his lilting accent, which was very obviously from the Highlands, I realized that I had been completely mistaken. Herbert Ross had not come to the town hall to attend a lecture. He had come, it seemed, to deliver it.

A quick glance at the banner hung up behind him confirmed this inference, a hand-painted sign that proclaimed: The Asiatic Society of Bombay welcomes Dr H.J.H. Ross of Edinburgh University, and the subject of his discussion, A Comparative Meditation upon the Accents and Dialects of Central and Northern India and the Greater Sub-Continent.

Letting out a muted groan, I realized I was trapped. Obviously, I had no choice but to sit through the rest of his lecture before approaching him. Leaning back, I half-closed my eyes and settled in to listen as he droned on rather pedantically, letting his words wash over me like a wave.

'It is often thought that language differentiates people into social groups, almost as much as ethnicity and race, but even within the broad confines of the study of linguistics, there are few subjects quite as interesting as the patterns of speech that emerge if you study the diversity of dialects. Not only do dialects change according to region, ethnicity and class, they are also influenced immutably by income, education and urbanization. Why, in Britain alone, there are more than forty distinct dialects.

'In my estimation, there is no clearer way to know the history of a people than through the study of dialects. Take Northumbria as an example. Within the borders of this single county, there are several noticeable local variations of spoken English, Geordie being the most famous, of course, having descended from the original Anglo-Saxon and particularly noticeable around the River Tyne. But equally pervasive is the subtype known as Wearside, which is prevalent in Sunderland and the port towns, and a curious new language known as Yakka, which has come to be the patois of the mine workers around Durham. And then, of course, there is the ancient Northumbrian tongue, which has two distinct variants demarcated by the River Tees. The northern branch is descended in large part from Old English, but it is interesting to note that the southern type, which is now sadly almost extinct, contains elements derived from Old Norse, most likely brought to the shores of England by Viking invaders when they raided the monastery at Lindisfarne in 793 AD.

'It is my belief that these creoles, these subdialects, so to speak, are cognate forms of language that coexist with traditional languages, that they must be considered the children of the same mother. And I am convinced that if we are able to study these linguistic patterns in exhaustive depth, we will be able to illustrate how it is that cultural assimilation works, that by studying how people speak, we can truly come to understand that both history and language are Darwinian, that they are not static but dynamic, and that they continue to evolve with the passage of time and the clash of cultures.

'Let us take our empire in India as an example. Frankly, India is a miraculous place for a linguist. As entailed by Grierson in his ongoing survey of Indian languages, there are over three hundred and sixty distinct spoken dialects here, the majority of them Indo-Aryanic and Dardic, thus sharing the same roots as English. That is why, I believe, India has proven to be such a fertile ground for the English language, the very reason why it has taken such firm root here in the pace of just two centuries.

'And that, in my informed opinion, is the greatest gift we have given the people of India. While our contributions have been many—the railways, institutions of higher education, the public works, law and order, modern banking—it is the gift of language that has been the most valuable.'

This pronouncement was greeted by a scattered smattering of applause, and one rather subdued snort on my behalf, if I may add.

'The people of India,' he continued, 'in their unique and inimitable manner have taken our tongue and made it their own. They have, in the space of a hundred and fifty years, turned English into something altogether Indian. Why, there are now over thirty-two recorded dialects of Indian English across the subcontinent, each with a unique lexicon, vocabulary and phonology.

'Thanks to the largesse of this venerable organization, which has seen fit to fund my explorations, it is my intention to travel across the length and breadth of India for the next seventeen months and compile a detailed study of the variable dialects of spoken English within the subcontinent. I am certain that my findings shall be nothing short of revolutionary, and I look forward to returning here and sharing them with you esteemed gentlemen.'

With that, he performed a brief and rather awkward bow, which was greeted by another, even more desultory, round of applause.

I did not approach him immediately. Instead, I hung back, waiting patiently when he descended from the stage and spent the next few minutes exchanging pleasantries with a small cluster of gentlemen, mostly office bearers of the Asiatic Society, I guessed, given that they were all wearing identical black gowns that made them look like a mismatched murder of crows.

Once he broke away from them, before he could make an exit, I cornered him.

'Mr Ross, is it? Herbert Ross?'

'It's Dr Ross,' he replied, peering at me curiously, probably because I was the only Indian in the room. 'I know you,' his eyes narrowed with recognition. 'You are the latecomer!'

'Ah yes!' I offered him an apologetic shrug. 'I really am terribly sorry about that. Perhaps I could make up for my rudeness by buying you a cup of tea.'

Sadly, this attempt at being charming fell utterly flat on its face. Rather than warming up to me, he continued to study me watchfully, biting his lower lip with a frown.

'That's an intriguing accent you have,' he said. 'Let me make a calculated guess. Judging by the way you overemphasize your S's and roll your R's, I would say you are from the Majha region of the Punjab. However, you also have the smooth eloquence of received standard, which makes me think you were schooled in England. Charterhouse perhaps, or Winchester? Am I correct?'

'Somewhat,' I replied with a grin, impressed by his acumen. 'I was at Eton briefly, and then Oxford, although I regret to say, I was sent down before I could take my degree.'

His frown returned at this mention of my expulsion. In most circles, being sent down from college was considered as grim a sin as worshipping Beelzebub himself, an opinion Dr Ross seemed to fully endorse, judging by the disapproval writ patent on his face.

'If I may return the favor, Dr Ross, while you have the cadence of a Cambridge man, the way you drop the occasional diphthong leads me to believe you were born in Aberdeen, or is it Dundee, within spitting distance of Ben Macdui?'

This riposte was what finally managed to break through his reserve. 'Oh, well done!' he exclaimed, finally giving me the slightest of smiles. 'Are you a fellow linguist?'

'I'm afraid not,' I said with a laugh. 'I have a much less interesting position.'

Extracting a calling card from my breast pocket, I offered it to him. 'Please allow me to introduce myself. I am the Maharaja of Rajpore. Sikander Singh is my name.'

'Oh!' The thin smile wilted, replaced by awkwardness. I guessed this was his first brush with genuine royalty, even someone as minor as myself. Unfortunately, as it does with most people, the experience managed to leave him a bit tongue-tied.

'A maharaja,' he said, his eyebrows rising in surprise. 'How very unexpected!' He looked me up and down curiously, as if I were a specimen in a laboratory. 'What can I do for you?'

'Well, I was hoping to have a word with you actually.'

He blinked several times, obviously confused. 'A word? What about?'

'As it happens, Dr Ross,' I improvised as quickly as I could, 'I found your lecture quite fascinating.'

'Is that so?' His face brightened. 'Which part exactly was it that you enjoyed?'

'All of it,' I said hurriedly before he could figure out I was bluffing. 'In fact, I was hoping we could continue the conversation.'

'I am afraid I haven't the time,' he replied apologetically. 'I am due to leave for Mysore tomorrow, and I really must get my baggage in order.'

'Are you sure? I really was hoping we could speak at length about your research, particularly what you said about Indian English dialects. It sounds rather marvelous!'

This stratagem worked, precisely as I had guessed it would. There are few things that academics enjoy more than a receptive audience, someone to whom they can demonstrate their superior intelligence and extol the virtue of their work. Dr Ross was no different. He simply could not resist the opportunity to hold forth about his one true passion, especially not to someone educated enough to understand exactly what he was talking about.

'Oh, why not?' he declared. 'I am sure I can spare half an hour for you.'

'Excellent! I noticed that there is an Irani cafe across the street. Would that suffice, or would you prefer something more gentrified?'

'Why not? I have never been to an Irani cafe before. Lead on, Mr Singh.'

Stroking his beard with a grin, he scurried after me as I turned and headed for the exit. 'Did you know, Sir,' he said, 'that there are two very distinct groups of Iranian immigrants in India? The Zoroastrians, who migrated at the turn of the thirteenth century; and the Iranis, who began to arrive quite recently. I believe they both have rather different accents. The Zoroastrians have a well-established Gujarati speech pattern, while the Iranis still display the same roots as the Dari, to whom they are closely related.'

Only half-listening to this monologue, I led Dr Ross out of the Town Hall. When we emerged, Uday Singh, who had been lounging against the bonnet of the Mercedes and smiling louchely at every pretty young woman who happened to walk by, sprang to his feet and scuttled to hold open the passenger door for me. I waved him off, telling him to stay put. His father, who was seated in the front seat reading a copy of the *Gazette*, gave me a pronounced scowl, as if he wanted to argue, before falling in silently behind me.

Dr Ross did not even blink, nor did he pause for breath, barely seeming to notice Charan Singh, in spite of the man's bulk and height. Instead, he continued to natter on, even as we crossed the road.

Directly opposite the Town Hall lay the Elphinstone Circle. Once, this had been a large maidan called the Bombay Green where bales of cotton had been sorted and stored. Now, it was lined by a crescent of handsome commercial buildings that housed some of the country's most powerful mercantile institutions enfilading a manicured oval garden, at the center of which a statue of Lord Cornwallis sneered down stonily at passers-by.

Opposite this monument, on the ground floor of a nearby building, a ramshackle white sign declared: Bayani and Co. Bakery and Restaurant since 1827.

I marched up to the entrance, but before I could enter, Charan Singh finally decided to break his silence.

'Huzoor,' he said to me in Punjabi, 'this place is not worthy of you. It is a haunt for scriveners, lawyers and ruffians.'

'Don't be ridiculous,' I replied nonchalantly, ushering Dr Ross onwards. 'It's a perfectly respectable establishment, old man. Stop being such a dratted snob.'

I must confess, I was being overly adventurous. It was my first time at an Irani cafe as well. Once inside, I couldn't help but grin. I had been expecting something akin to a Viennese kaffeehaus, but what greeted my eyes was a place of such unmatched dinginess that I couldn't help but fall in love at first sight. The walls were painted a drab ecru, covered with moldering calendars and portraits of Queen Victoria at various ages. The floor was black and white parquet, dotted with tables covered with dusty gingham tablecloths, which in turn were flanked by a mismatched variety of bentwood chairs. It was very crowded, packed full with customers who all seemed determined to ignore each other while reading their newspapers. I looked around for an empty table, trying to find a maitre d' to seat us, but the only employee in sight seemed to be a middle-aged manager wearing a topee, perched behind a marble counter. beneath a wooden sign which declared: *No talking to manager/ No smoking/ No fighting/ No credit/ No outside food/ No sitting long/ No talking loud/ No spitting/ No change/ No match sticks/ No gambling/ No newspaper/ No combing/ No beef/ No leg on chair/ No hard liquor allowed — By order.*

When I caught his eye, he gave me a disinterested shrug and pointed at a solitary table that was vacant, at the very back of the cafe. Stifling a laugh, I led Dr Ross toward the indicated table and sat down. Charan Singh shambled after us and took up a position in front of us, folding his arms across his chest, his width serving admirably as a screen. Dr Ross continued to ramble on, even as a dour-faced waiter materialized and looked him up and down before asking for our order. He was the sort of man, I guessed, who was afraid of silences. It is a malady shared by most intellectuals, I have found, a sort of verbal diarrhea that people often mistake for intelligence.

Choosing not to interrupt him, I picked an array of dishes at random from the menu, which was sandwiched beneath the glass table top. The waiter scurried away and returned with an impressive alacrity, bringing back two heaped trays of food. Much to my chagrin, I realized I had gone a bit overboard as he proceeded to lay out a veritable smorgasbord in front of us. There was an enormous kettle of tea, of course, and a platter piled high with buttered buns that was accompanied by a bowl of akuri, which is the Parsi version of scrambled eggs, spiced with chilis and onions. There was a plate of assorted biscuits, another piled high with some variety of glutinous tea cakes and a third, very intimidating bowl heaped with what seemed to be an indeterminate pilaf festooned with ochre-colored berries.

As the waiter backed away, I waved a hand at the doctor, inviting him to help himself. As it turned out, his eating habits certainly didn't match his loquacity. He took only a sliver of cake, one solitary biscuit and a half cup of tea. I was even more abstemious and tasted everything very briefly before fixing my full attention on Dr Ross, interrupting him as he nibbled away at his biscuit while pontificating, for some reason, about the language of the Malayalis.

'Forgive me,' I said rather brusquely, 'while I am fascinated by your research into the fifteen vowels used by Keralites, that is not why I needed to speak with you.'

'Are you certain?' he asked, rather crestfallen by this untoward interruption. 'I was just getting to the best part.'

'Perhaps we can resume the subject later, Dr Ross, but first, I was hoping you could speak about a young woman.'

'Ah!' he smiled, looking bewildered. 'That is not one of my fields of expertise, I am sorry to report. I am more comfortable with split infinitives than I am with members of the opposite sex.'

'Nonetheless,' I said, mirroring his smile, 'this is a young woman I believe you are more than comfortable with. Miss Hartley?' I paused, entirely for effect, watching his reaction very carefully. 'Mary Hartley? I believe you two grew rather close on the voyage out on the *Caledonia* , as thick as thieves.'

At the mention of Mary's name, Dr Ross's avuncular manner wavered, his eyes narrowing with suspicion.

'This is highly irregular,' he sputtered. 'You are trying to trick me. You said you wanted to speak of my work, but obviously, that was a fib.'

With an injured scowl, he started to rise, but I forestalled his departure with a curt flick of my wrist. 'Please, Dr Ross. Mary has disappeared. If I am to find her, I am in dire need of your assistance.'

That explanation gave him pause. Again, I watched him like a hawk, looking for even a hint of guilt, but all I could discern was surprise, followed by worry, and then a shadow of sorrow.

Letting out a vast sigh, Dr Ross sank back down. 'Disappeared, you say! Are you certain?'

'Yes, I am. Her fiancé was waiting for her when the *Caledonia* docked, but she never turned up.'

'And you fear something unfortunate has befallen her?'

'I cannot dismiss the possibility out of hand, not without further investigation.'

Frowning, Dr Ross took a minute to pull out a linen handkerchief from his vest pocket and mopped at his brow. 'How awful! How very dreadful!'

'Does that mean you will help me?'

'Of course ... of course,' he said. 'God, I just saw her, not two days ago.' Removing his spectacles, he massaged the bridge of his nose. 'Mary was, no, she *is* a friend.'

'Forgive me, Doctor, but I was not aware that polite society permitted single men and women to be friends.'

Dr Ross blushed, smiling shyly to reveal a pair of rather unexpected dimples that made him seem decidedly less bookish. 'Actually, Mr Singh, I think of Mary as more than a friend. As I mentioned, I am not a forthcoming man, nor am I the outgoing sort who makes friends, especially of the feminine variety. But Miss Hartley ... Mary, she was an exception to the rule.'

'I did not realize you were that close to her.'

'Oh, we were as thick as thieves, as you said so succinctly. I first became acquainted with her quite by chance. We were partnered during an egg-and-spoon race on the upper deck. She was the first leg, and I was the anchor. I made a right mess of it, I'm afraid, and ended up, quite literally, with egg all over my face.'

He grinned broadly, his eyes sparkling. 'Mary thought it infinitely amusing. She was kind enough to offer me a handkerchief. After I cleaned myself up, we got a cup of tea and began to chat.'

'Let me guess,' I said, trying not to roll my eyes, 'you were drawn in by her beauty. It seems most of the gentlemen aboard the *Caledonia* were enchanted by her. Why should you be the exception, yes?'

'Not quite,' Dr Ross replied. 'Certainly, she was an attractive young woman, but it was not my eyes that drew me to her. It was my ears.'

'I beg your pardon.'

'Her accent, Mr Singh. It was exquisite.'

'I'm not sure I understand.'

'Let me explain,' he said, sitting back. 'Being a man of keen investigative spirit, I'm sure you'll find this stimulating. Most people assume that accents are largely innate, that we are born with them. That may be true of dialect, but a person's accent isn't merely determined by their place of birth. Class, ancestry, education, breeding, ethnicity, migration, and more often than not, cultural osmosis all play a role in cementing an accent. And once that accent is formed, it is almost impossible to alter. A Norwegian may move to Newcastle, but he will not begin to speak as a Geordie, nor will he shed his Nordic dactyls.'

'I fail to see what this has to do with Miss Hartley's disappearance.'

'It will become apparent in just a moment. You see, what I am trying to explain is that accents are unique, Sir. To a trained ear, each is quite as distinct as these newfangled fingerprints.'

I finally grasped what he was trying to suggest. An accent as a forensic identifier. He was right; I was intrigued. I had never thought of accents that way, but to compare them to fingerprints was nothing short of revolutionary. Less than a decade had elapsed since Bose and Haque had set up the first bureau of exemplars in Calcutta and Alphonse Bertillon had used fingerprint evidence to apprehend a murderer in the Scheffer case, but in that all too brief period, this new technique had already revolutionized the solving and detection of crimes. *Could accents work the same way? Could you truly tell so much from the way a person spoke? And what if you could record and analyze those speech patterns? Would that voice imprint be enough to deduce the identity of a criminal?* I found my mind racing with the possibilities.

'Have you tested this theory?'

'I have,' Dr Ross continued. 'And one of the things I have concluded is that most people are rarely able to change their accents.'

'Surely that's a spurious conclusion,' I argued. 'What about stage actors? I once saw a performer in Paris who could switch from flawless French to German to Spanish, all in the same breath.'

'There are exceptions, of course, to every rule, small sub-groups who are able to practice diglossia.'

'I'm afraid I don't know what diglossia is.'

'It is the phenomenon, Mr Singh, when there are two distinct versions of a language that exist simultaneously. Take your Sanskrit for example, which is largely a written language, and Prakrit, which is the spoken version. In such cases, people are able to switch from one version to another, a phenomenon that exists to a limited degree in English as well, such as those who speak with a dialect local to their origins but are also trained to speak with received pronunciation, a number, interestingly, which constitutes less than 2 per cent of the general population.'

'Are you saying that Miss Hartley is one such, how did you say it, diglossial?'

'The word is diglossist, I believe. But to answer your question, no, not quite. You see, there is an even rarer breed of people, the polyglossists, who are able to intentionally change their accents through what is called mimicry, not unlike that performer you mentioned.'

'And you are saying that Mary Hartley was one of those ... polyglossists?'

'Indeed she was, and quite extraordinary at that. Ordinarily, an ear as discerning as mine can tell when a person is putting on an accent. There are always undertones, but with Mary,' he shrugged, 'over the space of an hour, I heard her change her accent not once, not twice, but six times, and on each occasion, she was pitch perfect.'

'You've lost me again, I'm afraid.'

'Let me explain it better. Take your accent, Mr Singh. As I deduced when we met, you have the veneer of received pronunciation, which suggests time spent in England, but beneath it, I can hear the cadence of the Punjab in your vowels. The way you stretch your I's and roll your R's; you will never be able to get rid of those speech patterns because they are ingrained in your engrams as surely as your memories. It makes you who you are, Mr Singh. The story of your life is articulated in the way you speak. But Mary presented a most unexpected case. She had a completely neutral intonation, Sir. It was uncanny, no cadence, no prosody. I had never heard such a thing before.' He let out a long, heartfelt sigh. 'It was really quite intoxicating, let me tell you. For a linguist, it's like the holy grail to find someone with a completely neutral accent and an innate gift for mimicry. That was why, Mr Singh, I made her a proposal.'

'What manner of proposal?' I sat up, hoping for something illicit.

'A chance, Sir, to be part of a truly glorious experiment.'

He took a sip of tea and cleared his throat. 'She was clay searching for an artist to sculpt her, and that is exactly what I offered. You see, while she had mastered the art of suppressing her origins, there were times—especially with my ear—when I could detect her wavering, the occasional twang of the Highlands and a stray hint of Edinburgh patois, especially when her color rose. The truth was that she was unschooled, and as a result, she lacked refinement. I thought it would be diverting to help her learn some of the mannerisms of the upper classes, concentrating most specifically on the accent. Received pronunciation is a tricky beast at the best of times, but with a gifted teacher, it really can be child's play.'

'Galatea,' I murmured. 'And you thought yourself to be Pygmalion.'

'This time, *you* have lost me, I'm afraid,' Dr Ross said, looking confused.

'It's a myth from ancient Greece. A sculptor named Pygmalion carves the perfect woman from marble, and she comes to life. It's a rather nice operetta by Gilbert and Sullivan, and also the subject of a new play by Bernard Shaw, which he has adapted quite admirably for contemporary times.'

'Why, I have seen that! Just this past month. A fine comparison, Mr Singh,' said Dr Ross, rubbing his beard introspectively. 'You're quite right. Mary did remind me so much of the young woman who is the heroine. Oh, what was her name?'

'Miss Eliza Dolittle?'

'Yes, that's the one. Mary had the same naive enthusiasm, Mr Singh, and the same drive to better herself.'

'Which is why she accepted your offer ...'

'Indeed, she did. And I confess, I am glad of it. When you are an academic, there are few things more gratifying than seeing your theories put to practice. Not to mention the fact that it made the journey a bit less onerous.'

Dr Ross paused, taking another sip of tea. 'You seem to be a well-traveled man, Mr Singh. As I am sure you know, long sea journeys are dreadfully boring, but thanks to Mary and the experiment, the next two weeks flew by. We fell into rather a pleasant pattern. Each morning, we would meet to take a constitutional on the upper deck and work on her diction. And for an hour before dusk, she would read to me for practice. There was a nice spot not far from the front stack, where we had a bit of privacy, and I would coach her on deportment and manners.'

'Did it work, this experiment of yours?'

Dr Ross's face broke into a self-satisfied smile. 'If I may toot my own horn, in sixteen days, I changed Mary from a common spinster to a proper lady capable of holding her own in the poshest salons in Mayfair. I remade her, Sir. It was nothing short of a miracle.'

'The Neptune Ball? You were involved in that, too, weren't you?'

'Indeed, it was. Our debut, so to speak. The acid test, which Mary passed with flying colors.' He paused. 'Every gentleman aboard the *Caledonia* had eyes and ears only for her.'

There should have been pride in his voice, even boastfulness, but I detected something else. *A hint of regret, perhaps, or was I reading into his words?*

'How did that make you feel? To see Miss Hartley surrounded by so many suitors? Surely you felt a smidgen of jealousy? It is only human. After all, you had been spending an inordinate amount of time together. It must have dismayed you, to see her with other men.'

'Oh, what rubbish! I'm sorry to say you are quite mistaken. Mary was an experiment to me, nothing else. Frankly, as I said earlier, I have little time for women, Sir. I am a man of habit; I have neither the patience nor the desire to endure their capriciousness.'

I almost believed him. It was a reasonable performance except for the faintest of involuntary tremors.

'You're lying, Doctor.'

'I most certainly am not.'

This time, he was even less convincing, a flimsy attempt at outrage that was the stuff of amateur dramatics, all sputtering and sniffing.

'Like you, Dr Ross, I also have a passion for language. However, it is not just the language of the tongue that captivates me, but rather that of the body. You see, like the words we speak, our bodies have accents, too, a dialect composed of twitches and tics, shivers and blinks. Most people tend to dismiss the language of the body, but when you have trained your eye to be observant, as I have, even the faintest of gestures carries a portent of meanings. Do you know why I am sure you're lying? Your right hand, Doctor, is your giveaway. Each time I mention Miss Hartley, it trembles ever so slightly. That means you're hiding something.'

I leaned forward until my face was just inches away from his. 'You were attracted to her, weren't you?'

'This is too much,' he started to bluster, but I refused to have any of it.

'Spare me the hyperbole. I know a man in love when I see one. Besides, that's the other half of the myth. Pygmalion falls in love with his creation, just as you fell for Mary Hartley.'

Dr Ross's eyes widened, and he winced. It was as good as a confession.

'You're correct,' he blurted. 'I have not been entirely honest. You see, I know Mary is fine, that she is in no danger.'

'What do you mean?'

I gave him a steely glare. 'If you know something, Doctor, tell me now.'

'Mary has not gone missing at all, Mr Singh. No, I hate to be the bearer of bad news, but the truth is that she has chosen to break off her engagement. My apologies to your friend, but she no longer wishes to marry him. She has decided to repudiate the arrangement.'

'What makes you so sure of that?'

'Because she is promised to me, Mr Singh. Mary and I ... we are engaged.'

Now it was his turn to offer me a determined frown. 'I will request you, one gentleman to another, to please leave us be. I'm sure your friend is a fine person, but the heart wants what it wants. Surely you understand that?'

'Where is she? I want to hear this from her.'

'I'm afraid that isn't possible. When we last spoke, she was en route to Mawand. She has an aunt there whom she wishes to visit. She will be returning in December, and we will rendezvous in Madras for the New Year. We intend to be wed there before setting sail back to England.'

That was it then. I sagged back. The bird had flown the coop. Part of me was tempted to go drag her back, but Dr Ross was correct. *What good would it do?* If she had decided to repudiate Peter, then that was the end of it.

Even as I mulled over that possibility, another, more sinister, thought occurred to me, inspired perhaps by what Miss Bennett had said about Mary.

'Tell me, Dr Ross, once she accepted your proposal, did you happen to loan Miss Hartley any money?'

This question took him by surprise. He colored a bright red and opened his mouth, as if to refute me, but then changed his mind and shut it so rapidly that his teeth clicked like castanets.

'I did. I gave her most of my stipend, almost ninety sovereigns.'

'Did you now?' I tried not to roll my eyes. 'Perchance, did she provide an address where you could reach her in Mawand, or the name of this aunt she was so eager to visit?'

His face fell as he started to gather the drift of what I was suggesting. 'No, she did not. But let me assure you, she has promised to send me a weekly correspondence care of the Asiatic Society.'

I stifled a groan. The lovestruck fool! I almost felt sorry for him. *Was he so naive to think that Miss Hartley reciprocated his ardor, or foolish enough to believe she would meet him in Madras as promised? Or was I being unnecessarily cynical? Could she have fallen for him quite as hard as he had for her?* No, I dismissed the thought as quickly as it had occurred. I had never met Mary Hartley, but after what I had heard of her, I felt I knew her well enough to say without a doubt she would never have settled for someone so pedantic. No, I was almost certain she had played him, just as she had played Peter, taking advantage of their trusting natures.

That realization gave me another insight into her character. When I had agreed to help Peter, I had imagined that Miss Hartley was a wilting willow, scared of her own shadow. But after interviewing the captain, the second officer, Miss Bennett and this hapless fellow, my suspicions were slowly cementing into conviction. It was becoming only too apparent to me that Mary was not an ingenue after all, nor was she a victim. She was calculating, an opportunist, not Galatea but rather Lorelei, the sort of creature who took advantage of men deluded enough to fall for her charms.

Dr Ross continued to study me with the befuddled intensity of a man utterly besotted. I was tempted, if for no other reason that the lovelorn look on his face was irritating me thoroughly, to shatter his dream, to reveal all that I had learned so far about his beloved Miss Hartley. Unfortunately, as always, I heard Helene's gentle voice in the back of my mind, urging me to be kind. I could not tell Dr Ross the truth about Miss Hartley. It would break his heart. No, in this case, it would be a genuine kindness to leave him in the dark.

I let out a vast sigh and rose to my feet. 'Thank you for your time, Doctor. This has been very helpful.'

He gave me a sheepish shrug. 'About your friend, Sir, it pains me to dash his hopes, but Mary and I are destined to be together. We will be happy, Sir. I will meet her in Madras come December, and we will be together until death does us part.'

'I hope you're right, Doctor. I truly hope you are.'

CHAPTER 14

Emerging from the Irani cafe, I offered Dr Ross a lift to his lodgings, which he declined and hurried away after bidding me a brusque fare-thee-well.

As for me, I paused, trying to consider my next gambit. Before I could make up my mind though, a shrill voice interrupted the cadence of my contemplations.

'Hai Ram! Give a helpless cripple a gift. God will favor you!'

Turning, I saw a beggar making a beeline toward us. He was indeed crippled. Both his legs ended in stumps at his knees, which were swathed in gory bandages, and he was seated atop a cart of sorts, a plank with four wheels attached to it, which made a dreadful clatter as he hauled himself forward using one hand like an oar. In the other hand, he held a tin bowl that he clanged on the rough pavement and then shook at me with a practiced vehemence.

'I am a veteran,' he croaked in guttural Hindi. 'I lost my legs in Afghanistan, at Saran Sar. Surely you can spare an old soldier a coin or two, your munificence!'

Charan Singh looked at me, asking if I wanted to be rid of him. I nodded no and pulled two coins from my belt, flicking them into the beggar's bowl.

I was not expecting any thanks, but the man surprised me by responding with a pronounced snort of disdain. 'Is that all? Two measly coins? I thought you were supposed to be a big maharaja or something.'

Charan Singh growled at his insolence, his mouth twisting into a scowl when the beggar made a rude gesture. He was about to resume his noisy passage, when I moved to obstruct his way.

'Hold on. How did you know I'm a maharaja?'

The beggar gave me a cheeky grin and then, like quicksilver, he was off. Reversing his cart, he dashed off in the opposite direction with a haste that would have put Mercury to shame.

'Get him!' I shouted to Charan Singh who took me quite literally. Taking two vast bounds, he seized the beggar's shoulders and lifted the man off the ground like he was a sack of potatoes.

'Aye, let go, you numbskull!' the beggar exclaimed.

My eyes widened in disbelief as the beggar's legs unfolded from beneath the bandages, almost appearing magically. He aimed a kick at Charan Singh. Taken by surprise, his grip loosened involuntarily, allowing the beggar to wriggle free.

Before he could do another runner, I was on him, grasping one arm and twisting it up behind his back.

'Who are you? You're no beggar!' I demanded to know.

'There's no need to be so rough, Sir,' the man replied in flawless English. 'I am Constable More from f Special Branch. Mr Hall-Caine sent me to fetch you.'

With his unrestrained hand, he pulled out a metal disc from his cummerbund and proffered it at me. Taking it, I saw that it was an identity token that confirmed that he was indeed who he claimed to be. Reluctantly, I let his arm go. With a grin, Constable More gathered up his cart, folding it as if it were a newspaper and tucking it under his armpit before giving me a bow.

'If you would care to follow me,' he said.

With a flourish, he spun around and headed due east, in the direction of the Crawford Market. Charan Singh and I exchanged a bewildered look before shrugging and setting off after him. Uday Singh followed behind, keeping the Mercedes at a respectable distance, close enough to be able to offer assistance if needed.

Much to my surprise, rather than returning to the Fort, our tattered guide trotted across the railway tracks and led us straight toward Carnac Road and the maze of lanes that lay beyond.

Most outsiders failed to realize it, but there was a very palpable demarcation between British and Indian Bombay. Carnac Road was the invisible boundary separating the two. Looping around from the Marine Lines to the last tram station just north of Pydhonie, it closely paralleled the moat that had once surrounded the Bombay fort. Until Aungier had ordered the ramparts to be torn down, this had been the border between the white city and the black town, as the English had so colorfully named the Indian quarter.

Even though the old walls were long gone, relegated to the dusty pages of history, the divide remained, only too visible to a trained eye. On the English side, everything was neat and orderly. The buildings were whitewashed and the streets kept well-swept. But on the native side, it was so crowded that it was difficult to move. The stench of open drains and the stink of middens at every corner clashed with the pungent smell of pepper and spices. The sound of the muezzin calling the faithful to prayer mingled with the peal of temple bells and the deafening din of a thousand voices speaking a hundred languages. This was the true essence of Bombay, death and life fighting each other, entropy and birth coexisting side by side, a barrage of color and noise so intoxicating that it could overpower an unwary traveler.

The constable pushed his way through the throng, turning off Carnac Road into Kalbadevi. Unfortunately, this was where we had to leave the car behind, as the road was not wide enough to permit vehicular passage. I gave Uday Singh a few curt instructions, telling him to take a different route and wait for us near the junction of Girgaum and the Esplanade.

As we entered the narrow lanes around Bhuleshwar, Constable More picked up his pace. We trailed after him as he led us across Sandhurst Road and through Khetwadi, and then past the Northbrook Garden to turn onto Grant Road.

Abruptly, he came to a stop at the junction of a narrow lane. Turning to me, he said, 'Just a little further, Your Highness!'

I glanced up at the signboard, which read 'Cursetji Suklaji Street', and let out a low whistle. To the north of this junction lay a labyrinth of congested alleys and warrens, including the infamous district of Kamathipura and the notorious cages of Falkland Road. This was the seething, unruly heart of Bombay, not the town hall with its imposing colonnades, but the red-light district, colloquially known as Lal Bazaar, an area with a reputation so evil that even the police thought twice before venturing into its by-lanes.

I knew these stories well enough to pause before carrying onwards, as did Charan Singh who offered me a wary grimace.

'Are you sure you wish to go on, Huzoor? This is not a place for a man of your breeding and background. Can you imagine the scandal if you were seen here by someone? Why, our nose would be forever cut. Enough, I implore you, let us turn back.'

I let out a laugh. 'You sound like an old woman,' I said. 'Besides, you know damn well that it is not in my nature to turn back, not when I'm having such fun.'

I waved the constable on, and he resumed his trek. At the next crossroads, he turned down a side street and then into a narrow cul-de-sac, coming to a halt in front of a warped doorway about three buildings down.

'In here,' he said and pushed the door open.

I stepped through to find myself in a dimly lit tavern. It was an establishment of the lowest kind, with an unpaved floor covered with dust and dried blood, and a mismatched array of clapboard tables and stools. Even though it was still an hour to dusk, it was very crowded, packed with at least two dozen men, all rough-looking customers, mainly laborers and coolies by the looks of them. I tried not to cough as the smell of the place assaulted my nostrils, a dank haze of sweat, charred tallow and sour liquor that made me want to gag. Next to me, Charan Singh let out a grunt of disapproval. He took one half step to stand in front of me protectively, glowering down at the array of villainous faces that had turned to eye us speculatively, wondering if our throats were worth cutting.

After a moment, they all turned away, obviously deterred by his bulk.

'This way,' the constable said, pointing to the back of the room, which was swathed in shadows. There, seated at a corner table with his back to the wall, Hall-Caine sat waiting, bundled up in a dark military overcoat and a matching Ascot cap. He looked utterly unaffected by the griminess of his surroundings, reading a newspaper while seeming as composed as if he were taking tea at Brooks's on St James Street.

'Ah, Your Majesty! Here you are at last,' he said expansively. 'Would you care to join me?'

The courtly formality of his manner was rather jarring to say the least, given the squalor of our surroundings. Stifling a snort, I sat down and asked, 'Could we get to it, please?'

'Of course. I have a lead for you. Another clue.' He nodded at the constable. 'Tell him.'

'Yesterday morning, a woman was picked up in Colaba by two men in a carriage.'

'Is that so? How does that concern me?' I asked.

'She was a white woman, sir. And the men who picked her up are known thugs, associates of the Duke of Bombay.'

This tidbit made me frown. 'Who is this duke ...? I've never heard of him.'

'It's a nickname. He's not a real duke, of course, but he is a bit of a legend,' Hall-Caine chimed in. 'Rumor has it that he runs the white trade in Bombay. Nobody knows what he looks like, what his age is, or where he came from. All we know for sure is that he has a fearsome reputation.'

'Does he now?'

'Indeed. He likes to cut off people's heads.'

'Surely you're joking?'

'Oh no. He's as bad as one of those Borneo Charlies. Why, last year, some Parsis tried to make a move on his territory. They all turned up headless, rotting in Mahim Creek. It was quite a scandal, let me tell you. The press had a field day with it. The commissioner nearly lost his job.'

'Where can I find this duke?'

Hall-Caine smiled. 'As it turns out, he owns this tavern. This whole street, actually.'

'Is that so?' I raised one eyebrow. 'Let me guess. You checked and discovered that the carriage that picked up the white lady in question was headed for an address owned by this mysterious duke?'

'Why, you're positively clairvoyant.' He gave me a grin and said, 'In fact, the carriage brought her to the last building in this very lane.'

I nodded and started to rise. 'Well then, let's go get her. Shall we?'

'Calm down, Mr Singh. You can't just march in and break the door down. This isn't Rajpore. It's Bombay. You wouldn't make it ten steps before the duke's men cut you down.' He beckoned for me to sit back down. 'What I would suggest is a touch of subtlety.'

'What do you have in mind?'

'Well, the building in question is a brothel. What I suggest is that we wait until dusk. Once the sun sets, the street becomes crowded with patrons looking for a bit of rough and tumble. Then, using the mob as cover, we can approach the duke's lair without suspicion and gain entry pretending to be punters looking for a good time. Once we are inside, I am sure I can find some way to corner this duke and arrange for you to question him.'

He sat back and gave me a triumphant smile, as if he had just hatched a plan to steal the crown jewels. I mulled over his scheme. It was clever enough, seemingly without any obvious flaws, much to my dismay. Unfortunately, it wasn't something I could work with, and I told him as much.

'That's a fine plan of action,' I said. 'However, it has one insurmountable defect. The problem, you see, is that I am not a patient man. I have always been one for direct action rather than playing the waiting game.'

Rising to my feet, I shrugged. 'I think I will go and have a dekko at this duke now. 'Would you care to join us, Mr Hall-Caine?'

'Oh no, not me! I am much too attached to my head, I'm afraid.'

'Very well. Come along, Charan Singh. Let us leave Mr Hall-Caine to his newspaper.'

'Hold on a minute,' Hall-Caine said before I could leave. 'Your man ... is he armed?'

'Always,' said Charan Singh, pulling up his achkan to reveal an oversized Webley revolver tucked into his waistband.

'What about you?' He turned to me. 'Have you a gun?'

'No, I didn't think I'd need one.'

'Here, take mine,' Hall-Caine offered me a small snub-nosed Browning pistol. 'Try not to use it unless you absolutely have to. We are very strict about guns here in Bombay.'

'I think I'll pass. I haven't yet had to use a pistol where my wits will suffice.'

'As you wish,' he said, making the gun disappear into his waistcoat as effortlessly as a cardsharp. 'You're a braver man than me, Mr Singh. Bonne chance!'

I rolled my eyes at such unnecessary drama and set off at a trot with Charan Singh on my heels, as faithful as a hound.

The building in question was a small whitewashed house with blue gables and windows. It seemed rustic, quaint even, quite incongruous amidst the squalor of its surroundings. We crossed the road and approached the door without any intervention. Charan Singh kept his eyes peeled for any sight of the duke's coterie, but no one showed up.

There was no bell at the door, only an old-fashioned knocker shaped like a laughing tiger. I tugged at its tail and a loud clack echoed, as violent as a gunshot. A long minute elapsed before an ancient munshi opened the door and peered at me curiously.

'I'd like to see the gentleman who calls himself the Duke of Bombay,' I said.

He looked me up and down before replying, 'Who may I say is calling?'

'The Maharaja of Rajpore, Sikander Singh.'

If I had expected my title to impress him, it failed miserably. He didn't bat an eyelid.

'This way, if you please,' he said, offering me a toothless smile and throwing open the door.

It was all very civilized. He led us past a row of curtained alcoves, behind which was the aforementioned brothel no doubt, judging by the array of lascivious grunts that could be heard emanating from within. At the end of the passage was another door, and beyond that was a small courtyard guarded by a cadre of tough-looking Afghans who exchanged scowls with Charan Singh. At the far end of the courtyard, the munshi conducted us into another house, up a flight of steps into what turned out to be a large room done up in Carrara marble and ivory chintz. It was most unexpected, an elegant salon that could have adorned a townhouse in Knightsbridge rather than a dingy tenement in Bombay's red-light area.

After ushering us into this peculiarly posh parlor, and having us seated on an overstuffed chaise, the munshi offered me a glass of sherry that I refused.

'If you would care to wait a few moments,' he said, 'I shall fetch my master presently.'

Perhaps five minutes passed before the elusive duke made his entry. He was a big man, not quite as large as Charan Singh, but broader across the shoulders and narrower at the waist. An Anglo-Indian, I surmised, for he was very brown but with a pair of startlingly green eyes. And a man who had seen more than his fair share of trouble, judging by his broken-nosed visage, which was as battered as a pugilist.

His accoutrement, however, did not match his thuggish face. an immaculate white silk dhoti and high-collared jacket, paired with round wireframe glasses that made him look more like a schoolteacher than a career criminal.

He gave me rather a friendly smile before taking out a pocket watch and tapping its face impatiently. 'I can give you ten minutes, gentlemen, I'm afraid, not a second more.'

His English was unexpectedly excellent, his accent pure Oxbridge with just the slightest of lisps. A testament to countless hours spent with a diction teacher who had no doubt been handy with a cane, I guessed, given the way he clenched his hands each time he pronounced a multisyllabic word.

'I take it you are the self-styled Duke of Bombay.'

'An unfortunate sobriquet, but yes, I have been called by that name.'

'I am—' I began to say.

'You, my dear fellow, need no introduction,' he interrupted me. 'I've heard of you, of course, Sikander Singh, the royal sleuth. Who hasn't, in my line of trade?'

'And what exactly is that?'

'Oh, a bit of this and a bit of that. They call Bombay the city of dreams, and you could say that I make some of those dreams come true.'

'Is that a polite way of saying you're a pimp and a procurer?'

I was trying to pick a fight, but he was much too smooth to take the bait.

'Come now, let's not be crude. Much as I would love to compare whose manhood is larger, I doubt you have come all this way to play such puerile games.'

He sat down opposite me and fixed me with a level glare.

'Shall we stop wasting time and get down to business?' he said, tapping the watch again. 'The moving hand, and so on.'

'Why not?' I retorted nonchalantly, 'We are here for the young woman you abducted yesterday.'

I had been expecting surprise, hoping for outrage, but he didn't miss a blink.

'Me ... abduct a woman? You make me sound like a villain from one of Miss Steel's novels,' he said. 'Don't be preposterous. As I said earlier, I'm just a humble businessman.'

'Don't try to deny it,' I said, much more belligerent than I had intended. 'We have witnesses who saw your men snatch a memsahib off the streets in Colaba and bundle her into one of your carriages. If you know what is best for you, I would suggest you hand her over to me. And before you get any ideas, let me warn you, I have a flying squad waiting outside. If you decide to try anything, they will come tearing in at the snap of my finger.'

It was a bluff, of course. For a moment, I thought I had him, that this naked show of aggression had managed to intimidate him. Instead, he threw his head back and let out a voluble laugh.

'You really are as reckless as the rumor mills say, aren't you?' he exclaimed. 'You come barging in here and try to threaten me in my own home.' Shaking his head, he gave me a sharkish grin. 'This is the first time in years someone has threatened me. I must admit, it's quite ... refreshing.'

The grin wavered and then vanished. I couldn't help but shiver. For the first time, I saw the truth under the convivial exterior, a hard-faced and cold-eyed killer.

'Let me tell you, Mr Singh, there isn't a policeman within three square miles who isn't on my payroll. And if I did decide to become unpleasant,' he nodded at Charan Singh who had involuntarily reached up to loosen the revolver in his waistband, 'even with your giant friend and the blunderbuss he has hidden away, they wouldn't find a trace of either of you ever again.'

And then, just like that, the moment passed. His mask slipped back into place, an impressive, if not somewhat unnerving, metamorphosis.

'But as I said, I have no desire to pick a fight. I'm a businessman, that's all.'

'A businessman who traffics in white flesh!'

He clapped his hands. 'Oh marvelous! There isn't an inch of give in you, is there? I appreciate that. You'd have made a brilliant criminal. Sadly, Mr Singh, I hate to tell you, but you have it all wrong.'

'In that case, please do correct my misapprehension.'

He chuckled. 'Miss Apprehension! How very droll!'

Rising to his feet, he indicated that I follow him. 'I think it would be best if I took you to the source. Come along, there's someone I'd like you to meet.'

Charan Singh and I exchanged a wary look. It could be a trap, I considered, but then dismissed the thought after a moment's consideration. If the man had wanted to kill us, he would have done it already.

I wracked my brain, trying to think what my next move should be. It did not take me long to come to the conclusion that my best choice was to go with him. I stood up. A heartbeat later, Charan Singh followed my lead, suspicion writ plainly upon his face. The duke gave him a grin and snapped his fingers. On cue, the munshi stepped forward and held out one hand. Scowling, Charan Singh looked at me. I nodded and reluctantly, the old Sikh handed over his beloved revolver.

'Don't worry,' the duke reassured him. 'I will make sure it is returned to you when we are done.'

Pulling aside a tapestry, he revealed another door hidden in the far wall.

'This way,' he said and led us into a small tunnel, which opened up into a curved stairwell. We went up two flights of steps and came to another door that was guarded by two massive Pathans, each half a head taller than Charan Singh.

'Here,' the duke paused, knocking on the door and waiting patiently until a voice announced, 'Come.'

Turning, he waved me forward. 'Do you know why I am called the Duke of Bombay, Mr Singh? It's because in my veins flows the blood of kings, for I am descended from Charles de Bourbon himself, who once ruled over half of Europe. I am his direct heir, in all but name.'

With that cryptic declaration, he eased open the door and urged me to enter. 'After you, if you please.'

Inside, I found myself in a study of sorts, a small room lined by leather-bound books, its center dominated by an ivory-topped table behind which sat an elderly woman. Her appearance was truly remarkable—skin so pale that she could have been an albino, silver hair tied into a simple plait, her bearing regal, her back as slim and straight as a eucalyptus, even though she must have been eighty. In her youth, she must have been very attractive. She still retained some of that sparkle, a humorous glint in her eyes, but it was backed by flint, I noted, as she put down the book she had been reading and studied me with a wary insouciance.

The duke leaned over to give her a peck on one cheek.

'This is my mother, Mr Singh. She is the real duke of Bombay, or shall I say duchess?'

The old woman grinned before waving me to a chair. 'I take it that my son has been boasting about my antecedents.'

'Is it true? Are you really related to the House of Bourbon?'

She laughed. 'I'm afraid my son is taking some liberties with the truth. The real story is slightly more complicated. You see, one of Charles de Bourbon's illegitimate sons, Jean Philippe, was forced to flee to India in exile after he killed a man in a duel. He ended up at Emperor Akbar's court and married an Indian Christian. Their descendants became soldiers of fortune after the sack of Delhi by Nader Shah, first in the service of Gwalior and then Bhopal. My mother, Eleanor, was born in Bhopal. When she was eleven, she was seen by the Nawab of Pathankot at a party, who offered to buy her to be his concubine. Rather than being sold into servitude, she ran away and came to Bombay instead. Here, she had many adventures and made a name for herself, first as a singer and then as a courtesan who was in much demand, especially as she claimed descent from European royalty.'

'That would make you ...?'

'Yes, if rumor is to be believed, I am the true Queen of France.' She laughed, and I laughed with her.

'It's a good story,' I said.

'It is, isn't it? But who can trust my mother's word? The truth is that whatever her beginnings, however grand her claims, she ended up as a whore who plied her trade in a brothel not two miles from here.'

'That is the only fact I do know for sure, Mr Singh, that I was born and grew up here, on these very streets. And that I was six years old when my birth mother succumbed to malaria, after which I had three other mothers who proceeded to take her place.

'My second mother was a Maharashtrian madam, Savitri. I was sold to her for six annas, but she loved me like I was her own flesh and blood. She taught me never to trust a man who was not family.

'My third mother was a Jewess from Syria, Esther. She bought me when I was eleven and taught me how to steal, how to tempt men with my eyes and how words are more lethal than the deadliest of poisons.

'My fourth mother was an Irish nun, Sister Siobhan O'Connell. She stole me away from the Jewess when I was thirteen, thinking she was rescuing me from what she called "this cesspit of sin". She was the one who taught me to speak English, enrolled me at St Mary's and promised me that I would be safe and happy when I found a good Englishman to marry. But it didn't take, Mr Singh.' She grinned.

I saw the girl she must once have been, a tempest, impossible to contain. 'Unfortunately, the cesspit was in my blood, and so I ran away and came back here, to Lal Bazaar.

'I guess I am a mushroom, white outside but with a heart that is brown. I like it here much more than in the white town. Here, the people are honest. Lust, greed and hunger; those are the inviolate truths of humanity. In Lal Bazaar, we don't try to hide behind a veneer of civilization. We *live*, Mr Singh, and that was what I wanted more than anything else, to live by my terms, not merely exist.

'After I came back, I became a thief and a pickpocket, and then a fan dancer. But my real business was information. Rumors and gossip, hearsay and secrets, that's the only commodity that is truly priceless, Mr Singh. That is what real power is. I suppose I might even have ended up a whore like my mother, if I had not tried to pick the billfold of one Charles Forjett on one fateful day. Perhaps you have heard of him?'

'Surely you don't mean Commissioner Forjett of the Bombay Police?'

'The one and the same, but I knew him as Madras Charlie.' She let out a bird-like laugh. 'I was his mistress, his bibi, for twenty-two wonderful years. We had all manner of adventures together, and he gave me six beautiful boys. Unfortunately, when he retired and went back to England to be with his shrew of a wife, he was forced to leave me and my boys behind, but not before carving the city into five parts, or territories, for us—the docks, the fort, the mainland, the marshes and the native town—and five dhandas—usury, smuggling, liquor, gambling, and hawala. One of our sons runs each territory and each business.

'And the sixth son? What about him?'

'Why, he is a judge, of course! One of the most successful in the city.'

'That's quite a story,' I said, clapping my hands. 'But it still does not explain, Madam, why this son,' I pointed at the Duke, 'is abducting white women off the streets.'

The duchess gave me a wounded look. 'I have committed many sins, Mr Singh. I am a hawaladar and an opium smuggler. I run gambling dens and sharabkhanas. I steal and lie and cheat, but I have never, not once, traded in women.'

'That sounds most unlikely, considering we are sitting above a brothel.'

I could see that my words had offended her. 'These girls? I do not own them. I merely offer them a chance to live life on their own terms, just as my mother chose for herself. They are all here of their own volition.'

She leaned back with a sigh. The Duke hurried to pour her a cup of tisane from a bone china kettle. 'I am sure you are aware that trafficking is a real problem in Bombay. From all around the Orient, women are spirited away and sold into sexual slavery, to satisfy the carnal cravings of soldiers and merchants. Jewish girls from Syria and Palestine, Arabs and Abyssinians, Kurds and Afghans, Japoni and Malay, and, of course, the most popular of all, white-skinned Tatars, Russians and Circassians who are down on their luck. They all wash up here, in Lal Bazaar, and this city eats them alive. Are you aware, Sir, each year over a hundred firangi women die in this district alone? Consumption, yellow fever, malaria, venereal disease, childbirth, and worst of all, violence. These girls, they live lives shaped by lust and desire, which consumes them like candles burning out too soon. So, if I can, me and my boy offer a service. We protect them, keep them safe and try to keep them alive, but only if they want our help. We do not coerce them or hold them against their wills.'

'Surely you don't expect me to believe that you're doing this out of the goodness of your hearts?' I asked sardonically, unable to hide my doubts.

Before she could answer, the duke decided to cut in. 'Tell me, Mr Singh, this girl you are looking for, what are your intentions toward her?'

'I have none, I assure you. I am merely trying to locate her for my friend. He is affianced to her and has asked me to make sure she has come to no harm.'

Now it was his mother's turn. 'And if you do find her, are you going to drag her back and force her to marry him?'

'Of course not. I am a detective, Madam, not a villain. I merely want to talk to her.'

'Very well,' she said. 'I can arrange that much at least.' She clapped her hands together imperiously. A moment later, the munshi, who had obviously been listening at the door, came striding in accompanied by a young white woman who looked at me warily.

She was certainly attractive, if in a rather battered way, with good Hibernian bones. Although one eye bore the shadowy remnants of a bruise, and her nose looked like it had been broken recently and had healed a bit crooked.

My heart sank when I saw her. This was obviously the memsahib Hall-Caine's men had seen getting into the duke's carriage. Unfortunately for me, she was much too blonde—her hair was practically the color of ash—which meant she could not be Miss Hartley.

'Here she is,' the duke announced. 'The young lady you have come looking for, who has led you on such a merry chase.'

'I don't suppose your name is Mary Hartley, is it?' I asked the question even though I knew what the answer would inevitably be.

The girl flinched. 'Miss Hartley? Oh no! You are quite mistaken. I'm Mrs Finchley, or at least I was until last week.'

When she said those words, I bit back a curse. *What were the odds?* It was the wrong memsahib, not Miss Hartley but another woman altogether, that too for the second time. What rotten luck!

'I hear you have come to take me back,' Mrs Finchley said, her voice querulous. 'I beg you, please leave me be. I don't want to return to my husband. I cannot. He's a brute, I tell you, an animal!'

With that exclamation, she started to sob. I took a hesitant step forward to try and comfort her, but she recoiled and quickly ran to the duchess, kneeling to bury her head in her lap.

'Please, please don't let him have me.'

'Slow down,' I said. 'Why don't you tell me the full story?'

'Go on, child,' the duchess said, stroking her hair gently. 'He won't hurt you.'

Mrs Finchley took a moment to calm herself and then turned to me, her eyes brimming with sorrow.

'I came out with the fleet three seasons ago. My husband, Andrew Finchley, is with Cockburn & Company. He manages one of their coffee plantations in Kotagiri. At first, it was a very pleasant life, even if a trifle lonely. I was like a princess, with khidmatgars to wait on my every need, with every comfort I could imagine. And Andrew! He was like a dream, as caring and kind as Darcy. But then, as time passed, after the first winter, I realized that the man I had married was like Wickham, Sir, not Darcy after all. He was an ogre, a monster masquerading as a gentleman. He liked to drink, you see, arrack by the gallon, and gin. And he is a degenerate, dissipated creature. He would beat me with a horsewhip and subject me to the most horrid of humiliations. Not only did he forcibly thrust himself upon me several times when I refused to do as he wished, he once made me submit to four of his friends while he watched, like I was a broodmare.'

'Is that why you decided to run away?'

'Yes, I had to. Before he killed me, or I killed myself. One of the railway men took pity on me when I told him my story and agreed to bring me here to Bombay. But then ...' her voice choked, 'he betrayed me, Sir. He took all that I had and left me with nothing.'

'How did you happen to end up here? At this address?'

'I have a cousin, a distant cousin, Margaret. She is rather a wild creature, the black sheep of the family. She is married now, to a pepper farmer in Ceylon, but years ago she had told me about the duchess and her establishment. When Margaret ran away from home and came out to India on the fleet, only to be rejected by her suitor, she worked here for a brief while, until she could earn enough to buy passage back to England. She confided in me about this place. When I found myself in the direst of straits, I did not know where else to turn.'

'So, you came here willingly, Madam? You would whore yourself out, of your own free will?'

The word 'whore' made her color rise, her face reddening with barely repressed outrage. 'I have no choice, Sir,' she said, her voice hardening. 'What am I to do? Live in servitude to a man who treats me like an animal? Let him beat me until one day he kills me and makes it look like an accident?'

She looked at the duchess who gave her a nod of reassurance.

'No, I refuse to be helpless any more. To paraphrase Mr Marlowe, it is far better to rule in hell than to suffer in heaven. Here, at least, I am my own mistress. I will make my way back home, on my own terms, even if it means laying flat on my back so that I can get up on my own two feet someday.'

'There you have it, the truth,' the duchess said. 'Now what do you intend to do, Mr Singh?'

I gave her a frown. I liked the woman, damn it. She had chutzpah! And I liked her son, too. He was more of a gentleman, in his own twisted way, than most of my peers in the Chamber of Princes. *But could I trust them enough to take their word?* They were criminals after all. Lying was their stock-in-trade.

I saw that Mrs Finchley was watching me, entreaty patent in her eyes. That was what helped me make up my mind, the piteous look on her face. No matter how dire her current circumstances, she was right. It was better to be a whore than to be enslaved to a deviant and libertine.

'Very well,' I said, rising to my feet. 'Thank you for your time, ladies. If you would excuse me—'

'Are you going to tell the police I am here?' Mrs Finchley asked nervously, interrupting me mid-sentence.

'I don't see how this is any of my business, Madam. You are free to do as you please.' I gave her a smile. 'Good luck, Mrs Finchley. If you wish, I can offer to cover your passage back to England, if that's what you truly desire.'

'Oh no, Sir!' she said proudly. 'I am not looking for charity. This is the path I have chosen. I will make my own way in the world.'

'In that case, let me leave you with a name. If you ever find yourself in trouble and need help, go to the police and ask for Mr Hall-Caine. He will help you if you mention my name. And I wish you the very best. If only I could track your husband down, I would very much like to teach him a lesson he would not soon forget.'

With that out of the way, I turned to the old woman. 'Madam,' I said, bowing deeply as I took her hand and kissed it. 'This has been a most interesting encounter. If you would allow it, I would like to come see you again. I am sure you have some truly filthy stories to tell.'

'Oh, that I do,' she grinned. Turning to her son, she gave him an imperious nod. 'He has done us a service, my boy. Now you must repay him.'

'Of course,' the duke replied.

Reaching into his waistcoat, he pulled out a coin and offered it to me. Hesitantly, I took it. Turning it over in my fingers, I realized it was a Portuguese moidore. At least three hundred years old, judging by the faded cross inscribed on its face and the Quinas on the obverse, which was so worn that it was almost invisible.

'I can't accept this,' I said.

'Please,' the Duke replied. 'It's a token of respect. If you ever find yourself in trouble anywhere in Bombay, just use the coin. We will make sure help gets to you, no questions asked.'

CHAPTER 15

Located at the westernmost edge of what had once been the islet of Bombay, Malabar Hill commanded a spectacular view, with the azure expanse of the Arabian Sea on one side and the congested sprawl of the city on the other.

Before the arrival of the Portuguese, its only inhabitants had been the dreaded pirates from which the promontory derived its name, who had utilized its rocky heights to keep a look out for vessels unfortunate enough to stray too close to their stronghold, thus becoming easy prey.

When the English had taken over the city, the hill was still covered by a verdant expanse of forest. It was Mountstuart Elphinstone who, during his tenure as the governor of Bombay, cut a road to the peak and built the first bungalow atop a ridge overlooking the curving expanse of the Back Bay. In the three decades since, Malabar Hill had become the most sought-after real estate in the city, especially for the Marwari and Zoroastrian merchants who had come to be the cornerstone of Bombay's business community.

In many ways, it was the Zoroastrians, or the Parsis as they were commonly called, whose wealth was responsible for turning Bombay from a dingy port into the modern city it was today. The word 'Parsi' quite literally meant 'of Persia'. That was where they were from ethnically, the fertile flood plains of ancient Iran. In the seventh century, the rise of the Islamic caliphates had forced the descendants of the Achaemenid and Sassanid empires to flee their homeland. A small group had migrated south from Iran to India. There was a charming story about their arrival, which my mother had once narrated to me. As chronicled in the *Qissa-e-Sanjan*, the first Parsi refugees had landed in the province of Sanjan in Gujarat, which had been ruled by a king named the Jadi Raja. If legend is to be believed, when the Parsis approached him and requested asylum, he rebuffed them by using a brimming bowl of milk as a metaphor, signifying that there was no place for migrants in his already crowded kingdom. The leader of the Parsis, a clever fellow whose name has sadly been forgotten by posterity, responded by taking a handful of sugar and sprinkling it in the milk, to suggest that rather than displacing the locals, they would assimilate with them and sweeten their lives.

The Jadi Raja was so impressed by this answer that he granted the Parsis permission to stay, provided they fulfilled three conditions. First, they had to learn Gujarati; second, their women had to start wearing saris; and finally, they were not permitted to carry weapons of any kind.

The Parsis stuck to these dictates assiduously and flourished in Gujarat, earning an enviable reputation as businessmen, merchants and traders. Nearly a thousand years later, in the 1600s, when the East India Company took over the seven islands of Bombay, they flocked there in droves and gradually came to occupy a unique position in the city's cosmogony. The English had chosen to trust them over the other communities and were quick to appoint Parsis to positions of power in the civil administration, the trading guilds and the public works department. The Parsis, in turn, were only too happy to embrace English habits, with an alacrity that was nothing short of astounding. In fact, that was where the other, more derogatory name for the Parsi community came from; 'bawa', supposedly derived from the Hindi word 'babu', which meant part-English, for they were about as anglicized as anyone could aspire to be, from their accents to their passion for cricket, Elgar, and tea.

It was near Malabar Hill that Bombay's Parsi community first settled, constructing their baghs and agiaries arrayed around the sacred dakhma, the tower of silence that had been built at the base of the hill in 1672.

As it turned out, the Billimoria manse was just a short distance away from this ancient landmark, at the center of a sprawling estate located in the shadow of the famous Hanging Gardens.

When the Mercedes slowed down at their front gate, I couldn't help but be gripped by an unexpected sense of déjà vu. It took me a moment to realize why the building seemed so familiar. Its facade was an almost exact replica of St James's Palace, except faced by an awfully brown sandstone, the sort that could only be found in Gujarat. I stifled a grin. The Billimorias obviously had more money than good taste, which meant that this interview was destined to be nothing short of interesting.

A little research had managed to uncover a fair bit of information about the Billimoria family and its antecedents. They were firmly new money, their fortune cemented very recently, acquired mainly from shipping and the China trade. The patriarch, Rustom, had a sound reputation as a trader, along with higher aspirations, it seemed, because he had acquired a title for himself just two years previously. As for his wife, she was rumored to be one of the invisible queens of Bombay society, hosting not just one but two of the summer season's premier balls. The family also sponsored a race at the Annual Derby, called the Billimoria Shield, where the winning horse received the princely sum of a thousand rupees.

As for the son, Percy, his reputation was much less exalted than that of his parents. If the grapevine was to be believed, he was said to be quite the lad about town, the very epitome of a young man born with far too much money and not enough good sense. That was exactly the detail I considered as I mulled over my options, trying to decide what was the best strategy to follow. If this was Rajpore, I could have barged right in, damn the consequences! But this was Bombay. I was a rank outsider here, and with Michael High-and-Bloody-Mighty O'Dwyer putting me on the constabulary's watchlist, I could not afford to stir up any trouble. That realization forced my hand somewhat. I would, quite literally, have to make my next move with a touch of finesse. Somehow, I would have to find a way to interview the boy face to face, which would be no easy task since I had neither an invitation nor a letter of introduction. That left me only one choice as far as I could see. I would have to play the airheaded dilettante, the wealthy wastrel, a role I thoroughly despised. Still, needs must, as they say. And this was the only route I could envision to bluff my way through the front door and gain Percy Billimoria's confidence long enough to hopefully get him to open up about his relationship with Miss Hartley.

Putting on my most vacuous smile, I dismounted from the Mercedes and ambled up to knock on the front door. There was no answer. I knocked again, more forcefully this time, but to no avail.

Just as I was about to lose patience and give up, I heard the soft sound of singing nearby. It seemed to be originating from behind the house. After telling Charan Singh to stay with the car, I set off at a brisk trot, circling the building until I found myself standing in front of a topiary maze so well pruned that it would have brought tears to the eyes of Inigo Jones himself.

It took me a minute to realize that this was where the song was coming from. Even as I entered the maze, the song swelled, nearing its crescendo. I paused, smiling as the words became more discernible. I could now recognize the lyrics, which were from a popular Parsi drama whose name I could not recall immediately. Although, if I remembered correctly, it was actually meant to be a duet between two women.

In this case, however, it was being sung by one singer, and a good one at that, because she was switching effortlessly between a deep contralto and a rich soprano.

'*Sisters, how sweet this sherbet is,*' she sang.

'*Drink—drink and enjoy it.*

Ha? Such are the world's ways that we drink sherbet, and men drink our sherbet.

What do you mean, sister?

Indeed, how would you understand?

You both are like flower buds; when the thirsty bees suck the flowers' honeydew when they bloom, you will understand.

So, were you, too, at one time a flower bud? And what was your bee like?

My bee is my rightful husband and none other.'

Stifling a laugh at the cheeky double entendre, I took a left and then a right until I arrived at the heart of the labyrinth. There, I came face to face with an older woman, perhaps sixty, who was engaged in planting orchids by the look of it.

When she set eyes on me, her voice wavered, and she fell silent.

'Who are you?' she snapped, obviously irritated at being interrupted. 'What do you want?'

'I was hoping to speak with Percy Billimoria,' I replied. 'Is he around?'

'Oh, Percy's not here,' she said. 'You can speak with me instead. I'm his mother.'

I hesitated, taken aback. I must confess, I had fallen victim to that most lamentable of traps faced by any investigator, namely preconception. The name Lady Billimoria had led me to conjure a vision of a tall, cantankerous Zoroastrian dowager in the vein of Miss Havisham, with one of those beaky snouts for which the Parsis were so renowned. However, much to my surprise, this woman was short and rather stout, almost dumpy. Rather than being clad in chintz and crepe, she was dressed more like a farmhand, in a pair of hickory stripe overalls and an immense straw hat that did little to tame a wild bird's nest of prematurely graying hair.

Ordinarily, I would have been a little shocked at the sight of a woman in men's trousers, but somehow, in this instance, it seemed very apt. This unconventional choice of accoutrement, coupled with the stern glare she gave me, told me everything I needed to know about her. Here was a woman who couldn't care less what people thought of her. I liked her immediately.

'Lady Billimoria, do allow me to introduce myself,' I said. 'I am Sikander Singh, the Maharaja of Rajpore.'

I offered her a quarter bow, just deep enough to be respectful. She did not reciprocate my greeting. Instead, she arched her back and let out a groan before briskly sweeping off her bonnet and mopping her forehead with one hand, leaving behind a broad steak of mud. Her face was handsome rather than beautiful, her cheeks and forehead wrinkled by a webwork of fine lines, which suggested she laughed often and wholeheartedly. She had made no attempts to make herself up, no powder nor rouge, and to my dismay, her nose was very ordinary, lacking any trace of that famed Parsi aquilinity.

The only striking feature she possessed were her eyes, which were the coldest of brown, gleaming the same molten shade as copper as she peered at me speculatively.

Faced with such unrelenting scrutiny, I tried not to cringe, feeling far too much like a recalcitrant schoolboy who had been hauled up in front of the headmistress.

'What do you want with Percy?' she asked very brusquely.

'I was hoping, Madam, to talk to him about a Miss Mary Hartley. I believe they came out on the *Caledonia* together just a few days ago.'

Lady Billimoria's reaction at the mention of Miss Hartley's name was quite unexpected. Letting out a dismissive snort, she turned away and knelt back down, fixing her attention on a startlingly purple narrow-stemmed blossom.

I waited patiently for her to say something, to tell me where her son was, but when it became apparent that she was bent upon ignoring me, I advanced and sank down in the mud next to her, entirely uncaring about the state of my trousers.

Wordlessly, I watched as she carefully pruned away the weeds surrounding the flower with a secateur.

'This is one of the rarest species in the world,' she explained after a minute or two, giving me a sidelong glare. 'It has taken me the better part of a decade to get it to take root here, in Bombay's uncaring soil. God willing, this is the year it will finally flower and all my labors will pay off.'

'I recognize it,' I said. 'Cypripedium calceolus, is it not? More commonly known as the lady's slipper orchid.'

Her mouth curved into an involuntary smile. 'Very good! And do you know where that name comes from?'

'As a matter of fact, I do. While most people tend to think it comes from the fact that the flower bears more than a passing resemblance to a woman's sandal, the actual botanical name can be translated quite literally from the Latin as "the shoes of Venus".' I grinned. 'Legend has it that a shepherdess was sent out by Goddess Venus to fetch her slippers from deep in the forest, but when she found them, she decided to try them on. In a fit of rage, Venus transformed her into this flower.'

Lady Billimoria clicked her tongue, as if to applaud this answer. 'Not just a pretty face, I see.'

'I enjoy a fine story, Your Ladyship, just as you do.'

It was undoubtedly the right thing to say because her manner seemed to change. The cold front thawed slightly as she gave me a grudging nod, as if to suggest she was willing to give me a chance.

Patiently, I waited it out while she snipped away at a few more errant weeds before straightening back up. I offered her my arm for support, but she waved me away, massaging the base of her spine with a groan.

'Oh, how I envy you and your young knees!' she declared.

'Hardly young, Madam,' I retorted. 'I am well over the hill.'

That reply earned a chuckle, a surprisingly girlish sound. 'If you are over the hill, young man, then I might as well be under it.'

'Pish tosh, Your Ladyship! Your best years are yet to come; I am sure of it.'

It was a base attempt at flattery, one which could have backfired drastically. Thankfully, Lady Billimoria was quite as susceptible to a compliment as any woman. Her dour face flowered into a broad smile.

'Oh, do stop all this ladyship-wadyship nonsense, won't you? Call me Persis,' she commanded. Turning, she beckoned that I follow her. 'Come along then, let's get a cup of tea.'

'Actually, Persis, if it isn't too much trouble, I'd much rather have a glass of champagne,' I said.

She let out a guffaw, amused by my boldness. 'Oh, why not! It's six o'clock somewhere!'

Pursing her lips, she led me out of the maze, to a nearby pergola covered with interlocked wisteria. Beneath the welcome shade of this bower, two rough benches had been arrayed on either side of a wide pine table, atop which was an array of half-potted planters and garden implements, along with an ice bucket inside which a frosted bottle was cooling, flanked by two cut-glass goblets.

I waited until Lady Billimoria settled on to the far bench and then took a seat opposite her. We watched each other, in companionable silence. Lady Billimoria made no move to uncork the bottle or pour me a drink. Instead, she reached into her pocket to pull out a crumpled packet of Chesterfields. Plucking out a slim cigarette, she lit it with a gas lighter and took a deep puff. I watched her, fascinated. She smoked just like a man, pinching the cigarette between her thumb and forefinger rather than holding it delicately, as a well-bred lady would.

Acknowledging my scrutiny, she offered me the pack, but I refused.

'I am trying to get rid of my bad habits,' I explained, 'before they get rid of me.'

'But you still drink?'

'Persis,' I rolled my eyes theatrically. 'Leave a man some reason to live.'

Another chuckle. 'In that case, far be it for me to stop you,' she said, gesturing expansively at the ice bucket. 'Go ahead, help yourself.'

Picking up the bottle, I gave her an approving grin. It was a Pommery 1902, a very decent vintage indeed, and rather expensive to boot. Either she was trying to impress me, or the Billimorias were richer than Croesus himself.

Pouring out half a flute, I offered it to her. She declined, waiting patiently until I took a long draught from the glass before fixing me with a glacial glare.

'Now tell me, Mr Singh. What is this nonsense about Miss Hartley? And what does it have to do with my son?' she asked, raising one razor-sharp eyebrow.

'As I was saying, I was hoping to speak with your son. I was informed by a reliable source that he had several, ahem, interactions with her on the journey out.'

Her eyes narrowed. 'And what, if I may ask, is your interest in this woman?'

'I have no personal interest in Miss Hartley, I assure you. I am sad to say that she has gone missing. Her fiancé, who happens to be an old friend, has asked me to locate her.' I gave her a meaningful glare, as if to punctuate the direness of my mission. 'It is imperative that I speak to Percy before it is too late. I am sure you understand.'

Lady Billimoria considered this explanation, pursing her lips until they were well-nigh invisible.

'Much as I would like to help, as I said, Percy is not here at present.'

'I am happy to wait, Madam, until he returns.'

'Then you will be waiting a very long time,' she sniped. 'I have sent him away to our estate in Gujarat, and he will not return to Bombay until he learns some good sense or acquires a suitable wife, whichever comes first.'

'I sense this is about a woman,' I said, stifling a grin.

'It is,' Lady Billimoria replied. 'Your Englishwoman, as a matter of fact.'

'Would you care to elaborate, Madam?' I asked, sensing the incipient appearance of a clue.

Lady Billimoria sniffed, her derision more than patent. Her eyes darted across the array of half-potted plants lying atop the table, settling at last upon what seemed to be an immature phalaenopsis at one end of the table.

'There! Do you see it?' She exclaimed.

'I'm not sure what you mean, Madam,' I said, peering at the orchid she had indicated, but I saw nothing notable, other than a tiny grasshopper with a bright purple thorax half-hidden behind one blighted leaf.

'That insect there, Mr Singh, the mantis.'

With one deft flourish, she reached out and plucked it off the leaf, holding it up between her thumb and forefinger without a hint of squeamishness.

'Hymenopus coronatus, or the orchid mantis, as it is commonly known. It mimics an orchid so perfectly that it can draw in its prey, which it then consumes.' Frowning, she crushed the insect, wiping her fingers clean of its ichor on her coveralls. 'Your Miss Hartley was not unlike this creature. She was a mimic, a very good one, but a fake nonetheless.'

'You have a low opinion of her, I see. Might I inquire why?'

'Oh, I had no opinion of her whatsoever for most of the voyage. To be honest, I didn't even notice her. That was my mistake. I normally keep out an eye for women like that and make sure Percy steers clear of them by a mile. But your memsahib, she managed to fool even my sharp senses. The first time I was introduced to her, I foolishly dismissed her as a complete non-entity. She was quite ordinary, you see, a quiet little mouse of a thing, at least until the Neptune ball,' Lady Billimoria said, her mouth twisting with a moue of distaste.

'As is tradition, the evening after we left Gibraltar and crossed properly into the Mediterranean, Captain Carruthers hosted a nautical-themed gala to commemorate the occasion. Rivers of champagne and dancing, and the like! It was supposed to be only for first-class passengers, but somehow, your Miss Hartley managed to swing herself an invitation. How, I will never know, but my goodness, she made quite a splash!'

'Is that so?'

'Indeed! Somehow, in the two weeks since we had departed England, she had managed to undergo a complete transformation. Quite like the fairytale, she had gone from a veritable duckling to a swan. And my goodness, did the little strumpet know it! She spent the whole evening batting her eyelashes at all the eligible men on board, both married and bachelors alike.'

'Including your son, I take it?' I observed dryly.

Lady Billimoria shuddered. 'Poor Percy! He's a good boy, but he has taken after his father, I'm afraid. He is a bit of a simpleton really, especially when it comes to matters of the heart. It's that unfortunate combination of being born stupid and wealthy. It's my fault, really. He's my only child, and I dread to say it, I have spoiled him awfully. He has grown far too used to having his way. He has never had to struggle, never starved, never had to wonder how to make ends meet.'

The way she spoke, with a wistful melancholy, made me want to know more of her story. Behind her diffident exterior, Lady Billimoria, it seemed, had hidden depths. At another time and another place, I could have spent a very entertaining afternoon getting to know her. Sadly, on this day, I hadn't a moment to spare.

'When it comes to disappearances, Madam,' I said, 'it is imperative that the missing person be located within seventy-two hours at the most. After that, the trail grows murky, almost impossible to follow. Miss Hartley has been in the wind for almost two days. That means I have perhaps twenty-four hours left at best, time that would be ill-spent having philosophical conversations. If you could tell me exactly what happened, that would be best.'

'She spun a merry web, Mr Singh, that's what happened. And Percy fell squarely into her trap. After the ball, she found every instance to waylay him, every pretense. She knew just what to say to him, and when to ignore him. She played the poor boy like a piccolo.'

'But you were not impressed by her, were you?'

'Not in the slightest! I can tell a zircon from a diamond, Mr Singh. I certainly own enough of them,' she said disdainfully. 'Naturally, when I found out that she had managed to get her hooks in my boy, I was alarmed, to say the very least. I gave Percy a very stern talking-to, absolutely forbade him from seeing her or spending any more time with her, but the little minx had turned his head completely. For the first time in his life, Percy stood up to me. No matter how much I chastised him, he remained adamant. He insisted on continuing to chase after her, like a dog in heat. And then, the night after we departed Malta, he declared that he intended to marry her.'

'Really?'

'Yes! Can you imagine it?' Her voice trembled with emotion. 'I can accept a shipboard romance. My Percy is young still, and all young men have oats to sow, but to decide to propose at sea, that too to a penniless chit; it was a scandal, I tell you, one that I had no intention of permitting.'

'So, you decided to nip it in the bud?'

'Of course, I did. I had to. After all I have been through to get here, I would never allow my only child to fall victim to a gold-digger intent upon finding a rich husband, not as long as I still have breath in my body.'

'That's rather unkind, isn't it, to accuse Miss Hartley of being a gold-digger? Perhaps she really did come to love your son. It isn't unheard of, you know. Shipboard romances are quite du jour these days. In fact, my uncle, Rajendra of Patiala, met his wife, Florence, at sea.'

'Perhaps you're correct,' Lady Billimoria responded, sounding unconvinced, 'but I highly doubt it. As I said earlier, I have an eye for gold-diggers. That girl was the best of them, or should I say the worst!'

'What makes you so sure of that?'

'Why, because I am one, darling.' She laughed, a discordant peal of noise that was rather too strident amidst our sylvan surroundings. 'Or rather, I was, a long time ago. I wasn't born a lady, you know,' she said. 'My husband purchased the title the year before last, along with a rotten borough in Cornwall. That's why we went to England, to sort it all out.'

Finally picking up her glass, she took a tiny, bird-like sip of champagne. 'I had a very ordinary childhood. My father was the priest up at the Saher Agiary. That is where I grew up, a poor dastoor's daughter surrounded by all the burra paisa-wallahs. But I did have one thing going for me,' she smiled, revealing a shadow of the beauty she must once have possessed.

'I may look like a frump now, but back then, I was quite a delicate rose.' Her eyes shone, gleaming with the diamantine patina of fond memories. 'In fact, that's what they called me, the Rose of Malabar Hill. I flirted with all the eligible boys, every single one of them, and all of them wanted to marry me. Why, I once got five offers in one week! But in the end, I decided upon Percy's father.'

'For his money?' I asked impishly.

'Oh no,' she shook her head, 'for his garden. In the end, that was what I fell in love with. Not the man, but this garden, you see.'

She let out a sigh. 'Anyway, that is how I recognized Miss Hartley for who she was. I saw myself in her, the same ambition and the same hunger. That was why I was certain she had fixed her sights on Percy, and why I took it upon myself to dissuade her.'

'By threatening her?'

'No, no! Nothing quite so inept. When a creeper threatens your prize bloom, my dear fellow, you don't cut it off. It will only grow back twice as dense. No, you *redirect* it. That is exactly what I did. I had a brief word with Miss Hartley's chaperone, an Italian contessa of some kind. I was very clever. I told her my husband had lost most of our money recently because two of our ships had sunk, and suggested that it would be so much better for Miss Hartley if she was to redirect her attentions toward one of the other bachelors on board. You know how these Europeans are. They can never resist a juicy bit of gossip!'

'And did it work? This ploy of yours?'

'Of course, it did,' she grinned triumphantly. 'Sure enough, less than a day later, Miss Hartley had lost all interest in my Percy and shifted her amorous inclinations to another gentleman. It was a masterstroke, I tell you, even if I say so myself!'

'You really expect me to accept it was that simple? What about your son? Do you expect me to believe that was the end of Percy's romantic longings? That he just gave up that easily?'

'Well, I did warn him I would disinherit him if he ever spoke to her again,' the grin grew wider, almost shark-like. 'I think that was what did the trick.'

I laughed. 'You really are formidable, Madam.'

'I have my moments,' she agreed. 'Well, there you have it. That is everything I can tell you about your Miss Hartley. For the rest of the voyage, she stayed well clear of my son, and I made sure Percy steered clear of her as well. And as soon as we made landfall, I had him packed off to Udvada, so that she could not track him down and try to hook him again.'

Putting down her glass, she gave me a frown. 'I hope that helps your cause, although I will say this much. Your friend is much better off without Miss Hartley. That woman, she is the sort who is destined for a bitter end. She is trouble, Mr Singh, with a capital T.'

CHAPTER 16

Unlike its very respectable neighbor, Green's Hotel had a less than salubrious reputation.

If the Taj was designed to cater to the sophisticated traveler, Green's was made for the adventurers. The interiors were dingy and the clientele decidedly unsavory, but not unlike Shepheard's in Cairo, Green's had a special something—a panache that was just the right mix of seamy and salacious.

Located directly opposite the damp edifice of the Gateway of India, it was an L-shaped, four-storeyed building with wraparound verandahs and wrought-iron balconies. On the ground floor was a decent restaurant called the Silver Grill, with an alfresco terrace that overlooked the Arabian Sea. Opposite it was the infamous Long Bar, where discerning punters could pick up Parsi, Khoja and Russian girls who were out looking for a good time. At the other end was the billiards parlor and a card room where gambling was permitted, and up on the first floor was the legendary ballroom, where Sylvie the Syrian did the dance of seven veils every Friday, as part of a truly outrageous cabaret revue.

The last time I had been here was almost three years ago, to attend a party hosted by my cousin Jagatjit, the erstwhile maharaja of Kapurthala, to celebrate his fortieth birthday. He had taken over the entire top floor and imported the full chorus line of the Folies Bergère from Paris, putting them up in grand style for six weeks. The press had dubbed them Kapurthala's flamingos, and Jagatjit's birthday had ended with a wild dance in the foyer by seven scantily clad Frenchwomen and one very drunk maharaja. As for me, I had little recollection of the evening other than drinking several magnums of a truly memorable Piper-Heidsieck and waking up seated on Prince Edward's black horse.

As the Mercedes drew to a halt outside the hotel and I dismounted, a lantern-faced Englishwoman emerged from the shadows and brandished a placard in my face that identified her as a member of the Bombay Temperance Union.

'Repent!' she roared. 'Do not get drunk with wine, for that is debauchery, but be filled with the spirit instead before your soul is damned for all eternity.'

'Would you care to move out of my way, Madam?' I said wearily. 'I desperately need a drink.'

She paused, looking bewildered. 'But ... but you must not drink. I have just told you, to drink is to face eternal damnation.'

'If I do not drink, Madam, then how am I to endure your horrendous face!'

That shut her up good and proper. Even as she turned puce with barely repressed outrage, I gave her a rakish grin and sidestepped past her, leaving her to hurl abuses at my receding back.

Once inside, I was glad to see that Green's was still as seedy as ever. Even more to my delight, I saw that the concierge remained the same, Mahbub Pasha, a dour Turk in a frock coat and a fez who greeted me with a wry smile.

'Your Majesty,' he said with a very correct bow, 'back for another birthday? I'm not sure we have enough champagne in stock.'

'Oh no,' I responded. 'Actually, I'm here on police business.'

'How very commendable,' he responded dryly. 'May I know who is the unlucky personage you wish to meet?'

'A captain named Gordon, of the Highlanders.'

'Of course, who else could it be?' He pointed toward the back of the hotel. 'You will find him in the small billiards room, Your Highness. It has become his haunt since he arrived. He has been drinking quite heavily and trouncing all our regulars most relentlessly for the last two days. And if I may offer a warning, you should be aware that the gentleman in question is rather a raucous sort who is given to brawling in the back verandah.'

Thanking him, I turned to Charan Singh. 'Take care of him, will you?'

'It never ceases to amaze me, Huzoor, how you seem to know every doorman, major-domo and maitre d' east of Morocco.'

'It's something my father taught me. If you take care of the gatekeepers, no door will remain closed to you for long.'

The old Sikh smiled. 'Just when I think I know everything about you, you manage to surprise me.'

The affection in his tone left me feeling rather embarrassed.

'Oh, shut up and get on with it,' I said, feigning irritation.

Charan Singh laughed, delighted that he had managed to throw me off balance. Leaving him to sort out Mahbub Pasha, I forged ahead, pushing my way through the milling crowd gathered outside the Silver Lounge. Even though it was just past six, Green's was already jumping. From the looks of it, the evening's revelry was well under way. I could hear the thumping beats of a ragtime band emanating from the ballroom upstairs, a throbbing tympanum that made me want to snap my fingers in symphony.

You are not here for fun, Sikander Singh, I had to remind myself. *You are on the case. Don't you forget that.*

Shaking my head, I made my way to the billiards room. It was a long, narrow enclosure that wrapped around the rear of the hotel. Inside, there were three green baize-topped tables arranged side by side. The walls were done in oak veneer, lined by a row of tall leather benches and matching cue racks. A preponderance of dim lamps kept the room swathed in a perpetual twilight. Overhead, a small electric fan turned slow revolutions, trying its best to dispel the muggy atmosphere but failing, leaving behind a miasma of cigarette smoke, sweat and too much testosterone, all mingling into an impenetrably noxious aroma.

As I entered, two gentlemen were squaring off, locked in a heated argument. One seemed to be a lawyer of some kind, since he was dressed in the black robe and white neckband of a high court advocate. The other I took to be our Scottish captain, given that he was wearing a kilt in the green and yellow striped tartan of the Gordon Highlanders.

'You're a bloody cheat,' the lawyer shouted, waving one ham-sized fist at the captain.

'So are you,' Gordon replied, smiling insolently. 'The only difference is that I am better at it. Now pay up before things get unpleasant!'

'Shut your mouth, you goddamned Sawney bastard!' The lawyer topped off this insult by taking a wild swing at Captain Gordon, who stepped aside deftly and responded with a quick uppercut of his own, which laid the man flat on his back.

It was nicely done, and I let out a low whistle of appreciation. Either the lawyer had a glass jaw, or our friend, the captain, had a brick for a right fist.

Even as the markers scurried to drag the insensate man away to a corner to recover, I approached Gordon with more than a hint of circumspection.

'Hello there, Captain Sahib. Could we have a word?'

Without sparing me so much as a glance, he said, 'Bugger off, won't you?'

With that curt dismissal, he called to the bearer to bring him a glass of rum punch.

I remained undeterred by this rudeness. Instead, I took a second to study the captain's face. After hearing tales of his prowess with the fairer sex, I had expected someone excessively handsome, but here was a truly ugly man, with a battered nose that had been broken more than once and a sloping brow that made him look almost a caveman. Still, in spite of his lack of good looks, he was possessed of a roguish masculinity, a simian charisma that was as unavoidable as a slap to the face.

'My name is Sikander Singh,' I started to say, 'and I am the Maharaja of Rajpore.'

'I don't care if you're the bloody Shah of Iran. Get out of my way!'

'It is imperative we have a conversation, Captain,' I persisted, trying not to let him ruffle me, 'about a Miss Mary Hartley. She has gone missing and could be in grave trouble.'

That made him pause. He finally looked at me, giving me a scowl so virulent that it could have curdled milk.

'And you think I have something to do with her disappearance?'

'Do you?'

'You're wasting your time. I have nothing to say to you.' He shook one calloused fist at me menacingly, 'Now leave, before I make you leave.'

I didn't move an inch. Instead, I returned his glare with a confident smirk.

'Let me make something clear to you, Captain Gordon. You seem to be the sort of man who is accustomed to throwing his weight around, but I should warn you, you do not scare me, not an ounce. I have faced Bob Fitzsimmons down for eight rounds at the Repton Boxing Club and looked into a lion's eyes in the Serengeti. I could take the bait you are offering and fight you, but I have a much better idea. How about I play you for the information? A wager? To the winner go the spoils!'

I could see immediately that it was the right gambit. From the way his eyes lit up, it was obvious he had a gambler's temperament and could not resist a bet.

'What did you have in mind exactly?' he asked warily.

'It's simple enough. We play a game. If I win, you speak to me about Mary Hartley.'

'And if you lose?'

'Oh, I don't know. A hundred guineas, shall we say?'

He frowned, considering my offer before shaking his head. 'No, I don't want money. I have money. What I will have is your pugree. They say you Sikhs prize your turbans above all else. It would be a nice little curio to have, a real maharaja's pugree. Maybe I'll put it on my dog's head and have him prance around.'

He was trying to rile me up. It may have worked with a Rajput or one of the Maratha kings, Scindia and the like, who were forever parroting on about their honor and nobility. But I didn't care about such inane rubbish. I knew enough of my family's history to understand that honor was a mutable thing. My great-grandfather had been a soldier of fortune; his father a notorious horse thief. Whatever honor my family possessed had either been bought and paid for, or won at the barrel of a musket. It would not be so easily lost by surrendering my turban in a game of chance.

'Very well. I agree to your terms.'

'Excellent,' Captain Gordon said, a bit bewildered by the speed of my acquiescence. 'What will it be then? Cards, darts, arm wrestling, a spot of snooker? What's your poison?'

'I had something more dangerous in mind. Tell me, Gordon, have you read Lermontov? 'The Fatalist'? It's quite an exceptional piece of writing.

I quoted from memory, 'And we, their poor descendants, wandering over the earth without conviction or pride, without amusement or anxiety, except for that involuntary fear that presses the heart at the thought of our inevitable end.'

Holding my hand out to Charan Singh, I said, 'Give me your revolver, won't you?'

The old man frowned, taken aback. 'What? Why do you want it?'

'Just hand it over, you great oaf!'

Reluctantly, Charan Singh complied, his earlier humor replaced by trepidation. Unbuttoning his achkan, he pulled his trusted Webley service revolver from his cummerbund and passed it over to me with an exceedingly worried expression, especially when I snapped it open and unloaded all the bullets except one.

'Here's the game, as Lermontov devised it. There is only one bullet left in here. We each take turns pointing the barrel at our heads and pulling the trigger. The first to flinch loses. Is that clear?'

Captain Gordon considered my words, arching one eyebrow. 'What if the gun goes off?'

'Then it's obvious who the winner is, isn't it?'

Snapping the cylinder shut, I spun it a few times before offering him the gun.

'You've gone mad, Huzoor,' Charan Singh gasped.

'You should listen to your man. If you think I'm afraid—'

'Does that mean you're too afraid to play?'

The slightest tremor of dismay flickered across Captain Gordon's face before he could control it, replaced almost immediately by a bemused smile. Taking the gun, he weighed it briefly in one hand before pointing the barrel straight at my head and pulling the trigger with a dry click.

I didn't even blink.

'I thought I would change the rules a bit,' he laughed and handed the gun back to me. 'Your turn!'

I raised the gun slowly. *Click!*

Trying not to shudder, I handed it back to him. Once again, he leveled it at my face.

Click! Another empty chamber!

Frowning, Gordon passed the revolver back to me. I saw his hand shiver just a bit. In that moment, I knew that I had won. Behind me, Charan Singh let out a groan. I put on a great pantomime of cocking the hammer very purposefully. Captain Gordon paled visibly, a bead of sweat glittering on his brow as I raised the gun, bringing it to bear directly between his eyes. Before I could even touch the trigger, he flinched visibly and turned his head away.

'Click!' I said with a grin and lowered the gun. 'I guess this means I win.'

The captain let out a vast sigh and shook his head. 'You're mad!'

'He's right, Huzoor,' Charan Singh echoed. 'You have taken leave of your senses.'

'Have I?' I whispered sarcastically and handed the revolver back to him. 'Or maybe I am just so good at sleight of hand that I palmed the bullet?'

Pulling the brass cartridge from my sleeve, I said, 'I took it out when you gave me the gun. There was no danger, none at all.'

Charan Singh rewarded this revelation with a ferocious glare. 'One of these days, Huzoor, your tricks will give me a heart attack!'

I left it to him to reload the Webley and tuck it back into his cummerbund. Meanwhile, I turned my attention back to Captain Gordon, who was watching me with a wary frown.

'You're a brave man. What if the gun had gone off?'

'Well, let's just say I would have lost a lot more than my pugree!' I gave him a cheeky smile. 'Now, shall we talk about Miss Hartley?'

He nodded, his frown tempered by the barest hint of respect. 'Very well. We had a gentleman's agreement, and I will uphold it. Ask your blasted questions!'

'I need your word of honor, Captain, that you will not lie, that you will answer what I ask without withholding anything.'

Captain Gordon bridled visibly. 'I am a man of Moray,' he growled, 'my honor is not something that can be impeached, not without a fight.'

I tried not to roll my eyes. *What a twit! My honor!* Blah-blah-blah. He sounded like a caricature straight from Walter Scott. Unfortunately, from the timbre of his voice, it was obvious that he actually believed every word, which meant I would have to give him the benefit of the doubt.

'You knew Miss Hartley quite well, I believe?' I was leading him, but he was smart enough not to fall into my trap, not just yet.

'After a fashion, yes,' his tone was very guarded. 'We were acquainted.'

'How did the two of you happen to meet?'

'It was the night out of Marseilles. The captain hosted a midsummer night's dinner for all of us in first-class, a costume masque. She had come as Titania, and I was Puck. We ended up seated next to each other.'

'Intentionally?'

'No, quite by chance. Although I will confess, I was quite intrigued.'

'And why was that?'

'Because it had only been a few days since we had departed, but already she had started to acquire quite a reputation,' He gave me an unexpected wink. 'Sea voyages are dreadfully boring, as I am sure you are aware. There is little enough to do other than poke about in each other's business. That's the sole distraction at sea, Mr Singh, gossip. The more, the better.'

'And what was the gossip about Miss Hartley?'

'That she was a bit of an angler, on the prowl for a fat catch, if you will forgive a bit of punnery. I thought she would be dreadful, one of those women who loved to play the lost naif, all sighs and bosoms, but she turned out to be quite delightful, by far the most interesting person I had met since I had boarded the *Caledonia*.

'As I said, we were both seated at the same table. It was a dreadfully boring evening, really. Not a bird in sight, only dowagers and that dreadful horse-faced Contessa and this awful couple, who were the worst kind of box-wallahs. Anyway, Miss Hartley caught me giving her the once-over. And do you know what she did? She pulled a face at me, crossed her eyes and stuck out her tongue. I was so surprised that I damn nearly swallowed half a glass of claret. It went up my nose and left me gasping.'

'It was an utter embarrassment,' Gordon exclaimed, shaking his head. 'And the cheek of that girl! She just sat there and started to laugh at me. She had a truly delightful laugh,' he said wistfully, 'unfettered, uncontrived and utterly uncaring of social propriety. We ended up chatting after that for almost the whole night.' He gave me a piercing glare. 'Do you know how it feels, Mr Singh, to really talk to a woman? To be listened to like you matter? Not for how you look, or how much you're worth, but who you are? It's an ecstasy that far eclipses any other.'

I tried not to roll my eyes. This was something I could not have predicted. Beneath the gruff exterior, the good captain, it seemed, was rather given to dramatics.

'What did you talk about?' I asked dryly.

'Oh, this and that, but mainly the truth.'

'She told you the truth? About her past?'

'She did. About her abusive drunk of a father and the hardships she had faced. She told me everything.'

'And what did you think of that?'

'That we had something in common. My father was a drunk, too. A harsh man who believed that to spare the belt was to ruin the child. Nothing I ever did was good enough for him. I told her all about him and about my childhood.' He shuddered. 'It was intoxicating. I have slept with many women, Mr Singh, but this was the first time I have bared myself completely to someone. That's what made Mary so special. She was not like any other women. She had this way of listening when you spoke, not just planning her next sentence or reply but actually listening, like she cared about what you had to say. And when she looked at you, it was like you were the only person in the room, the only one who mattered.'

'Let me be honest with you, Captain Gordon. In the past eight hours, I have heard Miss Hartley described as a gold-digger, a whore, an angel, a temptress and a fool. I still have not been able to understand which of those was the real Mary Hartley. I don't think anyone really did.'

'I did, Mr Singh. From the moment we met, we shared a bond.' He peered at me, his brow furrowing. 'Tell me, are you a spiritual man?'

'On occasion, yes. When I am drunk, mostly,' I replied.

He did not laugh. 'I am a member of the Theosophical Society. We believe that every person has an energy, an animus that makes them unique. Mary was one of those rare people whose energy was palpable, so forceful that it could reinvigorate even the most hardened of cynics. She had something special. A hunger for life, a passion that was infectious.'

'That's not what I have heard. Most of the people I have interviewed so far have described her as shy, even demure.'

'They don't know her like I do, Mr Singh. I made the same misapprehension when we were first introduced, but I assure you, beneath that plain-seeming exterior, Mary was quite extraordinary. Most people, especially women, rarely see past my cavalier exterior and my title. But Mary realized it was all an act straightaway. She was a listener, Sir, not a talker.'

He paused and gave me a glare, realizing that he was saying too much. The fervor in his voice and the light in his eyes made me wrinkle my brow suspiciously. *I already knew that he and Mary had been involved, but was there more to the story? Could he have been willing to risk his family name, his commission and his honor to help her break her contract with Peter? No,* I thought, *there was nothing reckless about Captain Gordon. Arrogance, certainly, and entitlement, but he would never place his reputation at risk, not for a woman.*

Still, I was missing something. I was sure of it. In spite of this nagging certainty, I decided not to press him about the exact nature of their relationship. No, it was better to let him reveal everything, at his own pace. That was the mistake most amateurs made. They thought they could browbeat a clue out of a suspect, but that almost never worked. If you wanted the truth, you had to wait for it. Like a cup of tea, you had to let it simmer. That was the only way to get to the truth. The art of detection, like gastronomy, took time and patience.

'To come back to the voyage, you said you and Miss Hartley talked for most of the night?'

'Indeed, we did. Before we knew it, it was almost dawn. All the other guests had long since retired, so I decided to ask Mary if she would care to return to my stateroom for a digestif.'

I winced. 'Gosh, was that really the best you could do? I thought you had a reputation for being a bit of a Lothario, Captain, a master seducer.'

For the first time, he grinned at me. 'I do, indeed. And it's well deserved, I assure you. Women appreciate my charms in a way that men never will. I think it's the sword. All women appreciate a bit of swordplay.'

I rolled my eyes at this blatant bit of double entendre.

'Miss Hartley, did she appreciate your swordplay, so to speak?'

His face drooped. 'No, she rebuffed me, and quite roundly. Frankly, I was more than a touch surprised.'

'You have a very high opinion of yourself, don't you?'

'And why shouldn't I? You see, on every voyage out, there is one catch, the big fish so to speak, who has wealth, standing and nobility. And all the ladies of the fishing fleet compete to try and land him as their husband. On the *Caledonia*, it was none other than myself. When I realized that, I was determined to exploit it for all it was worth, which was why I was pleasantly taken aback when she rejected my overtures.'

He chuckled. 'Do you know what she said? She laughed and told me I was callow, that my lines needed work. Can you believe it? I had half the women on board dancing to my whims, and this little nobody of a girl had the gumption to tell me my lines needed work. It was marvelously unexpected!'

'So, you abandoned your pursuit?'

'After a fashion. I called on her the next day. We had tea together. A most enjoyable afternoon, but there was not an ounce of romance. She was friendly but aloof. And we danced twice at the Neptune Ball, a waltz and a mazurka. She looked absolutely ravishing, and I took another sally. But once again, she rebuffed me. I realized I had no chance with her, so I decided to shift my focus of attention to someone else. There was this particularly nubile American, a bit tall, but she giggled like a schoolgirl every time I looked at her.'

'And that was the end of it?'

'Yes, it was.'

I leaned forward, fixing him with a scowl. 'Do you take me for a fool, Captain Gordon? Is there something about me that makes you think I am dim-witted or impaired in some way?'

'No, of course not,' he said, taken aback by my sudden ferocity.

'Then why are you lying to me? Is this what your vaunted Moray honor is worth?'

That made him wince, like I had slapped him.

'I know for a fact that you were involved with Mary Hartley. I have it from two different accounts. But here, you expect me to believe she rebuffed your overtures and you gave up. A man of your reputation simply abandoned the chase?' I shook my head. 'You promised to tell the unvarnished truth. That was our wager. Will you keep your word, or shall I let it be known that James Gordon of the Highlanders is a welcher?'

'I am not lying to you, Mr Singh. I am staying true to the spirit of the wager,' he said before letting out a long sigh. 'I did give up on Mary, I swear it, and abandon my pursuit of her. There were plenty of other fish, and I would have kept my distance, but then,' he paused, '*she* came to me.'

My eyes widened with disbelief. 'She initiated your affair?'

He nodded. 'Just before we docked at Cairo. I came upon her on D Deck, near the store room. I was trying to hunt down some Turkish tobacco when I chanced upon her and that box-wallah I had mentioned, Marsden. They were having a very heated argument, damn nearly at each other's throats.'

'Marsden? Do you mean Mason?'

'Yes, that's him. The very gentleman in question, although I would hesitate to call him that. A damn lout, that's what he was. You see, just as I chanced upon them, their argument flared into a full-fledged altercation. And do you know what that devil did? He laid his hands on her, the bastard! He pushed Mary so forcibly that the poor girl went sprawling.' Captain Gordon's jaw tightened with outrage. 'That's when I decided to become involved.'

'In what way?'

'Mainly a right hook, followed by a warning to get his hands off her. I would have given the bugger a proper thrashing, but she stopped me. Mason buggered off, sharpish, after that, quicker than you can say "how do you do?" As for me, I stayed to check on Mary. She was bleeding a bit, on account of having bumped her wrist and hand on a capstan. I tamped the cut with my handkerchief and escorted her back to her cabin.'

'Did you inquire what the argument was about?'

'I did, indeed. She refused to tell me, saying it was a private matter, and that I should leave it alone. I offered to stay with her a bit, and help her bandage her hand, but she chivvied me away.'

'But that was not the last of it, was it?'

'Not by a long shot. There was a bit of a squall that evening, a southwester coming off the Sahara. As a result, all the evening's entertainments stood canceled. I was in my cabin, polishing my boots, when I heard a knock on the door. It was Mary. I was about to ask her what had brought her to my doorstep on that cold grey evening, but before I could say a word, she kissed me.' He shivered, not with sorrow but with exhilaration. 'She said she wanted one last adventure before surrendering to a dull marriage. Who was I to resist? I am not one to kiss and tell, Mr Singh, but it was extraordinary. Mary was like no woman I have ever known. She was fire, Sir, not ice, and I was only too willing to be consumed by her, body and soul.'

He gave me a bitter smile. 'But it was not destined to last. That's the problem with sea voyages, isn't it? They are like dreams. They only exist until you awaken and open your eyes.'

The way he said those words, anger tinged with regret, made me realize what I had been missing.

'I have this all backwards, don't I? It was *you* who was besotted with her, not the other way around.'

Gordon nodded. 'Those four days I had with Mary were the best of my life.' His face lit up, rapturous. 'I had never experienced such passion before, such deep emotion. I am not a sensitive man; there is too much of the savage in me, a by-product of my Celtic ancestry. It is the very quality that makes me a good soldier. But Mary, she made me think of better things than drinking and fighting. She made me imagine a life of peace, with a hearth and a home, and two wee bairns. She was all that was missing from my life, Mr Singh. I knew that I could not let her marry another man.'

'You decided to propose to her?'

'I wanted to. I desperately did, but I could not do it. My rank and my name would never allow me to take someone like her as my wife, someone with her past and prior engagement. So, instead I made her an offer. I told her I would rent her a nice house in Bombay, and keep her in style, perhaps even pay for a small establishment she could run as she chose—a shop or a small lunchroom—with an allowance of eight hundred pounds a year.'

'I am guessing that she turned you down.'

He nodded. 'Of course, she did. I knew she would. That's why I wanted her. She would never allow another man to own her. She had too much chutzpah for that, too much pride. "I am destined to be more than a soldier's mistress," she said and made me a counter offer. She asked me to walk away from it all, the Gordon name and the inheritance that came with it. She said we could start over and build a new life together on the frontier, just the two of us.'

He shook his head mournfully. 'I admit that I was tempted for a moment, but I couldn't do it. I failed her, Mr Singh. I should have told her I loved her, asked her to spurn your friend and be my wife, but I was afraid, too weak to go against my upbringing and my father.'

His face tightened with anguish. 'We are no longer capable of sacrifices, for the good of mankind or even for our own personal happiness, because we know its impossibility and languidly go from doubt to doubt, as our predecessors threw themselves from one delusion to another, not possessing, as they did, either hope or even the undefined but great pleasure which greets the soul in every struggle with men or with fate.'

I frowned, recognizing the excerpt. It was Lermontov, from the same story I had mentioned earlier. It seems I had misjudged the captain. He was an educated man after all, not a brazen brute.

'She rejected you,' I mused, 'and that led you to resent her. That gives you a reasonably good motive to do her harm. A man scorned, and so on.'

Captain Gordon replied to this half-hearted accusation with a snort. 'Don't be ridiculous, Mr Singh. I have nothing but affection for Mary. And I will have you know, we parted on excellent terms. Why, I even gave her a gift of some money.'

'You did?'

'Yes, a hundred guineas.'

My dubiety must have shown on my face because he gave me a scowl.

'Don't look at me like that. You think she fooled me, but you are sorely mistaken. My story with Mary is far from over. I will wait a few months, give her some time to change her mind about my offer. Three months. That should be enough for her to break off her engagement and realize she made a mistake. Mary is too good for your schoolmaster. She deserves better, a man who recognizes her worth and who has prospects, not a drunken old sot. She will be mine, Mr Singh, I swear it by all that is holy. And if you know what's best for you, you will give up this chase and stay out of our way. Just you wait and see, she will come back to me. It's only a matter of time.'

CHAPTER 18

The district of Byculla derived its name, curiously enough, from a tree.

Before the construction of the Hornby Vellard and the joining of the seven islands, Byculla had been a swamp, populated only by flocks of migrating flamingos and groves of Cassia fistula, or Indian laburnum trees, which were also called 'bhaya' in Marathi.

Each summer, it was said, the laburnums had bloomed with brilliant golden flowers, making it seem as if the sea itself was on fire. These flowers were worshipped by the locals as a gift from Shiva himself and were considered disease-killers, mostly because they had been used from time immemorial as a laxative and purgative believed to cure gout and rheumatism.

Alas, the flamingos were long gone now, moving west to the mudflats of Sewri. As for the golden laburnums, they had been cut down until all that remained was a few sporadic specimens around Dadar and Gamdevi.

In place of the bhaya groves what had sprung up was a suburb not unlike Richmond or Kensington, row upon row of neat housing colonies arranged in serried ranks around a patchwork of parks and mansions. This new township quickly became a sought-after destination for the English community in Bombay, who moved out of nearby Mazgaon and its cramped confines in droves, eager to escape the mosquitos and the mills. By 1830,

Byculla had cemented its reputation as the poshest enclave in Bombay, home to the wealthiest and most powerful families in the city.

The apogee of the district's popularity had culminated with the opening of the Byculla Club in 1833. Distinctly 'Whites Only', it had quickly earned a reputation for its exclusivity. It was said that memberships could not be bought, only bequeathed. In fact, I had once heard a story that David Sassoon, then said to be the richest man in Bombay, had offered them a million rupees but been turned down. Consequently, he had purchased all the ice factories in the city and monopolized the Boston Ice trade, forcing the club's management to serve cocktails warm for one whole summer, until they voted to grant him entry.

Unfortunately, the golden age of Byculla came to an end with the bubonic plague of 1896. Caused by rats off a ship called the *Mandarin*, which had arrived from Hong Kong, the plague swept through Byculla, the docks and the mill district like wildfire. Over thirty-five thousand deaths were reported in a single calendar year, and the British authorities had been forced to set up plague camps and forcibly evict migrant workers from their chawls to bring the outbreak under control. As a result, many of the wealthier residents moved south to Malabar Hill and Colaba, abandoning Byculla and leaving it to fall into a state of slow decay.

Now, Byculla was populated largely by that lamentably vulgar breed known as box-wallahs. The mercantile class had always occupied a curious position in British Indian society. Until the Mutiny, most Europeans in India had either been soldiers or administrators. However, with the transfer of power from the East India Company to the Crown, India had become a vast market for the British Empire, rich with raw materials to be gathered and commodified. Cotton, indigo, coal, iron, tar and timber, all were farmed and mined in India and shipped to England, where they were turned into broadcloth and trade goods that were then sold back to the natives at ten times the price. It was the subcontinent that was financing the great Industrial Revolution and keeping the mills of Sheffield, Leeds and the Midlands afloat, all beneficiaries of the great robbery of India that showed no signs of abating.

At the forefront of this economic boom were the box-wallahs. Originally a pejorative used to describe the itinerant peddlers and salesmen who traveled the length and breadth of India, over time it had come to refer to the elite managerial class who worked for European-owned businesses. Whether it was the mills or the factories, the banks or plantations, all English businesses in India had one thing in common. They were run not by native Indians, but by English managers shipped out from the home counties by the boat load. These gentlemen—and I use the term liberally—were a class apart, ranked below the army and the heaven-born but much higher than the factory workers and railway and estate-wallahs, the very epitome of the burgeoning petit bourgeoisie that Marx and Engels so thoroughly despised.

A cursory bit of asking around had quickly established that Mr Mason, first name, Rupert (ha!), was most definitely one of this mercantile breed. Originally from Manchester, he had managed a cotton spinning mill there until he had abruptly decided to quit and come out to Bombay in the employ of Murphy and Co., a local company that specialized in building furnaces and steam engines. Interestingly, they had recently won a contract to build a factory and a power plant in Rajpore, a fact that had helped my investigation immeasurably.

It had taken some more determined digging on my part to find out what had really motivated Mr Mason to leave the comfort of the home counties and migrate to the colonies.

Thankfully, a telephone call to one of the company's lawyers had quickly revealed the truth. It seemed that he had been forced to resign from his position after ending a labor dispute a bit too forcibly. In fact, as my contact had explained, Mason had whipped a black worker half to death, resulting in charges being filed against him. Fortunately for him, the case was dropped when he agreed to pay the laborer a handsome settlement. His reputation, however, had been left in tatters, as a result of which he had been forced to leave England rather hastily.

It seemed Murphy and Co. had hired him only because he had a reputation for being a dour but efficient manager who always managed to get the job done, and under budget at that. All these fragments of information had led me to expect that Mr Mason would be a caricature of Mr Creakle—an aggressive and bumptious man who would not cooperate with me willingly. That meant I would have to either threaten or intimidate him, both of which were less than palatable propositions, considering I had no leverage to begin with.

On the manifest, Mr Mason had merely provided the company's name as a correspondence address. Fortuitously, my contact had been able to provide a current address for him. He was being billeted in one of the company's apartments, the eponymously named Murphy Terraces, which Uday Singh informed were located in the heart of Byculla, very close to the club and the Botanical Gardens.

As the Mercedes wound its way past the famous statue of Seth Cursetjee Manockjee Shroff, locally known as the Khada Parsi statue, my thoughts could not help but turn to my interview with Captain Gordon.

That meeting had left me more than a bit dismayed. It was obvious that Miss Hartley had no intention of going through with her marriage contract, that she had intended to jilt Peter all along. That was why she had built up such a neat nest egg. Taking money from Dr Ross and Gordon, and stealing from the Contessa, it was characteristic magpie behavior. *She had been planning something all along, but what was it? Was it the frontier, as Dr Ross had mentioned? Mawand and the Baloch plateau, where it was easy enough to disappear if you had the money to survive? Or had she never left Bombay at all? The fact that she had amassed such a tidy sum, could that have caused her downfall? And what did the Mr Mason have to do with the whole mess? As Captain Gordon had testified, he had seen the man physically assault Miss Hartley. What could have been the cause of that argument? What could have led an educated gentleman to become so incensed that he would lift a hand against a woman, that too in public?*

It was all very confusing, a Gordian puzzle that became even more complicated with each knot I managed to pick apart. Now that I had a moment to meditate upon it, there was only one thing of which I was still certain. I needed to find Miss Hartley, and I needed to do so quickly, if for no other reason than to ask why she would cause such pain to my old friend. Although, if I was being truly honest, I already had some small inkling of what that answer would be. She was looking for adventure, and Peter was quicksand. But that was the problem with adventures, wasn't it? In fiction, they may have ended with a happily ever after, but in reality, they almost always finished in tragedy.

This thought nagged at me as we arrived at the address my contact had provided. Murphy Terraces was a complex of six three-storeyed apartment blocks arranged in a hexagon around a central courtyard, not far from the Botanical Gardens. Emerging from the car, I frowned up at the estate's red brick façade. It was a drab imitation of the mansion blocks one could find in London, around Kensington, Battersea and the West End. There, the cream painted colonnades surmounted by Georgian gables and arched sash windows may have passed muster, but in Bombay it seemed incongruous, a mish-mash of architectural styles that made me want to shudder.

As I strode through the front portico, I realized I had arrived at rather an inopportune time.

There seemed to be a garden party underway. Rather a pretentious affair, it seemed, judging by the cast-iron lawn furniture and the preponderance of red and white bunting that looked like it would have better belonged in a carnival. In one corner, a violinist was doing his best to massacre Elgar's 'Chanson de Matin', even as a motley herd of box-wallahs milled about, sweating it out in formal evening togs, which was laughable considering it was hotter than the seventh circle of hell. Worst of all, there wasn't a drink in sight, not one solitary coupe of champagne, just an endless array of petit beurres and fizzy lemonade, which made me shake my head in disappointment.

Even as I glanced around, trying to spot my targets, a flustered-looking darban, dressed in a uniform so ornate it would have looked at home on one of Napoleon's cuirassiers, came rushing up to accost me.

'Do you have an invitation?' he asked brusquely in Hindustani.

'I do, indeed,' I said, brandishing my letter from the police. 'I am here at the express order of Commissioner Edwardes. I would like to see Mr Rupert Mason immediately.'

The darban ignored my credentials and clucked his tongue dismissively. 'You will have to come later, bhai,' he drawled. 'The party is for burra sahibs only.'

'I insist,' I said. 'This is a matter of the utmost importance.'

'Aye, you jumped-up son of a sow! Did you not hear me? Begone from here!' he said and reached out with one hand to push me back. But before he could touch me, Charan Singh surged forward and shoved him away with a growl.

'You will not dare to lay a hand on His Majesty. Not on my watch! Is that clear, you baboon?'

Even as the watchman promptly toppled over flat on his arse, a thin, pinch faced Englishwoman who had overheard the exchange came bustling over.

'You there!' she snapped irately 'Who are you and what do you mean by assaulting my chaprassi?'

'As I was trying to explain, Madam,' I said, switching to English, 'I am the Maharaja of Rajpore, here at the behest of the Bombay Police.'

I offered her my papers, but she barely spared them a glance.

'A real-life maharaja! How utterly wonderful!' She clapped her hands in delight. 'Oh, do come in, Your Majesty!' she exclaimed. 'I am Mrs Flora Mason. My husband and I are the hosts of this small soiree.'

Charan Singh and I exchanged an amused look. I could almost hear her brain clicking as she calculated the eminence that a man of my stature would bring to her party. Sadly, she failed to realize that I had come to ruin it.

Raising one bony hand, she waved at a man standing nearby, beckoning him over.

'Oh, Rupert,' she squealed. 'Yoo-hoo! Do come over here quickly!'

As the gentleman obliged, I took a moment to study both him and his wife more carefully.

They made for rather a mismatched couple. He was round-shouldered and plump, balding prematurely, with severe lips and a perpetual frown that had caused his eyebrows to grow into one another, making it look like there was a caterpillar poised atop his brow.

I recognized the type immediately. He was what was called a bean counter. That was the right phrase to describe him, for it was apparent that he was the sort of man who had an abacus for a heart, who chose to see people not as individuals but as numbers and commodities. And he was cheap, parsimonious to a fault. I could infer that from the cut of his dinner jacket, which was much too tight around the shoulders and midriff, and from his Oxfords, which were dreadfully scuffed.

Mrs Mason, on the other hand, was quite his opposite. She was thin to the point of being emaciated, with the sort of perpetually disappointed face that came from a lifetime of having her hopes dashed. Common born I guessed, but trying very hard to pass herself off as upper-class, as was evident from her proud manner and exaggeratedly plummy accent. It was obvious that she was someone who cared excessively for appearances. That much was evident from the way she wore her hair, cut short in a stylish bob, even though it made her look like a middle-aged Joan of Arc; and from her choice of dress, which was a blindingly gauche concoction of crinoline, taffeta and lace, complete with a flared bustle and frilled sleeves, ostentatious to the point of being laughable. Not only was it dreadfully impractical and ill-suited to Bombay's humidity, but it was also at least two seasons out of style.

'Rupert,' she announced. 'Come and meet this gentleman! This is Maharaja Rajpore Singh of the Punjab. He's real-life royalty, can you believe it?'

'A maharaja, eh?' Mr Mason looked me up and down greedily, no doubt making mental notes of what my jewelry and wristwatch were worth. 'What brings you out Byculla way? I certainly did not invite you.'

'Actually, I am here to see you and your wife,' I said.

'I am trying to track down one Mary Hartley. I believe you have met her.'

Their reactions were quite different.

The husband paled visibly. 'I think you should leave,' he said in a quiet whisper.

As for Mrs Mason, she let out a florid curse. 'Oh, that awful woman! I am plagued by that jezebel. A dreadful grasping creature! A brazen hussy, that's what she is.'

'That's a very strong opinion to have about someone you barely know.'

'Of course, we knew her. When you spend almost three weeks in close proximity, you cannot help but acquire more than a passing acquaintance,' Mrs Mason said with a grimace. 'Miss Hartley had the cabin next to us for the journey out, you see. She was sharing it with another young bride-to-be, but I cannot recall her name.'

'A Miss Bennett, I believe.'

'Ah yes, that's it. A pale little thing who spent most of the voyage locked away. Quite a sweet girl, but as timid as a dormouse. Your Miss Hartley, on the other hand, was anything but timid,' Mrs Mason let out a snort. 'She was cold and calculating, a charlatan, a chancer of the worst kind.'

Beside her, Mr Mason shifted uncomfortably, giving her a glare as if to suggest she was saying too much.

'Don't give me that look, Rupert,' Mrs Mason hissed. 'You know what I am saying is true. She had you fooled as well, just as she did me. I'll be honest, when we first met her, I didn't think much of her. I dismissed her as a bit of a non-entity, as a shy and demure novice. But she was quite the opposite, let me tell you!'

'We were seated with her the very first day out from England, at the captain's table, along with that dreadful Italian woman,' Mr Mason interjected.

'Contessa di Sforza?'

'If you insist!' Mrs Mason said with a sneer. 'She may have had the title, but she had no class. Her behavior was as common as dirt. That's probably why she took a shine to Mary Hartley, why she decided to take her under her wing. Birds of a feather and what not! Anyway, as I was saying, Miss Hartley spent most of the evening minding her own business, too scared to say more than two words. I didn't spare her a second look, not until later that night. It was just after the fourth course. I was telling the captain all about the Christian mission we had set up to reform the workhouses in Manchester and ameliorate the working and living conditions of the poor workers. For some reason, that set her off. She proceeded to harangue me, Sir, to lecture me publicly about how I knew nothing of the actual problems faced by the lower classes. It was in dreadfully poor taste, let me tell you.'

'She was just a bit drunk, Flora. She meant you no offence.'

'You know that's not true. She was trying to get noticed, and that too at my expense.' She shook her head. 'The nerve of that woman! Acting all high and mighty, but she was neither as strait-laced nor as innocent as she wanted us to believe, let me tell you.'

'What do you mean?' I asked.

'I recognized her the moment she started her tirade. I had seen her before, you see.' Mrs Mason dropped her voice to a whisper 'She was an actress, Sir, a second-rate stage performer. I had seen her at the Lyceum, in a musical revue. She did a most scandalous dance, I recall it only too well.'

'Are you sure? Perhaps you mistook her for someone else?'

'Of course, I am sure! I pride myself on my memory, Sir. I never forget a face. And Miss Hartley confirmed it herself after I took her aside and told her that I knew who she was.'

'What did she say to that?'

'She was utterly shameless, Sir. I warned her to be careful, that if she did not mind her p's and q's I would be forced to share the truth about her past with the other passengers. She told me she didn't care! She laughed in my face and told me to go right ahead. Can you believe that?'

'Why didn't you?'

'I didn't want to make a fuss, Sir. The last thing I needed was to be branded the local busybody. Besides, she pointed out that my reputation would be equally ruined if I revealed the truth about her because it would become public knowledge that I had patronized a music hall.'

Bravo! I thought. My estimation of Miss Hartley was growing. As far as ripostes went, it was very well-played, perfectly designed to keep someone like Mrs Mason, who probably cared about her reputation more than her husband, firmly on the backfoot.

'Was that the end of it? You decided to keep her secret and she stayed out of your way?'

'If only!' she said with a frown. 'Unfortunately, along with no manners, the woman had no sense. I made it a point to avoid her, watching from a distance as she swanned about. She was forever up in first-class, thanks to her Italian patroness, chasing after all the unattached men, while we were stuck down in second-class with the plebians.'

'But wasn't she already promised to someone? A schoolteacher, I believe.'

'As if that would stop the likes of her! She was an angler, a predator on the hunt. Her quarry was any man with an income and a roving eye. I can vouch for that. She went after most of the unattached men on board, and half the married ones, too.

'Including your husband?'

'Of course! That was the final straw!'

'Come now, Flora, you know that is not true,' Mr Mason said.

'Don't you deny it! I saw her making eyes at you, the shameless cow. Every day, she would track you down and pretend to ask all manner of questions about India. What she was really doing was cozying up to you and trying to supplant me. I am nobody's fool, Mr Maharaja! I've seen her kind before, the damned fishing fleet, angling for a husband. Well, I wasn't going to let her have mine!'

'Are you saying you confronted her?'

'You're damned right I did. As if it wasn't bad enough to be subjected to her hysterics in public, she compounded the offence by pursuing my Rupert. That is why I decided to put her in her place once and for all. It was just a few days after we left Marseilles. I approached her and told her that if she did not stop sniffing around my husband like a bitch in heat, I would ruin her.'

'And how did Miss Hartley respond to that ultimatum?'

'She ... she threatened me. She said that people fell overboard all the time, that no one would miss me, and that my husband would probably turn cartwheels to be rid of me!' Mrs Mason shuddered with outrage. 'I have never been spoken to so crudely. It was just too much to bear!'

'You assaulted her?'

'Not exactly! I was just trying to scare her a bit, so I poked her in the chest. I didn't mean any harm, but then she ... *she* attacked *me*, Sir. She slapped me right across the face. And then she told me to stay out of her way or she would kill me and feed my body to the sharks. Can you believe it?'

She shivered, reliving the shock of her encounter. 'I have never been treated so vulgarly, Sir, not once in my life. It was absolutely shocking! Miss Hartley may have pretended to be well-bred, but she was a savage. Utterly uncivilized, I tell you. Frankly, if she is lying in a ditch somewhere, it is her own doing, her own fault.'

I felt Charan Singh's shoulders stiffen, his expression of distaste mirroring mine.

'That's not a very kind thing to say.'

'You can't be kind with that kind of woman. They are parasites, Your Majesty, bottom feeders of the worst kind.'

I frowned. I had endured as much as I could of Mrs Mason and her waspish remarks.

'And you, Madam? What exactly are you? Playing the memsahib and putting on airs and graces, but your dress is two years out of fashion, and I can see the dirt under your fingernails. Do you believe that makes you better than Miss Hartley, just because your husband manages a factory?'

As I said that, Mrs Mason's face turned bright red. 'How dare you?' she squawked, giving her husband an affronted look. 'I insist you leave at once!'

I remained unruffled. 'I will leave, Madam, when I have found out what I need to know.'

'I have said all I am willing to say to you. Rupert, have him leave at once.'

'I think it would be best if you went, Mr Singh,' he said, but there was no real force behind it, merely a stolid resignation, as if he was more than accustomed to his wife's tantrums.

'Let me be clear, Mr Mason. I came here to see you, not your wife.'

'I have nothing to say to you.'

'Really? Are you sure? I was speaking to Lt Gordon not one hour ago, and he revealed something very interesting.' I fixed him with a frown. 'You see, I know all about the altercation you had with Miss Hartley.'

'Wait!' he exclaimed. 'Let's not talk about this here. Flora,' he said, turning to his wife, 'would you please go check on our guests?'

'But, Rupert,' Mrs Mason responded, giving him a bewildered look, 'what is he talking about? What altercation?'

'Please,' he repeated, more insistent this time. 'Do as I say.'

For a moment, Mrs Mason looked like she was going to refuse, but then she nodded and stalked away, giving her husband a scowl that promised there would be trouble later.

After she was gone, Mr Mason took my arm and hurriedly steered me away from the party, toward a secluded pavilion located in a distant corner of the lawn.

'I don't see what you think I can tell you,' he said evasively. 'My wife has already said everything there is to say.'

I gave him a level look. 'Are you sure you want to be difficult, Mr Mason? Let me be very clear. Either talk to me with absolute honesty, or I will be forced to make a scene and permanently ruin your entry into Bombay society. I am not sure your wife will take that too kindly, nor will she appreciate it if she found out that you were meeting unmarried women alone in the middle of the night and brawling with servicemen on the third-class deck.'

Mr Mason's face stiffened. I thought I had made a mistake, that I had pushed him too far too early in the game, that he was going to tell me to get lost. However, what happened next was surprising, even for a man of my experience.

While I had expected Mr Mason to bluster and deny everything, instead he sniffled volubly and then burst into tears. 'Oh no, what have I done? Damn you, Rupert, you've pronged it all up again! Now Flora will leave you for sure. You will be packed off in disgrace!'

I can't say what was more embarrassing, to watch a grown man cry, or to hear him chastise himself in the third person? I shifted uncomfortably, waiting for the furor to die down, but he grew more hysterical by the minute.

'I've ruined everything, haven't I? But it isn't my fault, I swear it!' he exclaimed desperately. 'She entrapped me.'

'Oh, for God's sake, take a breath,' I said, offering him my handkerchief. 'You're making a scene!'

Mr Mason paused and took the handkerchief gratefully, mopping at his eyes as he tried to calm down. It took three deep inhalations before he managed to stop hyperventilating and get himself under control.

'Now tell me exactly what happened with Miss Hartley? What is it that has you all tied up in knots?'

'It's her. Mary Hartley. Damn her to hell! She was a siren, Sir, a Lorelei. She lured me in with her song and stitched me up good and proper. What a horrible woman!'

'I can't understand a word you're saying, Mr Mason. You're not making a whit of sense.'

After another deep breath, he gave me a wounded scowl. 'What I am trying to say is that you have only half the story. Yes, I did have a rendezvous with her; I was weak and easily enticed. But I didn't make the first move. Miss Hartley did. We first met at the captain's dinner table, you see, as I mentioned. I was seated next to her, and we started to talk. She was very sweet and wide-eyed, rather too full of questions about India. Ordinarily, I find such people terribly tiresome. But in her case, it was quite charming, I admit, which was why I decided to entertain her. Also, it was quite flattering to have someone who wanted to listen. With my wife, she does most of the talking, so it was a pleasant surprise that Mary, Miss Hartley, was eager to hear what I had to say about my business, the factory and especially about my childhood in Quetta.'

'Hold on. You're a colonial?'

'Yes, indeed I am. Born and raised in Balochistan. My father was the principal secretary to Sir Robert Groves Sandeman. I am an old India hand, Sir. Not only do I speak Hindi and Urdu fluently, but I am also more than familiar with the habits and culture of the north and the south. In fact, that is why I took this job. It was a sort of homecoming for me, although it has left my wife somewhat bitter, I'm afraid,' he said, unable to disguise the resentment in his voice. 'She ... we had hoped that we had left India behind us for good.'

I nodded. That explained why Murphy and Co. would have been eager to hire him. It wasn't easy to find white overseers who were familiar with native habits and languages, especially now that the princely states were opening up for business. Someone like Mr Mason, who could understand the way India and the Indian mind worked, was sure to be an invaluable asset.

'What else did the two of you talk about?' I asked.

'As I was saying, when I told her that I had been born in Balochistan, she was beside herself with curiosity. She wanted to know everything about the frontier, the people, the tribes, the encampments, the social restrictions, and of course, about how difficult it was to travel through the hinterland.' He shook his head and added, 'She monopolized my company the entire evening. Flora was not happy about that, let me tell you. She kept elbowing me in the ribs, trying to get me to stop talking to Mary, but I was completely caught up by her, like a fly in a spider's web.

'Of course, I didn't know a thing about her then. It was only later that Flora took me aside and told me that she had recognized her, that Miss Hartley was an actress she had seen in Edinburgh. That should have been warning enough for me to stay away, but I confess, Mr Singh, I was intrigued. I had never spoken to one face to face, you know, someone of the dramatic persuasion. I always thought they would be rather bohemian, you know, frizzy hair and bold manners. But Mary, Miss Hartley, was really quite sophisticated. I thought that would be the end of it, but as Flora said, she sought me out, Sir. Not once but several times. She said she had more questions about Balochistan. I was wary, of course, but I was also very taken with her curiosity.' He cleared his throat guiltily. 'And then, Mr Singh, the night before we docked at Cairo, she made me a proposition.'

I frowned. 'What manner of proposition?'

'A rather lascivious one, I am sorry to say, that I rejected outright. That was what set her off. She did not take the rejection lightly and started to argue with me. She grew hysterical, Sir. I was trying to calm her down when Captain Gordon came upon us, misinterpreted the situation completely and assaulted me. That's the truth, I swear it. I am an innocent victim in this. What we have here is a misunderstanding initiated by Miss Hartley.'

'What are you insinuating? That she made a pass at you? You're twice her age, Mr Mason, and married to boot. You had nothing to offer her.'

'Nevertheless, Mr Singh, I am telling you, on my oath as a gentleman, that your Miss Hartley was a scarlet woman. I could not say it in front of my wife, but she solicited me ... offered herself to me in exchange for money.'

I almost believed him, except his right eyelid twitched ever so slightly. It was the most imperceptible of tremors, but for someone familiar with Darwinian nonverbal communication, it was as good as an admission of guilt.

'No. I think not. Your oath as a gentleman, I suspect, is worth the same as the veracity of that statement,' I said, giving him a stern scowl. 'You want me to think she was pursuing you, but it was the other way around, wasn't it? I think you propositioned her. You saw her being courted by the other men on board the *Caledonia* and assumed you had a chance as well.'

'I have never—' he began to object, but I cut him off.

'Oh, come on, Mr Mason! Do you take me for a fool? I know how the world works. Now, either tell me the truth or shall I go and fetch your wife and let her get the truth out of you.'

That threat worked almost too well. Mr Mason winced at the merest mention of his wife and raised his hands in abject surrender.

'Let's not do anything drastic,' he sighed. 'You're right. I was quite besotted with her, I am ashamed to say.'

He shuddered and continued, 'I had heard all manner of salacious stories about actresses, you see. A friend of mine who regularly patronizes the Palace of Varieties often told me that the lesser performers were always open to offering favors, provided the price was right.'

'What sort of favors?' I quipped, feigning ignorance even though I knew perfectly well what he was talking about.

'You know, romantic favors,' he said, blushing, 'of the intimate kind.'

'And you decided to ask Mary if she would offer you the same favors?'

'I most certainly did not!' he exclaimed. 'What I did ask her was whether it was true what they said about actresses. If they were known to charge gentlemen who wanted to spend more time with them, one on one.'

'And how did Miss Hartley respond to that question?'

'She laughed and played coy, Sir. She said that I would have to spend a lot of money to find out.'

He shook his head. 'Honestly, I had never contemplated paying a woman before, but I was very tempted by her, especially after the Neptune Ball. She was transformed, Sir, a vision so resplendent that it made my heart skip a beat. I knew then that I had to have her. I could not get that thought out of my mind as I watched her parading about with all the other gentlemen. I tried to get her alone, to get her to dance with me several times, but on each occasion she rebuffed me and said that I had had my chance, and not to waste her time unless I was willing to pay for it. That night, I couldn't sleep. I couldn't get her out of my mind, the gleam of her eyes, the dulcet musk of her voice, and those smooth shoulders,' he said, his voice shivering. 'The next morning, I approached her and told her I would pay her whatever she wanted.'

'And she agreed to your overture?'

'Yes, as long as I paid her fifty pounds.'

'That's quite a lot of money.'

'It is, but I was gripped by a kind of madness. I would have paid a hundred pounds, even two hundred. I wanted her at any cost; it was like a fire I needed to quench. It took me a few days to get that much cash together, especially under Flora's eagle eye. Finally, when we were approaching Cairo, I delivered the money to Mary, and we arranged a rendezvous on the third-class deck for later that night.'

It did not take a genius to see where this was going. Judging by my previous interviews, it was obvious that Miss Hartley had been playing him, and that he had fallen for the bait hook, line, and sinker.

'Let me guess. When you turned up that night, she decided that she had changed her mind?'

He nodded. 'She tricked me, Sir. I was the mark, and that was her scheme all along. She hooked me in with her flirtatious act and then bamboozled me. When I met her that night, I tried to kiss her. But she ... she laughed at me. She told me I was a fool, that I was deluded enough to imagine that she would ever be with a withered old prune like me,' Mr Mason hissed, unable to control his obvious outrage. 'And if that wasn't bad enough,' he continued, 'she tried to extort more money from me. She told me that she would tell everyone on board that I had tried to proposition her and ruin my reputation, unless I paid her another hundred pounds. That was the altercation Captain Gordon had witnessed! Yes, I lost my temper. And I am ashamed to say that I hit her, but it was her fault! She incited me, left me no choice. I couldn't endanger my job, or my marriage. I couldn't let her ruin me, ruin everything I have worked for. Most of all, I could not let her break Flora's heart. I had no intention of hurting her, I swear it. I just lost control, for one moment, a second of uncontrollable passion. Unfortunately, that was when that blasted busybody Gordon turned up. He came charging up like Galahad and slapped me about, like I was some common punter and I was forced to beat a hasty retreat.'

'What happened next? Was that the end of it?'

'I only wish it was. Your Miss Hartley sent me a note the very next morning, threatening to tell my wife if I didn't pay her. Can you believe that? The nerve of that woman!'

I couldn't help but grin. 'How much did you end up giving her?'

'A hundred and fifty pounds. It was all the cash I had on me.'

'You realize that gives you a motive to do her harm, don't you? How else could you keep her from coming back for more? Or perhaps you decided to get your revenge on her for making a fool of you? Is that what happened?'

I was fishing, and he knew it, because he replied with a pronounced snort.

'Don't be ridiculous!' he scoffed. 'If I wanted to do her harm, why would I have paid her a penny? No, the last time I saw her was the night of the altercation. We had no further contact after that. In fact, I made a concerted effort to avoid her. I was too embarrassed and much too afraid of becoming the laughing stock of the ship.

'May I be honest, Mr Singh?' he asked, giving me a solemn scowl.

'I would expect nothing less.'

'She played me, Sir, like a harpsichord. At first glance, she may have seemed innocent, but she was anything but that. She was a liar and a villain, but it isn't the money I resent. It's the fact that she emasculated me completely. I have never been so humiliated before. Frankly, my wife was too kind. I can only hope that bitch has got her proper comeuppance by now, wherever she is.

'Now, if we are done here, Mr Singh, please excuse me. I have a party to get back to and guests to take care of.'

As he strode off, Charan Singh came up behind me. 'It seems Rowan Sahib's memsahib is not who she is supposed to be,' he noted.

I could not deny that he was correct. What Mr Mason had just revealed confirmed what I had already started to piece together from previous interviews. Mary Hartley had run a proper grift on him. That was not the behavior of a debutante; it was something a career criminal would do. And then there was what he had said about Balochistan. This was the second time the subject had come up. *But how did it fit in with the rest of the puzzle?* I could not help but wonder what I was missing. I could feel the answer was right there, in front of me, but to my unmitigated frustration, I just could not articulate it into words.

There was only one thing of which I was now certain, and that was that the more I learned of Mary Hartley, the more I feared for Peter. He was a shy, unassuming man who wanted a quiet, scholarly life. The woman the Masons had just described to me seemed to be the opposite—a grasping, almost rapacious creature. Any relationship with someone like that could only end with a broken heart for my friend. *Would it be better if I abandoned my search?* I could simply lie about it. It would be only too easy to go home and tell Peter that she had vanished without a trace. I was an excellent liar, and Peter was always easy to lie to, far too trusting for his own good.

I dismissed the possibility just as quickly as I had considered it. There was the small matter of my professional pride. I had no intention of letting a case go unsolved, not to mention the fact that I owed Peter a debt that was far too great for me to lie to him.

Even as I mulled over this quandary, Charan Singh disturbed my reverie. 'It's just after eight, Huzoor. If we head back now, we can make it to Rajpore House for supper.'

'No, not quite yet,' I replied. 'What I really need right now, old man, is a drink.'

CHAPTER 19

I have always believed that if you want to understand a city, if you truly want to comprehend its quiddity, you must walk its streets at night.

All cities are illusions, and none more so than Bombay. By daylight, it seemed staid and imperial, even majestic on occasion, but it was only when the sun set and the gaslights dimmed that the real Bombay emerged, a squalid, sordid place filled with color, crime and carnality.

There were no more districts less respectable or more dangerous than the docks. Like every colonial entrepot—be it Singapore, Hong Kong or Bombay—the city's enduring prosperity was dependent on the dockyards. Bombay was one of the world's busiest ports. A thousand ships came in each day, unloading a million tons of cargo. It was here that a parallel city had sprung up to cater to the needs of the lascars and sailors who passed through the city. The English called it Plaguetown, because this was where the bubonic outbreak of 1896 had begun. It was a seething maze of victuallers and lading agents, of travelers' lodges and chandlers, of warehouses and taverns and brothels, and drinking dens so iniquitous that they would make even Lucifer blush.

Plaguetown was a lawless place, where Malay lascars from Batavia rubbed shoulders with Marseillais marins, and Cape

Dutch with Chilean empregados. I remembered reading that there were at least seven murders in the dock district each day, and that even the Bombay Constabulary was reluctant to patrol the dark alleys, preferring instead to leave it to the Military Police.

This was one quarter of Bombay I had never found cause to visit, but in this case, if I was to track down Hamid Ali the porter, I saw no other way. As it turned out, all I had to go on was the vaguest of descriptions. We were looking for a man of medium height, in his late thirties, clean shaven with his head razored bald. The only distinguishing mark that Mr. Mascarenhas had offered was that he had a tatau—a leaping dolphin on his right forearm—and three gold teeth that were the remnants of some past brawl.

Naturally, Charan Singh was not at all pleased to hear that I intended to venture deep into the heart of this most disreputable of districts. Uday Singh, on the other hand, turned out to be rather a surprise.

'We should begin at Carnac Bunder and work our way north. We can ignore Ballard Pier and Colaba, the drinking establishments there are too expensive for common seamen.'

'And how do you know that?' I asked, my curiosity piqued by this unexpected display of expertise.

The only reply I received was a mysterious smile, followed by a grunt of disapproval from Charan Singh, who gave his son a jaundiced glare.

I decided to take Uday Singh's advice, if for no other reason than to annoy his father. We began our search at an establishment named Portuguese George's, a dank hole in the wall near the Princess Dock that served a punch so pungent it could have been used as paint stripper. An inquiry with the owner, a Samoan with a wooden leg and a pierced nose, revealed that nobody fitting Hamid Ali's description had been there.

Though I was tempted to stay a while to watch George's sister, a very pretty mulatta, perform some sort of fan dance with peacock feathers, to my dismay Charan Singh insisted we move on immediately.

Our next stop was called China Bob's, a dingier establishment abutting the wall of a godown not far from Lakri Bunder. Its clientele consisted mainly of Orientals from the Macao trade, which led me to conclude that this was not the sort of place Ali would choose to patronize. Uday Singh then directed us to a slightly more respectable tavern called Paddy Goose on Reay Road. There, the alcohol was of much better quality, especially a very decent pale ale I quite enjoyed sampling. The patrons were mainly Royal Navy ratings, although there were a few merchant seamen scattered through the room. There was no sign of our quarry though, which meant we moved on after just one round, much to my chagrin.

By now, I was starting to feel a wee bit tipsy, inebriated just enough so that the next three places blurred together, all decrepit drinking dens serving rotgut of decreasing quality, tucked away in the lanes surrounding the Cotton Green. Unfortunately, there was still no trace of Hamid Ali, neither hide nor hair to be seen. I was about ready to give up when Uday Singh suggested we try one last establishment, a rather notorious public house on Nesbit Road named the Crown and Anchor.

It was a damp and low-roofed place, with mock Tudor walls stained permanently gray after soaking up decades of tobacco smoke, and a mismatched array of marble-topped tables. The grimy interior was almost deserted except for a smattering of sailors, two Arabs nursing a reeking hookah in one corner and several Africans playing some sort of dice game. As we entered, I scanned the room, pausing when I spied a likely suspect in the far corner, hunched over a mug by himself. He was almost exactly as

Michael Mascarenhas had described, a gaunt ferret-faced fellow with a trio of protuberant teeth capped in gold. This was Hamid Ali; it had to be.

'That's him, I think,' I said to Charan Singh, beckoning him over with a discreet bob of my neck.

'Are you sure?'

'Yes, look at his arm. Do you see it? The leaping dolphin?'

'It looks more like a dead sardine,' Charan Singh replied, peering at the man with a doubtful scowl.

'Nonetheless, this is our man. I am sure of it.'

'Should I bundle him up?'

I gave the big Sikh a withering frown. 'Perhaps we should try the civilized approach before you attempt to exercise your ample charms.'

After telling Charan Singh to keep his distance, so as to not spook the target, I wound my way through the tables, ignoring the questioning glances my presence drew from the other patrons, who were largely a rough and tumble lot.

'Why hello,' I said rather too cheerily when my quarry swiveled his neck and gave me a bleary glare. 'Hamid Ali, isn't it?'

To my dismay, this approach backfired utterly. It was obvious that I had chanced upon him at that stage of drunkenness where he was teetering toward aggressive rather than mellow. As a result, rather than being calmed by my effusiveness, my excess bonhomie immediately made him suspicious.

'Who the bloody hell are you, eh? What do you want?' He shook one fist at me. I noticed he was wearing a ring, engraved with a symbol I recognized all too readily, a square interlocked with a compass.

'I am a fellow traveler,' I replied. 'I have come from the West to seek knowledge in the East.'

Unfortunately, this ploy flopped even worse than the first.

He sneered at me, his brow knotting into a scowl. 'What are you on about?'

Rising to his feet, he looked me up and down so belligerently that Charan Singh took two hasty steps forward.

'If you are looking for a bum boy then just bugger off, won't you? Hamid Ali does not bend over for any man.'

I grimaced as the stench of the man assailed my nostrils. Hamid Ali smelled like he hadn't bathed for days. The reek of sour sweat and cheap alcohol surrounded him like a putrid mist.

Waving Charan Singh off before things got nasty, I tried not to gag.

'I assure you, I have no carnal interest in you or your bottom. I merely wanted to offer to buy you a drink, one member of the lodge to another, and ask a few questions about the journey out.'

The mention of free liquor served to allay his suspicions much more effectively than my attempt to masquerade as a Freemason.

'In that case, I'll have a pint, if you please,' he said.

'Of course,' I gave Charan Singh a nod. He came up and placed a tankard of cheap rum on the table with a snort.

As soon as he set eyes on the alcohol, Hamid Ali's entire demeanor altered; he became almost convivial. Reaching for the jug, he guzzled down half its contents greedily before turning his attention back to me.

'You're a right gentleman, Sir, and I am much obliged.'

'Nonsense. It is my pleasure.'

'Go on then,' Gathering up the jug, he took another vast sip and offered me a greasy grin. 'How can I help?'

'I have a few questions. You're the first-class steward aboard the *Caledonia*, correct?'

'Indeed, I am.'

'And you just arrived from London?'

'I did.'

'And on the journey out, did you happen to make the acquaintance of one Miss Mary Hartley?'

As soon as I mentioned Miss Hartley's name, the man's eyes widened. As I had expected, he tried to bolt. He was quick off the bat, I'll give him that. Aiming the jug squarely at my face, he jumped up as nimbly as a rabbit and made a dash for the exit. In spite of this display of agility, he did not get far. Even as I stepped aside, avoiding the recklessly flung jug, Charan Singh grabbed his shoulder and pinned him squarely in place.

'Let me go.' He squealed, 'I ain't got nothing to say to you.'

His objections were so shrill that they managed to attract some entirely unwelcome attention. From the corner of my eyes, I saw that a swarthy Goan, no doubt the owner of this disreputable establishment, was making his way toward us from across the room. He was flanked by the Janus from the door and two even more menacing-looking thugs, all of who were armed with wooden staves.

The Goan came to a stop in front of me, naked aggression writ on his face.

'Get out of here,' he snarled. 'I don't want your kind in here, causing trouble.'

Uday Singh moved to intercept him, but I forestalled him with a wave.

'It's no bother,' I said, before matters could escalate into something unpleasant. 'We'll be out of your hair in a minute. It's just an argument amongst friends.'

Reaching into my pocket, I extracted a coin and gave it to the Goan. He took it with a sour expression, even as I realized I had committed a bit of a blunder. I had meant to give him a sovereign as a tip, but what I had done instead was hand over the Duke of Bombay's token.

To my surprise, it worked like a charm. When the thug saw it, his attitude changed entirely. Paling visibly, he turned to his men and barked out a string of commands in Konkani. Immediately, they set to chivvying the motley of patrons out of the tavern, pushing them out one by one until I was left alone with Charan Singh, his son and Hamid Ali.

'Please take as long as you need, Sir,' he said, giving me an obsequious bow before handing the coin back, much to my delight.

The Goan retreated to the bar, followed by his henchmen. I replaced the token in my pocket, mentally thanking the Duke because it was turning out to be quite useful, and turned back to Hamid Ali, who was watching me with a sullen scowl.

'As I was saying, do you happen to know a woman named Mary Hartley?'

The man's face hardened. 'And what business is that of yours?'

'Are you aware that she has disappeared?'

A shocked look flushed across his features, but he refused to say a word. Instead, he gave me another scowl.

'Let me cut to the chase,' I said. 'I am trying to locate Miss Hartley's whereabouts. It would be best if you cooperated.'

Hamid Ali's only response was a very rude gesture involving his palm and middle finger.

Rolling my eyes at this childish display, I gave Charan Singh a curt nod. Grinning, he turned the man around roughly and delivered three slaps, one after the other, to his face. After the third blow, two of Hamid Ali's gold teeth came loose. He spat them out, choking and gasping.

'Stop it,' he groaned. 'I'll tell you everything, milord, just don't let the giant hit me anymore.'

I ordered Charan Singh to loosen his iron grip. Hamid Ali sagged forward, half collapsing into the chair after gathering up his wayward bicuspids.

'I barely knew the girl,' he whined. 'I sure as hell don't know where she is.'

'That's not what I was told. The second officer, a gentleman named Mascarenhas, said that she complained about you accosting her, that you tried to force yourself on her.'

'That's not true! He's trying to stitch me up. You've got the story all wrong, I tell you.'

'So, you are saying that Mr Mascarenhas is a liar.'

'No, no. She is, that harpy. Miss Hartley. She's a bloody liar and a tart to boot.'

I leaned forward. 'That's a serious accusation. Are you saying you did not make a pass at her? That you did not seek her out or try to molest her?'

'It's not what you think,' he started to repeat, but I cut him off by slapping the table so hard that it made him flinch.

'Then what is it?' I growled. 'Stop wasting my time and explain it to me!'

'She came to me just after we left England, asking for help.'

It was an interesting twist, and I found my curiosity piqued.

'*She* sought *you* out?'

'Yes, she wanted a favor.'

'What manner of favor?'

'She wanted me to allow her access to the first-class deck. I told her it would cost five pounds. She said she hadn't any money, but then she offered something else in exchange.'

'And what exactly was that?' I asked, though I had already guessed the answer from his prurient tone.

'You know, Sir. A bit of this and that,' he said and gave me a bloody smile. 'We came to a bargain. She let me have a bit of a pinch and tickle, and I agreed to let her up on the promenade deck every morning.'

'Hold on!' I exclaimed, unable to contain my skepticism. 'Are you saying that Miss Hartley, an educated and genteel woman, permitted you to behave inappropriately with her in exchange for access to the first-class deck?'

'Oh, she was a woman all right. I'll testify to that,' he whistled through the gap in his teeth. 'But I'm not sure about the genteel part. She was a minx, Sir, not the harmless little kitten everyone took her to be at first sight.'

Lowering his voice to a whisper, he said, 'What a proper piece of work that memsahib was, let me tell you. Once I let her come updeck, she was all over the nobs up there, parading about with a different gent every two days.'

'Is that so? And who were these gentlemen?'

'Let me see. There was this fat pudding of a Parsi. An heir, I believe, and filthy rich. And a military captain, Gordon or some such, a brooding fellow who had the look of a scoundrel about him. Then there was an odd little duck, a doctor of some sort, another Scotsman who caught her eye. Of course, not to mention high and mighty Mr Mascarenhas himself. She was forever making eyes at him and had him squiring her about like they were at Vauxhall bloody Gardens.'

'Let me guess. You felt left out and decided to take a second pass at her, because you thought she was available. But then, when she rebuffed your advances, you decided to take by force what she refused to give freely.'

Hamid Ali shook his head stiffly. 'That's not what happened. I admit, I lurked about a few times, trying to catch her eye, to see if I could cop another feel. And why not? You can't blame a man for trying. But that uppity bint ignored me utterly. So, after a week, I was happy to leave her to her devices. That is, of course, until she came back to me just after we departed from Gibraltar, looking for another favor.'

'What was it this time?'

He licked his lips and gave me a sly look. 'What's in it for me, eh? Surely, I should get something out of this? A reward of some kind? If you want me to say another word, you will have to pay me!'

I sighed, trying to hide my irritation. This was one of the inevitabilities of an investigation that I despised. Just when things started to get juicy, the suspect always decided to find a spine.

Why did criminals insist upon so much drama, I thought sourly. *Was there some sort of guidebook that ordered them to make things as difficult as possible? Why couldn't they just cooperate without forcing me to get nasty?*

As if he had read my mind, Charan Singh raised his hand and let the man have another stinging slap. Hamid Ali's third and final gold tooth came loose, skittering across the table even as he let out a moan and decided it would be best not to try and bargain any further.

'I have a side business,' he wheezed. 'I get passengers things they want for a premium, items that are sometimes difficult to acquire on board a ship.'

'And Miss Hartley wanted you to find something for her? What was it?'

'Two jars of Condy's crystals, Sir, and some laudanum.' He gave me a desperate grimace, terrified that Charan Singh would give him another whack. 'Rather a large dose of laudanum, actually.'

I wrinkled my brow. Condy's crystals was the trade name for permanganate of potassium which was mainly used as an antiseptic. Laudanum was the tincture of opium, a powerful sedative.

'Why would she want such a peculiar combination?' I murmured to myself.

'You know these upper deckers, Sir. All bloody reprobates. Why, once I had a passenger ask me to find him twelve ounces of liquid paraffin and a jar of magnesium. Anyway, I've learned it's best not to ask too many questions, and to simply get them what they want, as long as they are willing to pay the price.'

'And what was the price you set for Miss Hartley?'

'I offered her the same arrangement as before,' he said, offering me an oily leer.

'Is that so? How did she respond?'

'She laughed at me,' he hissed, trying but failing to hide the outrage in his voice. 'She said that once was bad enough for a lifetime. And then the bitch offered me five pounds. Can you believe it?'

'You took it, I presume.'

'Of course, I did. Money is money, isn't it? I kept up my end and got her what she wanted.'

'But that wasn't the end of it, was it?'

'No, it wasn't. When I asked her what she wanted the laudanum for, do you know what she said to me?'

He feigned an upper-class accent. '"Know your place, Mr. Ali". Can you believe it? Acting all haughty like I was dirt under her shoe.'

'So, you decided to teach her a lesson?'

'What I decided was to renegotiate our arrangement. I told her that if she wanted to keep coming up to the first-class deck, she would have to give me another taste.'

'And how did Miss Hartley respond to this ultimatum?'

'She laughed at me, Sir, and informed me she did not need my help, that she now had a patroness, some Russian hag who was sponsoring her access to First Class. And then she had the nerve to threaten me, to tell me that if I bothered her any more, she would complain to Mr Mascarenhas and have me whipped, before dismissing me like I was her bloody servant.'

'So, you decided you would take by force what she denied you willingly?'

'Oh no, I'm getting to that. It was the very next night, you see. Just after two in the morning, I was doing my rounds, checking the lifeboats, making sure everything was shipshape. That was when I caught her coming out of the priest's cabin.'

'Hold on a minute! What priest?'

'I don't recall his name. An Irishman, and a Catholic,' he said with pronounced disdain. 'He was headed to take over at Saint Mary's in Bandra, I believe.'

He gave me a conspiratorial wink, 'He's the one you should be talking to, not me. Him and Mary were as thick as thieves. Why I even saw them holding hands one evening, on the afterdeck, at the taffrail, behind one of the cowls.'

'A Catholic priest holding hands with an unmarried Anglican woman,' I said, unable to hide my dubiety. 'That sounds rather far-fetched.'

'I swear it, Sir, on all that is holy. Your memsahib spent an inordinate amount of time with that man. She was often in his cabin. Almost every night after Marseilles. I saw her going in and out with my own eyes.'

'You followed her?'

'I did, more than once, but I meant her no harm. I was curious, that's all, and a little put out by her behavior. I mean, the audacity of it! She rejected me, but took up with a man of the cloth. It's positively sinful, a proper scandal.'

'So, you confronted her because of your moral outrage,' I said, my voice dripping with sarcasm.

'I did. I cornered her when she got back to her cabin. I told her, in no uncertain terms, that I was going to tell the captain what she was up to.'

'And what did Miss Hartley have to say to that?'

'At first, she tried to bribe me with another five bob, but when I refused, she went utterly off her rocker.'

He shook his head, 'It was unbelievable, I tell you. One moment, she was perfectly normal, and the next she started to scream and bawl her eyes out. I tried to calm her down and get her under control before she woke up half the passengers.'

'By becoming physical and manhandling her ... ?'

'What else could I do? I may have shoved her around a bit, slapped her once or twice, but it was only to make her stop her caterwauling. But that wasn't the worst of it. There I was, trying my best to calm the mad woman down, and who should turn up? High and mighty Mr Mascarenhas himself. And what did she do when she saw him? She cried "rape, rape, rape", when all I did was smack her a few times.'

'Are you saying you did not try to assault her?'

'What I am saying, Sir, is that she assaulted me. If anything, I am the victim here. She set me up to take the fall. The vile bitch! I didn't touch a hair on her head, but I got a pasting for it, and was put ashore for no fault of mine. It's not cricket, I tell you, that she gets away with batting her eyelashes at all the fine gents, but when a working-class fellow asks for a bit of all right, she cries rape and goes screaming to that dago bastard.' He scowled, spitting ineffectually out of the corner of his toothless mouth. 'He'll get his due, just you wait. And so will she.'

'You realize every word you are saying, Hamid Ali, only serves to incriminate you further. A woman refuses to acquiesce to you, and has you hauled up on charges. That leaves you simmering with resentment, so you decide to have your revenge. And lo and behold, a few days later, she goes missing. It's a story as old as time,' I slammed one hand down on the table so hard it made him shiver.

'This is your last chance to confess. Where is Mary Hartley? Is she dead? Lying in a ditch somewhere?'

'You must believe me, I beg of you. I didn't touch her.' He gave me a desperate look. 'I swear it on my mother's life.'

I sat back, drumming my fingers on the table. It was a convincing performance. I doubted that Hamid Ali had the skill or the sobriety to fake it so effectively, not to mention the fact that if he was lying, why would he have confessed about the laudanum? After all, that admission alone was enough to cost him his job.

'What do you think?' I asked Charan Singh.

The big Sikh wrinkled his nose. 'I don't trust him. I think he's a liar, and he stinks.'

'I think he's telling the truth,' I replied. 'He's not smart enough to lie. Besides, I think if Miss Hartley was lying dead somewhere, we would have found her by now.'

'So, you think he's innocent?'

'I can't say for sure. All I can say is that he's a rather loathsome creature. That I am sure of.'

Hamid Ali, who had been listening to this exchange with an escalating degree of alarm on his face, decided to chime in at that moment. 'I can prove it, milord. I have been right here since the *Caledonia* docked, so I couldn't have done anything to your precious memsahib.' He pointed at the Goan desperately, 'You can ask him if you don't believe me. He will confirm what I am saying is true.'

I frowned and nodded at Charan Singh, who waved the owner of the tavern over to us.

The Goan rushed to oblige. 'How may I be of service?' he asked eagerly.

'How long has this fellow been here? In your establishment?'

'Since the day before yesterday, Sir. We throw him out in the morning, but he sleeps on the front step and is right back every night.'

I stifled a curse. I should have known it was too good to be true. Hamid Ali was very nearly the perfect suspect—not very bright, given to violence and with the countenance of a thug. The only problem was that he had an alibi, a rock-solid one.

Furrowing my brow, I contemplated his testimony. There were two exceedingly interesting pieces of information he had inadvertently revealed. The first was his claim that Miss Hartley had allowed a 'bit of pinch and tickle', as he had put it so colorfully, to gain access to the upper decks. That altered my assumptions entirely. In my mind, I had constructed a careful portrait of a hapless girl who had quickly lost her naivete on the journey out and decided to turn her circumstances to her advantage. All my previous clues—the false romances with Mascarenhas and Dr Ross, the way she had blackmailed Mason the boxwallah, the friendship with the false Contessa and Lady Billimoria's testimony that she was a gold-digger, not to mention her tryst with Captain Gordon—fit that profile perfectly. But this snippet suggested something else entirely. If true, it was not the journey aboard the *Caledonia* that had changed Miss Hartley. She had planned it all out even before she had boarded the vessel. That made this not a crime of opportunity but one that was premeditated, plotted out most likely even before she had accepted Peter's proposal.

The second and more interesting revelation was the priest. I made a mental note to check the manifest for his name. However far-fetched Hamid Ali's accusations may have sounded, I was intrigued. There were two reasons why Mary Hartley could have sought out a priest: either temporal or spiritual. Nothing in my investigation thus far had led me to believe that she was at all devout. In fact, the profile I had pieced together indicated quite the opposite, particularly given her rough treatment at her father's hands. Add to that the fact that she was Church of England while this priest was Catholic, which made it highly unlikely that she had reached out to him for religious guidance. That could only mean that her interest was entirely temporal, most likely romantic. It wasn't unheard of to hear about clergymen who lost their way. *Why else would a priest hold hands with a woman, that too an unmarried one? What other motive could have compelled Mary Hartley to visit a strange man's cabin late at night, if not a dalliance?*

I paused, taking a moment to consider if I could take Hamid Ali at his word. He was a drunk, a bully and a smuggler, and his hygiene was truly lamentable, but I couldn't help but feel there was some truth to what he was saying. Just when I was running out of suspects, he had provided me with one more. and a very interesting one at that!

'Will that be all, Sir?' the Goan asked, interrupting my contemplations.

'What is your name?'

'Gilbert, Sir,' he replied. 'Gilbert Vasco da Gama da Cruz.'

'Well, Gilbert, thank you for your help.' I palmed another fistful of coins, making sure none of them were the Duke's token this time before handing them to him.

'What should we do with him?' he asked, pointing at Hamid Ali.

I frowned, pondering an answer to that question. While it was true that Hamid Ali had an ironclad alibi, it did not exonerate him for harassing Miss Hartley. By his own admission, he had confessed that he had laid hands on her, which in my opinion was a sin that was damn nearly unforgivable.

'I want you to teach him a lesson he won't forget, then hand him over to the police.'

'As you wish,' my new friend Gilbert said with a broad smile, cracking his knuckles with such eagerness that it would have put John L. Sullivan to shame. 'We are only too happy to oblige.

He waved for his henchmen to come over. They surrounded Hamid Ali, who let out an anguished groan, even as Charan Singh turned to me with a weary look on his leonine face.

'It's past four in the morning, Huzoor. Are you done with this wild goose chase?'

Behind us, I could hear Hamid Ali's yelps of pain rising in volume as Gilbert set about meting out his punishment with grim efficiency. *Good*, I thought. *Serves him right!* No man should be allowed to assault a woman and get away scot-free.

'Can we go home now?' Charan Singh complained, 'I haven't eaten a bite all day.'

'Not yet,' I replied. 'We have one more stop to make in Bandra.'

'Bandra?' he exclaimed, glaring at me like I had lost my mind. 'That's all the way across the city. What on earth do you want in Bandra? All you will find there are mosquitos and Catholics.'

'Exactly,' I said with a grin. 'I think I am in the mood for some divine guidance.'

CHAPTER 19

The municipality of Bandra lay across Mahim Bay, located at the very tip of Salsette Island. Originally, Salsette had not been part of Catherine de Braganza's dowry, but in 1782, the English had signed the Treaty of Salbai and occupied the island proper.

It was only in 1845 that Salsette and Bandra were connected to the rest of Bombay, after the construction of the Mahim Causeway. The causeway itself had begun as the brainchild of William Hornby, the then-governor of Bombay who had initiated the construction of a seawall, a vallardo as it was called in Portuguese. Hornby had, by all accounts, been quite a determined fellow, one of those visionary Boy's-Own-Adventure types who had helped forge the British Empire with a combination of indefatigable tenacity and overweening self-righteousness. In Hornby's case, it had been his most fervent dream to see all seven islands of Bombay linked to each other by a common road. Even though the East India Company had bitterly opposed the project, Hornby had managed to push it through, ensuring that an embankment was built across Worli Creek, thus preventing the city from being flooded each time the tide came in.

After the Hornby Vellard was completed, the construction of three arterial roads followed in quick succession: the Duncan Causeway in 1803, which connected Parel to Salsette island; the

Colaba Causeway in 1838, which linked Bombay with Colaba and Old Woman's Island; and the Mahim Causeway in 1845, which united Mahim with Bandra.

Before that, the only route to Bandra had been via a marshy mire, accessible only by ferry or by hiring the services of native coolies who carried travelers across the sandbanks on their backs during low tide, like mules. But now, this fen was cut through by a single metaled road that had finally managed to connect the suburbs to the city.

By the time we reached the four-way traffic junction at Mahim, it was almost dawn. A night of drinking and wandering around the docks had left me with the most abominable of headaches, and the rising sun made me wince. Thankfully, there was little traffic. The Mercedes sped up, rumbling past a motley line of carts and a ragged cluster of coolies who hustled to get out of our way, shouting curses in our wake.

I sat back and closed my eyes. Beneath the throaty clamor of the car's engine, I could hear the rustling swish of the waves as they crashed against the embankment. As always, I felt a palpable sense of disconnection crossing from Bombay into Bandra. It was like entering a different world, leaving the hustle and bustle behind and crossing into a more rural, sylvan setting. Although Bandra was just a few miles from the Fort, it was a world apart from the city. There, it was a hectic mess of cramped lanes and dense crowds. But in Bandra it was the opposite, a quiet enclave of winding lanes lined with flowering trees, dotted with rows of low bungalows and a splendid assortment of churches.

For almost four hundred years, Bandra had been home to a cluster of humble fishing villages populated by the Kolis, an itinerant tribe who had been pushed out of Gujarat because of Muslim expansion. Then, in 1534, a Portuguese pirate named Deigo de Silvera had sailed up the Mahim creek and burned the villages to the ground, after which the first Christian settlers had quickly arrived. The Portuguese had been the first to occupy Salsette and Bassein, eagerly converting the locals to Catholicism. The English had followed soon after, and a large number of locals had converted to Christianity and flocked in droves to seek employment with the East India Company. This group had come to be referred to as East Indians, and it was a common enough mistake made by most outsiders to call them Goans, thinking them to be migrants from the Portuguese colony of Goa, which was located just south of the city. However, most of the Goans had arrived relatively recently, mainly the Casados, who were second-generation Portuguese born in India. They were migrating to the suburb of Santa Cruz, where an array of low-cost housing societies was being constructed, an ugly township of two- and three-storeyed buildings marching toward the distant hills like a concrete phalanx.

But around Bandra proper, especially between Perry Road and Hill Road, it was still mainly East Indian territory. The invisible boundary between these two districts was the Basilica of Our Lady of the Mount, which was where I was headed.

As the Mercedes turned up Hill Road, I could see the arched spires of the chapel in the distance, towering atop the peak, gleaming in the dawn like a pair of silver spears. Mount Mary, as it was locally called, was a relatively young church, but one with an ancient and remarkable history. This current shrine had been preceded by two previous incarnations. The first had been a humble mud oratory built by a Jesuit priest in 1570, inside which he had installed a wooden statue of the Virgin, imported from Lisbon. Unfortunately, in 1710, it had been sacked by Arabs from Muscat, when they invaded the island. They had looted the chapel and desecrated the statue, hacking off one of its gilded hands. However, before they could burn the building down, they had been assailed by a cloud of enraged bees, who had driven them off before they could do permanent damage.

In 1761, the church had been rebuilt, and then expanded again in 1902. The result was an imposing semi-Gothic structure with a pair of twin pyramidal spires very reminiscent of the Chartres Cathedral at Notre Dame. As the car drew to a halt, I paused to admire the building. Compared to the grand cathedrals of the continent, it was mawkish. Yet, there was something compelling about the place, judging by the long line of pilgrims congregating at the entrance, even though it was early in the morning.

Charan Singh forged ahead to clear a path for me. We pushed our way to the door, only to be obstructed by an elderly rector who was rather hard of hearing. After a brief struggle, punctuated by some inspired sign language, I managed to explain that I had come not to pay my respects to Our Lady of the Mount but to commune with Father Donovan.

Hesitantly, he escorted me to a small rectory and went off to summon the Father, who arrived a few minutes later. Given Hamid Ali's insinuations, I had expected him to be a young man, someone inexperienced and naive enough to be drawn into a shipboard romance by a lonely woman's overtures. Much to my surprise, he turned out to be quite the opposite. Father Donovan was sixty if a day, and an old India hand to boot, I inferred, seeing his skin, which was the color of boiled leather and his eyes which were a malarial yellow, permanently jaundiced after decades spent squinting under the harsh sun.

'Good day, Father!' I exclaimed and offered him my hand.

He shook it with a firm grip. Father Donovan was about my height, but much more powerfully built, with a stevedore's burly frame and powerful shoulders that strained against his cassock when he moved. His palms were knotted with old calluses, I noticed, the hands of a laborer and not a cleric, an observation that intrigued me.

'How can I help you, my son?' he asked, looking me up and down, scrutinizing me every bit as carefully as I had him. 'Do you find yourself in need of ecclesiastical guidance at this early hour?'

'Well, I am looking for answers, Father.'

He gave me a boyish grin. 'I don't have a great many answers to offer, my boy, but I do know it is the first step on the path to salvation when you start to ask questions of yourself.'

I reciprocated his grin with one of my own. 'I'm afraid my mortal soul is beyond salvation. But with your help, I believe we could rescue someone else who may be in dire trouble.'

'You're not looking for a priest, are you?'

'No, I'm not. Actually, to be honest, I'm looking for a woman.'

His impish smile grew wider. 'I'm afraid I cannot help you much with that either. As you can see,' he said, pointing at his collar, 'that is a subject well beyond my range of expertise.'

'What if I said it was Mary I have come to seek?'

'Most pilgrims come here seeking her favor, my friend. You will just have to wait your turn outside.'

With that declaration, he was about to leave when I said, 'I mean a different Mary, Father Donovan. Mary Hartley. I believe you knew her quite well.'

It was a brazen attempt to rattle him, and it worked almost too well. Even as I mentioned Miss Hartley's name, his manner changed. In a blink, the friendliness melted away and was replaced by a cold fury.

'What the bloody hell do you want with her?' Father Donovan snarled. 'Who sent you?' He advanced toward me threateningly, his hands clenching into fists. Alarmed by such vehemence, I took a wary step back. Father Donovan did not look quite as old as he had a minute ago, nor quite as benign. And while I was confident I could handle myself if it came to a scrap, he looked like he would put up a decent showing.

'Hold on now, Father, calm down! There's no need to come across like Jim Jeffries. I assure you, I mean neither Miss Hartley nor you any harm.'

He hesitated. I took the opportunity to offer him the letter given to me by Hall-Caine. Taking it, Father Donovan perused it with a frown, even as I made an effort to correct the oversight and introduce myself properly.

'My name is Sikander Singh. I am a friend of Peter Rowan, Miss Hartley's fiancé. He is worried to death about her, which is why I came to see you. She has vanished, you see, as surely as the white rabbit himself!'

This revelation stopped Father Donovan dead in his tracks. Taking a deep breath, he made a great effort to calm himself down.

'Not here,' he said evasively. 'Follow me, please.'

He led me into his private sacristy. It was a small enclosure, barely larger than a broom closet. the sanctum where he prepared for Mass, I guessed, judging by the chasuble and stole hanging on the clothes tree in one corner.

'Please have a seat,' he said, pointing toward a tiny wingback chair. Turning away from me, he stepped into an adjoining room, only to return a few minutes later with a pair of chipped enamel mugs.

He offered me one. I was about to decline when a whiff of the mug's contents wafted into my nostrils. I had been expecting tea, but this was coffee. Good Turkish coffee, by the smell of it.

'That's rather surprising,' I said, accepting it gratefully. 'To find an Englishman with a taste for coffee rather than tea.'

'Well, it's a good thing that I'm Irish then,' he said, grinning. 'My first posting was in Kenya. I picked up a taste for coffee there. I find tea rather insipid, I am afraid.'

'Speaking of which,' he opened a drawer and took out an amber bottle. Uncapping it, he poured half a measure into his cup before offering it to me. Given the pounding in my skull, I was tempted to decline, but it was not in my nature to refuse a drink, especially one that was free. I held out my cup and Father Donovan proceeded to dole out an even more generous measure.

Taking a sip, I savored it appreciatively. It was decent rye whiskey, Bushmills, judging by the taste..

'Here's to the Irish!' I exclaimed, raising the cup in salutation. 'And to a fine cup of coffee.'

'Down with the English!' Father Donovan retorted. 'And down with tea.'

Both of us laughed and sat back, enjoying another couple of sips in silence.

'Forgive me,' he said at last, offering me a sheepish nod. 'I have the devil's own temper. The curse of the Irish! It gets the better of me sometimes.'

I smiled. 'Whereabouts in Ireland do you hail from?'

'Actually, I have never been to the homeland. I'm an old Africa hand, born and raised in Johannesburg.'

'Is that so?' I nodded. So, I had been partly correct about his skin but entirely mistaken about the accent. What I had taken to be the broad lilt of Hibernian was really the thickness of Afrikaans.

'Yes, indeed. My father was an army surveyor. He died at Isandlwana. I was raised at the Children's Home in Cape Town.'

He grinned. 'I wasn't always spiritually inclined. To be honest, in my youth, I was quite a hell-raiser. In fact, I got into a spot of bother when I was seventeen, and they gave me a choice. To join the army, or to go to prison.'

'The army? Which regiment?'

'The Cape Rifles. I served seven years. I went in as a humble trooper and finished as a color sergeant.'

'Did you see much action?'

'Oh yes! I was at the Relief of Mafeking, and the retaking of Griqualand under General Warren. I took a bullet in the thigh at Faber's Put and was out of commission for the rest of the war. That was when I found my true calling.'

He finished the rest of his coffee before putting down the mug and giving me a wary grin. 'Anyway, that's enough about me. You wanted to know about Mary Hartley? You said she has gone missing. Is that so?'

'Yes,' I murmured, taking a sip of my own coffee. 'But you already knew that, didn't you?'

I peered at him, searching for some reaction, any tremor of emotion, but his expression stayed deadpan, as stone-faced as a statue.

'I'll be frank, Father. Do you know something about her disappearance? Has she done a runner?'

Father Donovan did not say a word. His smile remained cold, fixed on his face like a mask.

'It is a matter of dire importance that I find her,' I continued. 'As I said, she is engaged to a dear friend, and he is distraught at the thought that she may have chosen to break their agreement.'

'What if she does not wish to be found?' he asked so softly that I struggled to hear him.

'I beg your pardon?'

He shook his head and let out a mordant chuckle. 'A small joke, forgive my presumption. I am sorry to disappoint you, but I do not know anything about Miss Hartley's whereabouts.'

I put down my cup and leaned forward, dropping all attempts at conviviality.

'I don't believe you, Father. I think you are hiding something.'

Father Donovan responded to this accusation with a grimace. 'I have said all that I can to you. Now, if you will excuse me, I must prepare for the morning Mass.'

I decided to try something a bit different. If the direct approach wasn't doing the trick, then perhaps good old-fashioned guilt might work instead.

'I believe you know more than you're saying,' I said. 'If that is indeed the case, please, I beseech you, think of my friend. Surely, he deserves better than to live his life unsure of her well-being and her intentions.'

'I empathize with your friend,' Father Donovan said, pausing briefly, 'but as I said, I do not know where Mary is. However, I am certain she is safe. You can give your friend that assurance. I shall say a prayer for him, but I cannot help you any more than that.'

'Father, I need more than that. Why are you hiding the truth? Why are you protecting her? Who is Mary Hartley to you?'

He ignored me. Rising to his feet, he gathered up the cups and started to shuffle toward the door.

'Are you in love with her?' I asked.

That brought him to a dead halt. He turned to look at me, surprised by my bluntness.

'It isn't the first time a man of the cloth has been led astray by a pretty face,' I said. 'It's not unheard of. You're still a virile man, and she was an unattached woman, an attractive one to boot by all accounts. Did she entice you, make you question your vows? Like Simeon on the pillar, she was your most arduous test, wasn't she?'

I had hoped to offend him, to shock him into losing his composure, but Father Donovan merely laughed, a bark of disbelief.

'What a lurid imagination you have!' He shook his head. 'I hate to contradict you, Mr Singh, but you're entirely wrong.'

'I did not seek her out. It was the other way around. Mary came to me.'

'She did? Why?'

'She was having a crisis of conscience. She came to me because she was confused, and needed someone to speak to, a confidante.'

'Because of her impending marriage?'

'Yes, in part, but it was more than that. Mary's mental state was complicated, to say the least.'

With that cryptic declaration, he lapsed into an uncomfortable silence. 'I cannot say more than that.'

'Cannot, or will not?'

'What Mary said to me was a confidence made in the utmost sanctity. I am loath to violate the trust she placed in me.'

'A confession? She came to you for a confession. That makes no sense at all. Peter is Church of Scotland, the staunchest of Presbyterians. He would never become engaged to a Catholic.'

'She was not Catholic,' he said with a frown. 'That was why I told her I could not hear her confession, or offer her the sacrament. I did, however, offer to listen as a friend.'

'And what did she tell you?'

'As I said, I am loath to speak of it.'

'But you just said that it was not a confession. That means it is not sealed by canon. Surely, you can break a confidence if it could save her? Come now, she could be hurt or bleeding or worse, Father. What you say now could help me extricate her from whatever mess she might be mired in. If you truly care for her, it is imperative you tell me everything.'

He took a moment to weigh my words before letting out a sigh of surrender.

'She was not happy, Mr Singh, with your friend's contract. She regretted having accepted it and was worried if coming out to India had been the right choice.'

'She said that to you?'

'Yes, she did. In those very words. She had a stack of your friend's letters, which she read to me one by one. An intelligent man, but a staid one. Mary realized she did not want the life he wrote of, in a mofussil town like Ajmer, wasting away in the heat and dust.'

'And that was the only reason for her fears?'

'Not quite. She also told me that the real reason she had come out to India was to escape.'

'Escape what?'

'Not what, but who!' He gave me a stiff frown. 'What do you know of Mary's past, if I might inquire?'

'Not a lot, other than the fact that she lied to Peter about her antecedents, that in reality her father was a drunk who beat her, that he died violently when she was very young, and she was carted off to an aunt, where once more, her uncle tried to take advantage of her. As a result, she ran away to Edinburgh to try and be a performer. It was there that a nun named Sister Bridget brought her Peter's proposal.'

'That's only half the story. When Mary ran away to Edinburgh, she fell in with rather a rough lot, a gang led by a Fagin named Diamond Jim Menezies. It was his stock in trade to provide young women with protection. In exchange, he taught them how to pickpocket and shoplift. His particular innovation was to dress them up in taffeta and velvet, have them pretend to be high-born ladies, and sneak into department stores and dinner parties, where they would steal from the other patrons and burgle the hosts.'

'She was a thief?'

Father Donovan nodded. 'She did what she needed to survive. Unfortunately, it was her bad luck that this Menezies turned out to be an even bigger villain than her father and uncle combined. Not only did he force her to steal for him, but he also got her to act as a mule who transported his stolen goods to be fenced. And unfortunately he became dangerously obsessed with her. Mary said that he used her most horribly, Mr Singh, forcing her to do dreadful, depraved things.'

'He raped her?' I gasped, unable to hide my disgust.

'Yes, more than once. She was his thrall. He terrorized her constantly, stalking her every move. He told her often that he owned her, that she was his property and his alone. Mary was deathly afraid of him. She told me she ran away twice. but both times, he tracked her down and beat her half to death. Do you understand now, Sir? That has been Mary's cross to bear, all her life. She has had brute after brute try to control her, to own her. And that was why she accepted your friend's proposal on spec, not because she wanted to get married but because she needed to escape. She was trying to get away from the life of iniquity she found herself trapped in due to chance and circumstance, and from Menezies. She was trying to break his hold over her once and for all, and to start anew.'

I sat back, considering his words. If he was telling the truth, then Mary Hartley was on the run. That cast an entirely different light on her actions. It made sense now—her behavior with the Masons and her swindling of the fake Contessa and the hapless Dr Ross. It also explained why she had left her documents at the hostel, along with her luggage. If she was indeed fleeing from someone who was after her, it explained why she was trying to amass a neat little nest egg. It also made sense for her to start over with a clean slate, with a new identity and a new name that could not be traced. It also confirmed that she had planned it all out in advance, that it had never been her intention to meet

Peter at all, much less marry him. He had been her meal ticket, a means to an end, and her real plan all along had been to come to India and disappear.

What it did not explain however was how she had managed to set it up. *Where had she got the new identity? And a new set of documents? It was impossible to travel in the colonies without a proper set of papers? How could she possibly have managed that without help?* No, I was missing something. *What could it be?*

'There's more to the story,' I mused. 'There had to be!'

'Is this how investigations work? You ask the same question again and again until you get the answer you want?' Father Donovan asked, interrupting my thoughts.

'That's half the process,' I said, cracking a grin. 'But there's another side to it as well. In fact, it's the very thing which makes me a decent investigator, Father. Can you guess what it is?'

'The inability to take a hint,' he said sarcastically.

'Oh no! Although I confess I am as pig-headed as the worst of them. It's my nose, Father. I have been blessed with a very, very sensitive nose. I can smell a liar from a mile away, and I can tell when someone is keeping a secret from me, each and every time. And right now, I am sorry to say, but you absolutely reek. Here's what I think. You are hiding the truth because you and Mary were involved in some way, which is why you are covering for her. You see, I happen to know, and on good account, that she visited your cabin more than once late at night, far past a time that would be considered decent. Do you deny that?'

He did not answer, refusing to look me in the eye.

'Well, if you were not romantically entangled, why was Miss Hartley so keen to spend time with you? Surely, you don't expect me to believe you were praying in there until the wee hours of the morning?' I said, not bothering to mask my sarcasm.

There was still no answer from Father Donovan. All he did was close his eyes and purse his lips.

'Imagine, Father, how it would look if your flock found out you were spending time with an unmarried woman, that too one who was promised to another man? I can only imagine the scandal!'

His eyes snapped open. He gave me a steely glare.

'Do not presume your threats will intimidate me, Sir. I am a man of God. I fear no earthly prosecution!'

His voice was like iron. By God, I liked him. Not only did he have character, which was a rare enough thing, but he was also loyal, which was even rarer. *How was I to break him? What would it take?*

Luckily, he saved me the trouble.

'Are you a religious man, Mr Singh?'

I stifled a sigh. *What was it about Christians that everything inevitably became a question of piety? Was it that they possessed an inviolate devotion, or was it guilt that gave birth to this sense of righteousness, compelling them to reduce everything to a biblical debate?*

Personally, I was neither an atheist, nor quite an agnostic. If pushed, I liked to define my system of belief as syncretic, and my faith as fluctuating. The truth was that my morality was formed not from idealism and dogma, but from my explorations of the darker side of humanity. When you have seen the worst mankind has to offer, up-close and personal, the beastly instincts that hide in the most primal recesses of the sanest of minds, it becomes difficult to hold faith in the abstract and the intangible.

That was why I shied away from ecclesiastical discussions, but on this occasion, I realized I had little choice. *What else could I expect from a man of the cloth?* It was obvious that if I was to get Father Donovan to cooperate with me, I would invariably have to yield to this line of questioning, however tedious it may feel to a rationalist such as myself.

'I am not religious, no.'

'And why is that? What is it that caused you to lose your faith?'

It felt odd to be on the receiving end for a change. Ordinarily, I would have quashed any such questions in the bud, but in this case, I decided to play along, if for no other reason than it might serve to loosen his tongue.

'Honestly, Father, after the things I have seen, I have little belief in the nobility of suffering. That's what you sell, isn't it, all you religious types? Suffer now and you shall find redemption in the afterlife. I'm sorry, but the idea of redemption, whether in this life or the next, has always struck me as a bit of a confidence game.'

For the second time in as many minutes, Father Donovan managed to surprise me. I was trying to insult him, even rile him up, but he let out a bemused chuckle.

'Oh, in my experience there is no nobility in suffering. There is only suffering. That is the truest and most unavoidable of human conditions. All men are made to suffer, whether kings or beggars. But that is where you are mistaken, Mr Singh. We religious types, as you describe us, do not sell redemption. What we sell is hope. That is the only thing even more inescapable than suffering.'

'And that is why you were beholden to Mary Hartley? To offer her hope when there was none to be had?'

'Oh no! You have it backwards. She gave me hope, Sir. I owed her the debt, not the other way around. I have a secret, you see,' he said, 'one which I have never shared with anyone until now.' His face darkened palpably, turning a guilty shade of crimson. 'The perils of a misspent youth, I'm afraid. When I was a humble corporal, I paid a visit to one of the clergyman's daughters. It left me with a most unwanted souvenir, one which has been the cause of much of my subsequent suffering.'

It took me a moment to grasp what he was talking about.

'Gonorrhea,' I whispered. 'You have been a naughty boy, haven't you, Father?'

'What can I say? I was young and had a moment of weakness. I gave in to the temptation of the flesh one lonely night. It was a dalliance for which I thought I had been suitably punished. Truth be told, I thought it was behind me, but obviously my punishment was yet to be completed, my payment still due. Just after we left Marseille, I had an episode, for lack of a better word,' he said with a frown. 'I suppose I should call it a relapse. Honestly, I had endured such bouts before, but it had been some years since the last one, and it was never quite so bad. I imagine it was the tropics that brought it on. It seized me a few days after we entered the Med, a terrible itching in my nether regions. At first, I dismissed it as a severe case of prickly heat, but it quickly intensified into something much more painful, an ache in my gut and intestines, as if I was being devoured from the inside out. Each time I tried to pass water, it felt as though I was pissing glass. The pain grew, intensifying as we approached Egypt. Even though I tried to control myself, to try and manage it, I finally succumbed to a raging fever.'

'You didn't think of asking for help?'

'How could I? If word got around, I would have become a laughing stock. A priest with the clap! No, no. Surely, you understand! A ship is a closed world, which is why I kept it secret and refused to visit the ship's surgeon,' he said with a slight shiver. 'I had heard stories of how they put patients ashore, and I just couldn't risk it.'

'But you told Mary, didn't you? You took her into your confidence.'

'Oh no! She had an eagle eye, and noticed my symptoms. Somehow, I don't know what strings she pulled, but she managed to secure several doses of silver nitrate and potassium permanganate.' His face blushed a livid scarlet.

'It was desperately embarrassing. She washed me, Sir, a lavage twice daily of my most intimate parts. She kept it up for almost a week. There was a hurricane just before we docked at Cairo. The ship shook and shuddered. The waves crashed so high that I feared the vessel would capsize. The winds made the shutters clatter, the rain blustered in horizontally and drenched the deck, seeping in under the door to leave my cabin ankle-deep in water. And all through this maelstrom, despite the tossing and turning, I lay half-dead in a stupor. But Mary refused to leave my side, Mr Singh. She cared for me as if I were her own child. And in my fevered state, I came to see her for what she truly was. An angel, Sir. A creature of the divine.'

I frowned, considering what he had revealed. There were two questions that would not stop nagging at me.

'It's curious, isn't it, that a young woman apparently from a sheltered background, a good Christian, recognized the sailor's disease so readily? What's more, how did she know exactly how to treat it?'

'I thought so myself. I even asked her where she had acquired such unexpected knowledge.'

'And what was her answer to that?'

'She laughed and told me not to judge a book by its cover,' Father Donovan let out a sigh. 'You think you know her, don't you? You haven't a clue, Sir. Mary was quite extraordinary. She was special. You asked me if I loved her. The truth is that I worshiped her, Mr Singh, and not only for saving my life. I loved her because she was pure, a purity that was twisted by hardship, crippled by circumstance and buried away beneath suffering, but as palpable to anyone who cared to look as a blinding light. That is why I had to help her, Mr Singh. Not only did I owe her a debt that could never be repaid in full, but she was also my last chance at salvation, Sir, my only hope for redemption. By helping her, I could make at least part payment for my sins.'

'By assisting her in repudiating my friend? One sin for another?'

'Yes! I admit it freely, just as I have risked everything by telling you about my malaise. I gave her a letter of introduction to a friend in Lahore and a paltry sum of money, some ninety rupees. I also encouraged her to find her own way in the world, free from servitude to any man.'

'Why?' I snarled. 'Why would you do that? Why would you help someone deliberately perpetuate a fraud that would bring injury to a good man?'

'I have asked myself that not once but many times since I met Mary. The only answer I have is that it was because of her eyes, and because of the blood on my hands.' He paused, looking pensively at his palms. 'Here's the smell of the blood still: all the perfumes of Arabia will not sweeten this little hand ... my soul is too much charg'd with blood.'

Macbeth, I thought. A priest quoting Shakespeare, how very unexpected! I had expected something more biblical, but Father Donovan seemed to be a man of hidden talents.

Even though he had managed to pique my curiosity, I did not push for an explanation to justify this cryptic declaration. If there is one universal truth I have learned as an investigator, it is that everyone wants to talk. People only lie when it is easier than confronting the truth. More often than not, they want to reveal the truth, to confess their innermost secrets, to unburden themselves. The trick is not to push them but to wait, to give them time to trust you.

As I had hoped, my patience paid off.

After an elongated pause, Father Donovan offered me a mournful smile. 'Did I tell you why I became a priest? Truth be told, I was happy being a soldier. It is a simple life, to be told when to wake, when to sleep and what to eat. And I was a bloody good soldier. I was mentioned in dispatches thrice, and when I got hit, they put me up for the King's commendation. I didn't get it, of course, being African and not English born. And do you know how the burra sahibs rewarded me for gallantry? They posted me to Kroonstad because I spoke Afrikaans like a native. Have you read Milton, Mr Singh? "For those rebellious, here their Prison ordained; in utter darkness, and their portion set; as far removed from God and light of Heaven; as from the Center thrice to the utmost Pole."' Father Donovan shook his head sadly.

'If there is hell on earth, Sir, it was the camps. At Lord Kitchener's orders, we burned the farms and the homesteads, killed the livestock and rounded up the Boers, and herded them into the camps. Women and children mainly; the burghers were off on commando. "Scorch the earth," the generals said, "and the men will surrender,"' He shivered. 'They did not surrender, not one of them. They called themselves the bitter enders, and they fought on. The bravest bastards I have ever seen. No ammunition, no supplies and no shelter, but they kept fighting, even as their families rotted behind barbed wire, living in tattered tent cities we had hastily thrown up, without water or proper sanitation, surviving on little or no food. There weren't even blankets to keep the children warm.

'I was in charge of camp security. Our orders were simple but strict: nobody in and nobody out. If they died, we dug a grave and buried them. And they died by the dozens, Mr Singh, dropping like flies. Four months after I arrived, cholera swept through the camp, then typhoid, measles, diphtheria, enteritis, malaria, pneumonia and whooping cough, whittling the population down to a mere handful. Do you know how many people died in Kroonstad? More than two thousand children and fifteen hundred women, and we stood there in our blockhouses, turning a blind eye to it all.'

Letting out a groan, he went on. 'There was this little Boer girl they brought in one day. She was four years old, the only survivor from a skirmish near Constantia. She had hair like spun gold, Mr Singh, and the bluest eyes, as azure as a cloudless sky. When I dream, I still see her face and her smile. Such a beautiful, innocent smile!'

He fixed me with a solemn scowl. 'I watched that child die, Mr Singh, slowly wither away. I watched as her teeth and hair fell out, as her eyes turned dull and lifeless, until at last I put her in the ground. The very next day, I resigned and took the oath to serve God.'

Father Donovan let out a long sigh. 'I have done more evil than most men, Mr Singh. I have enough sins against my name to know that I cannot be saved, but I will be damned if I let Mary suffer the same fate as that child. I could not let this chance pass by, to do some good, even if it was only a drop in the bucket.'

His voice grew pensive as he continued. 'Mary had eyes like that child in Kroonstad. In spite of all that she had seen, all that she had suffered, she was still innocent, still full of life. She deserved a chance, Mr Singh. I could not let her die a slow death, shackled to a man who could not know the truth of her, slowly withering away until all that made her unique, all that made her special dwindled, and that the only thing that remained was a listless shadow.

That is why, I beg of you, one man to another, let her be. Let her make her own life, wherever she may choose to go. Let her chart her own course.'

He was persuasive, I will give him that. His eloquence was sincere. If it had been another man in my place, Father Donovan may have managed to sway him. But me? Helene has often accused me of being cynical, but the truth is much more basic than that. After you have seen the things I have—the darkness that hides beneath the thin veil of civilization, the savagery that lurks inside every man's soul—words, even heartfelt ones, come to mean very little.

'I ... cannot do that, Father,' I said solemnly. 'I, too, owe a debt, and I am known for paying my debts. A maharaja's word, you see, is worth somewhat more than that of an ordinary man.'

Father Donovan paused, biting his lip. Putting down his mug, he extracted the bottle once more and uncorked it before offering it to me. This time, I refused. He shrugged and brought it to his lips, taking a long swig before letting out a vast sigh.

'There is one more thing I have been keeping from you, one more secret Mary entrusted me with,' he said, looking me straight in the eye. 'Would it change your mind if I was to tell you that the person you are seeking is not Mary Hartley at all? That she was someone else altogether?'

This declaration hit me like a punch in the gut. I jackknifed up so suddenly that the bottle on the table wobbled and fell over.

'What are you saying?' I demanded.

'The woman you think of as Mary Hartley, well, that is not her name at all. It was merely a nom de guerre, a ruse, an alias.'

'I don't understand!'

'Her real name is Emily Malcolm. She told me so herself. You see, two days before the *Caledonia* was due to set sail, she was working her patch outside the Waverley railway station, when she happened to run into a young woman who was waiting for a train. When that woman went to the ladies' lavatory to freshen up, Emily decided to follow her and liberate her of her purse and carpetbag. That woman was Mary Hartley.

'You mean to say?'

'Yes, she is an impostor. A changeling, so to speak. Let me try and explain. You see, when Emily, much to her surprise, found a second-class ticket to India, along with a passport and your friend's letters while rummaging through the woman's possessions, she decided this was her one chance to escape, to start a new life in a country where no one knew her. The very next morning, she headed for London and managed to board the *Caledonia*, passing herself off as Mary Hartley. And the rest ... well, you know the rest.'

'My God!' I sagged back, stunned by this revelation. It was too much, just too incredible to absorb. But even as I struggled to comprehend all that Father Donovan had just divulged, I realized it made perfect sense. At last, the puzzle had come together, revealing a pattern even I could never have predicted.

'So, she had no intention of marrying Peter at all, did she?'

'I asked her that very question. She admitted that had been her initial plan, to take Miss Hartley's place in every way. But then, as she came closer to India, she grew afraid and began to have doubts. Not just that she would be caught, but deeper and darker doubts. It is one thing to steal a ticket and quite another to steal a life. She said that to me more than once. Added to that, she was assailed, of course, by the growing apprehension that your friend would turn out to be cruel, that he would hurt her, just like every other man in her life. "Why exchange one prison for another," she said. And she was right! I am not ashamed that I helped her, Mr Singh. In fact, I am proud of it, just as I am glad that she is free at last.'

Even as he made this declaration, another thought struck me as forcibly as a thunderbolt.

'Hold on a minute! I wonder, if your Miss Malcolm is an impostor, what happened to the real Miss Hartley?'

'I cannot say for certain,' Father Donovan replied. 'But I imagine she must be on her way out to India as we speak.'

'That means ...'

'Yes, it's more than possible that your friend has not been jilted after all. His missing memsahib might just arrive in Bombay on the very next tide.'

CHAPTER 20

Thanks to Uday Singh, we made it back from Bandra in record time.

He pushed the Mercedes to its limit, driving at breakneck speed. In the back seat, I held on for dear life. Charan Singh, who was hunched over beside me, kept up a steady stream of invective each time the car rattled over a pothole and caused him to bump his turban on the roof.

I couldn't help but laugh. What an unexpected twist! I had been prepared for a jilting, a kidnapping, even a murder, but I could never have imagined in my wildest speculations that this would turn out to be a case of impersonation.

Still, that meant good news for Peter. I did some quick mental arithmetic. If Miss Hartley, the real Miss Hartley, had departed England on the next ship after the *Caledonia*, she would arrive in Bombay within the week. That meant Peter would be able to go through with his wedding plans after all. A harvest wedding, just in time for Baisakhi! That should cheer him up.

When the car arrived at Rajpore House, I thanked Uday Singh profusely for his help and rushed in to tell my old friend what we had discovered, accompanied by Charan Singh, close in tow as always.

'Peter,' I shouted as I dashed through the front door. 'I have news for you. Bloody good news!'

Unfortunately, before I could take more than a couple of steps, Helene appeared to waylay me, a thunderous expression on her face. She had been waiting, I realized, half hidden behind a nearby philodendron, smoking furiously. The cigarette surprised me. She had quit almost a year and a half ago, and had been very assiduous about it, resisting every temptation. But now to see her puffing away like a factory chimney could only signify one thing, that I was in the deepest of trouble.

'*Bâtard! Menteur! Une merde! Sale excuse pour un homme! Vous me dégoûtez! Espèce d'horrible et redoutable bête!*' she exclaimed, stamping toward me like a rhino about to charge.

'English, Helene,' I said, rolling my eyes. 'I can't understand a word you're saying.'

'Sikander Singh, you are a dreadful man. I hate you.'

Beside me, Charan Singh cleared his throat and gave me a furtive look, as if to convey how uncomfortable he was to be caught in the middle of this exchange. I decided to take pity on him. It had been a long night, and as always, he had been my stalwart right hand.

'Hold on, my love,' I said to Helene. 'You can scold me to your heart's content in exactly one minute, but first, there is something I must do.'

Turning to Charan Singh, I commanded, 'Go and fetch Rowan Sahib from his bedroom. Tell him I have a surprise for him, that I have found his missing memsahib.'

Charan Singh gave me a relieved smile. Leaning forward, he whispered, 'The mighty oak breaks in a storm, but the supple reed learns to bend. Remember that, Huzoor.'

With that cryptic observation, he hurried off, heading for the steps with an alacrity that would have put a man half his age to shame.

After his departure, I turned back to Helene and offered her my most irresistible grin.

'You were just telling me how dreadful I am? Would you care to continue?'

Unfortunately, this attempt at being charming turned out to be a blunder.

'Answer me this minute. Where on earth have you been?'

'What can I say, my love? I was on the case. And what a case it turned out to be, let me tell you.'

For a heartbeat, I thought I had her. I saw the familiar glint of curiosity in her eyes, but it lasted only a second, replaced quickly by the cold glimmer of fury.

'I don't want to know about your blasted case. What I want is a proper explanation. You have been gone for a day and a night! That's unacceptable!'

'Let me explain—' I started to say, but she cut me off mid-sentence.

'You forgot, didn't you? You were supposed to take me to lunch. I was all dressed up and waiting for an hour and a half, and you forgot.'

'As I told you, my love, I was trying to track down Peter's fiancée.'

'You could have called at least, or sent your man to inform me.'

'I'm sorry, Helene,' I said, instantly contrite. 'I didn't forget. It's just ... you know how I am when I am in the middle of an investigation.'

'Enough, Sikander!' she shouted, her voice so shrill that it was almost a scream. 'I have had enough of your explanations and never-ending excuses. It's bad enough that you thought it was okay to leave me waiting and disappear all night, but how dare you leave me saddled with your dull misery of a friend? All the man does is drink and cry in his room. I can't bear him. I can't bear either of you. Merde!'

'I'll make it up to you, my love. Tomorrow, I promise. We will go out and paint the town red. But right now, I must tell you what

I have discovered. You won't believe it. Miss Hartley is not Miss Hartley at all. She is an impostor. The real Miss Hartley, Peter's actual fiancée, is in the wind. She has not jilted him after all. She never even arrived in India, so how could she possibly leave him?'

I fell silent as I realized that Helene was not listening. Instead, she was glaring at me, her brow bristling as her scowl deepened. I winced, readying myself for another broadside or two, but then something seemed to break inside her. Rather than losing her temper again, she let out a long sigh, a rattle of surrender.

'You have an answer for everything, don't you?' she whispered. Her voice was brittle, like it was made of glass.

'What's wrong, Helene?'

She did not answer and turned to leave..

'Don't go! Talk to me, please.' I said, grabbing her arm, 'Haven't I apologized? Haven't I explained why I was late? I'm sorry, but you were the one who encouraged me to get out there and find Miss Hartley. Haven't I done exactly that, Helene, that too in record time? It's not like I was out carousing and drinking. I was on the case!'

Helene remained unmoved. Wrestling her arm free, she pushed me away with unexpected vehemence.

'I don't want to hear it. There's always a case or a clue, always something, except me.'

'You're being unfair.'

'You're not listening, Sikander. You never listen to me.'

'Helene,' I said, 'that's not true, and you know it.'

'Isn't it?' she said, scowling at me, absolutely livid. 'I'm trying to tell you something. I'm tired, Sikander. I'm tired of your promises that you never keep. I'm tired of being constantly disappointed by you. I'm tired of taking care of you and receiving nothing but neglect in return, of being treated like a possession and not a person.'

Her words hurt me more than a punch to the gut.

'When have I ever neglected you? Or treated you badly? All I have ever done is to try and give you whatever you want. What is missing in your life? Comfort, luxury, wealth, security, you have everything!'

'That's where you are wrong. You have always given me what you think I want. Servants, jewels, pomp and circumstance; I don't need or want any of it. What I want is you. I don't want the maharaja. I don't want the sleuth. I want the man, the Sikander I fell in love with all those years ago. I miss our life in Paris. How we shivered under the same tattered blanket and made love to stay warm, how we scrimped and saved so that we could have ten francs to go for a boat ride on the Seine. How we danced all night and ate half loaves at dawn, fresh from the oven, and laughed while drinking sour Asti without a care in the world. How we walked everywhere holding hands, how you read poetry to me at midnight, when the moon was high. I want that man, not you!'

'I am that man, Helene. I have not changed. You are the one who has changed. You just don't see it.'

'Like I said, you have an answer for everything. You can never do any wrong, can you? The great Sikander Singh is always perfect!'

'Why are you doing this, Helene? Why are you being so difficult? So I forgot your birthday! So I missed our lunch yesterday! I'll make it up to you. Don't I always?'

'I'm being difficult?' she snarled. 'You think you're so smart and so intelligent, but you haven't a clue as to what is happening right in front of your face. Can't you see, Sikander, how unhappy I am? And how lonely? Damn it, I have been lonely for fifteen years. I have no friends, no one to talk to. I barely speak the language, and all of your people look at me like I am from another planet because my skin is white. I left everything behind to be with you—everything I am, my home, my family, my country. I have put up with it all because I love you. I never asked you for a thing, Sikander, other than you love me back.'

'When have I given you anything but love and affection, Helene?'

'Oh, you poor deluded man! Do you even know what love is? It is not the occasional gift, or a nice kiss every now and then, or a turn in the bed when the fancy strikes you. Love is trust. It is dependability. It is the willingness to put someone else's needs before your own.'

'When have I not done that?'

'You have never put me before your mysteries. Not once. I am the one who has always put everything aside for you. I have endured your eccentricities, your investigations, and even your dalliances, but I need more, Sikander. I need to get married. I need to have children before it is too late. I need to be treated like I matter, not like a plaything.'

Her voice was strident, the acrimony in her tone as sharp as a knife. I should have been more patient, but I am not a man who is accustomed to being shouted at. and I felt my temper fraying.

'Enough!' I hissed. 'Do not presume to shout at me. You forget your place, Helene.'

'My place?' Her voice took on a dangerous lilt and her left eyebrow arched, like a bowstring about to break. 'Oh, please do tell me my place, Sikander Singh. Educate me!'

Even as I said those words, I regretted them. Realizing I had made a cardinal mistake, I bit my tongue and tried desperately to backpedal.

'That's not what I meant. What I am trying to say is that you're being unreasonable. If you want to talk about this like civilized adults, then let's talk. We can fix all this, if only you would calm down.'

'Unreasonable! Is that what you think? That I am the one being unreasonable? Putain!' she screeched and launched into another tirade of French.

I tried not to wince as she spat out each word. I understood only every second sentence, but her descriptions of my hygiene and masculinity were anything but flattering, that much I could tell.

Just as she was warming up, beginning a vivid description of how my ancestors had been filthy pigs who enjoyed rutting in the mud, the door slammed open. Charan Singh rushed in, breathless.

The furious frown on Helene's face brought him trundling to a halt.

'My apologies, Memsahib,' he stammered, giving her a sheepish look. 'I did not mean to intrude, but this is an emergency.'

I was about to shout at him, to ask how dare he barge in without so much as a warning knock. But then, I noticed the stricken expression on his face.

The old man looked shaken, shocked to the core, his ordinarily taciturn features twisted into a dismayed grimace. It was unnerving to say the least. I had seen Charan Singh face armed gunmen without so much as a blink, but I could not recall ever seeing him so distraught, not since the night my mother had been murdered.

'What is wrong, old man?'

'Huzoor,' he said softly, his voice barely a whisper, 'you had better come immediately. Something terrible has happened.'

'Rowan Sahib is ... he is dead.'

CHAPTER 21

I have little recollection of the sequence of events that followed. The last time I had been gripped by such a madness was after my mother had been murdered. Then, I had been almost catatonic. Now, I felt manic, like I was being consumed by a nervous energy so profound that it left me unable to focus or think.

I remember retreating to the music room and gulping down most of a bottle of Pommery. I remember feeling entirely detached from everything, like every step or breath that I took had a dreamlike quality to it. Everything felt so unreal that I remember wondering if it was all a hallucination. *Peter's death, Bombay, the things and places I had seen in the past twenty-four hours, the people I had met; were they real or just a figment of my fevered imagination, as immaterial as Mary bloody Hartley?*

The cold ivory of the piano's keys beneath my fingers reminded me that it was all real. I pursed my lips and thought about what to play. *Something German, to suit the somberness of the occasion? Wagner perhaps? Or Liszt?* No, too grim. It had to be something else, something that epitomized Peter and his unique mixture of humor and stoicism, tinged by just a smidgen of despair.

Closing my eyes, I let my fingers be my guide. What came forth was a piece I had never played before: Chopin's 'Nocturne in E Minor'. It coursed through me, pouring out like a purging. I surrendered to its haunting, lilting melody, playing for all the people I had lost in my life—my father, my mother, and now poor, foolish Peter.

I played the same piece thrice, until every note rang perfectly. But still, it could not fill the void inside me, that gaping emptiness which ached at me like a hunger, even as I worked my way through a second bottle of champagne.

Just as I was contemplating whether to uncork a third, I heard the door ease open behind me. I did not need to turn to see who it was. Her perfume surrounded me, making my fingers skip a beat.

'Helene,' I said, 'have you come to scold me some more?'

Even as the words left my mouth, I knew I shouldn't have said them. I was lashing out at her, but part of me wanted the fight. I wanted to scream and rant, if only because it would stop me from feeling so completely numb. Unfortunately for Helene, she was the only target I had. I suspect she guessed as much, because rather than taking the bait, she chose to ignore my jibe.

'I have made all the arrangements. Your bogey will be ready to leave with the dawn mail train. As for your friend, I have had his body sealed in a coffin. It will travel with you to Rajpore. You can give him a proper burial there. It seems appropriate. He told me that the best time of his life was the years he spent as your tutor, that Rajpore was the last place he was truly happy. It is only proper that you find him a place there, in the soil that he so loved.

'That's a good idea. Thank you for doing that. Peter would have liked it.' My voice caught in my throat. 'If only he was here to say that to you himself!'

She frowned. 'You cannot blame yourself for what Peter did, Sikander. It's a choice he made.'

'I should have realized how fragile his mental state was. I should have seen the signs.'

Helene snorted. 'You were not his priest, Sikander. You were his friend. This isn't your fault.'

'Isn't it? I was harsh to him. Unduly cruel. Perhaps that is what pushed him over the edge and made him decide to do something so drastic.'

'You mustn't think like that. You had no way of predicting that he would choose to end his own life. How could you know what was going on in his head? You hadn't even seen him, or spoken with him, for well nigh a decade.'

'I should have known. There are far too many things I have failed to notice, it seems.' I shuddered. 'It is entirely on my head. Yet another sin I must add to my ever-growing list.'

I had been hoping for sympathy and tenderness, but Helene surprised me by rolling her eyes and clucking her tongue.

'Oh, shut up, Sikander. For once, stop being so dramatic. You have no right to feel guilty. It's just your ego talking. You like to think that you are somehow responsible for half the evil in the world, but that's rubbish, and you know it. Your friend's sins are his, and his alone. You are not God. You are a good man, but only a man after all. And all men make mistakes. The sooner you realize this and stop being so hard on yourself, the sooner you will be happy. And one more thing. If you're hoping for me to tell you how wonderful you are, I will not indulge you, not this time.'

She was being coarse, even unkind, but it was exactly what I needed to hear. Her words poured over me like ice water, making me shiver. Rising to my feet, I went to her.

'You're right, Helene. As always, you are right. You're a wonder! Have I ever told you that?'

I reached out to her, intending to take her in my arms and kiss her, but she brushed me away and took a step back.

'There is one more thing, Sikander. I ... I will not be coming back to Rajpore with you.'

Her face was as hard as a statue, all angles and granite. 'I have come to a decision. I think we should take a break.'

'That's a great idea,' I said. 'Where would you like to go? You name it. I will have Charan Singh book us a cabin on the next passenger liner out. What do you say? London, Rome, New York?'

'No,' Helene replied. 'You don't understand. I don't want to go on a break *with* you. I want to take a break *from* you, from us.'

Even as she said that I was struck by a momentary aphasia. I could hear her, I could see her lips moving, but I couldn't quite understand what she was saying. It was static in my ears, a blur of sounds.

'What are you saying?'

'I'm leaving, Sikander. I am going back to Paris.'

'You cannot be serious.' I wanted to take a step forward, but my legs refused to obey me.

'I have never been more serious about anything. I don't want to hurt you, but it has taken me a long time to say this, to come to this decision. I can't do this anymore. I cannot play second fiddle to you any longer.'

'But ... but I love you?'

'And I love you, mon chéri, but sometimes love is just not enough.'

'I cannot change, Helene.'

'You cannot, or you will not?'

'Both, I guess. I'm sorry, but I am what I am.'

'I know you are,' she said, shaking her head. 'Maybe that was enough for me once, but now ... now I am too old and too tired to wait any more, Sikander. I am finished.'

Her words bit at me, as cruel as a lash. I wanted to argue, to shout at her, but my voice dried up in my mouth.

'What are you going to do, Helene? Where will you go? How will you survive? You are forty-two years old. Do you really think you will find another man?'

Helene flinched and offered me a sad smile.

'You know, Sikander, you've been abrupt, short-tempered, neglectful, and sometimes selfish, but in the seventeen years we have been together, this is the first time you've been intentionally cruel to me.'

She gave me one last sad look before turning and walking out the door, slamming it shut behind her. I wanted to follow, but I didn't. I couldn't. I don't know if it was pride or shock that restrained me, but I found I could not move. A dizziness seized me, a confusion so consuming that I nearly lost control of my limbs and collapsed.

It was over! Seventeen long years, but I had buggered it up.

I had lost Helene.

After Helene left, I stood rooted in place, unable to move. My mind and body felt disconnected from each other. My brain would not stop racing, jumping from one inchoate thought to another. A conflicting storm of emotions welled up inside me, threatening to drown me. First, it was disbelief, then came sorrow followed by regret and, finally, an anger as corrosive as acid.

Turning, I strode to the side table and snatched up the half-empty bottle of champagne. Draining it in a single gasp, I threw it against the wall, where it shattered into a thousand shards. Like a lodestone, my feet led me to the piano. I sat down and began to play. An angry cataclysm poured out from me. It was supposed to be Liszt's 'Der Doppelganger', but all that emerged was a fury of discordant noise as I banged down on the keys so hard that my fingers began to hurt.

Behind me, I heard the door open once more. Abandoning the piano, I sprang up, hoping it was Helene, hoping that she had changed her mind and come back to me.

It turned out to be Charan Singh.

'I am sorry to intrude, Huzoor,' he said sorrowfully, his expression conveying that he knew what had elapsed. 'You have a visitor.'

'Get rid of them,' I said. 'Whoever it is, tell them to go away!'

'I tried my best, Huzoor, but the memsahib is very insistent. She says it is a matter of life and death!'

I cut him off, my voice rising to a screech. 'I said leave me alone, damn you!'

He took a step back, dismayed by my vehemence. That was when I noticed the person hidden behind his girth.

It was Miss Bennett.

She was dressed for travel in a belted blue serge jacket that emphasized her slender figure, paired with a fitted gabardine skirt, and a pair of high-ankled walking boots.

Seeing her, I was taken aback. For a moment, I was tempted to turn her away, but at the same time, her unexpected presence made my curiosity swell. It took all my strength to compose myself, to ramp down my despondence. With a mighty effort, I took a deep breath, trying to summon up a mask of cool detachment before giving her a brisk bow.

'What are you doing here, Madam? I thought you were off to Peshawar.'

'I have sent Malcolm on ahead and will take the morning train tomorrow. I gravely needed to see you, Sir.'

She paused, looking at me solemnly, a tremor of concern flickering across her face.

'Are you well? You seem ... distraught?'

'I'm fine,' I replied, my voice brisker than it should have been.

'I saw the police outside. Is something amiss?'

'It's Mr Rowan. He ... he has died by suicide.'

Miss Bennett let out a loud gasp, visibly shaken by this news. She shivered, so unsteady on her feet that I thought for a heartbeat she would faint. Hurriedly, Charan Singh moved to offer her a hand and help her to a nearby chair.

'I will fetch some salts and a glass of water for the memsahib,' he said.

As Miss Bennett struggled to collect herself, I watched her, more than a little surprised by the vehemence of her reaction.

'I wasn't aware you knew Peter.'

'I didn't,' she said. 'It's just ... what a tragedy! The poor man must have been terribly depressed.'

She offered me a sad smile. 'Are you okay, Sir? He was your dearest friend, wasn't he? Surely, you must be dreadfully shaken.'

'I do not think, Madam, you have come all the way here to inquire about my wellbeing.'

'No, not at all. Forgive my intrusion, but you did say I should call upon you if I found out any new information about Miss Hartley.'

She hesitated, biting her lip. 'I have a clue, Sir, about Mary's whereabouts.'

'Do you now?' From an ember, my curiosity flared into a wildfire. The despair I had felt just a few minutes ago receded to a dull throb. It sickened me a little, for it reminded me how right Helene was. I was indeed the worst kind of parasite, one who fed on misfortune and sorrow.

'What sort of clue?' I asked.

'A letter, Sir, from Mary. I found it just yesterday while packing my bags. She must have hidden it there before I disembarked from the *Caledonia*.'

Delving into her jacket, she pulled out a buff envelope and offered it to me. 'Here it is.'

Taking the letter from her, I unfolded it and started to read, mouthing the words in a soft monotone.

My dear Eloise,

Even though we have only known each other briefly, I feel I can trust you implicitly. I have grown to care for you, and to cherish your friendship. You are the only truly good person I know, and I can never repay you for your many kindnesses.

I thought that I could make a new life in the colonies, but now, as the shores of India draw ever closer, the prospect fills me with a monumental dread. It is an uneasiness that has been growing ever since I left England. When I embarked, the notion of a new beginning was something that filled me with hope, but now, as the journey draws to an end, all I feel is panic. What have I done? How will this be any different? I cannot bear the thought of being shackled to an old man in a loveless marriage. And what if this man I have never met, this Peter Rowan, turns out to be as much of a brute as my father or my uncle? What if he mistreats me, or beats me? Where will I run to? How will I escape? I know nobody in India, no one to whom I can turn to for support.

I have had a taste of freedom on this voyage, for the first time in my life. It has left me with two realizations. The first is that I will never be happy as Mrs Mary Rowan, a plain housewife to a schoolteacher, living a quotidian, monotonous sort of life. I deserve more. I deserve adventure and excitement; I deserve romance and desire. In fact, I have come to see that I crave these things, like a drug.

My second realization is that I will never be happy being shackled to any man. I will never allow myself to be a chattel again. I will never let a man treat me like I am a piece of property, someone with no rights and no power.

That leaves me, I believe, with no choice but one. It is all I can think of, the only avenue of escape left to me—the solace of a watery grave.

By the time you find this, I will be gone. I can only hope that I find some happiness in the afterlife, some semblance of the joy that has eluded me so far.

Do not judge me too harshly, I beg you.

Your friend always,
Mary

'Have you read this?' I asked, holding up the letter.

'I have.' Her voice wavered, and she clasped one hand to her chest. 'You do not think Mary decided to harm herself, do you?'

'I don't know,' I mused, contemplating the letter. 'I cannot tell. It doesn't fit. This letter is completely out of character for Miss Hartley. Going by everything I have learned about her over the last two days, by all accounts, she was too strong a personality to resort to taking her own life. It just doesn't make sense.'

'Life seldom makes sense, Mr Singh,' Miss Bennett said. Her hand moved to her collarbone, caressing a gold cameo she wore quite nervously. She rose and came to stand very close to me, so close that I could smell her perfume. It was much the same as Helene's, Guerlain and Yardley's powder, a scent so familiar that it left me a little intoxicated.

'We all have moments of weakness,' she whispered. Her voice was a throaty murmur. She leaned toward me, her eyes gleaming.

'Madam,' I started to object, but before I could say another word, her lips brushed against mine.

I have kissed my fair share of women, and as far as kisses go, it was nothing short of sublime. Miss Bennett's lips were urgent and demanding. She reached for my cheeks with one slim manicured hand, letting out a groan as her fingers caressed my beard. I should have pushed her away immediately, but I lost myself for a moment, caught up in the press of her slender body against mine, radiating a heat so eager that it was as if she was made of fire and not ice.

Who knows where that kiss would have led! But then, I saw Helene's face in my mind, her kind and disappointed eyes, and it broke the spell.

It took all my strength to push Miss Bennett away, all my wherewithal to break free of her embrace.

'Stop!' I growled, shoving her away so roughly that she nearly lost her balance. 'This is wrong.'

'Forgive me!' she said breathlessly. She seemed to be a different person. Her hair was in disarray and her pale complexion flaming, so vivid with color that I could scarcely recognize her. 'I forgot myself. It's just that you are a very attractive man, Sir.'

'Thank you for the compliment, Madam, but I am spoken for, as are you.'

I backed away hurriedly, putting some distance between us in case she decided to forget herself once more.

Miss Bennett refused to meet my eyes. Instead, she spent an awkward moment tidying up her hair, settling a few errant strands, fixing her blouse and carefully buckling her belt shut.

'I think it would be best, Madam, if you left. I am sure your fiancé will be waiting for you.'

'Yes,' she said, 'you're right. I just wanted to bring you that letter. I was worried Mary might have done herself some harm.'

She looked at me, her eyes brimming with emotion. 'Please, Mr Singh, you *must* keep looking for her. You mustn't give up. Promise me you will never give up.'

Before I could reply, the door creaked open once more.

'What is it now, you oaf?' I croaked, expecting it to be Charan Singh yet again. 'Have you completely forgotten your manners today?'

Rather than my manservant, it was Hall-Caine who came striding into the room, looking inordinately pleased with himself. When he saw Miss Bennett, he paused and raised an inquiring eyebrow.

'Well, hello,' he said, giving me a salacious smirk. 'Have I interrupted something?'

'What the hell do you want? I snarled. 'Have you come to enforce that god-awful order of externment I was just served by Commissioner Edwardes, and finish what your masters started?'

'Actually, Mr Singh, I came to tell you rather an important bit of news.'

His smirk widened into a self-satisfied grin. 'Your memsahib? We have found her. Her body washed up this morning, on a beach in Andheri.'

CHAPTER 22

Located some twenty-five kilometers north of the Fort district, the suburb of Andheri was the northernmost tip of Greater Bombay. Largely a fen of mangrove swamps that flooded each evening when the tide came in, it was bordered at its western edge by a half-submerged sandbar the Portuguese called Juvem, as well as a host of smaller islands that were accessible only at low tide. To its east lay the much larger basalt promontory of Salsette, and beyond that, Bassein and the mainland.

A lonely and rather desolate place, Andheri was populated mainly by itinerant farmers, toddy tappers who harvested liquor from the coconut and palm groves, East Indians who quarried the nearby hills for shale and limestone, and Koli fishermen who had migrated south from Gujarat after the Muslim invasions

Personally, I had never been this far north before. I watched the countryside flicker by outside the window, fascinated as the neat townships of Santa Cruz gave way to forbidding black hillocks and vast expanses of marshland. Beside me, Miss Bennett did not look happy at all. I had insisted she come with us, and she had agreed very reluctantly. With each passing mile, she seemed to grow more distraught, wringing her hands with a worried expression fixed on her pretty face. As for Hall-Caine, he remained as overly cheerful as ever, humming what seemed to be 'By the Light of the Silvery Moon' under his breath.

Unfortunately, the Mercedes could only take us as far as the local railway station. Beyond that, we were forced to shift to a pair of tangas, mule-drawn two-wheeled carriages that transported us down to the very edge of the Arabian Sea. There, we boarded a lateen-sailed dhow crewed by an ancient Koli boatman who was clad only in a loincloth, his skin as black as tar.

He rowed us out to the lonely island of Vesava, singing an old Koli folk song softly, keeping time with each passing stroke of the oars.

'*Aami Koli daryache raje haav, na baraan jaun hora bharun maashe hantaav* [We Kolis are the kings of the sea; even in stormy situations, we go to the sea and get boats full of fish].'

I knew enough Maharashtrian to get the gist of what he was saying. His nonchalance made me smile. Miss Bennett, unfortunately, mistook my bemusement for an invitation to chat.

'Why am I here?' she carped, all traces of her earlier amorousness gone, replaced by an implacable wariness instead. 'I should be on my way to the railway station, or I will miss my train.'

'We need you to identify the body, Madam,' I replied. 'Please be patient just a while longer. We are almost at the end of this adventure.'

Vesava was a small islet, barely two miles wide. In one corner was a large fishing settlement and a dilapidated Portuguese fort, at the other a decrepit church and a cluster of seven bungalows surrounded by fruit orchards. The rest was an expanse of arid rocks bordered by a smooth white beach covered with detritus, dead trees and an assortment of garbage that flowed out on the tide from the southern islands and washed up here—a tangle of rags, soggy paper, metal wires, tin sheeting, planks, and on occasion, human bodies.

About halfway down the beach, atop a natural breakwater of volcanic rocks that had piled up near the high-tide mark, a small group of fishermen clustered, gossiping, and watching two constables who were guarding what was obviously a corpse covered by a tattered sailcloth shroud.

As we drew closer, Hall-Caine gave one of the constables a brisk nod. He whipped the sheet back to reveal a horrific sight.

There was barely enough of the body left to identify it as human. After the better part of three days in the water, it had bloated to thrice its size. The skin had turned pale and mucilaginous, almost translucent. Fish and crabs had nibbled away at the extremities, gnawing the hands and feet almost to the bone. The only thing I could still recognize as what had once been a vibrant young woman was a mess of dark hair that surrounded the ruin of a face like dank seaweed, and one eye, pale and lifeless but still a striking shade of brown.

Behind me, I heard Miss Bennett let out a moan. She trembled visibly, but to her credit, did not lose control and fall into a faint. As for me, when I looked down at the wreck that had once been a living, breathing person, I couldn't help but be stricken by a deep sense of tragedy. What a waste! To come all the way out to India, only to die such a senseless and gruesome death. And to take Peter with you! *If only I had found you sooner*, I thought, *if only Peter had waited another day, if only I had gone to that damn priest first*. So many 'if onlys'! A wave of guilt rose inside me, like acid in my throat, making me want to retch.

'I'm sorry it had to end this way, old boy,' Hall-Caine said softly, coming up behind me. 'It's a shame, really, that such a happy occasion should turn to tragedy. First your friend and now her. What a blasted mess!'

'It isn't over yet,' I growled. 'There is still the small matter of identification.'

I turned to Miss Bennett, who looked decidedly green around the gills.

'Come here, Madam,' I said.

'Me?' she replied, her eyes widening with dismay.

She obeyed reluctantly, pausing near the body with her eyes averted, refusing to look straight at its horrific visage.

'Is this her?' I asked, pointing at the corpse, 'Is this Mary Hartley?'

Miss Bennett's only reply was a brisk nod, before losing control entirely. With a groan, she turned away and vomited, emptying her stomach violently.

'That's it then,' Hall-Caine said. 'Case closed.'

'Not yet! Hold on a moment.'

Kneeling, I took a closer look at the remains. ROCPET, as always. Rigor had come and passed. Her left side was completely abraded, no doubt by the current and the rough rock of the sea floor, leaving her torso and back dotted with signs of vascular marbling, like ink blotches on a sheet of paper. It looked like she had been dead for at least two days, judging by the pallor of her skin. Other than that, there were no obvious wounds. No cuts or bullet holes, no ligature marks. In spite of the warm weather, the cold water had ensured that she had not yet begun to decay.. The only palpable odor I could discern was the dank stench of putrefaction and salt, and a faint hint of what smelled like stale garlic. Wrinkling my brow, I leaned forward and peered into her one remaining eye. There, I found what I was looking for. A cluster of dull red patches around the cornea, like stains on the sclera.

I rose and turned to face Hall-Caine, who was watching me with a mixture of revulsion and curiosity.

'Well, if you're done mucking about,' he said, shaking his head. 'Since it is obvious that Miss Hartley drowned, and there is no evidence of this being anything but an accident, I'll have this marked down as a death by misadventure.'

'I cannot concur with that. You see, there are two things that you are wrong about, Hall-Caine. First, she did not drown. She was poisoned. You can confirm that from the petechial hemorrhaging in her eye. And second, this unfortunate young lady is not Miss Hartley at all. She is someone else.'

'What?' Hall-Caine exclaimed, utterly shocked.

Behind him, Miss Bennett let out an even louder gasp of disbelief.

'I have it from a source, you see, that Miss Hartley was robbed by a woman named Emily Malcolm before she even boarded the *Caledonia*. She never embarked from England in the first place, so how could she have drowned here in Bombay?'

'So, this is?' Hall-Caine frowned, obviously struggling to make sense of what I was saying. 'Is this the impostor who assumed her identity? Miss ... Malcolm, you said?'

'Not quite,' I said and pointed at Miss Bennett. 'Unless I am very mistaken, *you* are Miss Malcolm and that hapless creature was the real Miss Bennett.'

This announcement was greeted by a moment of stunned silence. For the first time, it seemed I had managed to dent Hall-Caine's ordinarily unflappable exterior; His eyebrows rose so high they looked like they would disappear into his hairline.

'Are you sure of this, Sikander?' He said, looking at me with an unsteady frown. 'It sounds rather unbelievable, to say the least.'

As for Miss Bennett, or rather Miss Malcolm, as I had pegged her, reacted by glowering at me with frosty disdain.

'This is nonsense!' she hissed. 'I have never been so insulted.'

It was a masterful performance, worthy of the Globe. She played the role of affronted memsahib to the hilt, right down to the look of beleaguered consternation writ on her face and the glance of entreaty she directed toward Hall-Caine, as if to say, Help, this foolish Indian has taken leave of his senses.

'She's right,' Hall-Caine said, drawn in by her completely. 'Do you have any proof of this assertion? Any concrete evidence?'

'There's an easy enough way to prove it. Her hair, have it washed out with lye shampoo. The dye will run, and you will see her true colors, so to speak.'

Miss Malcolm bristled at this suggestion. 'For God's sake, you cannot be serious. You cannot expect me to stand here and listen to this madman and his scurrilous accusations. I will not bear it a moment longer. Mr Hall-Caine, I have cooperated with you as much as I am willing. I insist you take me back to my fiancé immediately. Also, I demand you have Mr Singh stop saying these dreadful things before I have you both hauled up for slander.'

Hall-Caine gave me a squeamish scowl. 'I won't lie, old man,' he said. 'It's flimsy at best. I can arrest her on your say-so, but I will not be able to hold her for more than a day, not with some random theory about lye shampoo and hair dye. If you want it to hold up in court, I'll need something more, something substantive.'

'A day should be enough to prove me right. We can have someone from the *Caledonia* come down and identify her, the captain or the first officer, Mascarenhas. They will corroborate her identity and confirm that she is lying.'

As I said those words, Miss Malcolm began to panic.

'You can't be serious,' her voice was shrill, almost brittle. 'This is preposterous. I have had all I can take of this nonsense. I have a train to catch, if you will excuse me.'

'Hold on a minute!' Hall-Caine moved to intercept her. 'How sure are you of this, Sikander?'

'I have never been more sure of anything in my life. Don't bother to deny it, Madam. The game is up.'

She glanced around desperately, looking for any avenue of escape, even as Hall-Caine gave the two constables a wave. They began to move toward her, one on either side, trying to hem her in.

When she saw them advance, as I had expected, she tried to bolt. It all happened in a flash. I don't know where she was planning to go, since the only way off the island was by boat, but she turned and made a dash for the beach. I moved to stop her, as did Charan Singh. Realizing she was cornered, her face twisted into a rictus of fury. From somewhere within the folds of her skirt, she produced a gun, a snub-nosed pocket pistol that she brandished menacingly.

'Stay back!' she screeched, bringing the gun to bear on me. 'I don't want to hurt anyone. I just want to leave. Don't try to stop me!'

Charan Singh surged forward. trying to place himself between me and harm's way. But Hall-Caine was even faster. Like lightning, he lunged forward and chopped one hand down on her forearm. She squealed, and the gun fell from her nerveless fingers. In a trice, he had her arm in his grasp, pulling her off balance and pinning it behind her back.

'You aren't going anywhere!'

'You're hurting me,' she gasped and tried to wrestle free, but he was too strong for her.

'Calm down, Madam,' I said. 'It's pointless to resist.'

I gave Hall-Caine a nod 'Let her go. She will not give us any more trouble.'

He released her, and Miss Macolm stepped back, massaging her arm.

'How did you figure it out?' she asked, giving me an indignant glare.

'I almost didn't. You very nearly had me fooled, Madam. The hair and the accent were spot-on. But then, what else would one expect from an actress? The only mistake you made was that you overplayed your hand.'

'The letter?' she asked bitterly.

'Indeed! The letter! But even more than that there was your jejune attempt to seduce me. While you are a very desirable woman, Madam, you made one cardinal error. Your charms would have worked on a man accustomed to thinking with his heart, but I am ruled by my mind. I am a rationalist, not driven by base emotions like lust, which is why I was able to recognize your ploy for what it was, a feint.'

'I still don't understand,' Hall-Caine muttered. 'How exactly did you know she was an impostor, Sikander?'

'Once I had the pieces, it was simply a matter of putting the puzzle together,' I said. 'As I have already mentioned, I know from Father Donovan that you stole Miss Hartley's luggage, and with that, appropriated her identity and came aboard the *Caledonia* pretending to be her. Perhaps you even intended to honor her marriage contract to Peter in the beginning, but as the voyage passed, you began to have second thoughts. Marriage to an older man did not suit you, and you tried desperately to find someone who would help you get out of it. Like the professional grifter you obviously are, you ran your little schemes, gathering a handsome sum from your unwitting marks. But no matter how desperately you tried, you could not entrap another man into helping you repudiate Peter. As the *Caledonia* crossed the Med and entered the canal, it became obvious to you that you had painted yourself into a corner. It was only a matter of time before the ship docked in Bombay, and all that awaited you there was a man eager to be your husband, a man who had neither a fortune nor influence, who could only offer you a good heart. But that was not enough for you, was it? You were in it for the money, plain and simple. Everyone I spoke with told me that you grew more and more worried as the ship approached Bombay. It was then, I suspect, that you realized there was another way out.'

'The solution to all your problems was Miss Bennett, your unfortunate roommate. She was sickly and spent most of the voyage isolated from the rest of the passengers, which made it easy for you to supplant her and take her place. And then there was the fact that she was engaged to a younger, more vital and powerful man, a gentleman of rank and substance.'

'There was your opportunity,' I continued. 'And you, Madam, are not the sort of woman who stands by idly when an opportunity comes knocking. How did you do it? Was it the night before the *Caledonia* docked, just enough poison in Miss Bennett's food to render her insensate? And then, while she was in a weakened state, you took your chance! It's very easy to shove someone overboard. All it takes is a small push at the right time when they are dizzy. Is that what happened?'

'Stop it!' she shuddered, her voice breaking. 'You're wrong, completely wrong.'

'You deny you are Miss Malcolm,' I hissed, 'that you are an impostor?'

'Yes, my name is Emily Malcolm, but I am not a murderer. I killed no one. What I am is a thief,' she whispered. 'Yes, I stole your Miss Hartley's luggage and decided to assume her identity and take her place, because I thought I could have a new beginning.'

'But India? Why choose India of all places?' Hall-Caine chirped.

'Because this is where my mother is. This is where she came when she ran off and deserted my father.'

'So, you came to India to find her and reconcile with her?'

Miss Malcolm shook her head. 'It's too late for that. She died some years ago and is buried just outside Quetta.'

'That is why you were so eager to know about Balochistan. You wanted to find your mother's resting place and weep at her tombstone?'

'Oh no, Sir. I came here so I could spit on her grave. She betrayed me, Mr Singh, and left me when I was only seven years old, that too at the mercy of a drunk.'

It took me a second to connect the dots.

'The story that you told me was yours, wasn't it? It wasn't Miss Hartley's?'

She gave me a curt nod. 'After my mother left, my father beat me every single day, Sir. He was a bitter, angry man who came home every night from the knacker's yard, stinking of rotgut and death. Each time he beat me. I cried and begged him to stop, but he didn't care. I think, in some way, he blamed me for his life, for my mother leaving,' she said with a groan. 'Can you imagine it? A seven-year-old child, living every moment in mortal terror? I thought about killing my father many times, devising fantastical plots in my mind—rat poison in his porridge, pushing him down the stairs and making it seem like an accident—but I was never brave enough. I thanked the stars when he was stabbed to death four years later, because I thought I was free at last. But I could not have been more mistaken. In this world, a girl has no freedom, especially a child. I merely ended up trading one prison for another. I was packed off to my uncle, my mother's brother. He turned out to be an evil man, Sir, worse than my father, because he hid his malignancy under a mild exterior. One night, some three months after I arrived, he crept into my bed and started to fondle my breasts. When I screamed and ran to his wife to beg for help, do you know what she did? She blamed me, Sir. She said I was making eyes at him, and then beat me with an iron poker.

'I suffered his depraved attentions for almost two years, until I managed to steal enough money to run away. I found work as a skivvy maid, the lowest form of employ, with a gentleman named Mackenzie. At first, he was kind; he told me I was beautiful and gave me little presents: a pot of raspberry jam, a ribbon for my hair, a locket that had belonged to his dead wife. When he made an advance, Sir, I let him have his way because I thought he genuinely loved me. But I was wrong, yet again. He wanted to own me, like I was a possession and not a person. As time passed, his tenderness turned to something else, to dominance. He would tie me up and strap me. When I tried to resist him, he cut off all my hair. He told me I was his dog, that he owned me, that I was nothing without him, that I had no value.

'Once again, I stole some silverware and ran away, to Edinburgh this time. I thought I would be an actress, but all I could manage was a couple of small parts. Instead, I ended up making hats. It takes supple fingers, you see, a child's fingers to make the tiny stitches inside the brim. And the only place I could afford to live in was a poorhouse. They call them Magdalene Asylums in Scotland, a fancy name for what are shelters for broken and destitute women. I ended up sharing a dormitory with four other girls. Two were whores, one was a dancer and another a retarded girl who had been raped and was carrying a child.

Being poor isn't like what Dickens made it out to be, Sir. There's no romance and no hope, only dirt and hunger. I cannot forget the hunger, the constant starvation. It feels like your body is eating itself from the inside. But most of all, it's the fear that throttles you -—the beatings, the violence, the constant worry that someone will steal what you have, that they will hurt you, that they will cut or mutilate you, that some man will follow you and rape you. It is the fear thar wears you down to a shadow of a human being.

'I was a good hatmaker, but it barely paid enough to keep myself fed and warm. That was when I met Diamond Jim Menezies. I was making a delivery to Forsyth's on Princes Street when I first saw him and his gang at work. There were four of them: Diamond Jim; Sarah the Fox, named because she had hair as red as a fox's tail; Wee Wilhelmina, who looked like a child even though she was nearing twenty; and old Martha, who had been a thief for more than sixty years. They called themselves the Flash Mob because they liked to be in and out in a flash. Their specialty was going on the hoist, or shoplifting, as the police call it. They had it down to an art form. First, Mina would pretend to be lost and distract the guard at the door, then Sarah the Fox would flirt with a shop assistant at the jewelry counter, while old Martha grabbed what she could and palmed it off to Diamond Jim, who would tuck the haul in his top hat and swan his way out like he was Lord Fauntelroy himself.

'Anyway, that day, it was all going as smooth as clockwork, but it was their bad luck that an off-duty peeler was doing his shopping as well. He set upon Diamond Jim as he was making his exit, who decided to run for it. The policeman was trying to chase him down when he ran headlong into me, sending us both sprawling. Jim gave me a smile, helped me up and handed me the goods, saying he would find me later. That was how it began. He came looking for me a week later. I gave him back his package, untouched. He was surprised, to say the least, that I had not sold it all off, which was why I think he took a shine to me. The next thing I knew, he asked me if I wanted to come join the gang. I decided, why not? It was certainly better than rotting away slowly, working my fingers to the bone and starving to death. It was Diamond Jim who realized that I had a talent for playing a role, that I could mimic accents and pretend to be a high-born lady as good as Sarah Benhardt herself. He taught me how to play the hapless girl, the airy debutante, the hurried housewife, the nonchalant naif, the importunate ingenue, you name it! I learned all the tricks of the trade, and I was bloody good at it, let me tell you! It was acting of a sort, playing someone I could never be. And it let me escape, even if it was just for a few minutes. Once I put on one of those pretty frocks, a nice bonnet and a smattering of rouge, I became one of them, those fancy dames who lived up in the Grange. People looked at me like I was someone, like I mattered. It was intoxicating.'

She shivered, letting out a worn sigh. 'It was good for a while, but then I made the same mistake again, the one I always make. I trusted a man. When Diamond Jim decided to seduce me, I let him have his way,' she said, her face hardening. 'What is it about men that they cannot satisfy a carnal urge without imagining it as a form of ownership? Once I lay with Diamond Jim, it changed everything. He drove the other girls away from me, making them resent me. I tried to tell them that I was still their friend, but Diamond Jim drove a wedge between us. Worst of all, he was like a man possessed. He would follow me and keep a watch on who I met or spoke to. And if I so much as smiled at another man, he would go mad with fury. He once broke a barrow boy's arm because he raised his cap at me.

'When I confronted him,' she said, peeling back a sleeve to reveal a jagged scar on her forearm, shaped like a half-moon, 'he branded me with a hot iron, Sir, to teach me a lesson about who was in charge. I tried to run away twice. The first time, he found me before I could even get to the train station. He dragged me back and told the girls that I was going to rat them out to the police, after which they took turns beating me with broom handles. I broke two ribs and almost lost an eye. The second time, I made it as far as Glasgow. He was waiting for me there. He had let me run, like it was a game, like I was the hare and he was the courser. This time, when he took me back, he kept me locked up for two weeks and starved me. I almost went mad. When he let me out, he told me it was my fault, that if I tried to run away again, he would kill me rather than let me be free. I was too scared after that, until old Martha took pity on me. She bought me a ticket to London, gave me some money and helped me get away. We drugged the lot of them with chlorodyne, and while they were sleeping, I made a run for it.

'I was at Waverley station, waiting for my train, when I met your Miss Hartley. She was everything I was not, Mr Singh, sanguine, optimistic, and most of all, undamaged by the hardships of life. We started talking, and she poured her heart out to me. She told me all about how she was destined to head out to India on the fishing fleet, how she had an offer of marriage from a teacher, how excited she was to be embarking on this adventure and how she had everything planned out, down to the last detail, even the table napkins she was going to buy after she arrived in Ajmer. As I listened, I found myself thinking why her? Why not me? Why should she be so fortunate when I have had to suffer my whole life? When she went off the ladies to powder her nose, I decided I would take her place. It made perfect sense to me. What better way to escape Diamond Jim? What better way for me to start a new life? Who would think to look for me in India?

'I admit it, I stole her luggage, and took her place and didn't think twice about it. I boarded the train to Southampton and cut my hair so that it looked like hers. I even put on one of her dresses and boarded the *Caledonia* with her ticket. And nobody, not a soul, blinked or asked a single question. I would have got away with it, clean as a whistle, until you decided to get involved.'

'What about Miss Bennett? Why poison her?'

'That's what I am trying to say,' she said, her voice plaintive. 'I didn't do it. Why did I need to? I was clean away, and Eloise, the poor thing, was kind to me. She befriended me, Sir. She was the only true friend I have ever made, the first person who cared about me without wanting anything in return. She didn't care about my birth or my past. She was nice to me without expecting anything in return. I confess, I was wary of her at first. I hadn't expected a roommate, but as we left the Atlantic, I realized I had lucked out. Eloise was one of that rare breed who are genuinely good people, who haven't a mean bone in their bodies. Her only flaw, if there was one, was that she had a weak and nervous disposition, afflicted by what is commonly described as neurasthenia. She had led a very sheltered life, you see, and this was her first time alone. What I considered a grand adventure was an ordeal for her. She told me so herself, Sir.

'She was scared of everything—of men, with whom she had very little experience; of India, which she had heard was a savage place; but most of all she feared marriage, which was something she felt wholly unprepared for. She told me she had been forced into the contract by her family. The offer had originally come for her sister, Elspeth, but she had rejected it as she had decided to become engaged to another gentleman of her own choosing. As a result, Eloise had been compelled to accept it, since it was a matter of family honor. Her father, who had served with Colonel Boothroyd's uncle, thought him an exceedingly good match, not to mention the wealth and prestige such an association would bring. He had assured Eloise that she would be kept like a maharani, but Eloise confided in me that she was not happy with the arrangement. She told me often that she missed her home, her flowers and her cats, that she felt lost and uprooted, like she was being exiled for no fault of her own. Of course, it didn't help that she had an infirm constitution. The sea air and the ship's rocking made her sick to her stomach. She had a very rough time of it; the journey almost wrecked her.

'As we came to each new port, her neurasthenia grew worse. Most of all, it caused her fear of marriage to grow into full-blown hysteria. She had trouble sleeping, and when she did manage to get some rest, she was plagued by the same dream. She saw herself being stifled, slowly throttled to death by a large and faceless shadow. The only thing that helped her calm down was copious doses of paregoric mixed with valerian root. She was damn nearly addicted to it and spent most of her time in a sort of fugue, refusing to get out of bed. I tried to take care of her, to pay her back. I brought her meals and helped her bathe and change, but it was difficult to sustain as the journey continued. The more withdrawn she grew, the more confident I became. For me, the voyage was liberating. It changed everything—my outlook, the way I spoke and dressed, my sense of who I was and what I wanted.'

'Did you ever intend to marry my friend?'

'I thought about it many times. Part of me was willing to go through with the contract, but then I realized I didn't need to do it. I was free at last. Emily Malcolm was as good as dead. Now, I could be anyone I wanted to be. For the first time in my life, there was nobody to hold me back.'

'Is that why you played your games with Dr Ross, and the Masons, with Mr Mascarenhas and Percy Billimoria? Because you were having a bit of fun?'

She laughed. 'I admit, it helped pass the time. I blackmailed Mr Mason and duped Dr Ross. I tricked the porter and led poor Michael along because it helped me get up on the first-class deck. But that was all it was, a game! I meant no harm. My only regret was that I could not do something more for Eloise. If only I had been conscious enough to see what she was going through, perhaps I could have helped her, but I was too caught up in myself. And, of course, once we left Marseille, I all but moved out from the cabin.'

The regret in her voice was palpable. 'I only saw her twice after that. The first time, we had a dreadful falling out. She came to me after Cairo, to tell me I was being foolish. She warned me that I was getting a reputation as a fast woman. I mistook her concern for intrusion, lost my temper and was very unkind, I am sorry to say. Not only did I ignore her advice, but I also told her she was the one who was a fool. I called her a scared little girl too afraid to experience life, too worried to take a risk. "Go hide in your cave and rot for all I care," I said to her.'

'And the second time?'

She closed her eyes and let out a plangent sigh. 'The morning before we were to dock in Bombay, she sent me a note, asking me to come see her. I should have gone immediately, but I didn't realize it was a cry for attention. To be honest, with all the excitement, I forgot. I was with Lt Gordon, enjoying one last farewell. By the time I left him and remembered her note, it was too late.

When I got to the cabin to see her, it was after midnight. The ship had already moored and was waiting for the tide to change, so that we could begin disembarkation. I found the door locked. Luckily, I still had a key, so I let myself in.' Her voice caught in her throat, 'That was when I found her!'

'Dead?' I guessed. 'A combination of valerian and paregoric?'

Miss Malcolm nodded. 'It was strange. She didn't look dead. She looked peaceful, like she was asleep. On the table, she had left a small envelope for me. Inside it was some money, a brooch and a letter, saying farewell and wishing me luck, saying she wished she was more like me, that she was brave. I stood there a long time, Mr Singh, looking down at that poor, deluded girl. My only coherent thought was, what a bloody waste! She had everything to look forward to: a good offer, wealth, comfort, class, yet she threw it all away. And why? Because she was scared? That was when it struck me. Why let it all go to waste? I could do the same thing again. I could become her, just like I had become Miss Hartley. The rest of it was easy enough. I waited until just after the eighth bell was sounded. Then, as the watch was changing, under the cover of darkness, I bundled the corpse in a blanket and pushed it overboard. I repacked most of her luggage with mine, and the next morning, I disembarked as Mary Hartley and made my way to the hostel. After that, all it took was a bit of peroxide and presto, I became Miss Eloise Bennett.'

'And Colonel Boothroyd did not question you? He didn't ask any unpleasant questions?'

'Oh, he didn't suspect a thing! He fell for me the moment he set eyes on me.'

'You do realize, Madam, that he is not the sort of man who will let you have even an ounce of freedom. Men like Colonel Boothroyd want trophies, not wives.'

'I am well aware of that, Mr Singh. It was my intent to use him. He was going to get me out of Bombay and to Balochistan, where I was planning to desert him.'

'So, you could go to Assam?'

For the first time, she looked surprised. 'How do you know that?'

'I have my sources, Madam,' I said and looked at her sadly. 'It really was quite a clever plan, but I am sorry to say, it would never have worked. Sooner or later, you would have made a mistake and given yourself away. Nobody can sustain that degree of falsehood for the rest of their lives, not even someone as gifted at masquerade as you.'

'I could have. No, I would have done it,' she said, her voice like steel. 'I had no other choice, did I? Put yourself in my place for a moment. At least your Miss Hartley had a choice, as did Eloise. What chance did I ever have? Abandoned by my mother, beaten by my father, abused by my uncle, forced into a life of fear and bondage by every man I have ever met, treated like an object and not a person, and why? Because I am a woman? Told repeatedly that I am the weaker sex, that I need protection, a husband to be complete, to have value? No, Sir, I am done with that, done with men telling me what to do with my life. The day I stole Miss Hartley's luggage, I decided I would make my own way in the world. I would write my own destiny. Does that make me evil?'

I thought about it for a second before shaking my head.

'No, it does not. I agree with you, Madam. You have been dealt an unfair hand by life, and you have certainly suffered unduly for someone so young. Sadly, that does not justify what you have done. Your actions, while well-intentioned, have led to the commission of a great evil. Because of you, a good man has taken his life, a decent man. There is no escaping that fact.'

Her face fell. 'I understand that, and I will pay my dues.'

Turning to Hall-Caine, she asked, 'What will they do to me? How long will I get?'

Hall-Caine answered with a shrug. 'For the theft and imposture, six months at the least, three years at the most. As for abetting Peter Rowan's suicide, I cannot say. It depends on the judge. They may decide to send you back to England to stand trial.'

'No,' she said, stricken. 'Not that. I cannot go back. I will not go back. I will take my own life first.'

'You will not have to,' I interjected. 'Hall-Caine here will make sure of that. You will, won't you?'

Hall-Caine scowled, unhappy to be painted into a corner. 'I'll see what I can do. I can't make any promises, but I will pull a few strings to ensure you stay in India.'

'Thank you,' Miss Malcolm said gratefully. 'And after my imprisonment, I will be free? Truly free?'

'Yes,' I replied. 'You will.'

'Then I can wait a few more years, Mr Singh. After a lifetime, a few years are not much time at all,' she said with a smile, a wan grimace that was almost optimistic. 'About your friend, I am sorry for what happened, but it is not my fault that he took his life. That was his choice, and his alone. Surely, you understand that?'

Her voice was gentle, but it made my heart swell with immense rage. I wanted to argue with her, tell her she was wrong, that it was her fault that Peter was gone. But then, as I turned to look at her, so diffident that it was almost painful, my fury guttered, like a candle before a storm.

She was right, I thought bitterly. She was as much a victim in this instance as Peter. There were no winners in this case, only losers.

'Take her away,' I said to Hall-Caine.

Miss Malcolm gave me one last pensive glare, but I found I could not bear to meet her eyes, not a moment longer.

'What a goddamned mess!' I said to Hall-Caine as the constables led her away.

'What a goddamned woman!' he exclaimed, the awe evident in his voice. 'In another life, I might have married her myself.'

He shrugged, 'Well, for better or worse, at least it is over. Congratulations, you have solved another case! The legend of

Sikander Singh, the royal sleuth who never leaves a mystery unsolved, continues to grow.'

'Not quite. There is one more loose thread that needs to be tied up.'

'And what is that?'

'You, Hall-Caine! Why are you helping me? You have nothing to gain.'

'Well,' Hall-Caine said with a sardonic grin. 'There is a small matter of a debt I happen to owe you.'

'Preposterous! I hadn't met you before the day before yesterday. What debt could you possibly mean?'

'A few years back, you were very kind to a young woman named Jane Snowdon. Do you happen to remember her?'

I frowned. Of course, I remembered Jane. She had been both the perpetrator and victim of a rather confounding crime I had deduced a while back—the murder of the Resident of Rajpore, Major William Russell. During the course of my investigations, it had come to light that Major Russell had been a predator and a brute, and that Jane had suffered most unduly at his hands, which was why I had helped her escape prosecution after she had poisoned him. The last I heard, she was in Australia. *But how did Hall-Caine know her?*

'I met Jane last year in Canberra,' he explained. 'We fell in love, and she has been kind enough to agree to be my wife.' Hall-Caine bowed his head. 'She told me about her past and what you did for her. Do you see now? A debt *is* due, Sikander. While our circumstances may not permit us to be friends, I believe there is no reason why I cannot try to pay back at least part of what is owed. Does that answer your question?'

'I believe it does.'

'Good! In that case, let me be the first to wish you the very best of luck.'

'And I you! Good luck with your marriage!'

Hall-Caine laughed and shook his head. 'There's no luck needed, my friend, if there is love. I think that is the one lesson we have all learned from this case. Without love, we are all just mysteries waiting to be solved.'

With that, he tipped his hat to me before turning to follow Miss Malcolm to the dhow. As they approached the boat, he held out a hand to her, as if inviting her to promenade in Hyde Park.

She paused to give me a defiant grin, and then, with a toss of her hair, let him help her aboard. I watched them sullenly. I could not help but admire her, respect her for her audacity. It surprised me, but this time around, I did not feel the usual thrill that seized me after I wrapped up a mystery. Instead, all I felt was a looming emptiness in the pit of my stomach, an ache so intense that it made me want to groan.

'What's wrong, Huzoor?' Charan Singh asked, noticing my stricken expression. 'Ordinarily, when you close a case, you're over the moon.'

'What's the point, old friend?' I retorted morosely. 'I may have solved the mystery, but I've lost Helene.'

Charan Singh's craggy face softened. He frowned at me for a moment and then, to my surprise, he surged forward to hug me.

It was unexpected, to say the least. Such a blatant contravention of etiquette! We had an unspoken and carefully maintained détente. Even though he was my best friend and most steadfast companion, Charan Singh was very careful to respect the boundary between servant and master. But on this occasion, he broke every rule and enveloped me in his arms, cradling me to his chest like I was a child once again.

'Have you forgotten everything I taught you, Sikander Puttar? The fight isn't over until you are dead or knocked out. You are of the Khalsa! You never surrender. You never give in. You never back down!'

Releasing me, he held me at arm's length and gave me a stern smile.

'If Madam Helene has left you, never mind, you foolish boy. Let us go and get her back!'

EPILOGUE

After half a lifetime spent baking under India's scorching sun, Helene had all but forgotten how cold Paris could be; how desolate in the winter.

The memories she had cherished were of Paris in the summer—the delicate scent of cherry blossoms hanging in the air and the whispering laughter of the midsummer breeze blowing in from the Seine, as sibilant as a child's delight.

But now, the city she had returned to was cold and white. The Seine was frozen. The only wind was a bitter one, a mistral whistling in from the Alps, making her shiver. She pulled her shawl closer around her, hunching over, but the cold was as sharp as a saber cutting into her bones, a perpetual chill that made her joints ache and reminded her that she was no longer young.

It did not help that the apartment she was renting was in a particularly dismal corner of Les Halles. Very close to the meat and tannery district, it was a squalid area, haunted by women of low repute and dock workers. However, Helene preferred it to the more elegant parts of the city. That was where Sikander had offered to set her up, in a neat pied-à-terre not too far from the Place Vendôme, but she had refused him, just as she had refused his offer to provide her a generous pension. She wanted her break with him to be clean, free of any lingering doubts or attachments.

Instead, she had chosen to pawn a few pieces of jewelry and rent this place, a third-floor walk-up sandwiched between a brewery and a butcher shop.

At the thought of Sikander, a pang of pain bit at her heart. Helene gritted her teeth and hurried onward. She couldn't help but wonder how he was, whether he was drinking too much or getting enough to eat. That would never change, neither would the fact that she loved him. It had taken all her strength to make a clean break after all these years together. Part of her had never wanted to leave him, but another part knew that she could not be with him without going mad.

What she had not expected or planned for was how much Paris, her home, would have changed. She had grown up just a few kilometers south, in Rue du Jardinet, but that quarter was gone now, consumed by Boulevard Saint-Germain. This was a new Paris, Haussmann's city of avenues and boulevards, so cold and sterile that it made her feel like a relic. She hungered for the city she had grown up in, old Montmartre with its color and noise, but it was gone, only a ghost of what she had known as a girl.

It took her some time to haul the groceries up to the third floor, where her apartment was located. Unlocking the door, she paused to survey her meager kingdom. After her magnificent chambers in Rajpore, these accommodations were dismal, just two rooms and a small kitchen. A sour smell hung in the air, persisting no matter how often she scrubbed the floor. The only view was of a blank grey wall. There were no khidmatgars, no maids or servants, just a mangy cat that had taken up residence outside her window and hissed at her each time she tried to shoo it away.

To her surprise and dismay, she saw that the bedroom door was wide open. Helene frowned, trying to remember if she had left it unlocked. No, she had a distinct memory of kicking it shut before leaving. That could only mean someone else was in the apartment.

A thief! *Helene thought. Her back stiffened as she heard footsteps on the other side of the door. She checked her pocket, feeling the reassuring weight of the one gift from Sikander that she had decided to retain.*

'I have a pistol,' she said querulously. 'And I am not reluctant to use it.'

There were more footsteps, followed by a momentary silence before a familiar voice broke the tension.

'It is I, Madam. Charan Singh! Please do not kill me. My wife will never forgive me if I was to die in this godforsaken country, so far away from my beloved Punjab.'

The old Sikh emerged, his bulk filling the doorway. When she saw him, Helene was immediately assailed by two conflicting emotions: first reassurance, then immense irritation.

'What are you doing here? Did he send you to check up on me?'

'Not quite, Madam,' Charan Singh said and stepped aside.

She saw there was another man in the room behind him. It was Sikander, his sardonic face twisting into a smile when he saw her.

'You?' Her breath caught in her throat and her heart skipped a beat, love warring with consternation, leaving her wordless.

'Hello, my love,' he said, looking her up and down. 'You look tired.'

'Don't call me that. I am not your love, not any longer. What are you doing here, and why did you break into my house?'

'Ah yes, my apologies! However, I am not breaking and entering. It so happens that, as of this morning, I own this apartment. In fact, I bought the whole building.' He smiled. 'As to why I am here. It is to take you back, of course, to Rajpore.'

'I have no intention of going back. Not now, not ever.'

'Are you sure?' he said, stepping forward until she could smell him, a maddening mixture of tobacco and hair pomade. 'Is there nothing I can say to change your mind?'

He was shorter than her, but he still managed to look taller somehow, a trick of those thoughtful eyes and that monumental nose.

'What if I was to say that I made a mistake? No, you have heard that already. Many times.

Well then, what if I told you I have never loved another woman? No, you would never believe me. That leaves me only one choice.'

He nodded at Charan Singh, who stepped forward with an immense smile and handed him a small silk purse.

Sikander held it out to her. 'This is for you, Helene.'

Helene paused before reaching out to take it, unable to keep her fingers from trembling. Inside, she found a slim bangle. It was not gold; but beaten iron, covered with intricate carvings she recognized as Gurmukhi, the language of the Sikhs.

'This is our most cherished family heirloom. The great Guru Arjan Singh gave it to one of my ancestors. Loosely translated, the words inscribed on it read: "my love is with you; I see all other love as false." I want you to have this, Helene, and to have me.'

'What are you saying?' Helene gasped.

'I want you to marry me, Helene. I want you to be my wife and my queen.'

'But what will the people say? Your subjects in Rajpore? They will never accept a white woman as their maharani!'

'Damn them all! I may be a king, Helene, but in my heart, I am just a man. And I will never be complete without you.'

Helene paused, unsure of how to react to this proposal. Her whole life, she had waited for this moment. Now that it was here, she found herself at a loss for words.

'I ... I am not sure, Sikander. I don't know if I can play second fiddle any more to your sleuthing and your mysteries. I suppose I should accept it after all these years, but I cannot bear that you will always love them more than you love me.'

'You still don't understand, do you, Helene? After all these years? I do not love mysteries. I loathe them. I despise the unknown. That is why I cannot leave puzzles unsolved or riddles undeciphered. But you, my love, are the only mystery I never ever want to solve.'

Sikander took one of her hands into his own and caressed it gently. 'Please say yes,' he urged. 'Say you will come back to Rajpore with me.'

'I will,' Helene said, even as Sikander enveloped her into his arms and kissed her.

Behind them, Charan Singh choked back a sob and wiped a tear from the corner of one eye.

'Well,' he said with a satisfied smile. 'I do so love a happy ending!'

ACKNOWLEDGEMENTS

As any writer will tell you, the writing is the easy part. It takes a lot of people, a lot of work and a lot of pain to make a book possible and give it life.

I am grateful to Kanishka Gupta for being such a stalwart supporter of my writing and such a faithful friend.

I am grateful to Ananth Padmanabhan and HarperCollins India for giving Maharaja Sikander Singh and The Maharaja Mysteries a home.

I am grateful to my editors Rashmi Menon and Poulomi Chatterjee for their patience and their many kindnesses, and for the equanimity with which they have endured my many tantrums.

Most of all, I am grateful to my wonderful wife Masumeh Makhija for her unstinting love and support, and for the fantastic cover she put together with her team at The Creative Tribe.

A Very Pukka Murder came out almost ten years ago. That means Maharaja Sikander Singh has been part of my life for nearly a decade, and though this will, unfortunately, be his last adventure for a while, I can only hope he will be remembered by readers with fondness and perhaps a hint of class.

ABOUT THE AUTHOR

Arjun Raj Gaind is a writer of historical mystery, comics and literary fiction. *The Missing Memsahib* is the latest instalment in his bestselling Maharaja Mystery series, in which *A Very Pukka Murder* and *Death at the Durbar* are the first two. He is also the author of the critically acclaimed coming-of-age novel *The Anatomy of Loss*, as well as the creator and writer of several graphic novels, including *Project: Kalki, Empire of Blood, Reincarnation Man, The Mighty Yeti, Blade of the Warrior* and *A Brief History of Death*.

HarperCollins *Publishers* India

At HarperCollins India, we believe in telling the best stories and finding the widest readership for our books in every format possible. We started publishing in 1992; a great deal has changed since then, but what has remained constant is the passion with which our authors write their books, the love with which readers receive them, and the sheer joy and excitement that we as publishers feel in being a part of the publishing process.

Over the years, we've had the pleasure of publishing some of the finest writing from the subcontinent and around the world, including several award-winning titles and some of the biggest bestsellers in India's publishing history. But nothing has meant more to us than the fact that millions of people have read the books we published, and that somewhere, a book of ours might have made a difference.

As we look to the future, we go back to that one word—a word which has been a driving force for us all these years.

Read.

Harper Collins · Harper Sport · HARPER FICTION · HARPER NON-FICTION · हार्पर हिन्दी

HARPER LEARNING · HARPER VANTAGE · HCCB HARPERCOLLINS CHILDREN'S BOOKS · 4th · HARPER PERENNIAL

HARPER DESIGN · BOOKTOPUS · HARPER BUSINESS